VICTORIA
AND THE
HOLLOW RUBY

VICTORIA
AND THE
HOLLOW RUBY

D.B. MILLER

Charleston, SC
www.PalmettoPublishing.com

Victoria and the Hollow Ruby
Copyright © 2022 by D. B. Miller

First Edition

Hardcover ISBN: 978-1-68515-403-5
Paperback ISBN: 978-1-68515-404-2
ebook ISBN: 978-1-68515-402-8

In the midst of being haunted by the looming shadows and lurking creatures of the Black Needle Mountains, a surprising ability awakens within Victoria. Will she be able to use it to survive as she is forced into the woods and down a sinister path?

TABLE OF CONTENTS

CHAPTER 1

A STRANGE SHIMMER

SOMEONE WAS IN HER room. They stood between her wardrobe and chest of drawers, but it was too dark to determine more. Victoria had awoken to the chilly breeze of the first few true days of autumn nipping at her nose. The long curtains were billowing, her balcony door was open, but she was sure she had locked it before she had fallen asleep. Wondering if she was having a delusional nightmare, Victoria tried to move, but she could only stare with wide eyes. Her body was gripped in frozen terror as her mind ran in wild chaos.

Perhaps it was a thief. They were near her tall jewelry box, which sat on top of the chest of drawers. As the figure shifted toward her, she assumed they were gazing at her because she felt that tingling sense of unease. Her heart pounded in her ears, the blood in her veins churned. Suddenly, another figure entered from her balcony door and slammed into the first intruder. They both went down hard against her wardrobe, knocking the wall with a series of loud thumps as they wrestled. Both were trying to maintain the silence of the still night so only their panting was heard between the scraping of boot and flesh against the floor. As they rolled about, one hand shot up and clutched the side of her down duvet, ripping the silk.

Victoria flinched and shrunk back against the headboard. She wanted to scream but it seemed her throat was rigid and tight. She was having a difficult time getting enough air into her lungs. Then they rolled out the balcony doors, clamoring outside along the railing.

Victoria found her feet on the hardwood floor, pulling her body out of the bed and fleeing to the door. She desperately grabbed at the knob, and turning it seemed to take an eternity. Finally, it swung open, and she ran straight to her sister's room. She slammed the door and locked it soundly before climbing into her bed.

"Is it back?" Mabel asked sleepily.

"This time there were two," Victoria said. Mabel shuddered.

Victoria woke up to the familiar thud of Emily setting the porcelain pitcher filled with heated water near the washing basin. She grumbled softly as she opened her eyes to see Mabel's golden hair in a messy tangle beside her. Victoria slid out from the covers, pulling back the canopy bed curtains slowly. Still half asleep, she slipped a bit on her ruffled nightgown. Emily clicked her tongue, and Victoria straightened her posture.

Emily was an elderly lady with pale, wrinkled skin. Thin purple veins branched out along the edge of her eyelids like tiny lightning bolts flashing in the movement of each blink.

Her dry, bony fingers made Victoria cringe. She had little tolerance for children, even though Mabel was now thirteen years old. Emily still saw her as the little girl who had stained her best church dress red with the sticky handprints of freshly mashed raspberries from the garden.

"Good morning," Victoria said cheerfully but not loud enough to make Emily correct her with the thin ruler she always kept in the pocket of her apron. Although it did not look like much, it had a bitter sting.

"Good morning," Emily replied and gestured for Victoria to leave Mabel's room. Victoria quickly made her way back to her own room to make the bed, abiding by the unwritten rule of tucking the edges in neatly, hiding the ripped seam. She would repair it later today in secret so she would not get punished for the tear. She sat on the vanity stool so Emily could brush her hair. She was relieved to see light was sweeping the icky darkness away. She wished for the sunrise from her balcony, but she had been given the north-facing room. The large glass doors witnessed neither performance of the sun, instead it perfectly framed the Black Needles, the large mountain range to the north, reflected in the lake below. Like every morning, she shivered at the sight. The looming figures in the distance caused a strange unease. Always covered in snow, even in the hottest summers in the valley, they seemed harsh and bleak. There were several peaks, but the tallest jutted into the sky boldly while the others cowered before it. The continuous strange tales further proved her belief that they were indeed wicked.

When Emily stopped brushing, Victoria stood, secretly dreading her corset. Although it was tight and constricting, she needed to be a proper example for Mabel. So, she sat still until Emily tied the final knot.

Emily left to attend to Mabel. Victoria didn't need to look through the doorway as she passed down the corridor. She already knew the face Mabel would be making while her corset was laced. Making her way down the grand staircase, she practiced her poise, pointing her toes as a lady should on each step.

She slowed as she neared the entrance of the dining hall to peek in shyly. Presently Mother was sitting down for breakfast. She was a short woman; even Mabel had surpassed her last summer.

Mabel inherited her golden locks, although Mother's had slightly yellowed with age. She always wore it up, decorated with flowers, feathers, or beads. Her blue eyes were oddly paled, which Mabel also inherited. Although it perhaps made Mother more intimidating when they flashed,

Victoria thought they were remarkable. The last important feature was her thin lips, always tight and strained in a slight sulk. Accustomed to this, Victoria knew her mother was not angry, as others would assume. It was just her face.

Victoria stood waiting at the door patiently for Mabel, tapping her toes ever so softly in rhythm to a tune in her mind. Once Mabel arrived, Emily ushered them forward. Mother's hard glance swept them from head to toe. Not until she nodded did the girls sit down, relieved. Their appearance was acceptable today. They sat on the opposite end of the long table, properly folding their hands together and bowing their heads reverently until grace was recited in its entirety.

Then they were served delicate triangular slices of toast, which were accompanied by jams, jellies, and whole fruits. A small skillet of ham and fried egg was placed before her. As the first sizzling piece hit her tongue, she jumped. Everyone looked at her.

"Hot," she whispered more to herself than anyone else, smiling nervously. Only Mabel smiled back. No one spoke further, and the silent early morning resumed.

Once or twice Mother's eyes lifted, hovering over Victoria's face, an actual frown drawn as she buttered her toast. The scraping of the silver knife along the edge of the crisp bread grated painfully against Victoria's ears. Mother did not approve of her features.

Victoria's crimson hair was even a shade darker than her father's hair had been. Her deep blue eyes were not enough to satisfy. Men praised golden hair resembling the sun and eyes light blue like unto the heavens, an angelic face. She was constantly reminded that she needed to be even more charming and eloquent to snag a man.

Victoria once again lamented her appearance in the spoon she held. She looked to Mabel and back again at her own reflection. She stashed the discouragement away. Mabel continued to smile at her cheerfully, raising her spirits. Victoria could never stay mad at Mabel for long.

"Tell Mother," Mabel said, her voice seemed to shatter the silence harshly. Victoria shook her head quickly.

"Tell me what?" Mother asked, her eyebrows raised. Victoria sent a warning glance toward Mabel and Mabel shrunk under it.

"Just tell her," Mabel urged, her voice softer now. Victoria relented.

"There were two in my room last night—" Victoria began but stopped as she heard Mother give a disgruntled sigh.

"Victoria," Mother said. "The doctor said these delusions will fade if you stop letting them play out."

Victoria nodded and twisted her fingers nervously.

"And think of Mabel, you don't want it to spread to her. Fear is infectious," Mother said.

Soon they were shuffled to class with the instructor, Professor Leland Carter, in the library. They were educated each day until noon, and it was a terrible bore. Professor Carter was old and spoke in a dry tone. He was professional to a fault, always in a neatly pressed brown tweed suit and carrying a large carpetbag. He had arrived shortly after Father's passing, but he did not offer any sign of condolences in the way of slack. He demanded perfect attendance, discouraged any chatter during the lessons, and refused to linger a moment longer than necessary. He never mingled in the hallway, no matter how much Emily tried to engage him in conversation. Victoria did not understand. It seemed they would make the perfect match. Victoria would have felt bad for Emily and her failed attempts to receive more than a polite raising of his brown bowler if the woman was not such a snobbish pedant.

Perhaps it was this exact quality that attracted Emily to Professor Carter. He was relentless in assigning Victoria long hours of reading each night. Emily took it upon herself to oversee that.

Victoria looked up past his gold-framed spectacles that sat on the bridge of his nose lopsidedly and over his balding head to the painting on the wall between the tall shelves of books. It depicted a biblical scene with all varieties of animals ascending side by side on the ramp into the famous water vessel, a common story she had heard since she was little.

Although she had seen it many times before, today it seemed one particular animal stared directly at her with its small, beady eyes piercing from the canvas. It was a typical fox with a pointed muzzle and large ears. She shifted uncomfortably under its gaze, trying to force herself back into the lesson.

Soon it was lunchtime, the one meal not eaten with Mother, and although the food was light and the beverages rarely anything but water, Victoria found it to be her favorite. Victoria and Mabel sat on the veranda overlooking the garden, free to speak openly between each other. After lunch, Victoria wandered to her favorite place on the estate, the garden. She was told it was designed long ago by her great-grandfather.

After such a harsh winter, Victoria was amazed it came back full and green. Running fingers gently along the rosebushes, she was careful of the thorns. The light pink and red petals made her happy because they filled the garden with color. It restored fond childhood memories, the way it had since she was a little girl.

Birds settled into the trees lining either side of the cobblestone path; their singsong voices usually proved cheering, but today they were jarringly loud, some notes hitting a pitch that made Victoria cringe and cover her ears. She shooed them away. Finally, when the quiet was restored, she sat down on her favorite bench beneath the deformed tree. The rest stood tall and proud, but this one curled itself over in a hunch. Father used to say a friendly giant sat on it to rest his weary legs before making his way into the Black Needle Mountains. This funny little story always made Victoria giggle. The tree provided wonderful shade and perfectly curved to accommodate a weary back comfortably, so Father pushed a bench under it.

She once again was smiling at the thought of Father. His happy demeanor used to brighten even Mother's mood. She looked to the Black Needles again, scorning their inky, dark crevices. She pulled her book open to the embroidered ribbon she had made herself. Redirecting her concentration, she began reading about poise and proper etiquette. She needed to be the most respected young lady at the upcoming dinner party.

Suddenly a shadow hovered over her book, blocking out the sunlight. She looked up to see Mabel smiling. Mabel looked at her, holding her hand over her mouth to build on the suspense until bursting into a fit of giggles.

"Henry Johnson and his father are grooming the horses in the meadow today!" Mabel said eagerly. Victoria tossed her book to the side and followed Mabel as she hustled out of the garden.

They crossed an old wooden bridge to get to the fenced meadow. The rapid river rushed below to connect to the large lake on the edge of their land. Where the current ran slower, they could see down to the bottom with the smooth black and gray stones lining the riverbed like uneven cobblestone.

Once on the other side, the girls hung in the shadow of the tree line, watching for a few moments. Henry had light brown hair, but it was now bleached brighter from the days spent in the summer sun. It was long enough to curl about the ears and rustle in the wind playfully. He was tall with a rather large nose. His eyes were hazel, often different colors depending on the amount of light he was standing in. His clothes were continuously dirty, along with his hands, which were always calloused.

Henry brushed the horses' coats while they munched on the wild grasses in the field. Mother only kept dark chestnut horses, so Victoria was uncertain which horse was which, although she was sure he knew each one by name. But there was one horse she never was confused about; it was born last summer and was different in color. It was the same chestnut but had a white face and spots. Mother would have sold him at the marketplace if Mabel had not grown such an attachment, visiting him often. She had named him Nutmeg. When Henry turned his brush to Nutmeg, Mabel stepped out of the tree line and approached the fence. Victoria followed slowly but stopped when she heard a small splash behind her in the river. She turned to scan the water, but she could not see anything but the flowing current. Victoria followed Mabel.

Henry offered the oat bucket to Mabel and smiled at Victoria, tipping his hat in greeting. Mabel eagerly stuck out her hand to Nutmeg and stroked his mane while he ate.

"Good afternoon, Victoria," Henry said cheerfully.

"Good afternoon," she answered back. Henry offered the bucket to Victoria, and after a shy smile, she grabbed a handful of the feed. Nutmeg turned toward Victoria's outstretched hand and then snorted loudly, tossing his head. She stepped closer, trying to put the oats to his mouth. Nutmeg's ears flattened. Stomping his hooves and rearing, he let loose several hysterical brays before galloping off to the farthest side of the pasture.

"He has never done that before." Henry looked as surprised as Victoria felt. I don't know what has gotten into him," he said, giving a light shrug. Henry's father, Mr. Johnson, was approaching from the far side of the field. He was looking from the retreating Nutmeg and back toward their little trio standing along the fence in curiosity.

Victoria nodded and said goodbye, too uncomfortable to linger any longer. She felt hot and perhaps a bit weak. Mabel was slow to follow now. She waved to Henry a few times before catching up to Victoria.

"How embarrassing!" Victoria huffed as they reached the edge of the bridge.

"I think it was funny," Mabel said and made a silly face, lightening the mood. "Nutmeg has developed a good taste!"

Victoria could not deny Mabel's bubbly disposition, so they tittered together as they crossed the bridge. Victoria noticed a small flicker of movement in the lake out of the corner of her eye. Looking again, she saw a shimmer glisten over the ripples of the lake, but she was too far away to do more than squint. She crossed back onto the bridge, but it was gone. Mabel closed in behind her.

"Victoria? What are you looking at?" Mabel scanned out into the water and looked back at Victoria.

"Nothing," Victoria said and motioned for them to resume their walk. Mabel quickly bounded from the bridge and back toward the manor. Victoria cast a final glance toward the lake. The sparkle resurfaced, and Victoria threw herself against the railing, leaning far forward.

It was a bright shimmer with a golden hue. It moved slowly across the surface toward the tiny island in the middle of the lake. Victoria wished the sun was not so bright today. She tried to shield her eyes with her hand, peering farther. Raising her second hand to fully block the rays, she leaned against the railing, resting on her hips, on the highest tippy-toes, while calling out to Mabel.

"Do you see that?" Victoria called out.

Victoria blinked, and the shimmer was gone.

"I don't see anything. It was probably a muskrat," Mabel yelled back.

"No! Something is over there!" she said as she flung her arm hard in frustration, motioning toward the spot. Then a terrible thing happened. The old wooden railing creaked and groaned as the top structure snapped. Victoria only had a second to process Mabel's terrified face as she experienced the rush of falling.

She plummeted forward into the river and hit the surface headfirst, taking the full sting of the chilly water against her cheek. In a panic, she whipped her arms up and kicked her legs mightily. Her dress wrapped about her limbs, making the effort more strenuous. Finally, she pierced the surface, gasping for air.

Mabel's panicked screams was the first noise Victoria could decipher among the commotion of the water. She fought through the thick folds of her fabric as she struggled to keep her head above water. The river's current was fast and continued to sweep her along. It was deeper than anticipated when she tried to find footing, and instead she found herself under again. Kicking fiercely, she was able to poke her chin out and slap the water enough to keep alive. She bumped painfully against the large rocks despite her best efforts.

She heard Henry's voice, but she was unsure where he was calling from. There were several more petrifying moments before his arm was about her waist, pulling her toward the bank. Soon they were both knee-deep in mud and filth. Victoria lost a shoe as she trudged alongside Henry. Feeling the red-hot mortification flushing her face, she tried to retain whatever poise remained despite coughing periodically. Both Mr. Johnson and Mabel were standing at the bank, looking concerned. Victoria realized her dress was sticking to her. Silently she thanked Emily that she was not wearing her white cotton dress today.

"Are you okay, miss?" Mr. Johnson asked politely.

Victoria nodded, shaking from the cold. She stepped onto the dry bank, standing lopsided without her left shoe. She spied it floating on top of the river rapids, floating far away from the muddy bank, but pretended not to see it. Praying no one else would notice it either, she coughed a few more times dramatically. Dripping head to toe, her carefully constructed curls were now frizzy with the bow sagging to the side.

"What happened?" Henry asked, and Mabel just laughed, unable to control herself any longer. She just pointed up at the bridge.

"The railing broke!" Mabel could barely breathe, and that was the only sentence she could get out between the fits.

"Do not go on the bridge anymore until it has had the proper repairs," Mr. Johnson said in a firm tone. Then they began toward the house.

As Henry stepped out from the shadows of the tree line, the sun hit him brightly. His white cotton shirt was now transparent. The water drops gleamed on his skin. He had a hairier chest than she expected, and Mabel stopped laughing, which perhaps was more obvious than if she had continued. She sent a quick smirk, and Victoria tried to ignore it, hoping Mabel would stop because she was not by any means subtle.

Mr. Johnson held out his jacket to Henry, who gratefully took it, wrapping it about Victoria's shoulders without hesitation despite his own shivers. She thanked him kindly, her eyes to the ground. Pulling her shoulders back under the jacket and correcting her posture, she tried to preserve whatever dignity she had left. She started toward the manor, but to her further humiliation, Henry offered himself as an escort. It would have been less embarrassing if Mabel had not giggled the entire way from behind.

Mother happened to be outside, correcting the gardener, to Victoria's dismay. Mabel fell silent, slipping out of Mother's sight slowly. Victoria enviously watched Mabel disappear into the back door as Mother began the dreaded lecture.

"Victoria? What have you done?" Mother asked with tension in her voice, trying to contain a dainty whisper while her lips curled downward in an unflattering frown. Victoria's skin felt hot with embarrassment.

"The bridge broke! I fell into the river," Victoria explained.

"Victoria! I expect a lot more from you. Start acting like a young lady! You should not have been anywhere near the bridge today. You must have missed your harp lesson entirely! Go inside and get out of those wet things!" Mother commanded, flashing another suspicious look at Henry, who was humbly looking down at the ground.

"Did you have anything to do with this?" she asked Henry curtly.

"He saved me," Victoria defended him quickly. Mother furrowed her eyebrows at the jacket about her shoulders and then looked to Henry. She whipped off his jacket from Victoria and, in one swift movement, tossed it back into Henry's face. Mother gave him a last glance and shooed him away with a flick of her wrist. She then turned back to Victoria.

"If you two had not been by the river, you would not have needed saving! Unacceptable behavior!" Mother scolded further.

Victoria went through the door and hobbled up the stairs, the wet and heavy dress making quite the opposing rival. Once in her room alone, she accidentally ripped her sleeve seam while struggling to get out of it. She hopped about in a frenzy of shaking and twisting until all the wet fabric was finally loose.

"Arghhh!" She huffed and stomped on it several times in frustration. She slipped a bit and had to awkwardly whirl her hands in the air to try to regain her balance. She finally caught herself on the edge of the dresser. She dropped her head down on the shiny wood with a soft thud and gave a heavy sigh.

Once in a dry gown, she hung her wet one on the marble balcony. Victoria looked over the valley and then timidly at the Black Needle Mountains. Mabel slipped inside her room closing the door behind her. Now that Mother's scorn was over, she was cheery again. Her large grin made even Victoria slightly smile.

"You should have seen how you fell. It was so funny!" Mabel said, giggling once more as she acted it out, flopping forward onto the bed. "I could see your bloomers as you fell in!" she said.

"It was so shameful!" Victoria said in a huff. Both girls wandered quietly into Mabel's room and out to her balcony, which overlooked the pastures. Mabel just giggled while they looked out at the horses. Victoria felt another pang of embarrassment as she spied poor Henry resuming his chores in his wet clothes.

"And Henry saved you! He is your hero," Mabel said.

"He is so handsome," Victoria agreed.

"And hairy!" Mabel giggled, and Victoria joined in. They fell completely silent, standing upright quickly as Mother appeared. Gliding along the floor until she stood side by side with her daughters, she stood peering out the window with them for several long moments. Neither girl dared move.

"Victoria and Mabel, I know that you have been taught that lying is a sin," she said in a stern voice, still looking out over the estate.

"Yes, Mother," they both responded in unison.

Mother's gaze fell upon them heavily. "You lied to me today about what happened at the river."

Both girls exchanged a look of confusion but dared not say a word until Mother was finished with her accusation.

"Tell me that Henry pushed you, perhaps trying to be playful or draw your attention?" Mother turned to look her straight in the eye.

"No, Henry had nothing to do with it. The bridge is in dire need of repair," Victoria responded as boldly as she dared. As anger flooded in her, she felt a prickle on her leg. It was so keen she could not help but scratch at it furiously. Mother gasped with further disgruntlement at another rule of etiquette being broken right before her eyes.

"Well, I think that it is time for me to ask Mr. Johnson and his boy to find work elsewhere," Mother said shrilly.

"No!" Victoria could not restrain herself, knowing how devastating the job loss would be for the Johnson family. "It was my fault. I was clumsy."

"Perhaps they can stay if you promise to keep yourself distant from that boy," Mother said.

Victoria nodded adamantly. "I promise," she quickly said.

Mother looked a bit relieved and gave a small sigh. "You must think of your future. Mingle with those lower than your station and you will deter any proper suitors," Mother said and turned swiftly on her heel, shutting the door behind her.

"I can't believe this!" Victoria said crossly, pacing the room. Her heart was pumping hard, and her cheeks burned. Anger welled in her stomach and up into her throat, making it hard for her to breathe. Mabel looked sorrowfully back at the field.

"Does that mean I can't see Nutmeg anymore?" Mabel asked. Victoria flashed a warning glance toward her.

Another itch made Victoria scratch violently at her face. When her fingers crossed over her cheek, she felt a tuft of something soft. She pulled at it, but it stuck. Looking into the full-length mirror on the opposite wall, she realized dark red hair, the same shade as the hair on her head, had sprouted out of her cheek. Gasping, she tugged at it again, pulling a few strands out painfully. She covered her face with her hand and stepped back, noticing the hair now popping out of her arms and hands.

"What is it?" Mabel asked in response to Victoria's sharp inhale. Victoria turned away from her quickly, hunching over to further hide.

"Nothing," Victoria screeched and pulled a blanket from the bed, covering herself. As Mabel approached, reaching out, Victoria reeled back and sprinted for the solitude of her own room. Sadly, Emily was just making it to the top of the stairs with a huge basket of clean linen. Victoria collided with her painfully, and both went down in a sprawling mess with a loud crash. The wicker basket thudded down the stairs with the linens billowing behind, lining the steps and railing.

"Victoria!" Emily exclaimed from the frazzled heap.

Victoria hopped to her feet and fled up the stairs into the nearest doorway, reentering Mabel's room. Slamming the door shut with a bang and locking it soundly, Victoria leaned against it, breathing heavily. She jumped as she opened her eyes and saw Mabel looking almost as confused as she was.

"What is wrong with your face, Victoria?" Mabel screamed. Victoria groaned in pain and whipped her arms about wildly. Mabel jumped on top of the bed, holding a defensive position with one of her candlesticks, standing ready to swing.

"Back!" Mabel said.

"Mabel!" Victoria huffed and took another peep in the tall looking glass on the wall. She screamed as pain erupted in her gut. She tore at her gown, and every bit of skin she could see was covered in hair. She burst into tears, screaming uncontrollably as a new wave of pain hit.

Intense pressure shot through her nose and up to her head. She looked back into the mirror to witness her nose actually moving. It was lengthening, and her nostrils were growing closer together. The skin bub-bled into a series of tiny bumps, turning black and textured. She fell to the floor, doubled over into the fetal position. Feeling as though all the bones in her body were breaking, Victoria ground her teeth in agony. Her high-pitched squeals escaped louder and louder, yet they were unable to drown out the pain.

Emily was now pounding on the door, demanding to be let in. Victoria looked to Mabel, who was frozen against the headboard, staring in disbelief.

"What is going on?" Emily was shrieking. Well, Victoria was sure she was because the pitch of her voice was very high and spoken with much haste, but the volume was soft, and although she was sure Emily was still pounding on the door with a tight fist, none of it was more than a whisper. It was getting fainter, echoing in from far away as the room darkened.

CHAPTER 2

AN INSTINCT

WHEN VICTORIA CAME TO, she opened her eyes to see Mabel looking down at her with a loving facial expression. Emily was no longer yelling at the door. Victoria welcomed the silence and the fading pressure on her nose. Grateful the pain was gone, yet fearful it would return, she dared not move.

"Don't worry. Everything is fine!" Mabel shouted down at her. "I told Emily that it was just a . . . um . . . rodent! She went to tend the laundry again!"

Victoria felt odd. Mabel looked huge. Mabel's touch felt heavy as it landed on her head rhythmically. She pushed out of Mabel's hand with a squeal, but the noise that met her ears was not her own. She looked down at herself. She tried to scream, but her tongue would not move properly. The sound that met Victoria's ears was a strange whimper.

Her body was covered in a thick pelt, and she held up her hands to see paws in their place. She raced to the mirror and had to sit on her haunches to see into the bottom part of the frame. Her face was no longer human. She had a pair of pointed ears and a snout. It took a few long moments for her to believe the reflection after bobbing up and down and whipping from side to side.

She was a red fox, the type men hunted with a brigade of hounds and brought home as trophies for sport. Her heart pounded so fast it hurt to breathe.

"Look at you, Victoria! You are so cute!" Mabel exclaimed and tugged at her fluffy large tail. Victoria shook, and it followed, bouncing from right to left. She whirled in a circle, and it followed. She then sprinted about the room, dodging between the furniture. It was still there. Mabel giggled as Victoria went under the bed and looped back toward the door. Finally collapsing near the mirror again, the tail landing in her face, she pushed it out of her eyes to once again peer into the mirror with skepticism.

"You are so adorable!" Mabel caught her about the stomach and hoisted her into the air, giggling. Victoria went on a crazy ride high into the air. Her stomach wrenched, and she instinctively bit Mabel's hand. Shrieking, Mabel dropped her. Victoria fell all the way to the floor and hit hard. She let out a cry of pain, but all that met her ears was another animal yelp.

Mabel ran toward the door. Victoria zipped under her legs and beat her there, trying to tell her to stop. She hissed, another strange sound coming from her own mouth. Mabel jumped back and scrambled onto the bed.

Victoria did not know what caused her to bite Mabel, but she immediately felt regretful. Victoria sat on the floor, smelling the blood from the wound, feeling guilty as she listened to Mabel's sobs. She tried to apologize, but all that came out was a weak yip. Mabel stood on the bed, which was too tall for Victoria to climb. She only could put her paws up on the sideboard and stare up at Mabel in dismay.

"Get back! Get back!" Mabel screamed, her voice so loud it seemed to vibrate down Victoria's spine.

Once Mabel had stopped crying, Victoria scratched at the frame of the bed again and tried to look harmless. Mabel gingerly pulled her on the top of the bed. Victoria's nose was overwhelmed with the strong smell of blood although the wound was relatively small. She rejected the wild impulse to lick it. She pushed the strange notion from her mind and concentrated on snuggling by Mabel.

"Victoria, can you hear me?" Mabel asked in a booming voice. Victoria nodded her head and rolled her eyes, trying to convey the obvious, and Mabel gasped in delight, clapping her hands together.

"If you stay like this forever, will you be my pet?" Mabel shouted happily, petting Victoria's head and tickling her tail. Victoria was unsure how to express her irritation, so she just pushed her head against Mabel's hand.

They sat like that for several long minutes, and then Mabel began to tell her all the places she would carry Victoria to in her purse. Victoria began to fall asleep, feeling too exhausted to resist. As her heart fell back into a regular pattern, she began to feel itchy again. She snapped upright in anticipation of another wave of pain. She noticed a few patches of fur were missing on her tail. Victoria scoured the bed for the hair, but none was to be found. She looked at the balding patch and realized the hair was disappearing back into her flesh. It was sickening to watch as each hair strand began to shrivel as the pore opened to envelop it fully. It was indeed very uncomfortable, having no fingers to scratch. She resorted to biting at herself.

She gritted her teeth as another painful sensation exploded all over her body. Her arms registered a new depth of pain. Her paws were growing, lengthening into fingers. Her back paws were now looking like her toes again. Her muscles felt as though they were on fire. She felt herself being stretched long and tall. But this time, unfortunately, she did not black out from pain.

She winced and rolled about, unable to concentrate on anything but the agony. She fell off the bed and hit the floor beneath. It was nothing compared to the pain inside.

Although intense, the pain was fleeting. As the pain subsided and Victoria gasped for air while lying face down on the floor, too exhausted to move, a flood of relief washed over her as she wearily looked at her human hand again.

"I am me again!" Victoria said breathlessly. Although the relief gave her some energy, she still felt too sore to move.

"Um, you are undressed," Mabel said, diverting her eyes.

Realizing Mabel was right, Victoria slowly gathered her gown and dressed between a series of long breaks. Her entire body ached, and her head was dizzy. Once strong enough, she went to the mirror and welcomed her own image again. She hugged herself and then Mabel.

"I am back to normal!" Victoria sighed happily. Victoria took another look at her familiar image and then finished dressing completely. She had never embraced the sight of herself so wholeheartedly. She smiled as she touched her skin and hair.

"I was just dreaming. This is a dream!" Victoria exclaimed.

Then she stopped, turned about, and looked at Mabel fiercely.

"Mabel! Even though this was all a dream, I would most definitely have to ask you not to talk about this at the dinner party." She opened the door with a shaking hand and ignored each explosion of weary pain from her muscles as she made herself walk to her own room. It was even hard to lift herself onto her bed. As she pulled the covers over her head, she sang the odd little lullaby her father used to sing to her. She did not remember the words, so she sang gibberish sounds to the melody, but it stilled her heart and cleared her mind.

She sang this until she fell into a light nap, as much of a nap that can be taken when it's only midafternoon. In this state, she dreamed about a little mouse in Mabel's room hiding under the bed.

Upon opening her eyes, Victoria saw Emily, Mother, and Mabel all gathered around her bed.

"I hope you are feeling better, miss," Emily offered politely. Victoria looked at her hands and felt her face.

"Oh, I am wonderful," she sighed.

"First, you defile your clothes by swimming in the dirty river as though it was a large bath! Then such a ruckus exploded from your rooms! You were so loud we could hear you from the parlor!" Mother was exasperated, eyes wide and lips tightly shoved together in an angry pucker.

Victoria's intense sense of smell was fading, but enough lingered for her to notice the round wounds where Mabel's skin had been ripped open at the knuckles. Victoria understood the red look about her eyes. Victoria's stomach clinched. This was her fate as well.

"You will never behave like this again. Do you understand me?" Her mother waited in silence until Victoria eventually met her eyes. Then Mother nodded to Emily. Mabel was excused from the room as Emily pulled out the familiar wooden ruler, ever stained. Victoria obediently climbed out of bed and stood facing Emily, raising her hands and forming two fists.

As Emily proceeded to rap them fiercely, Mother nodded and left the room. Once Mother was out of sight, Victoria felt relieved, although the sting continued. She let the tears fall freely, not caring if Emily saw her cry. Emily's strikes were too swift and fierce to keep count, but it was the longest Victoria could ever remember. Emily's forehead had beads of sweat, but she continued until blood stained the ruler. Victoria supposed she, too, was in for some sort of punishment for not minding them closer.

Emily gave one more glance of displeasure before leaving, shutting the door behind her quickly. Victoria knew this meant she was confined to her room until further notice. She sat down on the bed, holding her throbbing hands.

After a while, she stood out on her balcony. She peeped for Mother, but the courtyard was empty. She rested her knuckles on the cool marble, and the lingering chill from the darkened sky soothed her hands. Large ugly scabs formed, and she hoped they would heal before the upcoming dinner party.

The Black Needles stood proud; their hideous, sloping face sneered at her in the twilight. Father had told many stories about them. Anything strange that happened in the valley, Father credited to those mysterious peaks. Few ever ventured in, and even fewer returned. They were filled with bandits, thieves, and those banished from society.

Father somehow always returned from his many travels and retained a respect for the mountains. He would tell and retell silly stories full of strange and wonderful creatures he had encountered there. Mother usually interrupted to explain he was pretending, but it did not break Father's spirit. Although he had never written it down, Victoria had memorized the tale of sparkling fairies with shimmery dust that shed from the tips of their tiny wings with every flutter. They twinkled among the leaves even without moonlight on the darkest nights. He would squat on the ground and shake his fists into the air, imitating goblins with a series of grunts. They were small but fierce and nasty. He acted out running from them in fear, and Mabel fell in line with him, her tiny feet tapping along with his until everyone was laughing. Then he would describe how green and lush the grass was in the valley where men with lower bodies and legs of mighty elk ran freely, each crowned with a pair of majestic antlers. He spoke of women with wings like birds, with voices so sweet it far surpassed any note a mere mortal could muster. He would try to mimic the song, and everyone would end up singing along, even Mother. He danced along as he sang. He said the nymphs taught him how to dance, which was rare because they were shy. They could hide anywhere in plain sight by changing colors quicker than a chameleon.

All these stories made Victoria and Mabel want to venture into the mountains. Father had promised them one day he would show them, when it was safe. He couldn't say when. He just always said *one day* with a hopeful gleam in his eye.

But the reason one glance at those mountains could cause such fear was the final story Father had told her—only her, just once. He returned from the mountains much later than expected. In fact, Mother had started to worry he was not coming back at all. She never told of her doubts, but Victoria could read it on her tight and rigid face. Each evening, she set another lantern ablaze, hoping to lead him home.

It was in the dead of night when he arrived, stumbling into the yard, and hollering weakly. Mother was the first to his side, screaming for Emily hoarsely. The screams had slipped into Victoria's room and stirred her from sleep. His back held lashes from a whip and his chest had several large bruises, the few fractured ribs underneath evident. Both his pinkies were missing completely. He could barely breathe. Mother said he was robbed by thieves. She had told him not to go and pestered about his foolishness for not listening. Then when the doctor arrived and shook his head quietly in the hallway, she grew quiet.

Father lay in his bed, barely able to hold his head up. Mother kept hushing him as he tried to speak, but when she left to fetch a fresh pile of linens, he mustered all his strength to tell a story with such urgency Victoria stood frozen. She leaned over him as far as she dared. Even in the dim candlelight, she could see all the blood and muck caked on his skin.

His voice was frail, and Victoria made out the pieces she could. He told a frightful tale with wild, rolling eyes of terrible ancient beasts who were hairy and fanged. They lived off raw flesh. He raised his hand weakly, gesturing to the cuts across his face. When he spoke of them, he waved his hands high above his head, stopping to cough several times before continuing about their height and build. He said their strength was greater than ten men. Then he clawed at his neck, startling Victoria as he began the second half. It was about monsters who only drank human blood, unfit to see the day of light, yet living forever in their shame. His face grew pale as he testified of their agility, speed, and hypnotic beauty.

He was interrupted when Mother bustled back into the room, shaking her head and checking his forehead for a worsened fever. He stopped trying to talk, the effort too demanding between the coughs. Mother sent Victoria out.

Victoria ventured to his bedside after Mother had fallen asleep in the chair in the hallway, her exhausted form slumped, still clutching another cold cloth for Father's forehead in her lap. Victoria was all alone as she slowly pushed open the door to Father's room. The moon spied through the window, a giant watchful eye, as she began a story. She was sure it would cheer him up. Perhaps if she shared a good enough story, he would get out of bed.

He huffed as he listened, the pain obvious, but he did not say a word until she was done. He weakly gave a smile and stroked her cheek tenderly, using the last reserves of his strength. The stub of the missing pinky made her shiver at its sight, and Father tucked his hand back into the blankets quickly.

Motioning for Victoria to come closer, he whispered in her ear.

"Much I have left undone." He struggled to form the words properly, and Victoria had to sort them a bit in her mind to figure out what he said while he turned to cough.

"You are fine. You will get better," she whispered while praying with all her heart.

"Keep this safe. This is the answer," he mumbled as he slipped his hand over hers, placing a small black pebble in her palm. It was from the river outside. She wondered what he thought he was handing her. Perhaps in his fevered mind, it was a diamond or a shiny gold piece. The beads of sweat on his temples indicated his fever clearly. She ignored her impulse to touch his forehead, knowing it would imply her disbelief. Instead, she gave him a gracious nod. She sat with him, unsure what to say.

"Don't forget to sing," he reminded her in the frailest voice she had ever heard escape his lips. Victoria felt useless watching him struggle to breathe.

No one knew Victoria was there when his chest stopped heaving. Red skin turned cold blue. The color unnerved her, and she stood up, unsure whether to call for someone or try to shake him. But before she decided, he faded to a pale white. His dull eyes stayed open, eerily pointing straight at her until she slunk out into the hallway. She hurried away to her room, where the mountain peaks seemed to creep closer, watching her cry into the hem of her blanket.

Spring felt cold and icy as they grieved. Even the summer heat could not thaw their hearts. As autumn stripped the trees and withered the remaining stalks in the fields, things seemed bleak.

"Impractical! There are no such things," Mother had repeated each time Victoria begged for a room facing the completely opposite direction of those horrid mountains. The sharp silhouettes biting into the sky were an awful reminder of what had been stolen. Every night she would put a chair against the door leading to the balcony after locking it soundly. She would wake with awful nightmares of the beasts and monsters described so vividly she could imagine them in their entirety. She was sure she could hear them fighting outside.

Sometimes she would wake and see a figure standing on the railing, looking through the glass door. She would rub her eyes, and then it would be gone.

As Emily and Mother pushed eagerly to prepare her for the reality of her future, Victoria had to grow out of such scares. Mother repeatedly insisted Father was only fevered and hallucinating.

"Impractical! There are no such things," she repeated this to herself again now, letting the phrase catch hold and settle until she had convinced herself she had only dreamt a horrible illusion of being an animal. She looked at the plain black pebble sitting next to her brush and powder on the dresser. She meant to cast it back into the river, but, somehow, she never found the time.

A swift knock on the door pulled her from her thoughts. She gave one last glance to the mountains and shut the balcony doors behind her. Once she opened her bedroom door, Emily nodded, giving her permission to join dinner. Victoria followed with a heavy tread. The memories stirred inside, leaving a terribly large pang of sadness. It was like a thick blanket wrapped tightly about her, and it always took a while to shake off. She should not have let her mind wander into the past, not tonight.

As they sat down to dinner, Mother did not look at them. Mabel and Victoria sat side by side, trying to avoid eye contact. When no one was looking, they chatted in hushed tones quickly.

"How are your hands?" Mabel asked when her cup was lifted over her lips.

"They are smarting something sound," Victoria said, turning her face away as if avoiding a cough. She shook them under the table.

"Mine too." Mabel winced. A servant entered and offered a black-and-purple envelope on a silver platter. Shaking in excitement, Mother ripped the top off with much more gusto than needed. Mabel muffled a snicker as the strip of envelope landed on Mother's plate, right in the gravy.

"We received the official invitation to the Harvest Masquerade Ball today from Charlene!" Mother said with a smile while lifting the elaborately decorated invitation for them to see. She read the full letter out loud in its entirety, and Victoria slowly ate her meal, only half-listening to it. Mabel, less tense now with Mother smiling, had stacked most of her food into a little pile in the center of her plate and was shaping it with her fork into a smooth slope. Victoria finally gave into the fun and flung one of her peas. It landed right on top, to Mabel's delight. Mother was too intent on reading to notice.

Queen Charlene always hosted two balls a year. They had never been invited before. Now that Victoria was of age, the invitation arrived. Although Victoria would be in the spotlight this year as a new eligible lady, Mother and Mabel would accompany her. The one early in the year was called the Spring Tea. As Victoria gathered from older friends who had attended, it consisted of dressing in white and soft pastels and celebrating the end of winter. The second was the Harvest Masquerade; it required elaborately decorated masks and basking in the bounty.

Mother affectionately stroked the black envelope and traced each gold letter on it with her finger. Eligible bachelors from all around would be attending.

Soon Victoria and Mabel were scooted off to bed, climbing the grand staircase to the top and separating to their own rooms.

A creak made Victoria look up at her large glass door and she saw a tall and silent silhouette. Victoria held her breath, frozen in fear. She gripped her blankets tightly, unsure whether to scream or run or perhaps do both. It slid down and out of view.

Only the moon in the sky and a few freckled stars between the clouds remained. It took several long moments to push her shaking legs to move out of bed and cross the room. Lapsing into old habits, she placed the chair against the knob and pulled the curtains shut so she did not have to see out. A nervous pang left the candle burning bright until Mabel came in. She welcomed her sister happily as she scurried under the covers.

"I think you made a very beautiful fox, Victoria," Mabel said.

"Impractical! There are no such things." Victoria knew she was lying but saying so helped her nerves. Mabel only responded by stroking one long strand of her crimson hair, which Victoria gathered into a braid and placed on the other side, away from Mabel's reach.

For most of the night, she stared at the curtains, fearing the figure was still out there. It was a windy night, and the glass door rattled relentlessly. When she could not stand it anymore, she climbed out of bed and opened the curtains slightly, just enough for a sliver of moonlight to enter the dark room in an ominous ray. She peered out into the clear night sky. She watched the distant treetops sway and searched for anything peculiar.

Finally getting back into bed, she listened to Mabel's soft snores while casting weary eyes toward the window. Victoria felt something was staring back at her, even if she could not see it. Unsettled, she pushed herself to close her eyes, only to reopen them a few moments later when the window rattled again. Not until the glorious sunshine peeked in did she actually fall asleep.

Then Emily let herself into the room. She whipped the chair from the door with a dreadful screech across the floor. After she tied the curtains back fully, bright sunrays flooded into the room harshly. Emily tapped each girl on the head thrice. Victoria could not stir herself to wake. Emily impatiently pulled the covers off and shoved Victoria into her bath, still in her nightgown.

Victoria had no choice as Emily completed the rest of the morning routine, snapping at her for being drowsy and slow. When the time came for the corset, Emily's rough tugs woke her up completely, and she gasped in pain. Mabel had awoken to Victoria's groans and was making the bed. Emily urged them out of the room and shut the door, making sure Victoria was halfway down the stairs before turning to Mabel. Emily squeezed Mabel's arm tight in her hand while Mabel looked wide-eyed at her frown.

Once Victoria was at the threshold of the dining room, she leaned against the wall. Falling into a light daydream, she was stirred awake again when Mabel arrived. Together they entered and sat down for breakfast. As Victoria reached for a slice of toast, Mother gasped loudly. Every eye turned to Mother.

"Emily!" she exclaimed.

Victoria snapped awake, looking at Mother in alarm.

"Why did you spare Victoria from her punishment?" Mother asked with flashing cold eyes.

"I completed her knuckle rapping as soundly as Mabel's . . .," Emily said defensively. "Did you not see them last night at dinner?"

"I was far too preoccupied with the invitation to ensure you had completed a simple request." Mother pointed at Victoria's hand, which was still holding the piece of triangular toast in midair, quite forgotten in the commotion.

"No, you did not! I see no sign of punishment!" Mother said, looking from Victoria's knuckles to Emily and back again. Victoria looked at her own hands, dropping the toast completely as she looked upon her smooth knuckles.

There were no scabs or broken skin of any kind. She rubbed them in disbelief. She looked at Mabel's knuckles, still sore and broken, the scabs bright red. Emily looked most horrified.

"I swear I completed the task. She must have healed in the night," Emily said. Her voice slightly rose, defensive.

"Impossible! Mabel has not healed. As I recall, I took my leave shortly after you started, trusting you would complete your responsibility," Mother said with scorn. Emily looked baffled.

Victoria was excused from the breakfast table, only partially finished.

It was particularly hard keeping her composure while puzzling over her soft hands. Then she faced another difficulty, trying to stay awake during another lecture from Professor Carter. She fluttered her eyelashes each time she held a blink too long. She tapped her toes and whirled her thumbs in circles about each other between her palms.

"Victoria!" Mabel whispered when Professor Carter turned his back to gather another book from the high shelf using the ladder.

"What?" Victoria said.

"Do you remember yesterday?" Mabel asked quietly.

"Yes. I was punished for following your suggestion to go see Henry," Victoria replied.

"No, not the river; you were a fox!" Mabel whispered back.

"No, that was only a dream!" Victoria said with frustration. Mabel was bringing up the same thought Victoria had been struggling to keep locked away.

"A dream? How could it have been a dream if I remember too?" Mabel asked. Victoria had to agree with this logic.

"Impractical! There are no such things," she said frankly.

"And yet it still happened," Mabel said.

"No, it did not. We both had the same food that morning. Maybe it was old. Emily probably let it sit too long unattended. It was just a figment of our imagination, perhaps a hallucination. That brook water had a slight greenish hue, which must mean some sort of fungus . . ."

"No, it was not. I remember your fluffy tail." Mabel giggled as she motioned the shape of the tail.

"Do not speak of it again!" Victoria lightly slapped Mabel's hands while using the same tone Mother had used for years.

"I liked you better as a fox," Mabel snapped. Professor Carter grunted at her outburst. He looked at them sternly before resuming the reading. His voice was rhythmic and stayed in the same tone without variation. Victoria continued writing on the piece of parchment, careful to record everything noteworthy. It soon whirled together, though. Victoria lost her place and then found it again. She tried to keep taking notes, her pencil scratching shrilly on the page.

"Wake up, Miss Victoria!" Professor Carter's deep voice vibrated in her ears. She opened her eyes and realized she was lying on the desk, face smashed against her book as though it were a pillow. Professor Carter pointed with his crooked finger.

"Drawing on paper reserved for instruction too, Miss Victoria?" he asked.

"No, I would never!" Victoria instantly replied as she looked up at his face earnestly.

"Your mother will surely hear of this." As he blathered on, Victoria looked at where his crooked finger sat. At least a dozen pictures darted around the words and borders of the page. She furrowed her brows as she leaned closer to look at the sketches.

All of the drawings were foxes. There was a fox lying on its back, one nestled for sleep, and others hopping into the air. She did not recall drawing them.

Wearily, she paraded to the garden after a grueling day. She sat on the bench and leaned against her favorite tree whose trunk, once again, seemed perfectly curved to accommodate her weary back. She tried to obey the rules and study her book, but soon she was fast asleep, the book flopped upside down on the ground.

She had a dream that was vaguely familiar. She had been there before, recurring with beasts and monsters plaguing her imagination. She awoke with such a start she fell right off the bench. Something poked her painfully underneath, and when she arose, she saw her book's spine was completely broken. She quickly picked it up and dusted it off, smoothing the wrinkled pages. Once again, she had the distinct impression someone was watching her.

"Hello?" she yelled out at the rose bushes. "Who is there?" she said while looking for a long moment, waiting, hoping someone would come out and explain themselves. She heard a rustle and dove toward it without a thought as to what she was doing. Her body moved without her conscious effort, and her fingers wrapped tightly about something soft. She pulled a cottontail bunny from the undergrowth with reflexes she never knew she had the capability to muster.

She stood looking at the kicking and thrashing bunny in her hand, dumbfounded, until its back foot scratched across her collar bone.

"Oh, oh, I am sorry," she called out as the little bunny hopped away in a wild panic.

Grateful no one witnessed what had just taken place, she shook the tuft of hair from her hands in disgust and dabbed at her bleeding collarbone with her handkerchief.

It was probably near dinnertime, and Victoria felt another twinge of dismay. There would be no excuse for being late to dinner. She lifted her skirts and sprinted as best she could to the manor. Arriving out of breath, she collapsed into her seat. Mother flashed her eyes at the blood drips staining her white collar.

"Why are you late and bleeding?" Mother asked, her cheeks reddened, which only made her blue eyes fiercer.

"I caught . . . in the bushes . . . I . . . um—" Victoria sputtered.

"Victoria! Collect yourself and begin again," Mother corrected. Mabel was looking at Victoria with wide eyes and nodding her head, trying to offer support. Victoria straightened her back and took a very deep breath as she quickly laced words together in her head.

"There was a bunny in the rose bushes. It startled me, and I fell into the thorns." She nodded as if to further sell the lie by agreeing with herself. Then after the third nod, she forced herself to stop and meet Mother's unblinking gaze. Victoria broke eye contact by watching a fleck of cracked black pepper spin around in her soup. She waited for Mother to continue the lecture but was pleasantly surprised. When she shyly looked up, Mother was once again stroking the invitation to the ball, rereading it with a gleam in her eye. Victoria was grateful for Charlene and her overdone parties.

After dinner, Victoria came straight back to her room, wanting to sort her thoughts alone. She pulled out the small key to her large jewelry box. She kept it tucked between the pages of her favorite book. It was a classic fable book filled with adventurers taking epic quests. It was for children, so of course she did not read it anymore, but somehow it was the book she relied on to protect the key. She usually slid the key alongside the illustrated page depicting a large tree filled with tiny fairies hiding in its leaves with a large moon peeking above the top of the tree. In the background was a lovely white palace perched on top of a hill. She took another moment to admire the artistic detail, and then she unlocked the box. She quickly glanced over her sparkling hoard and her eyes came to rest on the necklace in the back. It was big and heavy. Father had given it to her after his father had given it to him. It was part of their antiquity. Father had reminded Victoria to keep her jewelry box locked.

Although it was valuable, cast from pure gold and precious rubies, she had never actually worn it anywhere. Mother said it was too gaudy and old-fashioned. On further examination, she had found a finely crafted tiny hinge fastened on the edge of the largest center ruby. It had elegantly carved clasps holding it in place and connecting it to the gold chain. She opened the ruby by pulling on the delicate latch attached to the front with her fingernail tip. As usual, she peered inside and turned it over to shake it once or twice, merely tolerating her curiosity a bit further. She wondered who had forged this piece and the worth of a hollow ruby. Why would someone go to such lengths to craft such a tiny pocket? She guessed it could barely hold more than some grains of sand or ash. She hoped it was not supposed to hold the ashes of someone dear. She remembered dancing and jumping around, playing dress-up with it about her neck as a child. The thought of an ancestor's ashes dusting the room made her queasy.

Mother knocked at the door. Victoria set the necklace down and settled into her bed. Mother came to her room and turned toward the lavender dress hanging on the wall.

"Oh, your dress is almost finished. It will be splendid once it is properly altered!" Mother said, running her fingers along the seams. Mother noticed the necklace out.

"Oh, you are taking Father's old necklace to the ball?" she asked. "Are you sure you do not want to take a piece more in today's fashion?" Mother gestured toward the dainty silver necklaces in the front of the box.

"Well, it has been in the family for many generations," Victoria said, stashing her smirk behind an eager expression, giving large innocent eyes with tiny lips. "Father always took care to store it properly in his finest chest. If it was important to him, I want to wear it to such a grand event," Victoria explained slowly, relishing the obvious dilemma playing out on Mother's face.

"All right, if you wish," Mother said, a bit of unexpected emotion seeping into her voice. She looked at it for a few long moments before setting it back on the dresser. Victoria was slightly puzzled at her mother giving in so easily. A wave of shame rushed over her. As Victoria tried to shake it off, Mother did another unusual thing. She sat down on the end of the bed. Victoria was already in her nightgown, tucked squarely in the center of the bed, determined to sleep tonight. She slid over to give Mother room.

"Now, Victoria. What is the matter? You have been so strange lately," Mother asked, anxiety soaked her face, pulling on her lips, eyes, and forehead.

"Mother, I am a young lady now, but I do not feel like one," Victoria admitted.

"Yes. Explain to me what you have been feeling," Mother said in a tone Victoria had long forgotten. It unlocked distant memories. Victoria began to vaguely remember it from a time when she was very young. It was pleasant and oddly reassuring. Perhaps she could ask her mother for help. Maybe she would have an answer.

"I have changed into something unladylike completely." Victoria looked down at her hands and rubbed them together nervously. Mother just nodded, still listening, so she continued.

"I found it very difficult to stay calm when all these changes happened to me," Mother said, sounding more nurturing in that one sentence than she had all year.

"Really? It happened to you? You know what I am speaking of?" Victoria sat up in her bed, pulling the covers up to her face and holding her breath. Mother nodded.

"Abnormal changes?" Mother asked.

"I grew hair where it should not be," Victoria answered in a tight whisper.

"That is perfectly normal," Mother said, giving her a knowing look.

"And the pain was the most intense I have ever felt, like I wanted to vomit. All I could do was huddle in the corner and cry," Victoria went on, mumbling a bit, but she could not slow down her words.

"Yes," Mother agreed. "Was this the reason for all the misbehavior, Victoria?" Mother asked, still tender and kind.

"Yes," she said and could not help but wrap her arms about her mother in desperation; both were almost knocked off-balance. They teetered on the foot of the bed. Victoria pulled her mouth close up to Mother's ear and whispered.

"Yesterday I turned into an animal!" she finally said it and gasped as if the very walls would judge. Her mother pulled away quickly, looking straight into her face.

"No need to be alarmed, Victoria," her mother said calmly.

"Really?" Victoria breathed, trying to strain her ears to make sure she was hearing correctly.

"Yes, I went through it, and I was scared at first too. But it is just a part of growing up," Mother said with a slight smile.

Mother stood up to leave, straightening her dress. "That is how you will bear my grandchildren, my dear." Mother once again smiled, a bit bolder now.

"Good night, sleep tight," she said, returning to her usual emotionless tone.

Victoria felt a rush of embarrassment as she realized they were not on the same subject at all. She hunched her back, indignantly brooding over the impossible situation. Mother tapped her own shoulders and nodded toward Victoria. Victoria tried to salvage what little composure she had left by smiling as she sat up straight. Mother smiled back in approval before shutting the door. Once alone, Victoria instantly slumped back, discontented. It was a mistake trying to tell Mother. She could never understand.

Victoria glanced at the curtains, fearing they might have fluttered. She then lit the candle. Placing the chair under the knob, she rearranged the curtains to be overlapped, definitely closed. She was on the edge of sprinting out of the room, perhaps to the south wing of the manor. She made herself lay under the covers and try to sleep.

A creak made Victoria jump and gasp.

"Mabel?" Victoria asked, spying her sister standing near her bed. She had brought her teddy bear, which meant that she, too, was feeling the unease.

"I hate nighttime. This house sounds weird at night," Mabel said in a whisper as she climbed into the bed.

"Me too," Victoria finally admitted.

"And you were a fox," Mabel said, sounding a bit excited about the matter.

"Impractical! There are no such things," Victoria said, once again hitting Mother's pitch perfectly. Mabel just sighed and soon was asleep. Victoria eventually fell asleep, ignoring the tapping noises echoing into her room, exhaustion taking over.

CHAPTER 3

A CHEERY HARVEST

VICTORIA FORCED A SMILE as Mother discussed the dress particulars for the Harvest Masquerade. She was on a pedestal, and the seamstress was pinning the dress to the proper measurements. Mother chose lavender-colored silk edged with a darker purple lace and thread. She hovered close to the seamstress, following each movement. Victoria felt irritated, and with a quick glance exchange with the seamstress, she realized she was not alone.

Mabel sat on a cushioned chair, quietly embroidering Victoria's initials onto yet another handkerchief. Mother said she needed many more. Victoria was to give one to each gentleman who asked her to dance with him.

She knew Mabel was only half-paying attention to the conversation. Precious few days of sunshine remained, and she was trapped indoors embroidering.

Mother assigned plenty to do, and Victoria felt grateful for the distractions today. Tonight was a dinner party Mother had planned. Many of the suitors' mothers would be attending to get better acquainted with Victoria. She was expected to answer each question with poise and have a graceful demeanor.

The evening came faster than expected. Soon she was being whisked down the staircase and into the dining hall by Emily. She spoke reassuringly to Victoria and gave her a smile before disappearing into the kitchen. Emily's unexpected kindness gave Victoria a boost of energy as she entered the room.

It seemed loud despite all the whispering women, each trying to retain the delicate image of the modern lady. Victoria thought it sounded like a room full of mice squeaking, and the shuffling skirts sounded like little paws scampering across the floor. She straightened her face and tried to regain a proper pose. Fan to her lips, trying to mimic her mother's eyelash flutter, she felt ridiculous all the while.

Mary Johnson, Henry's mother, was the first to acknowledge her. Mother saw the entire Johnson family as nothing more than servants and treated them as such. The only reason Mary was invited tonight was simply because it would look impolite to not invite her since her son had been invited to begin attending the masquerades last year.

Victoria saw where Henry inherited his hazel eyes in Mary's face. She smiled at the thought of Henry. Victoria had gathered from their limited encounters that Mary seemed to be under the assumption that her son was to marry Victoria. Mary would be proud. Mother would be infuriated.

"You ask the first question, Mary," another woman named Gretchen spoke. She had dark brunette hair, pale porcelain skin, and burnt sienna eyes. Victoria knew that was the best way to describe the color of her eyes because the day they had met last summer, Victoria had been painting and among the assortment of colors one was labeled *burnt sienna*. She liked the way it sounded. Gretchen had a friend named Hannah. Hannah's black hair and lovely deep-almond skin always seemed to glisten in the light. Victoria often wished she could touch her cheek to see if it was as velvety soft as it looked.

They were almost inseparable. Wherever one was, the other didn't seem too far behind. They laughed between themselves so often Victoria found herself shying away from them. Victoria knew it agitated Mother as well, but it would be impolite to discuss their rude manners, so Victoria had to listen to the hissing whispers while she tried to enjoy her tea.

She had to pull her thoughts back and give a pleasant smile.

"Oh no, Gretchen, you can go first," Mary said. And so went their banter until they decided the topic of Victoria's talents was the focus of the discussion. Victoria found herself reciting Mother's list.

"I am excellent at embroidery and skilled at playing the harp and flute," Victoria said dryly. "I have practiced daily on all three talents since I was a small child, except, of course, on Sundays. This is reserved for religious study."

"Very impressive," Hannah said. Victoria gave a small bow in response.

"Henry would love to hear you play. Will you play for him sometime?" Mary asked.

"Of course. I look forward to it." Victoria nodded and then tried to hide her eager expression.

Mother looked appalled for a brief instant but quickly resumed her polite mannerism. The women were pleasant, all using the same tone as Mother, which was stripped of any emotion. Victoria felt lonely amid the constant bombardment of inquiries.

It was getting uncomfortable and tedious. The noise seemed to be getting louder. She put down her fork and placed her hands in her lap. Her fingers brushed something soft. At first, she thought it was the fabric of her skirt, but a quick glance down stirred fear.

Red hair was sprouting over her hand and climbing up her arm. Victoria felt her cheeks getting warm. She started using her fan with the other hand, the tiny gust not nearly enough. She pushed her chair back and stood. Mother's head snapped toward her, cold eyes commanding her to sit back down. Victoria ignored her and hustled out of the room.

She rushed through the hallway and out the front door. The refreshing night air hit her face. As she made her way farther from the house, she scratched at her neck and felt the familiar tuft of hair. She ran to duck out of view, away from prying eyes. She finally came to a stop, surrounded by the red and pink rosebushes on every side. She could not hear anything but the slight rustle of wind through the trees. She looked up into the sky and at the stars.

She thought calming her heart rate could evade the transformation, but she was wrong. Her body continued to crumple in pain. She gasped sharply. It was unbearable, and she had to stifle her screams into her gown. She did not know what else to do but to watch as her hands turned into paws. Kneeling on the cold cobblestone, she cried into the night.

When it was finally over, she opened her eyes and noticed it was much easier to see in the dark as a fox. She looked about in amazement for several long moments. She turned her large ears toward the manor. She could hear the silverware clanking against the dishes and the women chattering. She stood in the pile of fabric that made her dress. It seemed too heavy as she tried to pull it in her teeth to move. She needed to get it off the ground to avoid any stains or debris, but soon she gave up. Leaving the noisy dinner party behind, she wandered through the garden.

Turn human! she snapped in her mind. *Human!* Nothing happened.

A gentle gale ruffled her large ears and fluffy tail. The distinct chalky smell of smoke filled her nostrils. She followed it curiously. She went through the garden and down the courtyard, along the white fencing. She now saw the odd blue flames near the tree line. It was burning so hot the tree nearest it, although lush and green, was charred solid black in every place the blaze had touched. Suddenly, two figures dropped from the top of the tree and landed heavily on the ground. One of the shadowed figures caught the blue sparks on the edge of their cloak and erupted in bright white-and-blue fire. She watched in horror as the two-legged figure ran into the trees, disappearing from view. The other silhouette reached his hand up toward the burning tree, and the fire leapt from the branch into his hand.

Victoria was too stunned to do anything as she replayed the sight of the fire vanishing into his palm over in her head. He turned and looked around. She pressed her ears flat and ducked below the bushes, hiding herself as the being passed by. His face was hooded, so she never caught more than the tip of his nose. It took several long moments before she was sure she was safe to venture back to the garden.

She did not know what else to do, so she went to her favorite tree to wait. She was too small to reach the bench, so she sat underneath it. Poking her little head out to look up at the stars, she waited. When she saw Mabel approaching, she felt a tinge of irritation. She wanted to brood alone.

"Hey, Victoria," Mabel said in a casual voice. "I thought I would find you here." She took a seat on the bench. She put her hand down, and Victoria climbed into it, feeling slightly incensed at Mabel's easy acceptance of her new form. Mabel pulled her up onto her lap and petted her ears softly. "Mother is really mad. I guessed you'd be here. It is the only place to hide tonight," she said.

Victoria yipped, which was strange to her ears, so she stopped and sat quietly.

"I think Father would have liked you like this," Mabel said. Victoria felt a pang of loss again. Mabel was younger than her, but she, too, remembered well enough to know it was completely true. He would have thought it was fascinating. Mabel breathed heavily as she cocked her neck up to see the sky momentarily, as if expecting to see his face in the stars. She then looked back down upon Victoria.

"I want to be an animal! If you are one then I bet I am going to be too! Maybe I will be a pony or a butterfly." Mabel then sat Victoria down and stood on the bench, acting as if she were flying.

"Mabel!" Mother's voice rang out. Her approaching footsteps drove Victoria deep into the brush. "Have you seen Victoria?"

"No, I have not seen the Victoria you are looking for," Mabel said.

Victoria rolled her eyes. Mabel always thought she was so witty.

"Well, it is off to bed with you; I still have guests and can't be worrying about you too."

"Yes, Mother," Mabel said obediently. She shuffled by the bench, pausing for a moment. Victoria jumped into her skirts, and then Mabel slowly made her way to the manor. She marched all the way up the stairs and did not stop until they were in the safety of Victoria's room with the door locked behind them.

"Okay, change back!" Mabel said as she waved her arms in the air as if casting a spell. Victoria looked at her. If it was that easy, she would have done it already.

"Just think human. Be human!" Mabel said. Victoria just put her paws up on her bed frame and looked over expectantly. Mabel picked her up and set her on top of the blanket with a giggle.

"You would be the best pet in the world!" Mabel said happily. "But you should change back now. Mother looked really mad."

Victoria kept thinking *human*. She spied her wardrobe and looked at the dresses. She needed two arms and a pair of legs to wear them. She needed to be taller and less furry. She kept picturing herself as a human. It was exhausting after a while. There was no pain or patches of hair going away.

Mabel began to sing the usual lullaby Father always sang to them. She just sang the gibberish, the real words long forgotten. The melody remained embedded in their minds. It had slow low notes at first and led into higher notes until the highest note was sometimes hard to hit, especially now as Mabel's throat was coarse from whispering.

Victoria tried again, focusing on Mabel's voice. She wanted to be human again. She was going to be human again.

"Oh, look, it's working!" Mabel said.

Victoria felt a familiar tingling sensation followed by the intense pain, harsher now due to her dreaded anticipation. Victoria gritted her teeth, and it took everything in her power to not scream. Time moved impossibly slow as they both sat in a hushed silence, watching the hair disappear. Mabel held her paw, which painstakingly transformed back into a hand. The nose shrinking was the most painful part. It shot agony up through her nostrils, past her eye sockets, and up into her head. Finally, Mabel held up a robe, and Victoria put it on while trying to ignore the ache of her limbs.

"I am glad to be back," she said, once again looking into the mirror and touching her face. "Okay, we have to go get my dress. It is in the garden. Hopefully Mother has not found it yet." As Victoria said this, she opened the door to find Emily coming up the stairs. She was holding the dress over her arm, looking curious. Victoria slowly came out of her room, smiling politely.

"Did you take leave of your dress in the garden, Miss Victoria?" Emily asked.

"Yes! I can explain." Victoria said.

"There is a perfectly logical explanation," Mabel added quickly.

"Um, there was a spider in my skirts, and I was frightened," Victoria threw out the first thought that came to her head.

"A spider chased you out of your dress, and you ran in your undergarments all the way to your room. How is it that no one witnessed this?" Emily asked.

At this, Victoria was at a loss. She needed to bargain. "Please don't tell Mother."

"Why should I lie to your mother?"

"Because I will start folding my own laundry," Victoria quickly offered. Emily gave a long pause to examine Victoria's face. A small smirk crossed her face as she dropped the dress into Victoria's desperate, outstretched hands. Mabel had already crossed the hall into her room where she was climbing into bed obediently.

Perhaps I can control this, Victoria thought as she walked down the steps. Mother caught her by the arm.

"Where have you been, child?" Mother hissed.

"I, um—" Victoria winced as Mother squeezed harder, yanking her down the hallway.

"Ow, you are hurting me," Victoria said.

"Hush. You behave." Mother let go as they neared the entrance, gliding gracefully into the dining hall, wearing a smile as if perfectly content. Victoria followed obediently.

"Victoria is feeling much better now. The slight dizzy spell has passed," Mother told the concerned-looking women. After they heard this announcement, they smiled and began asking more questions. Victoria forced back the tears and smiled. She curtsied and laughed accordingly.

"My son Fredrick loves to fox hunt. Would you ever ride with him on the hunt?" Hannah asked.

Victoria felt like she just swallowed a dozen bees that were now flying in her belly. She only smiled and nodded at the irony.

"If that is his interest, so shall it be mine," she said pleasantly. Out of the corner of her eye, Victoria saw Mother nod.

Hannah agreed and began a story about Fredrick. From the way his mother described him, Victoria promised herself to avoid this Fredrick at the masquerade. Victoria wished the night would come to an end rapidly. There was dessert and tea served afterward, but even the berry tarts were sour on Victoria's tongue.

Finally, the guests were dismissed, and Victoria was sent to bed. Victoria turned into Mabel's room. Mabel woke to her entering and patted the space beside her.

"Let me tell you about the burning tree I saw this evening," Victoria said. Mabel eagerly scooted closer to hear.

CHAPTER 4

A CHARRED PETAL

THE PREPARATION FOR THE Harvest Masquerade started before the sun rose. Mabel shook Victoria awake and then pranced about the room.

"What are you so excited about?" Victoria asked in a drowsy voice. "The Harvest Masquerade means nothing to you yet."

"It means finally being done with all the preparations. I have embroidered so many handkerchiefs for you. My fingertips are still numb from all the needle pricks." Mabel was still prancing. "And Mother said that when Emily went into the market, she overheard two of Queen Charlene's cooks discussing their recipe for a strawberry trifle that will be served."

Victoria sighed and pulled the covers over her head, falling back into a light doze. Too soon, Mabel scrambled back to Victoria and told her Emily was making her way up the stairs. Victoria was unsure if she was just lethargic or if her apprehension was taking an unusually strong manifestation. Victoria seemed to be slower than reasonable, and Mabel noticed.

"Do you not want to go to the ball?" Mabel asked.

"No, I do. I want to go." Victoria had to push an energetic tone into that statement and found it exhausting. Mabel gave her a look and then pointed at her as Emily walked in.

"Victoria is ill," Mabel said flatly.

"Oh, what is wrong?" Emily asked, sounding concerned.

"No, I will be all right. I am just a bit tired," Victoria said.

"Tell me if any other symptoms occur," Emily said as she began their morning routine.

They made their way outside with Emily carrying their luggage behind them. Mr. Johnson and Henry approached, leading the horses. Both were dressed in the black suits Mother had chosen for them for this particularly important event. Victoria gave Henry a quick smile when Mother was not looking. He nodded back, raising his arms to further show off the fancy suit. She giggled at his expression as he held the door open for her, offering his hand with much flourish.

"You look quite handsome," Victoria whispered. Henry beamed as he helped her inside the carriage.

She admired it once again as she climbed inside. It was sleek black with her family crest engraved into the wooden sides. It was accented with a bit of golden paint, and the window frames were longer and narrower than most. All six of the chestnut horses were vigorously brushed until their coats shone. Victoria gave Henry a final smile as he closed the door after Mabel and Mother.

"Hopefully you will meet Mason. He is the only heir of Charlene, not to mention the most eligible bachelor in the land," Mother said. Victoria did not want to think about how unbearably pushy Mother was going to be the entire night, so she just politely smiled.

Victoria sat with Mabel on the bench inside, facing the front. Mother sat on the larger pillowed rear-facing seat. Emily was sent to the front with the coachmen. Victoria silently wished they could trade places. She looked out the window as they traveled ever closer to the Black Needles as the first rays of dawn peeked over the horizon.

Victoria secretly hoped that the sun would rise too close to the hillside and burn the mountain's haggard face. She imagined the snow melting and running down in streams, as if tears, over the charred blackness. She blinked, and the Black Needles were still tall and proud. They scoffed at her as she traveled toward them. Part of her wanted to lunge out of the coach, but Mother's stern face kept her sitting in her seat.

When they passed the white fence line, Victoria eagerly looked at the tree she had witnessed burning last night. It was half green and growing and the other half, split right down the middle, was black. Victoria and Mabel looked from the tree to Mother, wondering if she would notice. Gratefully Mother was preoccupied with her needlework.

Victoria sighed in relief and took up her book. She pretended to study but lingered on the same page she had drawn the little fox pictures. She had tried to erase them, but the imprint was still visible in this bright sunshine. She now stared at them, letting her mind wander.

An unexpected stop of the horses jogged her thoughts. The coachmen hollered for them to stay in the coach, but of course, Mother ignored these commands. She was sure she was behind schedule, although they had passed by three other manors that were just strapping their horses to the coach.

"What is it?" Mabel asked as Mother got back into the coach, looking pale. She shushed her and pulled the curtains shut on both windows sharply. Victoria and Mabel dared not ask by the sight of Mother.

When they reached the market, Mother was distracted by some friends and began to talk. Victoria's curiosity was itching more than her anticipation of getting caught, so she turned to Mabel and begged for silence.

"On one condition," Mabel said, sounding older than her years, with negotiation.

Victoria sighed. "What do you want?" she asked.

"You have to tell me what you find out. You have to!"

"Okay, agreed," Victoria nodded.

Mabel smiled, and Victoria was already out of sight, heart pounding slightly.

She shuffled to the coachmen's barn. Hiding in the shadows, she listened to them greet and swear at each other. She peeked inside as she heard Henry and his father talking with the others, resting themselves over a table of cards and booze.

"Lying dead in the road. Just lying there, blood-covered. It was a man, his body shredded by something awful," Mr. Johnson said. A few others stopped talking to listen to his husky voice.

"You're drunk, Johnny, and making up tales."

"It's true!" Henry said.

"No creature I've ever seen can do that kind of harm," Mr. Johnson said, shaking his head.

"We only got wolves here," another man said.

"Well, then, a very large wolf," Mr. Johnson said, mumbling the last bit as he took another chug from his mug. The other men laughed.

"You're blathering now. Anything that big would only stay in the Black Needle Mountains."

The conversation died down as they began the next round of cards. Her imagination ran wild, faster than her brisk walk back to Mabel. Father had described the creature in such detail, she was sure it was a beast who had killed the man. She imagined them hunting and feeding on travelers' flesh. When she saw Mabel's eager face, Victoria reminded herself it was impossible, shoving her mind back into reality.

"Um, it was a dead horse," Victoria lied.

"Gross," Mabel said. "Just there in the middle of the road?"

"They guessed it was exhausted and collapsed," Victoria added lamely.

"Oh, that is really sad," Mabel said with large eyes, her face crinkled in sadness, further justifying Victoria's lie.

"Yes, quite a shame. People just do not know how to treat them properly," Victoria said.

After Mother was satisfied with her shopping at the marketplace, they rode up the rest of the hillside and turned inside the large brass gates toward the palace.

The smell of rose seeped into the coach cabin. It was so thick Victoria was puzzled when the door opened and there was not a rose in sight. Then she saw a large wagon filled with the brilliant red, disappearing behind the corner toward the servant entrance. The tall white stone archways and twisting towers rose high into the sky. Victoria had to tilt her head back to see the top spiral. Mother looked as though she would faint, and instinctively Victoria held her arm, offering balance.

A butler came to greet them and directed the Johnsons to the stables.

"My word!" Mother gasped, awe breaking up her usually bored expression. Mabel and Victoria exchanged looks of genuine excitement as they fixated on the large fountain standing in the center of the front yard. It was enormous, deeper than the average pond. There were several grand statues arranged in variety of positions, so the water streamed down from their intricately carved pots or bowls. A swan with outstretched wings shot water high into the air from its delicately shaped beak. It was so breath-taking Victoria found she had forgotten herself entirely and stood with her mouth agape. The spell was broken when there was a little splash and Victoria raced to the edge, Mabel right behind her. They sat on the marble stones and looked down into its depths.

"There are golden fish in there!" Mabel said in delight. Even Mother watched the fish swimming for some time, the three of them enjoying the masterpiece together. But the moment was interrupted by the impatient butler. He cleared his throat loudly and gestured toward the palace. Victoria understood, their luggage was heavy. The butler held two of their bags and his assistant, a young boy, teetered under the weight of Mother's carpetbag.

Mother gawked at all the paintings and tapestries. Then she ogled the furniture. Mother could not stop herself; she rushed into the large ballroom and was greeted with the shocked faces of the servants at the intrusion. They were arranging the large bouquets of deep red roses into dozens of tall violet vases. Victoria admitted it was a breathtaking sight, but she felt more curious to find the explanation for such thick curtains. It was one of the last remaining warm days full of sunshine and beauty, yet all the curtains were tightly drawn over the windows.

"Why are all the curtains drawn?" Victoria asked out loud. None of the servants raised their eyes to answer; they were busily attending the preparations.

"Who cares? Look at this fabric!" Mother said while running her fingers over them affectionately. "I would want to show this off as well."

Mother stepped into the next room, and as she disappeared behind the doorway, Mabel wrapped herself in the nearby curtain panel mockingly. Victoria laughed silently as Mabel fluttered her eyelashes, pretending to adore the curtains by lavishly petting them.

"Gracious me! These curtains are divine!" Mabel whispered and shimmied to and fro, using the curtains as a dress. Victoria could not stop herself from giggling and tried to stifle it with her hand, which resulted in a snort. Mabel pointed at her with a gasp, and Victoria shook her head. A servant stopped to look at them, opening her mouth and then shutting it again before continuing on. Unraveling herself from the window, Mabel straightened up and Victoria quickly followed, extinguishing her laughter the best she could.

Mother's constant admiring of the walls, floor, and everything else down to the little pillows set on the benches was so ecstatic she was almost out of breath when she finally regained her composure. An annoyed butler escorted them to their room.

"This will be your quarters for the duration of the week." He gestured toward the bell on the wall. "Please do hesitate to ring for service," he ungraciously offered with a frown.

"Oh yes, thank you," Mother said, oblivious to the insult as she impatiently fussed with her hair in the mirror. Victoria and Mabel exchanged a smile as he shut the door louder than necessary.

Commanding Mabel to hold the pins, Mother did not notice Victoria slip out of the room. She hoped she could remember how to get back. She wandered until she finally had to ask a passing servant.

"Which way to the gardens?" Victoria asked.

The servant looked at her indifferently and pointed directly behind her. She turned and looked at a huge door. It was engraved with many symbols in its dark wooden flesh. The knob was massive, and she had to use both hands to pull it open. The thick smell of rose flooded in, and she closed her eyes to breathe it in.

She stepped out, leaving the door ajar, unsure if she would be able to get it open again from the outside. Blinking a few times in the bright sunlight, she rubbed her eyes. As she looked over the garden from the balcony, she gasped. Every petal on each rose held no bright color. They were all black, darker than a June beetle's shell.

She stepped down the stairs and found herself plucking a velvet petal and holding it up to the sunlight. Black. The stems and leaves were green and growing. The roses smelled wonderful, but there were no bright reds and pinks. Even white or yellow roses she would have admired. The roses were undoubtedly forsaken.

Without a backward glance, she marched back up the steps of the balcony and into the castle. Flinging herself inside, she slammed the door shut. Leaning against it, as if holding the dark at bay, Victoria only breathed again when they were out of sight. She stroked the ruby necklace hanging from her neck. It was heavy. Perhaps she would not wear it all night long. Realizing her eyes were closed, she felt a bit silly. She opened them to find a man strolling down the hallway toward her. He walked past her but stopped and turned on his heel in his shiny shoes until both polished leather toes were pointed directly at her.

"Miss, are you okay?" he asked. His light brown hair was combed in place, looking as proper as the house he stood in. She recognized the crest on his cuff links and knew it could only be the famous Mason.

"Yes, I am quite all right. Thank you for your inquiry," she said quietly, trying to muster all her mother's mannerisms as she curtsied.

"Did you enjoy the garden?" he asked with a gesture toward the door to the garden he had just seen her come through.

"Oh, um . . . It was . . ." She desperately wanted to say what she was supposed to but was appalled when she heard her own voice say, "No, it was horrible." She covered her mouth afterward, suddenly embarrassed. She looked away, hoping that he was not offended.

"Really?" he said in a voice sounding more curious than insulted. At this, she looked up at him. He wore an amused smile. "I have never cared for them either. My name is Mason Fossey."

"Yes, I know. Prince Mason. Only living child of Charlene Fossey, heir to the throne." She stopped, feeling silly once again reciting Mother's words. "I am Victoria." She lifted her gloved hand to him, and he kissed it as was proper.

"It's a pleasure to meet you," he said with an intrigued smile. Victoria was unsure what to say next, so she curtsied again. He bowed again, and Victoria giggled.

"We are going to lose ourselves in the theatrics of proper etiquette," Mason said. "Let me give you a tour of the palace. I can escort you." He offered his arm graciously, and she took it a bit nervously.

"Are you excited for this evening?" she asked politely as they continued down the long hallway.

"Yes, I enjoy meeting new people, especially when they are so beautiful," he said, giving her a sidelong glance. The overdone compliment was unexpected, and she had no idea what to do with it, so she remained silent.

"Are you excited?" he asked, saving her the embarrassment of dead air.

"Somewhat," she said hesitantly, realizing how rude it was to say to the host. "I mean, I am happy to attend," she corrected herself, then looked at Mason, who was now standing in the middle of the stairs, waiting for further explanation.

"Have you ever noticed anything peculiar happen here?" she finally asked. His eyebrows struck a curious arch. "I mean, you live right here on the foothills of the mountains, and I have heard rumors," she said and then stopped herself from saying anything more, hoping that he would elaborate. He just resumed walking.

"Well, what have you noticed?" he asked, dodging the question smoothly.

"On our way here, it was said that there was a dead man in the road. It delayed our carriage," she said, now feeling a bit absurd as she heard herself speak.

"Anything else?" Mason asked with his strange mahogany eyes searching hers.

"The black roses were a bit ominous," she said.

"Well, thieves and robbers line any road, not just the Black Needle Mountains. As for the black roses, Charlene paid extra for them, imported from foreign lands," Mason said. "You have nothing to fear. Please enjoy your stay here; this is supposed to be fun."

"Charlene? You call your mother by her name?" Victoria asked.

"Ours is a tried relationship. Calling her mother proves harder, I can assure you," he said. They continued the tour, and she was sure she would lose her way if left alone in the palace. He opened most of the doors, showing libraries, studies, parlors, and conservatories.

"This is a huge palace. How long did it take you to learn your way around?" she asked.

"I have been here all my life. It seems small compared to other places I have visited."

"You would laugh if I gave you a tour of my home. It would take only a few moments." Victoria giggled, imagining herself showing Mason up the one flight of stairs. Mason turned to her and looked her in the eyes again. She wished he would stop doing it because every time he did, she felt very small. It was a funny feeling, and she almost let her begging feet take off running down the hallway.

"I am sure your home is lovely, based solely on the fact you live there," Mason said, pulling on a strand of loose hair and tucking back behind her ear. Victoria could not resist a smirk. She tried to stifle it, but enough escaped Mason pulled back.

"What?" Mason said, looking alarmed.

"I know it is terrible for me to ruin your moment, but it seems a bit rehearsed," she said, pulling an apologetic smile.

"No, you are right. I have been giving plenty of tours today," Mason said frankly.

"Sorry, I was impolite," Victoria said, and then she felt a bit self-conscious and fell silent.

Mason cleared his throat lightly and looked around. "You are right. This is all a bit dreary," he said, pulling her hand to follow him down another hallway. "This is not part of the tour, and you are not permitted in this wing of the palace," he said, looking about as he drew a small key from his pocket. He unlocked the door and stepped inside before beckoning for her to follow.

It was a landing to a steep spiraling staircase, and the last steps ended in complete darkness.

"Um, no, thank you," she said, turning to flee. Mason gave a chuckle, a real laugh—not a polite banter, but one from deep inside his throat.

"No, no, do not be afraid. It is worth the walk." He reached across her, his knuckles ruffling her skirt a bit as he grabbed the candlestick perched on the long table. "Here, you can even hold the flame," he offered graciously.

Despite her inner voice screaming at her to not follow a stranger into darkness, Victoria found herself stepping down the stairwell. As they descended, Victoria noticed the drop in temperature. She was sure they were now underground.

At the end of the staircase, there was a long hallway with many doors, but Mason walked straight past them until they curved down another hallway. There was an echoed scream in the distance. Victoria jumped. Mason laughed again, but his voice sounded sinister in the shadows of the dancing flame.

"Probably a mouse. The servants are dreadfully afraid of them when they come down here," Mason said.

"Yeah." She laughed nervously, mentally counting the steps from the staircase in case she had to make her way back without light.

"My mother will be wondering where I have gone . . .," Victoria said with a shaky voice. "I do not think your tour was dreary. It was good. I was quite enjoying it. Perhaps we can finish it upstairs," Victoria continued to murmur under her breath.

Mason did not say anything. He just pulled on her arm a bit harder. Dragging her to a door that he took another key out to unlock. He opened it and beckoned her inside. It was too dark to see anything, and Mason let go of her arm. She stood frozen in fear, unsure if she should call out or try to run.

Suddenly, he lit a lamp, and the entire chamber was aglow in its cheery light. She was standing in a room filled with desserts—cakes, pies, cookies, and tarts on every shelf.

"This place stays cool and dry, perfect for the baked goods to rest. The bakers have been working all night," Mason said, sliding two berry tarts and a small cake into a basket. He grabbed a few handfuls of different berries and tossed them into the basket as well.

"Here, try some of this chocolate buttercream. It is made by a specialty baker Charlene hired personally." He dipped a spoon into the bowl and gave it to her.

"Wow, I have never tasted anything so delicious!" she said, all fears faded.

"The chef who made it has been perfecting the recipe for years until it is ready to be revealed tonight."

"It is like nothing I have ever tried before," she said.

Mason gave a smile. "I would think the daughter of Richard would have tried more exotic things," he said.

"You knew my father?" Victoria asked, feeling her stomach churn at mention of him, the familiar pang of sadness grasping her heart once again like a heavy blanket.

"Oh, I apologize. I assumed you knew he worked for Charlene," Mason said. Victoria just shook her head. "Well, your father, rest his soul, was one of the bravest men I have ever had the pleasure to meet. He had no fear wandering into the Black Needle Mountains," Mason said respectfully. When Victoria did not answer, he shifted his feet. "You knew he went into the mountains, right? I am sure he brought you back all sorts of souvenirs?"

"Well, I knew he traveled there, but, no, he didn't mention he was on an errand for your mom, nor did he bring anything back for us," Victoria said.

"I am sorry. I should not have mentioned it," Mason offered.

"I know you did not mean to offend," she said with a slight nod, looking at her feet.

"Let me make it up to you!" he said, trying to draw some cheer back into the room. "Let's have ourselves a picnic," he said, pulling more food into the basket.

As they made their way back toward the staircase, a faint voice echoed in the hallway, and Victoria whipped around to find the source of the noise, causing her shoe to slip off her heel. There was nothing to see in the long hallway except a few torches burning slowly, resting in their wall mountings lazily. She had to exhale before bending in her corset, she then slipped it back over her ankle, fighting the folds of her dress all the while. As she looked down, her eye caught a strange marking along the wall. She dropped down onto both knees to read it closer.

smile raises concern
blood flames burn
tainted black petals turn
stomach churn
silver to yearn
sunlight slowly fills the urn

She reread it quickly, puzzled still. Mason did not acknowledge her stop, and his light was fading in the distance. She had to hurry to catch back up to him. He pressed onward up the stairs, and once they reached the top, he locked the door behind them.

"We shall enjoy these treats in the other garden, away from the roses you found so disturbing," Mason said, and they soon were on the balcony overlooking a series of hedges cut precisely into giant rectangular sections and forming a sort of maze. The balcony was so heavily shaded Victoria had to lean over the railing to catch the sunlight on her face and arms while she puzzled over it.

"I would get lost down there."

"Many do," Mason said with a lighthearted laugh. Victoria forced another giggle, a bit unnerved.

He placed the basket on the glass table and offered her a chair.

"This is the fanciest picnic I have ever been to," she said as she picked up the engraved fork, her little pinky extended dramatically. Mason frowned.

"Oh, no, I was just having a bit of fun. It is nice," Victoria said apologetically, lamenting on her actions. She needed to stop acting silly and grow up. Mason returned her smile, but like all his smiles, it was reluctant and short.

"Why are you so anxious?" Victoria asked.

"Me? I seem anxious?" Mason asked. "Hundreds of people are coming to my house this evening, and I am supposed to be the courteous host, and my mother hopes I choose a bride this very evening."

"Oh, understandable," Victoria said, offering a sympathetic tone. "If you have other things that need your attention…"

"No, this has actually been quite refreshing, meeting Richard's daughter," Mason said, sighing pleasantly. They sat for several long moments of silence together. The soft breeze blew through her hair, pricking the goosebumps on her arms and neck. She ignored the impulse to rub her arms for warmth.

"What else do you remember of my father?" she asked curiously.

"I only met him a couple of times, but I was always impressed by his ingenuity," Mason said.

"Do you know why he went into the Black Needles on his final trip?" Victoria asked. "Was he on your mother's errand?" When Mason gave her a curious glance, she quickly explained, "Mother never wanted my father to discuss business. She thought it was dull."

"I do not know either. Sometimes Charlene is very secretive," Mason shrugged. "He never told you anything about his travels?" he asked.

"No, we never really talked about it. He only told me fun little stories he made up about them," Victoria said with a small smile reminiscing. Mason looked at her and encouraged her to go on with a slight nod. "Well, he would always talk about fairies, goblins—" Victoria realized how it sounded and tried to end her sentence quickly. "And mermaids," she finished with a slight scoff.

Mason gave a short chuckle. "Mermaids?" he repeated.

"Yeah, for my little sister's entertainment," she said, trying to deflect any childish demeanor from herself.

"That sounds like a fun story. Tell me one," Mason demanded intently, pulling his chair closer. Victoria felt flattered by his interest.

"Really?" she asked and shivered under his expectant gaze.

"Could we pull back these shades and let the sunlight in? I am a bit cold," she asked, giving in and rubbing her arms twice before making herself stop.

"Please continue your story," he encouraged and pulled his jacket off and wrapped it about her shoulders. It was made from such soft silk Victoria had to grab it quickly before it slipped off entirely.

Victoria began the first story, summarizing it a bit because it was quite lengthy. At the end of each story, she stopped, searching to see if he was bored only to find he was actually more intrigued, leaning farther off his seat. She tried to remember the details and even started to act out the voices the way Father had.

"Any other stories?" he asked as a maid refilled their teacups. Victoria shook her head, tucking the last story away in her mind. She hoped she did not look too obvious and quickly sipped her tea, burning her lip.

"Ah!" Victoria winced and pulled the teacup back quickly and set it down, trying to ignore the sting. "No, that is all of them."

"Did he ever write these down or draw a picture?" he asked.

"No," Victoria answered, puzzled.

"Well, it seems to be a delightful tale. It could enchant many children here in the valley," he added quickly.

"Oh no, they were just bedtime stories. I don't think they will ever be much more than that."

"You are too modest," Mason said. The maid slipped a letter to him, and he opened it with a flick of his wrist. Victoria wondered how he moved so gracefully as he quickly glanced over it.

"I am sorry. I have to attend to some business, but I will escort you back to your hallway," Mason said. His genuine smile was gone, replaced with another one of those short tugs of his lips. She could tell he was once again anxious. He politely walked with her but remained silent, nodding to each guest they passed in greeting.

She was so turned about that when he pulled to a stop, it took her a minute to recognize the guest room doors.

"Thank you for the wonderful time," he said and stepped closer. Victoria held her breath as his face was only inches from hers. He caught her between his arms. His eyes seemed to burn into hers, unblinking. Then he pulled the jacket from her shoulders, and the moment was over, leaving Victoria to wonder if it had been as long as she thought it had been or if it was just a trick of her mind. Victoria realized she had forgotten to release her breath.

"I will find you tonight at the ball," he said as he stepped back, the jacket slung over his shoulder.

She nodded quickly, looking down to hide her blushing face and clutching her ruby necklace again absentmindedly.

Mother was still anxiously bustling around, demanding more decorations on the dresses and wigs. Mabel noticed Victoria's entry and gave her a trying look. Victoria mouthed an apology for leaving.

"Where have you been, child?" Mother asked.

"I was with Mason," Victoria said sheepishly.

Mother flung the feathers in her hand madly above her head as she twirled to look Victoria in the eye. "Mason? That is wonderful!" Mother breathed. The feathers drifted down lazily between them while Mother's voice continued to flow out of her mouth and hurl itself at Victoria. "Tell me everything!"

"Well, we had tea together and—" Victoria said, swiping one feather as it floated past her face, tickling her nose.

"That is what you were wearing?" Mother interrupted. "With that gaudy necklace?"

"You chose this dress this morning. What is wrong with it now?" Victoria asked, stroking the ruby necklace defensively.

"It is not Prince Mason worthy! Take that thing off now! We must get you into your lavender gown this instant!" Mother demanded with a stomp.

"What was he like?" Mabel asked.

"Confident and a perfect gentleman, too perfect," Victoria said. "I suspect he is mischievous, falling on the side of untrustworthy."

"It is a perfect match!" Mother exclaimed.

"Oh, no, I don't think I would want—" Victoria started to explain but was interrupted by a small knock on the door. Mabel opened the door, and there stood a girl matching her height in a navy cloak. Her hood was drawn up over her head, only her nose poked out and her shining eyes two little stars amid the darkened hood.

"I am here to help with the preparation for the ball tonight," she explained shyly.

Mother wasted no time putting her to work, and she frantically tried to assist. While she was fetching the skirts, Victoria noticed her face still remained hooded.

"What is your name?" Victoria asked.

"Ann," she said obediently, head still lowered.

"That is a pretty name," Victoria said sweetly. Ann thanked her quietly and then pulled her hood tighter about her head.

Mother unpacked the boxes she had been hiding deep in her luggage. Eagerly she handed them out. Mabel had hers open first. It was a lovely mask, delicately handcrafted by an experienced artisan.

"Oh, these are fantastic!" Mabel squealed, pulling it out and dancing around with it balanced on her nose. Hers was a pink bird with a small pointed golden beak and large feathers along the top ridge. It would look lovely with her soft pink ball gown. They continued to unbox. Victoria's mask was white with purple ribbon and lace along the edges symbolizing a bunny. Small, pointed ears rounded out the top, and fine white horse hair laced under the triangular nose to make whiskers.

"Do you like them?" Mother asked excitedly.

"They are lovely," Victoria admitted.

"Don't look at mine!" Mother said, her eyes flashing with mysterious mirth as she snatched the last box up. Victoria and Mabel laughed, exchanging happy smiles and cherishing every moment, as Mother was in such a rare mood. Mother hid behind the dressing stand. She dramatically stepped out from behind the curtain to meet a loud applause from her daughters. She was wearing a green-and-blue mask representing a type of lizard that matched her dark blue dress.

"I am a dragon!" she said proudly. The jewels on her mask glinted in the fading sunlight pouring in from the large balcony windows.

They started down the hallway, and Victoria stopped.

"Oh, I almost forgot my necklace!" she said, touching her neck.

"I thought we had decided not to wear that gaudy thing," Mother said but did not say anything else as Victoria scurried back to the room.

Ann gasped as Victoria opened the door. Victoria stared in shock before she could stop herself. Ann had a balding head. Her hair was so thin only a few strands remained. Her scalp was peeling, and the inside of her hood was filled with skin flakes. Some floated down to the floor like snow in a tiny blizzard. Her entire face was bumpy, and there were many discolored splotches, especially around her lips and eyes. Victoria realized Ann hunched over a bit, a large bulge on her shoulders. Before, Victoria assumed it was extra fabric from the large ill-fitting cloak, but now she realized her crooked back.

"Sorry," Ann said, quickly pulling her hood back on tightly around her face.

"No, it is my fault. I am sorry to startle you." Victoria gave her a reassuring smile, but Ann pushed past her in embarrassment and rushed away.

Victoria wondered if she should chase after her. She stood for a long moment, trying to formulate some sort of reassurance she could give but nothing came to her. She had never seen any birth defects of such magnitude. Empathy filled Victoria. She wondered what sort of life Ann could lead with such a misfortunate disfiguration.

She shifted about, looking for her necklace. She thought she had left it on the bureau but found it on the floor. Perplexed, Victoria rubbed the ruby, feeling the cool smooth surface. She smiled, unsure whether she liked wearing it more to remember Father or to perturb Mother. Her smile faded as worry crept back into her mind. She had to control herself. There could not be any transformations tonight.

CHAPTER 5

A BLOOD FLAME

THE MUSIC FLOODED THE solemn corridors with cheer, inviting them from their rooms. Victoria felt normal for a change. There was no sign of the transformation happening.

"I am human tonight," she whispered, hoping saying it out loud under her breath would make it so.

They followed the crowd to the grand staircase. Mother instantly began chatting, soon consumed in conversation. The persuasion of the thick crowd pushed her down each step. One man stood still among the commotion. Perhaps he caught Victoria's eye since he seemed out of place, leaning against the railing lazily and looking over the crowd with little consideration. He wore a crudely made snouted mask. A pair of jagged pointed ears were pinned lopsidedly on the top, a red streak lined the narrow, slanted eyes, resulting in a rather menacing demeanor. With no other decorations or designs, the coarse mask seemed unfitting among the sea of bright colors.

Although his square jaw protruded from the mask boldly, it was his eyes that seemed to draw her attention. They were a brilliant dark green, looking like emeralds shining from his otherwise coarse face. Casting her eyes to his feet, she noticed his suit was an inch too short in the leg, his anklebone showing. She wondered why he would not have his suit properly tailored before such an important event. He wore no socks, yet somehow his nonchalant manner added charm.

He remained immobile amid the flurry of excitement with no regard to the enticement of the music as the crowd shimmied down the stairs. She watched as his eyes glanced over the crowd, suddenly landing on her. She looked away. She stared hard at the ground as she passed him. Her heart seemed to skip a beat as her ear nearly grazed his chin, the crowd pushing her toward him.

"Let's go get some food. I am getting lost in all this grandeur," Victoria said, impersonating the snobbish butler from earlier this evening. Mabel laughed loud, and the sound was lost in the noise of the crowd. The staircase led them to the base of the ballroom. No expense had been spared in decoration. The chandeliers of pure crystal reflected the candlelight. Each sparkling splendor seemed to float above their heads, illuminating the dance floor. She stepped cautiously, afraid of slipping on the shiny motionless lake of marble beneath the ripples of her dress hem.

Numberless benches were pushed against the walls with purple candles shelved above them. Each had maple leaves, trees, and other landscaped scenes etched into the wall of wax—such artistry she had never seen before. Part of her wanted to blow out the flames so as to not let it melt the hours of work no doubt a small army of artisans had taken to complete. Victoria was enchanted by the strange glow each flame held.

"How do they get it to burn red?" Mabel asked.

"It must be some sort of chemical in the wick," Victoria guessed. They proceeded to the buffet. Rounded tables with dark red or burnt orange tablecloths held pumpkin centerpieces. Each one was carved with fascinating detail, the same designs as the candles held but on a much larger scale. A flickering candle flame brought the carved pumpkins to life. It, too, was red. Both girls puzzled over it for a long moment before turning to take in the rest of the room. The mixture of roses, scented leaves, cinnamon sticks, and orange slices gave a cheery mood. They headed toward the large tables burdened heavily with food piled on silver and gold platters. It was all to represent the harvest.

Victoria knew Mabel was eyeing the tall trifle in the middle of the table. It was layers of soft fluffy cake followed with custard and fresh berries. It repeated this pattern several times, alternating from layers of strawberries to raspberries and then blueberries. It looked so splendid that Mabel timidly stood staring hungrily, too embarrassed to be the first to cut into it. Victoria grabbed the blade and slid it through. She lifted two slices and placed them on the small serving plates.

Giggling, they ate the dessert as if they were small children. Feeling much more content, they wandered into the ballroom, looking now at the people in the crowd.

Victoria gasped as she saw a large bouquet of black roses. She stepped closer, staring at the ugly things in a rage.

"Earlier these were red," she said.

"What, Victoria?" Mabel asked, scooting closer to hear her better.

"These were red when we arrived," she said louder.

"There are so many decorations in here. I am sure the red ones are here somewhere," Mabel offered.

"No, I remember. They were delivering these today when we arrived. They were red. I recognize these vases. All of them were red!" Victoria said.

Mabel turned to her and laughed. "Maybe Charlene is just picky," she said. "Think if Mother had this much wealth. You know she would declare it unfit if something wasn't exactly as she had imagined in her mind."

Victoria could not argue with this logic and nodded her head. In a small gesture of discontent, she stomped her foot. Then feeling a bit silly, she shifted her eyes toward the festivities in an effort to ignore the flowers.

Victoria took time to examine each person's mask, uniquely designed and bejeweled. A variety of fowl recreated, some beaks pointed and long, others short and stubby. All were colorful and bright. She found other masks of the proud lion and the fearsome bear. Children a bit younger than Mabel danced about as a mouse, a squirrel, and a little pig. Then there were some that were fearfully bold. She was perfectly entertained until Mabel handed her a handkerchief.

"You have to hand out at least the ones I stitched. I spent forever on them for you," Mabel said impatiently. She held several handkerchiefs up close to Victoria's face, waving them impatiently until Victoria finally nodded and took them. Victoria shoved them into her skirt pocket. She looked about; she couldn't recognize anyone.

Finally, she noticed Henry dancing with the other servants in the far corner. Although Mother had spared no expense in his coachman suit, Victoria now realized she intentionally excluded a mask, perhaps to discourage his attendance to the great ballroom. Henry wore a humble portrayal of a horse; obviously he had made it himself. She silently scolded herself for noticing his mask was not as fancy as the rest.

"How are you doing this evening?" he asked, pulling his mask from his face as he gave an awkward bow. When offered his hand, she happily smiled, and soon they were gliding on the dance floor.

Mother was determined and was at her side immediately once the song ended with an eligible bachelor to her standards. After the introduction and a dance or two, she was prompted to give him a handkerchief. Victoria enjoyed herself the first couple of hours, but her heart sank as

Mother approached for what seemed like the hundredth time. A man with thick curly hair accompanied her. He wore it tied back in a black bow. His stiff collar came straight up to his chin.

"This is Fredrick; you have already met his mother. You remember Hannah of course?" she asked, expecting Victoria's automatic agreement.

"Yes, such a charming woman," she lied, sending Fredrick an over-drawn smile. She remembered making a mental note to avoid the ever-celebrated Fredrick, the fox hunter. He crinkled his nose at her slightly before taking her hand forcefully.

"Why did you wear that necklace?" He asked. "It is a bit much, isn't it? Perhaps you wear it in compensation?" He asked.

"What are your hobbies?" Victoria asked, steering the conversation into a safe territory before she said something she ought not to outloud.

"I am a skilled hunter." Fredrick announced.

"Oh, that is wonderful," Victoria said automatically using the standard polite response. "What do you hunt?" She already knew the answer, but it was the only question on her mind.

"I have brought home many muskrats, sable, and fox," he said proudly. "But I plan to bring home larger game this season."

"I think foxes are kind of cute with their large fluffy tails," she said defensively, trying to keep a soft, ladylike tone.

"Ugly, nasty things. They are vile creatures, and they carry numerous diseases," he said with a curled lip. She could tell the look of disgust on his face was not only meant for foxes, but for her opinion on the matter. They danced in silence, and Victoria wondered why this song was ten times longer than any of the others the musicians had played all night. When he did speak again, she was sure she would have preferred him to remain silent.

"I am a very talented trumpet player as well. I play daily, and my family greatly enjoys my talents. I mastered the tongue of the native islanders who dwell on the islands in the ocean south of here. It is a delightfully simple language, and I have traveled there twice already to relax on the beach."

"That sounds nice," Victoria said dryly, hoping he would lose interest soon.

"It was very invigorating. I doubt you have traveled much further than this estate. Am I right?" he asked smugly.

"Yes, this is the farthest I have traveled," she confirmed his assumption, feeling annoyed at his arrogance, yet now slightly self-conscious.

"Now, my mother said that you play the harp and the flute. Which do you play best?"

"I suppose I play harp the best," she said.

"Well, I think you should play for me and I can critique you," he said. "I seriously doubt your tutor is pushing you hard enough," he added.

"Probably not to your standard," she admitted, concealing the sarcasm she desperately wanted to convey. Relieved when the song ended, she shoved a hand deep into her pocket, snagging all handkerchiefs tightly in her fist, suddenly terrified one might fall out and be mistaken as an invitation. Mother was nodding at her from a distance. Victoria pretended not to see as she glanced back to Fredrick with his hand outstretched, waiting. People were leaving the dance floor while she was momentarily frozen between two frightful people.

Mother's lips were thinning in frustration at Victoria's hesitation. Still, she could not lift her hand to release the handkerchief.

Mother stood from her chair, making her way forward while Fredrick cleared his throat expectantly. Victoria's heart thudded in her chest, pounding along with the introduction of the next song. She could not endure another dance with him. In a shaking panic, she whipped away from Fredrick, and she grabbed the nearest available man, praying he was in a charitable mood.

She could see his eyes widen in surprise behind the mask but she quickly hushed them with her silently pleading ones.

"Whoa," he said and whirled her farther from Fredrick and Mother and into the center of the floor. She was relieved that she recognized the voice.

"Mason, thank you," Victoria said.

"No, I thank you. I wanted to dance with you this evening, but it has seemed impossible to get close to you. Your mother seems determined." Mason said as he expertly guided her through the dance steps.

"Yes, it has been frightfully dull," Victoria said.

"I suppose so. Frederick is unbearably boastful. It would make my ears bleed," Mason said as he looked back toward the spot Victoria was attempting to flee.

"Yes, I fear mine are already," she said. He gave a small chuckle. Victoria ignored the urge to look back at Fredrick or Mother's face. She focused on his mask in front of her.

"Your mask is unusual," she said. Surely it was some sort of animal, but it looked almost demonic to her.

"Yes, I didn't choose it. My mother had it made for me, gaudy thing. Honestly, I don't understand why we must wear these at all, makes it awfully confusing already. I have a hard enough time sorting names to faces. Throw an entirely different element into the mix and I am doomed," Mason said. "No, mine is just another mask. There are over a thousand here tonight. But your necklace is quite unique. I have never seen anything like it," Mason said as he pulled on the ruby, his fingers grazing her collar bone. Perhaps she had been too hasty in her disapproval of him.

"It was my father's," she said timidly. "Well, I mean, he never wore it, of course." She chuckled at the thought. "It was given to him by his father. It is a family heirloom."

"You wear it always?" he asked as he continued to glide across the floor, each movement seemed smoother than the last and he directed her through each one with not only perfect technique but with a fancy flourish.

"No, never actually," she said, enjoying the thrill of being turned about and guided by his firm and skillful hand.

"But you have worn it twice now by my count." he said.

"More to annoy my mother. She says it clashes with my dresses," Victoria said, but while she said it, she immediately felt like a liar. A sudden pang in her gut made her realize it was indeed to hold something of his close to her.

A blast of trumpets took her by surprise, and she jumped. Mason gave another one of his short smiles to her. She fidgeted with her dress, trying to calm her nerves. They announced the arrival of Charlene. Everyone turned to the grand staircase as she gracefully descended. Her long blond hair fell in thick ringlets around her bare shoulders. Her dress wrapped about her bosom tightly down to her hips, and the skirt layers whirled about her legs down to the floor. It was unlike any dress Victoria had seen before. The crowd fell silent, and Charlene began a speech.

"Wow!" Victoria breathed.

"Yeah, she knows how to make an entrance," Mason whispered.

"She looks too young to be your mother," Victoria whispered back.

"Believe me, she is much older than you think," Mason said.

"And her face—it is like porcelain."

"She avoids the sun; you can't imagine what it would do to her complexion," Mason said with a smirk. Victoria knew all too well the lengths taken to preserve skin's youth, but his amusement puzzled her. Perhaps the joke was to a reference she had missed earlier that evening.

"She is lovely," she offered quickly, trying not to hinder the conversation.

"Only on the outside," a deep voice interrupted, startling Victoria. Mason gave a huff as he turned expectantly toward the intruder.

"Gor, I do not recall sending you an invite," Mason said in his usual nonchalant tone, but by the nervous shift of Mason's posture, she detected his uneasiness.

"No, you did not." A large, burly man dressed in an old, stained suit stood behind them. He was probably nearing the end of middle age, with a streak of gray zigzagging through his hair.

"What do you want?" Mason asked, stepping closer to Gor until they were face to face, although Gor was a couple inches taller.

"I only came for the food," he said as he dug his fingers deeply into the nearest cake. He held up a chunk and took a bite. "Yum. Is this your treat for the evening?" Gor pointed his icing-covered hand toward Victoria. His dirty fingernails, almost black from filth, gave Victoria a shudder. "If not, could I take a snap at her?" He bit in the air toward her, thrusting his chin out in the gesture. His vulgar conduct was frightening. He strutted toward the food table again. Mason motioned for her to stay where she was, and he followed Gor, looking agitated. Victoria could not help but slowly trail them, once again curiosity getting the better of her.

"You must leave. I will escort you out if need be," Mason said, looking about while trying to keep his voice steady. Luckily all the guests were busy listening to Charlene's toast of harvest. As the applause echoed, Gor shoveled more food into his mouth, letting large chunks fall out of his mouth and back onto the table. Victoria was relieved she had already eaten some of the trifle, for now he was leaning an elbow into it as a prop. He looked at Mason lazily.

"I really should come to these gatherings more often," he said with his cheeks full of turkey after ripping the meat from the whole bird with his teeth. He tossed it to the side, and it flopped with a heavy thud on top of the other platters. Some crashed to the floor. A few people in the back of the crowd turned to look.

"Gor, leave now," Mason commanded.

"No, I am having too much fun," he said and winked at Victoria. A slow jagged smile crossed his face with the thinnest lips she had ever seen. His teeth were large in comparison, giving her a shiver. He came closer to her. Victoria stood her ground, feeling the urge to mask any fear. Gor leaned to take a long sniff of her hair, pulling some of it to the side with his dirty fingers. Sticky crumbs dribbled down her collarbone and landed on the front of her dress. She stood frozen in sheer shock. Mason watched, his hands in fists and jaw set like stone.

"Get out!" Mason said forcibly.

"I think that a more polite tone should be taken with me," Gor said.

"What do you want?" Mason's voice rose.

The crowd cheered as Charlene finished her toast. Everyone raised a goblet high into the air. Gor grabbed the nearest person's goblet from their hand and thrust it into the air, letting out a hearty grunt in mockery before chugging loudly. He threw the cup down and yanked on Victoria's arm, forcing her down on the floor. Mason stepped between them, and Gor dropped her arm. Gor shoved his fist deep into Mason's stomach. Victoria screamed as Mason grunted in pain. Gor pushed him to the ground and held his neck fast under his boot. Others turned, and a loud uproar sent the guards running toward them with outstretched swords. Two guards were closing in on Gor now, and he moved away from Mason. The first guard blocked Gor's punch while the other reached for his arms to hold him fast. Gor headbutted the first guard so hard he fell flat on the marble floor. Using strength Victoria had never seen, he lifted the other guard over his head and tossed him into the table. Food platters fell with heavy clanks. Now all movement had stopped, and the crowd's anxious faces peered at the scene, their gasps echoing into Victoria's ears.

Gor let out an inhumane bellow, arms out wide in invitation at the remaining guards. Everyone in the crowd stepped back cautiously. Mason got to his feet and clutched the nearest object, a silver pie server. He whipped it with speed Victoria thought impossible. Pie sprayed out into the crowd as the server sliced through the air. The triangular shaped head ended in a sharp point which lodged straight into Gor's back, below his shoulder blade.He roared out in pain as the silver dug deep into his flesh. He was in a fury as he twisted back his arm awkwardly, but it was beyond his reach. He jumped toward Mason, and they continued the heated brawl face to face. Mason was thrown headfirst onto the table on his belly. Food was flung everywhere as his body upturned the remaining platters as he slid. Mason came to stop after landing on the floor with a thump and collapsed from pain. By the time he stumbled to his feet, Gor was there to kick him in the stomach, ignoring the screaming crowd.

As the rest of the guards dashed through the crowd, Gor looked up. He was outnumbered and sprinted out into the night, the silver handle glinting in the candlelight as it bobbed slightly, still embedded in his back. All the guards followed.

Mason's head turned toward the ballroom, scanning the scene while he held his side, wincing in pain. Victoria followed his gaze. She did not see anything but scared faces. Then she noticed one figure weaving through the standstill.

Victoria felt frozen as Charlene glided toward them.

"All is well! The intruder will be brought to justice. Please do not let his feeble attempt ruin the evening." She nodded to the musicians, who took up a cheery song. The crowd resumed their laughter and dancing. She looked over the mess and broken furniture till her eyes fell on Mason, then Victoria.

"Mason," Charlene said in greeting, calm as ever. "Who is this lovely lady?" Charlene asked, looking at Victoria with interest without a mention to Mason's bloodied form.

"This is Victoria, daughter of Richard," Mason grumbled, wiping his split lip with the back of his hand. Charlene's eyes flickered and fell upon the necklace.

"Oh, my child, I have to say your father was a brilliant man," she said.

"Harriet, I offer my condolences about sweet Richard," Charlene said in greeting to Mother as she shifted her way out of the crowd. Mother curtsied with a broad smile, the biggest Victoria had ever seen.

"Thank you, it is much appreciated," Mother said. Charlene turned back to Victoria.

"What an interesting piece of jewelry! Victoria, I am a collector of interesting things. I must have this!" she exclaimed, stroking the ruby with a delicate finger. "You will have a chest of gold in exchange."

Mason grunted, holding his ribs tighter. Charlene looked at him with a swift click of her tongue. Mason fell silent.

"Are you going to be all right?" Victoria asked, ignoring Charlene's obvious annoyance of the interruption. Victoria caught him under his arm and helped him balance.

"Your hand is burnt!" Victoria gasped in sheer confusion, unsure when he had touched anything hot enough to scald his skin so severely. But no one seemed to hear her, they were too distracted with Charlene's presence.

"Charlene, if you would like the necklace, it is yours for the mentioned price," Mother said.

"Wise decision. It will be taken into my personal collection," Charlene said.

"But I—" Victoria said, with a slight huff under the weight of Mason. "It was my father's," she said softly before Mother gave her a threatening glance.

"I don't want to part you from something you hold dear," Charlene offered. "Of course, it is up to you."

"We should summon your physician," Victoria said worriedly, trying to guide Mason toward the door of the ballroom leading to the kitchen.

"Perhaps," Charlene said, beckoning them to follow her. Victoria hobbled with Mason until two attending servants gathered him into their arms.

"Do you want me to come with you?" Victoria asked. Mason offered her a small smile but shook his head before closing his eyes in pain as the servants carried him away.

"Let me show you my collection. I assure you your necklace will be admired by all." Charlene turned her attention squarely on Victoria, without a second glance at her son.

Down a hallway lined with countless oil paintings and fine tapestries they walked until arriving at a large room filled with pieces of jewelry, pottery, and other antiques of value. Each piece sat on its own column table. Some pieces were displayed on the wall, while others had their own glass window box. Victoria could not believe the glass itself and gingerly touched the case. There were no bubbles or traces of lines where the craftsmen had worked. It was flawless.

"These are my prized possessions," Charlene said. "I have been working on this collection for years now," she continued as they looked around. Victoria had never seen so many jewels and precious stones.

"Of course, you can wait till the end of the evening to decide," Charlene said. "It will be cared for in the most respectful manner and you are free to visit it anytime you want. It is obvious it holds great sentiment to you," she said with a smile as a servant opened a chest of gold coins. "This is yours if you decide," she said and nodded as she left, allowing them to discuss the matter a bit more privately in the corner.

"Mother, please, we can't sell it," Victoria said in a shaky voice, pulling on the chain defensively as it hung about her neck.

"We need the money, Victoria," Mother whispered through gritted teeth, smiling at the other people mingling around the art in admiration. "We have not been doing so well without your father," she said, and Victoria understood the tone. Her mother was almost pleading. "There are other items we can keep to remind you of your father," she said, her voice softening. "I know this is hard but think of the family." Mother stepped away, venturing about the rest of the collection before returning to the ball.

Victoria sat down on the carved marble bench near the entrance. She looked down at the necklace and sighed. She could feel her throat scratching the way it did before her eyes began to well up with tears. Despite her best efforts, a few drizzled down her face while she tried to stifle the sobs stirring in her chest.

She did not look up when she heard another shuffle from the doorway, but as the pair of shoes stopped near her, she glanced up. It was the man with the green eyes. He was gazing at the different pieces thoughtfully. She flinched as he turned toward her. She straightened her skirts in a fidget, hoping he would take interest in someone else in the room so she could continue to sulk in peace.

"I could not help but notice you are upset," he said. When he spoke, she felt a flush of annoyance.

"And I could not help but notice your lack of socks," Victoria whipped back defensively. He looked down at his ankles in consideration. Realizing how harsh she sounded made her feel a bit guilty, so she offered a small apologetic smile among the sniffles. He returned her smile good-naturedly and gestured toward the bench. She slid over in reply.

He gave a short huff as he sat beside her. His shoulder grazed hers as he drew off his mask, scratching at the sides of his chiseled cheek where the ribbon had held the mask in place. He was indeed handsome.

"There is too much involved in dressing up nowadays," he said in annoyance, unbuttoning the top of his collar and loosening it with a slight tug. He settled against the wall in a slump. His ill-tailored suit seemed to groan against its seams as he rested his arm on his knee lazily. Victoria understood his discomfort and ignored her own urge to adjust her corset. She removed her mask in response, conscious of his gaze while she wiped her eyes and patted her nose.

"I am sorry," she offered. He accepted her apology with a nod.

"Gregor," he introduced himself.

"Victoria," she answered.

"I tried to offer you a dance, but I was overlooked in the crowd climbing over themselves to get a chance," he said after a long moment. Victoria could feel her face flush. He must be just offering a compliment. Surely, she would have noticed him.

"I would like to dance with you, so I will keep an eye out for you once we are in the ballroom again," she offered. He gave a small nod and continued twiddling the mask between his fingers.

"What is your mask supposed to be?" she asked while eyeing the red slit for eyes and hollow snout.

"This is just your typical beast," Gregor explained, lifting the mask in his hand, two fingers protruding from the snout as though fangs. He made a couple low growls, and the mask lunged toward her face playfully. Victoria laughed, and this made Gregor smile.

"A rabbit doesn't suit you," Gregor said, tugging at her mask ribbon.

"Why?" she asked curiously.

"You are not prey. You are much too clever," he said.

"Is that so?" Victoria asked. "How do you know?"

"I can tell," he reassured her.

"Did you get a chance to try any of the cake before it was destroyed by that guy?" Victoria asked.

"No, I was not able to. Had you?" Gregor asked.

"Yes, it was delicious."

"Well, now I might have to go back and eat some off the floor if it is as good as you say," Gregor said, and this made Victoria laugh out loud. Once again Gregor chuckled at her amusement.

"Did you hear anything about the impostor?" Victoria asked with a shudder.

"Nope, they always seem to have a crazy or two show up to these things," Gregor said.

"I wouldn't know. This is my first one," Victoria said.

"Ah, you will tire of them as I have," Gregor assured her.

"You don't look much older than me. How are you already bored of them?" Victoria asked, puzzled.

"I have been coming to this palace for what seems like my entire life," Gregor said.

"Oh, so you live close to here?" she asked.

"Close enough," Gregor said. "My father keeps making me come back."

"My mother was pretty insistent I come here too. I could see myself growing tired of these soon enough," Victoria agreed.

They sat for a long moment together in silence. It was different from the usual dead air. It wasn't rigid or holding tension. She felt his comfort just sitting beside her, and she shared in the moment.

"Would you be interested in seeing the famous rose garden? I am headed to the balcony overlooking it," Gregor invited casually.

"No, I don't like those black roses. I . . .," she fell short, unsure how to explain the trepidation caused by a flower. Gregor nodded pleasantly, but Victoria caught the slight fade of his smile before he propped it back into place before leaving.

Victoria blinked a few times, feeling silly to be still smiling down at her hands. She wiped her eyes carefully looking at her reflection in a nearby shiny vase and applied a second coat of lip color before she wandered back toward the ballroom. As she approached, the music flowed louder in her ear, and she turned away. She wanted to be an obedient girl and return to her duties, but, somehow, she was unable to face the entire crowd Mother had undoubtedly assembled.

Flashes of Gregor's enticing smile in her mind lured her toward the large door with the oversized knob. Her heart thudded a bit as she touched the handle, unsure what she could say to match his allure.

She straightened her dress once more, shaking the ruffles into place and adjusting her corset. The chilly autumn wind blew about her face, tinkling her earrings. Stepping out, she used as much poise as she could muster and lifted her skirts daintily. The door shut behind her, blocking the cheery light.

"Gregor?" she whispered into the dark. No one answered. She could barely make her way across the marble as her eyes adjusted to the dim lights cast by the lanterns hanging on the wall. The wind whistled over the several statues, making it feel all the more forlorn. She sighed and stepped out to the nearest statue, placing a hand on its cold stone, trying to remember what they looked like in the light because the shadows made them look a bit ominous. She turned toward the railing and gave a hesitant glance out over the edge. The ballroom light from the distant windows cast its glow weakly over the garden; the dark, cursed petals seemed more menacing with their pointed shadows. As she looked out, she noticed the stars were bright overhead and the moon shone. She guessed several more days and it would be full.

She then felt foolish, waiting idly. Perhaps Gregor got distracted by another lovely lady; there were so many here tonight. Then she sighed softly. It could have been a perfectly romantic moment. They could have looked up at the stars together and furthered their conversation. The faint hum of the music faded into the still night air, and as it reached her ears, she pictured dancing under the moon together. The music faded away as the song ended.

"Oh, I am glad you changed your mind," Gregor's gruff voice interrupted her thoughts.

"It was getting a bit stuffy in there," she agreed. It was then that the musicians began to play a slow song and it flowed into the garden with a romantic hum.

"I would like that dance now." Gregor said. She happily gave her hand to his outstretched one. He began to lead and after only a few steps, she realized he was truly a terrible dancer. She could see he was trying to mask his frustration at his lack of knowledge of the steps by plastering on a smile. Victoria tried to give him full control, following his rigid movements best she could, but it was slow going and out of rhythm with the music. Soon his smile faded as he plunged himself into serious concentration.

Victoria tried to stifle her groan in pain as he stepped on her toes. He apologized quickly. He was determined and continued trying to guide her with shaking hands until the last notes of the music faded. He tried to save it by twirling her, but he was too forceful and sent her off balance in an awkward spiral. Somehow, Victoria ended up on the balcony floor, all her skirts and petticoats fluffing about her. She swatted her skirting down as she began to laugh, interrupting his flurry of apologies. He came over but rather than offer his hand to help her to her feet, he slumped down beside her.

"I saw that going a lot smoother." He lamented. "I honestly tried to practice before I arrived, but the broom is not a worthy partner when compared to you." He said. This sent Victoria into another fit of giggles.

"It is alright." Victoria said. "That was the best dance I have had all night." At this Gregor gave in and laughed too.

"You are everything I have imagined you would be." Gregor said, leaning closer and looking directly into her eyes. Victoria, leery of his sudden flattery, froze under his stare.

"You are a bit too forward, sir," she said, looking down at her hands nervously. His body gave off a tremendous amount of heat, and she realized he was blocking most of the chilly wind from hitting her face.

As he closed the last of the gap between their bodies, she was unsure whether to scootback or perhaps push past him. His lips were on hers in a clumsy lunge, and he grabbed her about her waist, his fingers climbing her neck and stroking her back passionately. As soon as she could recover from pure astonishment, she yanked herself away from his grasp, looking at him with a mixture of emotions.

"I am a lady. I do not presume to know what you were thinking, but I am not available to any man on merely a whim!" she said with as much force she could muster while sliding back, enough to place ample space between them, no longer concerned with politeness. Gregor looked stunned and muttered under his breath before lifting his head to meet her glower.

"I apologize. I have forgotten my manners. I promise not to bother you further this evening," he stammered as they both scrambled to their feet. She gave him a scowl as he turned to leave. She waited with her arms firmly crossed for a long moment before letting herself breathe again, partly afraid he would return. Then she lamented on her own foolishness. Perhaps when he had invited her to see the garden, he had not really wanted to see the garden? It was dark out. The garden was barely visible in the dim lantern lighting! She flushed hot with embarrassment.

She was not at all ready for any of this, and she wanted to go home. Maybe Mother would let her hide in her room. Then she realized that was impossible. Perhaps if she was sick—but she would have to prove how sick she was. She wondered how well she could pretend to vomit.

By looking up at the night sky, she avoided the thorny flowers below. As another chilly wind blew through the balcony, she shifted her shawl about her shoulders, her hand grazing her collarbone. That is when she realized it was bare.

"My necklace!" she exclaimed out loud, sprinting after Gregor. "Guards! Guards!" she screamed but to no avail. They were all probably still pursuing that horrible man Gor. Down the stairs and past the merry music, she spied Gregor as he slipped out the front door. She had to run if she was going to catch him, and she managed well enough in all the skirts, but the shoes were terribly awkward.

As she yanked the heavy front door open, she looked out into the courtyard, spying Gregor's shadow fading out from the large, decorated gate.

She darted round the corner of the brick wall and sprinted after him. The courtyard was much larger than she remembered when she entered earlier by horse carriage. In the dark, it seemed almost impossible to catch him, but she did not give up. She sprinted past hedges and the tall statues, pushing herself. She caught his arm and squeezed angrily while frantically sorting his many pockets. A sheer look of astonishment registered on his face.

"Give back my necklace!" she yelled. He tried to shake her loose and run, but she clung to his arm. After a moment or two, he finally stopped and turned toward her.

"Go back!" he commanded, pointing toward the palace.

"Not without my necklace!" she screamed, realizing her voice was louder than necessary due to the fact her face was right by his ear. He looked at her with annoyance, and she glared back.

"Get out of here!" he shouted back angrily. His deep voice scared Victoria, but she shoved back the fear as she felt the necklace under her fingertips among his wallet and pocket lint. She snatched the necklace, looping it back around her neck. He caught her arm by the wrist and held it while his face became very serious.

"Please!" his voice cracked a little in the anxious plea. It was then she spied Mr. Johnson and Henry walking in the distance behind Gregor.

"No, don't!" he hissed, but Victoria had already begun to scream, waving her free arm toward them.

"Help! I am being robbed! Help!" she shrieked as loud as she could muster while trying to kick Gregor.

Movement among the row of statues in the fountain caught her attention. Then she froze, realizing the count of statues was one too many. A figure unfurled, rising from the water as it stood on thick legs. Its large outline silhouetted against the stars. At first, she thought it was a man, but the neck was thicker, connecting to the shoulders with an oversized muscle, which resulted in a sloping hunch. The shoulders themselves were huge and rounded. Her gaze followed down its arms, which were longer and wider than proportion should have allowed. A low rumble escaped its throat as it stepped on its hind legs toward her, light catching its face. Victoria's stomach clenched at the hair-covered face with a row of sharp teeth beneath a long snout. One pair of fangs showed even with its mouth shut, like the legendary saber-tooth tiger she had read about in books. Its demonic red eyes glowered beneath the heavy brow and sloping forehead. As it moved forward, she turned to flee.

Her futile movements proved pointless as the beast sprung toward her, easily catching her about the waist as the folds of her dress flew up all around her.

"No!" she heard Gregor yell from somewhere below while she was being pulled through the air. She tried to scream, but the sheer terror gripped her throat. All she could do was watch with wide eyes as the creature yanked her over the edge of the wall like a rag doll. The last sight was Gregor staring, his eyes wide in surprise, mouth agape.

CHAPTER 6

A SINISTER PATH

SHE WAS ASTONISHED AS the beast jumped easily over the outer wall and escaped out into the night. Victoria turned as best she could to look forward, determining which direction it was taking. It entered the forest without hesitation. She was finally able to make her body listen to the commands she was demanding, and she began to scream and kick. Its arm grabbed her legs tighter, holding her fast against its shoulder. She pounded her fists into the fur covered back, continuing to scream. She noticed a silver handle sticking out of its back, blood dripping down, matting the fur in a gross blob. She tried to reach for it, but the moment her fingers touched the rim, it felt hot, like it had been sitting directly on the stove. She flung her hand back, sucking on her fingers in pain. Her mask fell, and she prayed someone would find it. The creature continued until the trees were so thick Victoria could barely see the moon above.

Charlene's palace was far in the distance and out of sight when they finally came to a stop. The beast dropped her, and she landed with a painful thump. She staggered a bit as she stood, trying to keep steady on her shaking legs. The beast snorted right above her head. Its hot breath bellowed against her hair, ruffling it most unpleasantly. It continued to stare at her hungrily while Victoria stood frozen in a new wave of terror. It snarled at her, scraping the ground impatiently while Victoria whimpered, back pushed against the nearest tree trunk. It barked at her, and its horrible breath flooded over her face. She sputtered, disgusted and afraid. Again the screams were choked up in her throat; she could barely sputter for air. Then the creature stepped back, turning its back toward her and hunching over.

Victoria stared in wonder as its spine writhed and shook, breaking with a bloodcurdling crack. The silver trembled but remained embedded in its flesh. It whimpered. Then fur began to disappear. The large snout sunk back into its face, and the claws shrank back into fingernails. It happened much faster than she could ever imagine herself changing. It seemed to only experience a slight tremor of pain. Despite her situation, she stared wide-eyed until the transformation was complete. She gasped in surprise when she realized she knew the man. It was Gor. He was the gray beast.

Then she quickly averted her eyes in disgust, realizing he was undressed. As he clothed himself from a bag he obviously had stashed earlier beneath an overturned root, she kept her face toward the ground, trying to ignore the intense impulse to flee. Her face felt hot in anger and fear. Trying to run was pointless. She searched for any other means of escape but found nothing.

"Get this thing out of my back!" Gor demanded. He stepped toward her, and she flinched. A gloved hand slid between them and yanked the pie server out with a sickening gurgle from Gor. He groaned and walked around, shaking from pain. As she turned her head to follow along the arm to its owner, Victoria blinked in confusion. Gregor stood holding the silver handle, and then he dropped it quickly when he saw her staring at him with her lips apart, frozen in a silent gasp.

"Gregor?" she asked, her voice barely above a whisper. Her face must have shown pure astonishment because Gregor looked at her with his brows low, close together, the corners angled, an expression of sadness—or maybe it was apologetic. Her heart sank. He was not there to save her.

"Well, give it to me!" Gor shouted, interrupting with his gravelly voice, unnerving and impossible to ignore. His eyes rested on her necklace while he stood with his hand outstretched impatiently.

"It is mine!" she yelled out before she could stop herself, knowing too well she was in no position to make demands. Gor began to step closer, and his awful breath hit her face again. She slid back, trying to avoid it. He shot his hand up about her neck, clutching her throat tightly. Victoria gagged as she frantically pulled on his fingers, trying to free herself.

"No!" Gregor intervened, and Gor looked at him, his brow furrowed angrily at his interjection. Gor stared Gregor in the eye, and Gregor shifted uncomfortably. After another painfully long moment, Gor released. She slumped against the nearest tree, gulping for air.

"No funny business. Your father tried, and you know how that turned out," Gor said with a crooked finger pointed at her.

"She does not know about any of it," Gregor said flatly. Gor looked at Gregor and back to Victoria. She stared at him in confusion.

"I am sure she knows much more than she is telling," Gor said. He held his face close to hers inquiringly.

"No, she does not know anything. Her pa never told her. Remember when Richard admitted she wasn't even his? I have been there for long enough to confirm this. She doesn't even know about that," Gregor said, gesturing to her necklace. "I had everything under control," Gregor said. "You did not need to get involved."

"You were taking too long. You were almost caught. We could not risk it because you can't handle one little girl," Gor jeered back.

"Well, we got the ruby. Let her go," Gregor said.

"We will let Brutus be the judge of that," Gor said. "He might want to talk to her."

"In the city? Are you going to enact bellum?" Gregor asked alarmed.

"Yeah, she might be useful," Gor said, looking at Victoria and then clearing his throat loudly and spitting.

"Trust me, she is useless," Gregor said. Gor huffed.

"Let her return. She is slow, and by the time she gets back, we will be long gone," Gregor said harshly without a glance at her. Victoria felt a pang of humiliation, feeling confused at his suddenly cold demeanor.

"I think not. Looking at her now, I think I would like Richard's daughter atoning for his deception," Gor said. "Let's go to Bellum Gate. I am feeling revived by all that food from the palace." He raised his arms up to flex his biceps and gave a hearty laugh.

"No, she belongs with the other humans down in the valley," Gregor said. Victoria was astounded by the speed at which Gor was upon Gregor, yanking him by the collar and forcing his face into his.

"Don't tell me what you think. I am the boss around here!" Gor held him fast while Gregor squirmed under his iron grip. Not until Gregor gave him a slight nod in submission did Gor toss him reeling back.

"Get the necklace," Gor commanded. Gregor found his balance and walked over to her slowly. He looked down at Victoria and opened his mouth, and then he shut it again. Shifting his eyes away from hers quickly, he tried to retrieve the necklace with his fumbling hands, catching it in her hair.

"Ow!" Victoria flinched. Gregor's rough fingers brushed against hers as they both tried to untangle it. His mannerisms were completely changed, no longer charming and relaxed. He now seemed like a cold, stone statue, jaw squared and eyes emotionless. Gor turned his back, the blood staining down his shirt from his open wound.

"Get moving!" Gor shouted from a distance, interrupting the awkward moment. Gregor turned to walk, and she watched the ruby disappear into his pocket. Feeling helpless as she fell into line with their steps, she noticed the increasing shadows as they plunged deeper into the forest. The moon was barely visible above the thick canopy. The trees were wider and taller than she had ever seen or even imagined. Orange, red, and golden leaves were falling all around. The jagged branches reached into the night sky like gnarled fingers. Each step held a mighty crunch underfoot, and it echoed into the gloom.

Noises erupted about her. Crickets and owls persisted to make all sorts of commotion. There must have been a pond nearby; the toads' unmistakable croaking met her ears consistently. There were other noises she could not identify, but she reassured herself they were just animals.

Restless with fear, she continued to search for any sign of escape. Soon she gave up, only concentrating on each step before her. Her feet were starting to smart something sound in her dress shoes. The ground was barely visible; her ankles seemed to disappear into the black furrows between the overturned roots. She tripped repeatedly and had to stop to whip ants and other creepy, crawling things off her calves before they scurried higher up her legs. The trees were now even taller and wider, blocking the moon out of view and leaving her in darkness. Following the sound of Gor's heavy footfalls seemed the only guide. Gregor trailed behind, keeping himself distant.

As they hiked deeper, she began to slow in sheer terror.

"Move it!" Gor shouted back toward her. Victoria could not see him but knew the scowl he held on his face. Pushing forward, she felt confused at the ease with which Gor and Gregor wandered through the forest.

"How are you two not stumbling?" she asked in frustration. "I can't see anything!"

"Stop complaining!" Gor said. "Will she ever shut up?" Gor asked Gregor, but Gregor did not respond. He was lagging behind somewhere. She could only hear him faintly.

She drew her mind back to civilization. Mabel was probably searching desperately for her now. Soon Mother would be in a tizzy, trying to contemplate which was worse, losing her daughter or the expensive necklace. The wind whistled against her, interrupting the thought. She shivered, pulling the sleeves of her dress down to her wrists. Her hem was torn and muddy. Her hands were sore and cramping from holding the folds up, the dress feeling heavier as the time passed. She leaned against a tree, taking deep breaths.

"Come on!" Gor shouted back to her. She could hear his footsteps approaching.

"Hold on!" she pleaded, reaching under her skirt and untying the large hoop and all the petticoats. Stepping out of them, she felt lighter and moved easily. She left them there, hoping if there was a search party, they could follow the trail. She cast a hopeful glance behind her, but there were no torches or bright, shiny guard armor. No one was coming to her rescue.

Gor pulled her forward, grasping her arm tightly. "C'mon," he said.

"Ow! You are hurting me!" Victoria said, struggling to free her arm. Gor let go, and she fell backward, landing in a pile of leaves. Gor laughed at her.

"Now, hurry up!" Gor said. Victoria got to her feet, brushing the dirt from her dress. She could hear Gregor was now only a few steps behind her as they wandered further. The wind began to blow harder, whipping her face and sending shivers down her spine.

The moon was high overhead now, its light shifting weakly through the treetops and leaving them in almost darkness. Victoria stumbled over a root and fell hard, landing painfully.

"Get up!" Gor barked.

"I can't. We have been walking for hours and it is freezing!" she pleaded, searching to find anything among the darkness.

"Get up!" Gor repeated. Victoria was surprised he found her easily in the dark. His blow stung sharply on her cheek, and she fell back.

"We cannot rest here!" Gor shouted at her, yanking her to her feet. He dragged her two or three minutes painfully before letting her arm free, the bruising grip hot on her flesh.

She had no choice but to continue on. Trudging along, her feet felt heavy, each movement slow and cumbersome. Tripping between the folds of her dress and the overturned roots underfoot, she huffed in aggravation as her arms and face stung from numerous scratches.

"You are the loudest and slowest creature on this mountain. All your huffing and sighing is driving me nuts and every other being here can hear you too! We are going to get attacked if you do not shut up!" Gor thundered at her threateningly. Victoria tried to move silently after that, biting her lip when she stubbed her toe and sucking in her breath when she walked through a thick and sticky spider's web. But when she stumbled over some sort of creature's burrow, she fell head over heels and rolled down several feet into the thick vegetation.

A distorted gargle reached her ears from nearby. Victoria looked about, catching a pair of black eyes gleaming from the brush. They were low to the ground and small, so whatever it was, it could not be worse than Gor. Another small gargle and hoot erupted as a tiny round-bellied creature with thin limbs crawled out from under the upturned roots.

It was barely as high as her knee, and she smiled at its little jagged face. Its cheeks were slender, coming to a jutting point at its chin. It had large floppy ears and big bright black eyes with a thin ring of gold encircling the pupil. It was completely naked with pitch black skin, a few red designs tattooed over its boney forearm. Victoria giggled at its round belly with a knobby button. With only one tuft of hair sprouting from the middle of its head, it seemed adorable to her. She bent over, stroking its bare head tenderly as it cooed up to her.

"Where is your momma, little guy?" she asked, and it put its arms up for Victoria, melting her heart. As she bent down to scoop it up, suddenly Gregor stomped down on top of it. It gave a sharp yelp as his boot crushed its skull with a crunch. Gregor wiped his feet against the ground, rubbing off the blood and muck.

Victoria gasped as he stepped over the body with no more than a grunt. She looked down at the small remains with tears streaming her face.

"I am going to end this now, Gregor. You were right, she is useless and loud. She is going to get us killed," Gor huffed, and she trembled as she heard his angry footsteps coming at her. Suddenly Gregor was scooping her up in his arms. His chin grazed her cheek as he stood.

"Oh, you are going to carry her now?" Gor asked with a mocking chortle. "I thought you said she was useless."

"I don't want to die as we pass over goblin territory," Gregor stated in an emotionless tone.

"Yeah, good thinking," Gor said.

Gregor did not answer. He kept his head looking straight ahead. Victoria was still crying for the poor creature he just murdered in cold blood, and then Gregor had the audacity to push her face into his chest, stifling the noise of her sobs. She thrashed about angrily, trying to inflict serious pain with the heaviest punches she could muster against his chest and face, but it was a weird angle, and she couldn't do much damage. He simply tossed her over his shoulder and continued onward.

She wanted to punch him some more, but her body was just too tired to move. She let her muscles relax as Gregor carried her, planning her escape.

She guessed it was another hour or so before Gor finally stopped in front of them. He dropped his bag, and she could hear him groaning as he sat on the ground. Victoria was surprised when Gregor did not rest after he sat her down. Rather he climbed in the nearest tree and hung out on a sturdy branch to pull his chest up to the branch again and again with his arms. Victoria was puzzled, surely, he must be spent carrying her for such a distance. He continued for longer than Victoria would have deemed possible before climbing down and settling against a tree trunk between Gor and Victoria. Gor was already snoring. Gregor pulled a worn, shabby blanket from his bag and tossed it at Victoria without a word. She looked at him, but he avoided her by crossing his arms and tucking his chin down into his jacket collar. He leaned back and closed his eyes.

Soon his breathing was slow too. As the moon rose higher in the sky, its light threaded through the canopy overhead to weakly shine on their little camp. She could see their sleeping faces. She stayed awake, staring into the dark shadows in fear. Eventually, she must have fallen into a light stupor because she was startled awake by a rather large centipede crawling over her arm. She flicked it off with a silent shudder. The morning light was just enough to make out both her captors' faces.

A burst of anger and hatred consumed her, and she fought the urge to attack Gor, which she knew would be a feeble attempt. She had never killed anything bigger than an insect. She was not even sure how to inflict pain. She silently prayed he would never wake up. Then she stopped herself, sorting the foul feelings. She needed a solution rather than sulking. After several long breaths, she mustered the courage to stand, letting the blanket drop onto the forest floor.

She could barely breathe. She wished she had some sort of weapon and clung to the folds of her dress with tight fists. She took a deep breath and then crept on tiptoe toward Gregor. Taking each step slowly, each crunch below felt like an earsplitting shriek. Cautiously, she leaned over Gregor; the pocket with the necklace was within her grasp. Gor snored loudly, his snore raspy and unsettling.

The moments seemed to pass tantalizingly slow as she reached out her arms, fingers eager to hold the necklace again. With a slightly shaking hand, she reached inside, feeling for it. As her fingertips closed about the gold chain, she breathed a short sigh of relief. Carefully she drew it out, preventing the soft clinks.

Gregor was still asleep, and she looked toward Gor. His savage face held a snarl, even in his sleep. His scars and sun-damaged skin made his face look like the tanned leather hides they used to cover furniture. His continued snore gave her the courage to pull away, gathering the rest of the necklace in her hands. The large red ruby glinted in the soft glow of the dawning rays.

Gregor shifted against the ground, and she froze, staring at him in fear. His rough, unshaven jaw and cheekbones seemed striking as the sunrise touched his cheek. As she stood in the momentary lapse of judgment, she quickly assured herself it was just the lighting. Then she turned to tiptoe back out of sight, tripping over the vegetation, which unfortunately she had quite forgotten.

With an uncontrollable gasp in surprise followed by a loud smack of her hitting the ground, she quickly looked over her shoulder from the forest floor to see Gregor's eyes flutter open. Their eyes locked, and for a moment, neither moved.

His eyebrows lifted, his lips parted slightly, and Victoria was unsure what he was thinking. As his eyes wandered over her face, Victoria knew he was reading her expression, which she was unable to conceal. She was sure there was no mistaking the fear and desperation.

Victoria made the first move, not breaking eye contact while gathering herself slowly. She continued to match his gaze as she shifted onto her feet, heart pumping, the adrenaline burning, yelling at her to run, but she maintained her slow, controlled movements. She forced a shaking leg back, deliberately small steps, taking an unaggressive pace. She was almost out of sight behind the first large tree. Gregor shifted into an upright position, a look of bewilderment crossing his face.

As his eyes continued down her body, they came to rest on her hand, still holding the golden chain tightly. His face creased in anger, brows furrowing deep. He sprang to his feet much faster than Victoria expected, and she shrieked in panic, hearing her own voice thrash against her ears. It was an awful sound. Fleeing as fast as her feet would allow over the brush and under the low-hanging branches, disregarding the abysmal cry of sore muscles, panic rose inside her as she heard Gor shout.

"Go get her," Victoria heard Gor huff in annoyance at Gregor. Ducking under a low tree limb and pushing through some bushes, she ran.

CHAPTER 7

A WATERFALL

A WHISPERY ECHO FLOWED through the chilly wind, whistling in her ears, stirring her soul. The fading shadows crept around dead twisted trees arching in rotten angles. Their roots jumped to claw at her feet, snagging her between the dark furrows of their domain. The struggle slowed her, and she saw Gregor running close. Farther ahead in the forest, odd little sparkles danced along an uneven path. Large stones provided a dry bridge across the stream; Victoria saw this as a beacon of hope. As she hit the dry ground, she felt the pebbles and dirt fly under her upturning feet. Maybe there was a chance of escape. Coming to the edge of an uneven hill, she decided she would need to jump to avoid the slow navigation through the jagged path. It was high enough that a moment was needed to prepare herself, but it was interrupted by Gregor's heavy footfalls landing right behind her. She jumped, shoving hard against the edge, propelling faster toward the ground below. The brief rush fueled another blast of adrenaline so as her feet touched the dirt, she felt refreshed, ready to run forever. The feeling was immediately doused. She had grossly underestimated his speed. Gregor had already landed right behind her, catching her about the waist.

Although it was futile to resist such unyielding force, she instantly tried to pull away, and he tightened his grip, yanking her closer. Her back was pressed against his chest, and as she struggled, she could feel his heartbeat quicken.

As she turned her body toward him, her hair brushed against his cheek. Her chest now pressed right against his, she forced herself to look up into those deep emeralds, searching for mercy. There was a flicker of doubt across his face, a small chip in his stone-cold gaze.

He closed his eyes, turning his face. His grip loosened momentarily. Although surprised, she didn't hesitate to twist free and dart into the trees. When she dared to look behind, he was slumped, fists slammed into the frozen ground. The obvious struggle inside raged on his face in a terrible grimace. An awful groan escaped from his lips, spooking the ravens from their perches in the trees. The blackbirds rose into the air like a dark cloud as she ran past. Hoping to place as much distance between her and him, she did not stop running, even after stumbling multiple times.

The trees were growing so close together she had to weave a crooked path. Too soon it took its toll. Feeling a bit dizzy, she staggered to a halt, leaning back against the cold bark of a nearby trunk. She slid down until her legs were sprawled out on the ground, arms limp on either side in sheer exhaustion. She imagined how she looked with dirt streaked on her face and a torn dress. She knew her hair was a mess, falling loose around without any bow or clasp. She sighed. For the first time in her whole existence, she did not quickly fix it. It would have to wait until she could move again.

A rustle in the leaves in the distance woke her from her light slumber. Victoria gasped, knowing her hiding place was wanting. She gave a relieved sigh as the little female fox appeared from the thick underbrush. She giggled at its big bobbing tail and tiny paws.

"If you can find me, I am sure they can as well." Victoria sighed, fear once again racing up her spine and tingling into her neck.

A whisper drifted through, and at first, she assumed it to be the wind playing more tricks. But when the fox dashed off and into a nearby burrow, she listened intently. Soon the voices grew louder, accompanied with heavy footfalls. She identified two pairs of boots stomping closer, and Victoria knew they would find her, but she could barely move. Her eyes followed the trail the fox had taken to the burrow only a few feet away.

Animal, be an animal! she shouted to herself in her head. *Fox, fox, fox!* she silently screamed. At first, nothing happened, and her stomach lurched in panic. She concentrated hard, trying to drown out the terror with images of a fox. There was little more than a stitch in her side as a response. As the boots neared closer, she scrambled underneath the thick bramblebush, trying to fit herself under the prickly vines. Her skin was pierced by the thorns painfully, stabbing her arms and her back. Her cheek was grazed, and blood dripped onto her top knuckle as she lay on her hands, holding her breath. All the while she commanded herself to transform.

When a tuft of hair sprang out over her hand, she felt a rush of relief. Swallowing the shrieks of pain inward, she gave no sound, except the soft rustle of her dress shifting over her small body. Mustering the last of her strength to drag the necklace into the burrow with her, she collapsed just inches from the opening as a large boot stepped into view.

"She stole the necklace right out of your pocket?" Gor screamed in frustration. Gregor grunted angrily.

Gor shouted out with a squeal of delight. "Looksy here! She is either naked or dead," Gor said, and Victoria realized they had found her dress under the brush. "It's still warm," he cooed.

"There is blood on it—" Gregor said.

"If we are lucky, her body is close around. We can get the necklace back," Gor said. The shifting footsteps fell away.

Victoria soon relaxed as silence offered safety. Although it smelled musky, the burrow was warm. She welcomed sleep as it overtook her, she hoped she could stay in animal form while she slept.

She woke up with something licking her wet nose, and she snorted a few times. Opening her eyes, she looked to see the small fox licking her face. She decided to name her. She settled on Cuddles. Then she looked past Cuddles and toward the outside. The sun shone brightly into the burrow entrance.

Apparently, she could indeed hold her form while sleeping. She checked to make sure the necklace was still underneath her paw. As she scampered from the burrow, she quickly realized how small she felt compared to the giant trees overhead. She could move with much more ease. The sun's rays shifted unevenly through the thick canopy overhead, and it was closer to the horizon than she hoped.

Deciding quickly, she grabbed the necklace in her teeth and clumsily shoved it into the pocket with her lipstick in her small leather purse on her dress. She had to chew through the strap and tie the ends together, but soon after she was wearing it as some sort of animal satchel. She gave one last glance to her dress, still lying abandoned in the dirt, before diving under the bushes. Each overturned root no longer a hurdle, she easily made her way across the forest floor. Her huge ears detected the slightest flutter of an insect or scurrying rodent.

As she continued trying to navigate down the mountain, thoughts ventured to Gregor's odd behavior. He let go. He simply let her go. She replayed the moment in her head, puzzling over it again and again, but came to no conclusion. She tried to fasten her mind on her hate of him, but somehow it was fading.

Soon she heard water flowing nearby; she was sure it would lead her out of the Black Needle Mountains. When she came to the edge, there was ice lining either side, but the middle still ran fast and strong. Carefully she pattered to the water's edge, paws sliding about. Finally, she was able to drink. And she drank from the water with no reservations, letting gluttony fill her belly.

The leather purse dipped in as she drank, and she pulled it back with her teeth. She continued to drink, feeling as though she could never be full. It slid to the front again, and before she could pull back, it slipped off. Clumsy from the cold and unable to catch it quick enough, it grazed past her teeth and into the river. The current snatched it up and thrashed it harshly about, pulling it farther and farther away. The leather was waterproof and kept the purse bobbing on top of the surface. She dove her head into the water, but it was already out of reach. She ran awkwardly along the ice, paws slipping and sliding on either side. She tried to swipe the necklace with her paw, but the current was too fast.

Jumping again toward the edge, all four of her legs lost their traction and she went down on her belly, sliding over the ice in a total sprawl. By the time she was able to get up, the necklace was far downstream. She screamed in agitation but all that reached her ears was a series of yips. She stood and regained her motivation.

As she trotted along the water, searching, hoping it got snagged on a jagged rock, Cuddles fell into step with her. Cuddles was enthusiastically making all sorts of noises kicking up the leaves playfully. Cuddles yipped high and loud when she found a twig she could chew on, carrying it around proudly. Bringing it to Victoria as some sort of prize, she growled when Victoria did not grab it with her teeth. She kept growling until Victoria finally gave in and carried it for a few feet. Cuddles sprang around her happily and took it again, running down to the water's edge to toss it in, watching it float away.

Victoria wondered if she saw her lose the necklace. Perhaps she was smarter than she assumed, but as she thought this, she looked up to see

Cuddles chomping at an insect buzzing around her head. Maybe not. However, she appreciated her company.

Then she spied the purse again being carried downstream. Victoria's heart sank. There was a waterfall up ahead. She watched the purse go over. When she got to the edge, she looked down. The drop was much farther than she could ever jump and survive. She started scanning the easiest path to venture down. The necklace had to be in that bottom pool.

There were wild mint bushes everywhere, and she had to run through them to continue. Cuddles disappeared again, and Victoria did not think too much of it. She would probably show up again later. After passing through a few more bushes, her eyes were watering, and her nose and ears throbbed. She sniffed and wondered if it would remain on her hair once she turned back human. Her eyes were too blurry to tell where she was going. She wandered about, trying to make sense of her surroundings.

THUNK! She had run straight into a boot in mid-step. She sprang up to dash away, but the dizziness hit, and she collapsed. Her right back paw stuck out awkwardly in the fall and landed under the boot as it came down. She yelped in frantic pain as a sickening pop was heard.

"Oh!" Gregor's voice made it to her ears before everything went blurred and dark. When she finally was able to sort through the pain, she realized his huge hands were holding her by the nape of her neck, rendering her teeth useless. She had very limited range of motion and could only kick frantically.

"Sorry," Gregor said to her as he pulled her paws together so she could not struggle anymore. Victoria tilted her head up to see as far as she could, and her stomach flipped. She was terrified to the point of nausea, but that perhaps was due to the pain. He held her up for Gor to see.

"Foxes aren't good for eating. Too lean," Gor said, disinterested, while continuing to scrutinize the forest below thoroughly.

"She has an excellent pelt. This deep red is rare," Gregor said. He combed his fingers through her fur to her thick, bushy tail. Victoria's head spun as the shivers went down her spine.

"She?"

"Yes, she is a girl, see?" And to Victoria's embarrassment, he turned her over onto her back, underside exposed, and pointed.

"It will never make it with that foot," Gor said bluntly, and Gregor grumbled in agreement. "Might as well kill it so it doesn't suffer," he said, throwing a stick he had been fiddling with at Gregor in irritation.

"She can't have gotten far," Gor scanned the forest. "I wonder if that Snal is helping her. That could be the only reason she has eluded us this long unless the goblins are having some fun."

"Do you ever shut up?" Gregor asked in a grumble.

She again tried to squirm free from his grip to no avail. Thankfully Gregor did not snap her neck as Gor insisted. She was surprised when he began walking again, carrying her in his arm. Gor followed with a huff.

They made their way down the slope, and Victoria eagerly looked at the waterfall and the surrounding banks, searching for any sign of the necklace.

Victoria happily realized they were headed for the pool and anxiously searched every part as far as she could see. When they arrived, she examined each rock and crevice, hoping it had been washed ashore. She did not see anything glint among the ice-lined banks or the protruding rocks in the river. With utter frustration, Victoria wanted to scream. Then she saw it, the pouch had drifted from the waterfall and now rested tucked in between two rocks near the bank. She hoped neither man would spot it.

The men gathered water to drink, careful to keep their boots dry. Gregor held her mouth close to the water until she timidly drank. They ventured away from the wet, muddy bank between the trees until they found dry ground so Gor could start the fire. Gor looked at Gregor, cradling Victoria in his arms.

"Your new pet is pathetic. I have a pair of wolves. They will gut anyone I command them to," Gor said proudly.

"I think my pa's creature, Samson, beats anyone's pet," Gregor said defensively.

"Yeah, Brutus bit us both, but Samson's body rejected the curse. Instead of just killing him, he became a creature uglier than death, so ugly the shadows hide his face and—"

"And no woman would have him, so he went raving mad," Gregor continued, dryly. "Yes, I know. You have told me the story many times."

"It is not a story. It is my memories. I was there, I lived it. I saw Samson try to transform!" Gor continued, to Gregor's obvious annoyance.

"Have you ever seen Samson?" Gor asked.

"Yes, once. Pa brought him out into the bright sunlight, no trees or shadows. Just an open field, and then I could see him," Gregor said, his face crinkled in disgust.

"He got stuck in transformation. He is not man nor beast but hideously twisted with both. One eye is round and the other is a slit. He has shredded, torn-up skin where the fur started to come through but never finished. I am not sure if he is able to think, but he cannot talk," Gor said enthusiastically.

"I wish we knew how to help him complete the transition," Gregor said.

"I tell you these things because your pa would spare you the hard truths. Before you were born, we were as close as brothers. That is why he gave you my name, but then began the pampering of the little prince. 'Don't spin the baby, Gor. Gor, don't hold the baby upside down. Gor, you cannot take the baby on your hunt.' Your pa is too protective over you. He has made you soft. And your mum—" Suddenly Gor shut his mouth.

"What about my ma?" he asked anxiously.

"Nope, nope. I am not telling you anything about her. Your pa has already beaten me one time too many on what I have told you," Gor said.

Gregor shifted the ash near his foot.

After that, they fell into an uneasy silence.

If Gregor decided to cook her, she would have to transform and make a run for it. So, she sat, trembling as the flames licked the wood and began a roaring torment.

Then Gregor pulled out a knife from his belt, and Victoria yipped from fright despite trying to be brave. Gregor pulled out something else from his bag. After the parcel was unwrapped, Victoria sighed in relief. It was bread and cheese, and he used the knife to slice it roughly. When he offered a portion, she was too hungry to feel the humiliation of eating out of his hand.

"Where could she be?" Gor said after a few circles around the campfire, kicking leaves into the fire angrily. "We should hunt for her tonight with the help of the moon."

"Fine," Gregor said, shifting Victoria off his knee and leashing her to a trunk nearby while Gor mocked him mercilessly for it.

"Don't mind him. He is old and bitter," Gregor whispered, patting her head softly and rubbing her ears tenderly. "Stay here and rest. Don't run away. I will be back soon." He stood and turned toward Gor, who was standing with his arms crossed.

"Can you track her smell?" Gor asked.

"Yeah," Gregor said shortly. "If she is anywhere nearby, I will be able to find her."

"Then c'mon. Let's not waste any time," Gor said, pulling his clothes off quickly while Victoria again looked away in disgust.

Gregor sluggishly removed his boots while Gor finished changing and howled at the moon. Victoria felt it was a bit melodramatic, and she could tell Gregor agreed as he shook his head slightly. Then she wondered why he, too, was removing his boots.

Suddenly everything clicked. Gregor was obviously a moon creature thing, too—his height, his stamina, his strength. He pulled his shirt over his head, and Victoria tried to ignore his physique by reminding herself how angry she was at him. She nibbled at the rope in discontentment, trying to determine how long it would take to bite free. When he looked at her, she stopped, afraid he would be angry at her chewing. This seemed odd when she thought more about it, and she resumed chewing. Gregor came over and patted her on the head, and she wished he had not. She shut her eyes tightly, feeling indignant.

Then he transformed, and Victoria was astounded at the speed and ease, such control she could only wish she possessed. Covered in dark chestnut fur and over six feet tall, his figure was quite intimidating. His large snout pulled back in a snarl to show a set of sharp fangs. The longest were the pair of canines, but they did not protrude out the way Gor's did. His paws were large and covered in hair with black claws where fingernails should have been. The palms were padded like a paw, but he retained his thumb and individual fingers. Momentarily, she lost her fear in sheer awe. He was the flawless blend of beast and human, resulting in a far superior predator.

He sniffed toward her, and she shrank under his gaze. Then he shook his head, sputtering a bit from the strong mint. Victoria felt very fortunate to be covered in it until Gregor cast her a glance.

She was sure he did know, even through the hair and fangs, she could see that readable expression of realization. Gregor turned his head and barked to Gor, leading him into the woods.

Victoria waited anxiously until they were far out of sight and then tugged at the rope. Finally, she started to chew through it, but it was thick and would take too long. She looked again to ensure both were nowhere in sight.

She concentrated hard on being a human, thinking of her peach skin and, oddly, her opposable thumbs. She turned quicker this time although the pain was still unbearable. She wondered how many times she needed to turn before she could be instantaneous like Gregor.

Her plan was all panic and had not been thought out. The rope was now pressed against her throat, and she could not breathe. Her ankle shot a fresh new pain from taking half of her body weight instead of the three paws keeping it lifted.

She looked around hysterically as an owl hooted from the tree. Its large eyes stared at her. She screamed inside to turn back into an animal.

Smaller, smaller animal neck! was all she could scream at herself, chanting in her head while her throat felt like it was on fire. She welcomed the agonizing pain as her neck slimmed down, and she gasped. It was not until after several deep breaths she realized she did not have the proper tail. Instead of her fluffy fox tail, she had a large plumage of owl feathers.

Looking at the plumage, she got an idea. She told herself she wanted to be an owl, a tiny owl.

After some intense pain in her face and head, she looked down the front of her to see a beak obstructing her view. She guessed it would take a while to get used to having a large beak on her face. Then she realized she still had her fox body, only her tail and head were an owl. She wondered if she would ever get it right. She easily slipped the rope over her head and let it drop to the ground. She screamed *human* again and again in her mind.

After she was done, she collapsed on the ground, gasping for breath. She made a fist with her human hand and pumped it weakly in the air once in triumph.

A small creature approached from the distance. A spark of hope warmed her heart as she welcomed Cuddles into her arms.

"I can't believe you found me again," she told her while scratching her ears. She pawed at her playfully.

"Wait here," she said. "I will be back. I just need to get the necklace." Cuddles curled up beside the tree and chewed contently on the rope.

She stood, but the pain was intense. Her ankle was swollen and tender. Cuddles watched as she limped away, freezing as the chill of the night air hit her bare skin. It was slow going as she tried to push herself along, afraid at any moment the beasts might return, but it seemed impossible. Slumping from one tree to another for support was immensely time-consuming. As she reached the bank, she had to say goodbye to the last tree and limp until she reached the ice. Then she got onto her knees, crawling to the edge. Forcing herself into the water took all her might. As she dipped into the water, she tried to prepare herself, but nothing could keep the excruciating chills from rushing over her.

Avoiding noise by moving slowly, she glided on the rocky bottom, trying to move quickly to keep the blood flowing into her numb limbs. It was much easier to move in the water with her swollen ankle. The waterfall bombarded her face and dampened her hair with constant splashing of icy cold droplets.

She saw the leather purse still wedged between the two rocks. She continued and the water was over her waist. A large fish wiggled against her leg, making her jump with a splash. She cried out in surprise but quickly jammed her mouth shut, covering it with her hand. Looking behind her, she saw only the trees swaying in the wind. No other movement from the bank. Taking another deep breath between the severe shivers, she knew she had only a few moments more in the water. Already her toes and fingertips were crying out in pain.

A snap of twigs made her turn toward the sound, but once again, only the wind replied. She took a breath before stepping further and dipping deeper into the water, reaching for the necklace. Suddenly there was a heavy splash and she turned to see Gor's deformed lips slither into a smirk, a cruel greeting. Her scream echoed against the rocks as he yanked her arm, gripping her so tightly in his hand it was sure to snap in half.

He thrust her face into the pool. Water flowed into her open mouth and filled her nose painfully.

"Where is the necklace?" Gor shouted the question at her and pulled her out so she could answer. She sputtered and screamed hysterically. He shoved her face back down into the pool. He never flinched as she struggled with all her might. He pulled her hair hard, yanking her face again into the freezing air. She spat water and coughed until she could frantically swallow the precious air.

"Tell me!" Gor said and gave her a punch in the cheek. His knuckles stung like fire against her cold flesh. She had never been punched before, and it was indeed every bit as painful as she imagined it to be. She could barely gasp for breath, let alone utter a single word as her very bone felt shattered. Gor was impatient. Victoria cried out as he planted her into the water on her back, her face was upturned so she could see Gor's eyes flash flecks of red. Victoria believed it was his blood boiling up to his eyeballs with hot temper.

Gregor's face came over Gor's shoulder, distorted by the watery veil. Victoria watched with wide eyes as he slammed into Gor. As the two collided into the water, Victoria wiggled free the moment his hold lifted. She popped out of the water immediately, greeted by the earsplitting shriek of Gor screaming in pain.

Victoria could only watch as she uncontrollably spewed water from her nose between gasps for breath. Gregor and Gor turned toward each other in fierce anger.

Gor burrowed his head into Gregor's gut with a brutal slam into the sharp edges of the ice. Victoria pulled herself out of the water and crawled off the ice, ignoring the pain of her ankle while begging herself to turn into a fox. All she could imagine was soft, thick fur. Welcoming the familiar throb of pain, soon the red coat appeared. When she looked up and back toward the pool, Gor was staring right at her before Gregor yanked him back into the water.

Even though she wanted to run, she could only hobble on her three paws through the underbrush. She passed the campfire, which was still smoldering. She pulled up to a stop as she noticed Cuddles sitting by her rope, waiting.

"Run!" she tried to warn, but only high-pitched yip came out. She tried to beckon her to follow, but she just matched her energy with some playful hops and jumps. The more she tried to push her out of sight, the more Cuddles just pawed at her tail lightheartedly. Gor's frenzied mumbles approached closer.

Gor stormed up the bank, yanking Gregor behind him. He pushed Gregor down and left one foot on his head as he shouted at him. He turned and kicked Gregor in the gut hard. Then he grabbed his hair, pulling him up to punch him several times in the jaw. Then Gor bit him, sinking his teeth into Gregor's shoulder. Gregor screamed. It was horrifying to see Gor's human teeth dripping with Gregor's blood.

"Are you going soft? Brutus has no need for a wimp in his army!" Gor said, spitting out the blood in his mouth. "It is your fault. I will not lose any blood for your mistake!" Gor shouted down at Gregor, and then he straightened up, looking around.

"Richard lied! His wife was not unfaithful. Victoria is his! She can shapeshift, just like he could. Beneath our very noses! She made a fool of us!!" Gor screamed angrily.

Victoria edged farther away in the underbrush, hiding safely out of sight. Cuddles joined her as they entered the small clearing. Gregor looked at Gor expectantly, waiting for him to provide proof.

"You don't believe me, but . . .," Gor took a few long sniffs, "I smell her!" Victoria realized the mint had washed away. She cringed as Gor stepped closer, but Cuddles gave into panic, springing out to flee.

"There! There she is!" Gor screamed and hurled himself forward, catching Cuddles about the neck. Cuddles let a yelp of pain as Gor shook her violently. Victoria barely could breathe as she gazed at the scene in horror.

"Change! Change right now!" Gor screamed at Cuddles. "You are a fool for choosing a fox form again! We know who you are! Change!" he yelled again as Gregor looked with confusion. "Change!" Gor said, trying to plead his cause. "I saw her change!"

Gregor shook his head in unbelief as Cuddles continued to squeal in pain.

"Drop her," Gregor's voice wavered and then cracked in emotion as he begged Gor. Gor looked at Gregor, his brow furrowed and lips slithering into a crooked smile as he broke Cuddle's neck with one swift movement. Tossing the small lifeless body on the frozen ground between them, Gor spat. Gregor grunted as it hit with a disheartening thud. Victoria gasped; a sickening pile of guilt bore down on her heart. Both men stood rooted where they were, looking down at the carcass expectantly. After what seemed like an eternity, Gregor snorted at Gor, infuriated.

"I don't understand!" Gor said in disbelief. "It was her—I am sure of it. Perhaps the transformation needs more time with these things," Gor said quickly, kicking Cuddles as though that would spark some sort of change. Gregor stood to face Gor.

"Then she would be dead!" Gregor shouted, anger flushing his face.

Gregor landed a punch squarely in Gor's jaw. Gor stumbled back and regained his balance.

"You took me by surprise just then, but I am older and stronger than you. I will kill you!" Gor threatened, and the fight exploded between them. Victoria was lost in a panic, anxious as to who would emerge the victor. Although it seemed Gor was more experienced in combat, Gregor was in a fit of heated rage. Gor twisted Gregor's arm until there was a sickening snap. Victoria gagged at the sight of Gregor's limp arm dangling uselessly to the side. Gor kicked Gregor, and he fell down against the tree. As Gor finished bashing him hard in the ribs, Gregor jammed Gor's chin in a heavy uppercut with his other fist, and a tooth flew from Gor's mouth, landing out of sight, lost among the mess of leaves. When Gor reeled back in pain, Gregor lunged, dragging him down to the ground.

Gregor growled violently like a rabid animal although he was still in human form. Gregor pounded on Gor until Gor snatched his broken arm, giving it a mighty shake, and Gregor shouted out in pain. Gor mercilessly dragged Gregor down and slid over on top of him, pressing his face hard into the dirt until Gregor began to choke and gag. Gor did not let up until Gregor stopped moving completely. Victoria was sure he was dead.

Gor held his bleeding face with one hand and spit on the other, lathering his saliva into his cuts and bruises along his cheek and under his eyes. Victoria gagged as she watched but then was astounded to see Gor's broken skin heal right before her almost instantly. He licked his hands and his arms and even bent down to lick the cut on his calf.

"I grabbed the wrong fox, but she can't be too far! Imagine our reward if we not only bring back the necklace but a true daughter of Richard!" Gor said. When Gregor did not move, he shifted restlessly.

"Get up. Stop acting like such a spoiled prince," Gor said.

Gregor slowly moved, his arm dangling uselessly at his side. Victoria cringed as Gor walked over and popped it back in place without warning. It must have hurt even more than it sounded because Gregor thrashed wildly while his throat released a howl of agony.

"Now we have to find her," Gor said. "This time we know what to look for. I bet she can't change into anything but a fox yet."

CHAPTER 8

A GREEN SOLUTION

VICTORIA SLOWLY CREPT FROM her hiding spot, her whole body shaking from the violence she'd just witnessed. She respectfully covered Cuddles as best she could; her paws could only dig so far in the frozen soil. Then she covered the rest with leaves, giving a silent prayer in the same manner she had been taught since childhood.

She wandered away, looking for a shelter from the chilly wind as it whistled through the branches loudly. She followed a musk-scented trail to an abandoned rabbit burrow. Once nestled inside, the wind continued to whine outside, mixing with the replaying screams and shrieks of Cuddle's last moments of terror echoing in her head. She tried to quiet them to no avail. Eventually she was able to lure herself into a light, dreamless sleep, hoping the sun would come back soon.

As the strong light of the sun filled the entrance, she reluctantly left the safety of the den. Her ankle was now tolerable as she made her way down to the pool again. She was surprised at its speedy recovery. The sun shone through the waterfall with a small rainbow, which lifted Victoria's spirits. When she changed, she pushed herself to quickly see her fingers and toes. It was harder now, being all alone. Her fear and adrenaline seemed to help hasten it. But soon she could touch the familiar high cheekbones of her face, she gave a small smile, which soon faded as she remembered the necklace.

She reluctantly entered the water, which seemed to be even colder in her anticipation. She quickly moved to grab the purse. Once it was in hand, she gritted her teeth as she made herself dip a few times to wash her hair. She looked at scratches Gor had given her, an ugly row of scabs on her arm. Looking at her reflection in water's surface, she noticed a purple bruise remained on her face from the painful punch. She shuddered, thinking he was still out there somewhere in these very woods. With that thought, she swam to the edge and climbed out. Still shaking, she grimaced as another chilly wind whipped about her body.

She rummaged through the remains of the campsite. Thankfully in Gregor's hurry to gather his things, some of his clothes were left behind, and she quickly dressed herself in the pair of trousers and coat. She wrapped the remaining cloth about her feet, unsure if she could manage out of the mountains without frostbite should it snow. Although the clothes were dirty and smelled fiercely like sweat, she was grateful the musk would hide her scent. Much warmer now, she moved on, following the river downstream.

The trees all looked the same. She was sure she was lost. She sang the lullaby from her childhood again and again in her mind. It seemed to soothe her. She was too afraid to stop, so she continued to follow the stream in a desperate hope. She walked all day, ignoring the pain of her sore limbs and the blisters on her poorly protected feet. As the sun started to sink, the first snowflakes wafted down around her. She looked at them with discontentment and frustration.

A shadow crossed overhead, and she looked up to witness a tall and particularly thin creature hunching in the large tree. He had long frail limbs lined with knots and bumps. His rounded head held a few twigs covered with green leaves, which were combed back, creating a sort of hairline. Shifty eyes under a high brow arch, large orbs of black, were surrounded by a thin brown ring. There were small flecks of gold sprinkled in the iris, making her stomach knot. As her eyes moved down his greenish brown body, they were met with a horrendous sight. Rather than the calves connecting to ankles and eventually feet, the flesh split and writhed in moving strands. Where his feet should have been, there were green vines with small roots branching in every direction, perching it atop the branch. Victoria had a difficult time trying to even determine what he was and could not imagine trying to explain him to Mabel if she lived to tell the tale. He was a strange creature indeed. She decided he could only be identified as a type of living plant, like one of the weeds she pulled from the garden.

She screamed, throwing everything within reach at him, which consisted of a rock and a couple of sticks. They bounced off the creature with a soft thud and fell into the hardened, snow freckled dirt. In a swift, effortless movement, it dove from the tree and stood with one long thin hand against her mouth, muffling her screams.

"Is she lost?" His voice was raspy and thick, and Victoria could barely decipher it. "There are plenty of creatures who would love to feed on her flesh." As he said this, his forked tongue slid across his top teeth, making a soft smack. Victoria wondered if it was an overview of her near future. She shuddered as his bizarre face stared at her.

"Her body to freeze, snow-ridden hair," he said with a chuckle, pulling on her hair roughly. Victoria screamed out.

"I am trying to get out of here. Can you point me in the right direction?" Victoria asked nervously as the creature circled about her.

"Out?" He chuckled. "You won't make it . . ."

"Please," Victoria asked, trying to ignore the unblinking stare.

"Oh, she doesn't know." He laughed and vanished into the forest underbrush without a single burnt amber leaf displaced. Victoria pushed her hand into the exact spot. A shuffle of branches moved under her fingertips, and several of the autumn leaves fluttered to the ground.

"How did you do that?" she called out. His face popped out from a high tree branch behind her, once again leaving the delicate leaves undisturbed.

"She dies," he said, his eyebrow arching high. "Frozen and alone."

"Is she me?" Victoria asked fearfully. "You do not make a lot of sense."

"She has no coins," he said with a snide tone. Snickering again, he merged back into the remaining foliage.

"Please," she asked softly.

"Please?" he said, voice cracking in enthusiasm. "Please . . . she begs for death!" he mimicked her with a shrill, whiny voice. As he mocked her, Victoria gasped at his horrid humor.

"Rid her of her human stench," he said, rubbing his gnarled fingers over her, leaving a sticky sap down her clothes. She backed away.

"My name is Victoria," she said, trying to avoid more goo.

"He knows," he said. "Eldest daughter of Richard, bearing the hollow ruby," he said, looking at her neck where the necklace sat underneath her collar. She fastened the top button, ensuring the gold was completely concealed, and disturbed that he knew of it.

"How long have you been following me?" she asked uncomfortably.

"Snal," he said loudly and pointed to his chest. He began to walk, beckoning her to follow. She pushed her hair out of her face and followed.

"How do you know my father? Snal?" She struggled to say his name with the same dialect he had used. "Please tell me how you know my father." She eagerly ran to join his side. When he did not answer, she asked again. He just grunted and continued walking, weaving up into the trees and back again on the forest floor gracefully. The riverbank being left far behind made her a bit nervous.

"Where are we going? What are you?" she asked, fishing for any answer. All the while, she curiously watched him move along the forest floor. He was the most unusual creature she had ever seen. She could not take her eyes off the several roots sinking into the ground with every step.

"Daughter of Richard does not know anything of nymphs?" Snal asked.

She followed him through the trees and jumped when he began making a series of peculiar noises, low rumbles. A musical chorus of high-pitched whispers answered back, almost as though a song. Victoria recognized it as the haunting echoes she had heard earlier, but now closer, they offered a calm melody. Victoria found herself walking slower and enjoying the feeling of peace that suddenly overcame her. No longer afraid, she wandered about, looking at the dazzling flowers that were in full bloom. "She will freeze," Snal hissed in a tone Victoria could not discern.

"Aren't nymphs supposed to be beautiful women sung about in legends?" She jumped a bit when he stopped and turned toward her sharply. His face came right to hers, their noses touched, and his huge eyes stared straight into hers. His hot breath hit her face, and a strong waft of garlic made her eyes water. She squirmed a bit under his somber gaze.

"Would she sing about him?" he asked expectantly, stepping back slightly to gesture toward himself. When she did not answer, he gave a pointed nod.

"Help me or leave. I don't have time," Victoria said flatly.

He smiled and returned to his unblinking stare as he pulled a long green cloak off his shoulders. Wrapping it about her with an eerie silence, his thin, gnarled fingers grazed her cheek, rougher than tree bark.

She looked at the fabric, realizing it was made from green leaves woven together in an intricate pattern with some sort of silky thread.

"This is incredible," she said, snuggling into its warmth. "It's so soft!" she exclaimed.

He then gestured toward the pair of boots he yanked from somewhere in the messy tangle of his roots. The outside of the boots was thick, and she could tell they were meant for snow, although she could not figure out what they were made from. It seemed to be some sort of leather, but it was too green in color to be anything she knew. The laces were also white, velvety to the touch but strong enough to lace tight about her feet. They were tall, covering up to her knees.

"What is this?" she asked as she tied the final knot. She stood, and immediately her feet felt better, protected from the thorns and cold. She wiggled her toes in delight.

"Laces are of spider silk," he said, watching closely to enjoy her expression. Victoria was disgusted, but she did not want to take them off. They were too comfortable.

"How do they harvest spider silk?" she asked, although she assumed she wouldn't get an answer. After a long pause she finally said. "Thank you, Snal!"

She hugged him in a tight squeeze. His rough skin scratched against her with a rustle.

"He wanted to give it to you. He cares for you," Snal said, immediately pushing her away.

"Well, thank you, Snal. I care for you too," she said, pulling the collar of the cloak about her cheeks.

"He doesn't care," Snal said, gesturing to himself with a face full of disgust.

"But you just said—" Victoria said, confused, but it was too late. Snal already vanished back into the trees. She knew he was watching from his hiding place, but it was impossible to see him. She nestled deeper into the cloak, cherishing the warmth.

Victoria noticed another nymph approaching curiously. She had the same green color of skin, but it was completely smooth, unlike Snal. She was lovelier than any story or song could describe, with a petite slender body and long waves of golden hair that rippled down past her waist. Victoria did not understand how it was so shiny, even in the sunlight. Her pale green skin was strangely beautiful. Victoria could not stop staring at her large violet eyes. Her tiny feet did not make a sound moving through the forest, as though she blended into the surrounding vegetation seamlessly. This puzzled Victoria because she had fully formed feet, unlike Snal.

Before she could find words to ask about it, movement shifted about her in the trees, more peered down at her. Their bright eyes caught hers. No two pairs of eyes were the same color or shape, but all of them had soft, smooth green faces. Victoria now turned every way, trying to catch another in movement. The forest was still again. They had come as close as they dared. She could feel their eyes on her. Finally, she turned back toward Snal, who once again stood before her. They held strange instruments that made an odd yet sweet music. Victoria listened and could not resist swaying a bit in rhythm. She noticed one holding a handheld harp, the strings stretched taut over a bright green vine curved into a semicircle. She pulled the piece to her and began to strum it as Professor Carter had taught her. She was grateful for the painstaking hours of practice now as the nymphs began to dance around her happily.

"Many creatures doubted she would undertake such a task. So puny! Unable to fulfill her destiny," Snal said.

"What are you talking about?" Victoria asked.

When she looked up again, Snal was nowhere to be found.

"Snal!" she cried out. The singing had faded away, and she was now standing alone. It seemed darker in the forest than before. All the trees were tighter together, and she could not determine which way she had come from. She started to run in one direction and then back again in the other.

"I am completely lost! Snal!" she called out, fear erupting inside. She stood still, trying to take long, deep breaths to calm her racing heart. She heard a small echo in the distance.

"Snal!" she called out and ran toward the voice. There was a glow in the distance, and she sprinted toward it, too out of breath to call out. When she was only a few yards away, a large vine whipped across her chest, slamming her to the ground with a huff. Snal's hand was again muffling her mouth.

"Shush," he said. His slimy fingers twisted over her, leaving sap all over her face and neck. He pointed to where Gor was coming from the other direction, and Victoria ducked behind the nearest tree, dropped down low, and squeezed into the brush, ignoring the spider web she had disturbed and all the muck oozing over her hands. Her knees were tight against her chest, and for a full minute, all she could hear was the beating of her own heart.

She watched Snal slide into the vegetation, abandoning her. Hope seemed to disappear with him. She gingerly peered out.

"When I find her, I will make her suffer!" Gor said to Gregor, and he stomped angrily. Victoria was surprised their faces were back to normal. There was not even one scratch from the brutal beating they had given each other. Gor stopped short, sniffing the air. Victoria held her breath, every muscle in her body poised, ready to run.

Gor sniffed again, a gleam in his eye. She crouched down deeper.

"He's better looking as a beast," Snal interrupted Gor's concentration. Victoria listened intently now. She was unable to see them from her hiding place.

"Get out!" Gor said in a deep voice, almost as terrible as his growl. "Snal, I do not have time for your games."

"He angry," Snal said.

"Yes, he very angry," Gor yelled, and Victoria could tell he chucked something at Snal because of the huff he gave followed by a heavy clank. Victoria ducked down lower. Snal chuckled.

"Give him shiny," Snal said.

"No, go away," Gor said. Victoria assumed he disappeared because silence resumed. "I hate nymphs," Gor uttered, and she heard him stomp onward, to her relief.

"Oh, he is a wise one!" Victoria heard Snal say. Victoria heard the unmistakable sound of coins clicking together. She closed her eyes, frustrated she had no idea what was going on.

"Don't do that—don't give it money!" Gor angrily shouted, his footfalls returning.

"Just let me know if you see her," Gregor's voice cut through all the blathering insults Gor was tossing around like confetti. Then silence.

Victoria ducked lower, listening. There was nothing but the rustle of leaves and of course the constant pounding in her ears that had not gone away since the moment she was snatched out of the courtyard days ago. *How many days?* she wondered, trying to count the number of sunsets, including this one, she had watched with a sinking heart.

Presently Victoria felt a cold tickle beside her and gulped while turning her head slowly, seized in terror as Snal's roots slithered over her arm.

"She here!" Snal said smugly, gesturng with both his arms, a wicked gleam in his eyes.

"Get her!" Gor hollered. Gregor was already in motion. Victoria did not have time to cast Snal a scowl; she was already sprinting. The harp was still in her hand.

Each passing moment in the fading darkness lasted twice as long as it should have while she dodged between the tight vegetation, taking paths she knew Gregor could not follow as easily due to his tall stature.

A pair of gleaming eyes blinked at her from a distance. Then a bony hand gestured her into a narrow hole, and she could see faint light on the other side. The creature looked like the other one Gregor had crushed earlier. The hole was barely wide enough for her to squeeze through. She dropped the harp and got onto her knees to crawl. Victoria winced as thornbushes around the entrance tore at her skin. Gregor tried to snatch her leg, but she was too quick, pulling herself inside while he shouted at the entrance. His shoulders could not fit through.

"No, come back here right now!" he demanded angrily. She could hear him trying to dig out the tunnel, scraping at the sides and then shouting some more.

She scooted along on her elbows as fast as she could, following the creature. She could hear Gregor still yelling but could no longer make out the words. When she reached the other side, she realized she was in a ditch carved out by the little creatures with thick bramblebushes on either side, overgrown to form a thick ceiling. It was long but not very tall. She could barely sit up and had to keep her head ducked. She saw over a dozen pair of eyes venturing closer to her. Their coos were soft and welcoming. The trees overhead parted slightly, so a sliver of the setting sun shone down through the thorns.

"Shh!" she whispered, listening intently. She could hear Gregor's shouts diminish. She just needed to get out from this bush somehow and she could navigate her way home. As she turned about looking for an exit, she realized the tunnel was the only clear path. She would need to cut out of these branches, which was much harder because they were covered in thorns. She tugged at the first branch, careful where she placed her hands. It was green and bendable and took a lot of effort to twist and finally break. She sighed. It was going to take time to clear a path large enough for her to worm through.

As the adorable creatures snuggled against her, she smiled. She continued to twist and break each branch of the interwoven thorny vines and stopped often to shake her fingers, which were now bleeding in several places.

The creature nearest her licked her bleeding shoulder and then climbed on top of her. It gurgled to the others, which seemed to excite all of them. Some began to smile, and she smiled back at them, now noticing how sharp and pointy their teeth looked. Their tongues slithered out of their mouths, forked like a serpent. She gasped, feeling suddenly alarmed. As more clung to her, she tried to wiggle from their scratching nails.

"Ow, you are hurting me," she whispered, but they ignored her swats and pushes.

She turned to crawl back out through the tunnel, deciding she would take her chances with Gregor, but they blocked her way. There was now a lot more than before, and she couldn't move in any direction.

"Oh dear," she said hoarsely. She tried to scoot them away, and the moment she pulled the first one off, its sweet voice turned into a high-pitched squeal. The others joined, their eyes no longer a lovely golden shade, but red. Forked tongues were all around her. Tiny arms were pulling at her limbs and hair. They hopped onto her back, pushing her down. They sucked the blood from her wounds and then started to bite. As she struggled to yank one off, its teeth dug deeper into her flesh. It took all her might to get it off, and another replaced it.

She kicked one in the face, and it shrieked, sending the others into a frenzy. They were now chattering loudly. She screamed in panic as they swarmed over her. She could feel her hand itching, that usual patch of hair sprouting. She welcomed the change, asking it to take over because perhaps as a fox, she could wiggle out between them and through the tunnel. Her train of thought was interrupted as she heard a loud thwack, stopping the change. Another wave of panicked yips erupted between them. Victoria realized Gregor's large knife had cut through the bramble, stabbing the nearest creature in the head. He pulled it out and hacked at the thorns until there was an opening. She crawled slowly toward Gregor's outstretched hand and grabbed it. He pulled her out, the thorns tattering her dress and catching her bare skin in multiple places. She winced in pain but did not stop to look.

Several of the creatures were clinging to her. Tearing two from her body at once, Gregor bashed their skulls together. A shower of warm blood rained down over her back. Whimpering while kicking two more away, she finished crawling out of the bramble while the horde tore at her. Gregor pulled her to her feet and freed her leg of another creature. They both ran, Gregor in the lead, but he grabbed hold of her hand and yanked her whenever she almost tripped. When she finally looked back, she saw they were still close on their heels. Gregor stopped short and slashed at the nearest. They lunged at him, and he had to hack and hack to keep them at bay.

Gor jumped out from somewhere behind her and began to kick and stomp on the creatures. Together, Gregor and Gor took on the horde. Victoria estimated at least thirty, maybe forty, were still hissing and jumping at them. It was hard to count; they were moving so fast. Eventually the creatures saw their battle was a losing one and scampered back into the forest in a full retreat.

"Oh, she might be a shape-changer, but she is completely useless because she doesn't even know about goblins!" Gor shouted. "We are leaving you here. Feed them with your hide. You are going to get us all killed. They are coming back, you know. They are coming back with more! There are always more!" Gor was so furious he was spitting as he spoke, and then he stomped away.

Gregor stood, wiping his knife on a cloth from his pocket, waiting as she leaned against the nearest tree, shuddering. Once she regained her composure, she stumbled to him on shaking legs. She looked down at the dead goblins near her. One's mouth hung open, with a thin forked tongue dangling over the razor-sharp teeth. Taking a deep breath, she looked up at him.

"Thank you," she breathed between gasps. Gregor barely looked at her. He pointed toward Gor, and she nodded.

"I know, I know, get going," she said, stepping over the bodies and following.

Gregor only gave a grumble, pushing himself a few more feet ahead of her to avoid further discussion. She stayed close behind him, peering into the foliage in fear of seeing another pair of eyes. In her haste to keep up, she accidentally bumped into him and he flinched, pulling away from her quickly as though the thought of touching her was repulsive. Gor was determined to leave her behind even if it meant abandoning Gregor as well. Gregor did not talk to her, but he did not run ahead to join Gor, although she knew he could easily do so. The goblins were creeping behind them, Victoria spotted some in the trees and others crawling under the upturned tree roots. They flashed their sharp teeth and flicked their forked tongues, tormenting Victoria.

Soon the goblins' blood dried and became sticky on her skin. When they finally caught up to Gor, he was already sitting down and eating a rabbit raw despite the large campfire roaring by his boots. When he spied Victoria's look of disgust, he pulled the intestines out with his teeth, twisting the head one way and the feet the other. He chewed eagerly, making such a commotion Victoria had to turn away.

"Oh, you are still coming along?" Gor asked in a sarcastic tone. Then he stood and stomped toward her. "If you want to stay with us here, safe from the goblins, you need to beg," Gor said with a rude smile sliding across his face. "Beg for your life."

Victoria gave short, ragged breaths and began to open her mouth, and Gor shook his head and gestured to the ground. Victoria's face burned hot with indignation as she knelt down.

"Please, let me stay," Victoria said with the combination of embarrassment and the staggering probability she would in fact die if she tried to navigate her way home alone. She could see at least a dozen little beady eyes staring at her right now from the forest, hoping she would try again.

"That is a good start," Gor said with a hearty laugh, looking triumphantly toward Gregor. Victoria noticed Gregor did not even look up from the book he was writing in. Obviously disappointed with the lack of interest from Gregor, Gor huffed in defeat.

"Wait, where is the necklace?" Gor asked, spinning Victoria around with a sharp twist of her arm. Victoria grasped at her neck. It was gone. Gor shouted and slammed his fist into the nearest tree trunk several times, bark flew out all around him. "You—you lost it to the goblins!" Gor hollered at her angrily.

"Calm down. Where do all the goblins take their loot?" Gregor asked, still not looking up from his book.

"To the Goblin Queen," Gor said with a gasp as he finished his last punch and leaned against the trunk, panting. "We will get reinforcements and come back," Gor said, and he sat back down to continue devouring his rabbit on the stump he was using as a sort of stool.

After a while, Gregor put the book away and pulled his pack open, handing her a slice of bread with cheese. He drank from a flask and offered it to her.

"Oh no, I don't drink," she said. Gregor lifted it closer and gave a grunt. She was too thirsty to deny it a second time. She gingerly took it, her finger grazing his, and she noticed he flinched. She smelt the flask and then eagerly drank; grateful it was water.

Gor shoved his bag under his head and propped his boots on a nearby stump lazily.

"Go, try to run home," Gor said to Victoria rudely before shutting his eyes and muttering under his breath. "And next time I won't come save you."

Victoria sat as far from Gor as possible in the narrow clearing of trees, not just because she hated his vulgar demeanor, but his smell was intense.

She sat against one of the massive tree trunks. She looked up at it in awe. They were so tall and wide that she was sure she could easily stand inside with her arms stretched out and still have room before her fingertips touched the edges. Feeling small and insignificant, she curled her legs against her chest, wrapping her stained cloak over her like a blanket.

One place in the middle of her back registered the most pain, feeling tender to the touch. She ran her fingers over it and realized something was stuck inside.

Victoria struggled to pull the sliver from her back. Although Gregor kept his face turned toward the flames, she caught him watching from the corner of his eye.

She huffed in frustration, but when Gregor leaned over, stretching out his hand, she scooted away.

"No, I can do it myself," she said defensively. He pushed her neck forward, forcing her back flat for him to see in the firelight. She could not wiggle away from his grip. As he pulled at the sliver, she looked over her shoulder with a wince of pain, catching his eyes. For a moment, he held her gaze, a flash of green emeralds. He shifted his eyes away. His face resumed the stone-cold expression, eyebrows once again furrowed. She grimaced in pain as he pulled the object loose. He let her up but only after another moment, long enough to remind her he was only letting her go because he was good and ready to and no amount of fight in her could change that fact.

It strangely did not make her angry, not the way Gor's strength was so extremely infuriating. She felt helpless against Gor and loathed him for it. But Gregor, for some reason she could not exactly express . . . well, it made her stomach flutter a bit every time she saw him flinging a log like a toothpick or pushing a boulder closer to the fire as though he was sliding a stool across the floor. He had an odd habit of moving anything and everything around, always pulling himself up on the sturdy branches or pushing himself up and down on the ground. He was constantly moving until he would settle down to sleep.

She turned to face Gregor now, wondering what was lodged in her back. He quickly hid it in his fist.

"Well, what was it?" she asked expectantly, wondering if she could entice more than three words from him today. He shifted nervously. Victoria impulsively grabbed his hand, and he gingerly opened his palm. Victoria gasped in disgust when she spied the razor-thin tooth covered in blood. Gregor chucked it into the fire.

"That was in my back?" she screeched in revulsion. Gregor, as usual, did not reply. He only turned away from her. Victoria wondered if she had imagined his charming demeanor at Charlene's palace.

"Well, are they venomous? Am I going to need a physician?" she asked. Gregor only shook his head without looking up at her.

In the morning, she was so sore and tired she could barely flutter her eyelids open. Gor's relentless commands pushed her aching body through the forest. She wondered how much further they expected her to march.

The forest thickened the farther they traveled. The trees were taller and more menacing with gnarled, bare branches. The heavy layer of leaves underfoot made a hard crunch with every step. As the forest grew more silent, Victoria slowed her pace.

"Why is it so quiet here?" she asked out loud.

"Keep walking. We aren't answering questions," Gor said.

Snal appeared again from the treetop, swooping down to stand in front of her.

"She is alive!" he said in disbelief.

"Yes. I am alive," she huffed angrily. "No thanks to you!"

"Hush!" Snal hissed, his vines thrashing loudly about her while his eyes flared, sharp teeth snapping close to her face. She shrunk back. "He goes no further," Snal said, his roots burrowing deeper into the ground.

"Yeah, run away, you nasty little ragweed," Victoria said in a mumble, and he disappeared into the brush. The autumn chill had stripped their leaves; they now were only darkened, looming shapes. A pathway of broken branches was evidence of something trampling through madly.

She ignored the strange sensation of being watched, knowing Snal was smirking somewhere above while she fought the gnarled and dead branches to reach the dirt road Gor was already on.

She lost track of time as they walked along, the massive trees lining either side.

Ahead was an enormous gray-and-white stone wall. The forest on either side had been chopped down, leaving a funnel that widened near the gate, forming a circle. There was a wide line painted in the dirt outlining the curve in a vivid red. The chatter from the crowd ahead drowned out the wagon wheels crushing against the road.

Victoria followed the crowd's eager faces to watch the gatekeepers performing their task. Their red badges matched their red hats. Apparently, this city was not very well off because of the lack of proper uniforms. The shade was vibrant though and seemed to pierce through their mishmash of variant clothing, uniting them under the tattered red.

She didn't understand why there were over a dozen men sitting or standing near the wall, watching everyone entering the city.

Victoria gasped as she saw a strange woman standing in the line. A feline human mixture, some sort of she-beast with the tail and ears of a cat, pulled a large wagon filled with grapes. She wore a blue shawl and a plain cotton dress with a hemmed hole which let her tail hang out freely. Her bonnet had slits to let her ears poke out on either side of her head. She kept her gray-and-white-striped furry face down and stood shaking a bit.

That is when Victoria realized, aside from the she-beast, the rest of the crowd were men. When it was the she-beast's turn, the gatekeeper looked at something marked on her pointed ear and nodded. She began toward the gate. One man stood from where he sat with his back against the wall and spoke something. Another man came toward them, and he stood looking at the first man. He repeated the same word the other had said. Victoria couldn't make it out perfectly, but it had the same number of syllables, so she assumed it was the same word.

Then the first man stood facing the other, looking him up and down for a long moment. The first man was a bit shorter and smaller and promptly shook his head and returned to sitting by the wall. The other man then turned toward the woman, and this time Victoria heard the word clearly.

"Bellum," the man said. The she-beast watched nervously as the man pulled a couple bunches out. She seemed surprised when he stepped back. No, not surprised—she looked relieved. She actually smiled as she pulled her wagon with the remaining grapes into the city. Victoria was so confused.

"He just stole from her, and she is fine with it? Why didn't the gate-keepers do anything?" Victoria asked Gregor in a whisper.

"He was generous to the widow," Gregor whispered back. She began to argue the point, but he hushed her. She continued to watch this bizarre ritual. Someone stood at the entrance with their goods and others would approach and look at each other and say that funny word. Then the goods were divided, somehow.

A man stood with a pile of fur pelts draped across his back. He stood tall and proud, meeting the eyes of all those sitting along the wall. Three men came over and stood around, all eyeing each other. The gatekeeper motioned for the first two who had approached to step inside the circle. Immediately, a fight broke out between them. Victoria waited for one of the gatekeepers to stop them, but to her astonishment, they just watched. He was not just watching; he was waiting. He waited until one man fell to the ground and did not try to stand up again. Then he motioned the winner to turn toward the next man waiting to defend himself again. The winner from the next battle was then presented to the original man who held the pelts. He set his pelts down and adjusted his belt. Then the fight began between them. Victoria secretly cheered on the man who was trying to keep his own belongings.

To her relief, the pelt man won, and the challenger lay on the ground shaking his head in defeat. The pelt man produced a small chunk of metal from his pocket and passed it over to one of the gatekeepers who stood near the firepit. A bookkeeper sat writing the outcome down in a large leather-bound book. The piece glinted in the sunlight, and Victoria made out some sort of carved symbol, perhaps an initial for a name. It was crudely made with a thin square handle connected from one end to the other.

She watched as the gatekeeper helped the pelt man brand the inner lining of each fur in the center until the entire stack was stamped with his initials.

"Bellum?" Victoria repeated it softly to herself. She had now heard this word over a dozen times and was starting to understand it was some sort of challenge.

Now they were near the entrance. Gor was idly leaning on the cart in front of him so when a man in a black hat pulled a gray donkey forward, Gor had to shift back on his feet to avoid falling over as the cart moved away. He huffed and stood crossing his arms. Gregor stood behind them, clutching his satchel strap tightly. Victoria wondered if perhaps he had something important in his bag and was worried he might lose it. Only the donkey and its owner stood between them and the city. The donkey lazily chewed on a bit of grass as the man stepped into the circle and pulled the rope until the donkey's hooves were all inside the circle too. Many stood and some started toward him but then changed their minds when a particularly grouchy and tough man stomped up and said the word.

The man in the black hat obviously did not want to lose his donkey because he fought relentlessly, standing up and trying again and again to conquer his challenger. The fight was a lot rougher to watch when Victoria could see the sweat dripping off their foreheads and hear the thud of their fists landing hard. Worse still was Gor chuckling along while he watched the fight, obviously entertained. The dust flew around their shifting feet, stirring up a cloud. Victoria coughed. Gregor's grip on his bag tightened as he looked not at the fighting pair but the others watching along the wall. He was anxiously scanning each of their faces and Victoria wondered why.

The conquered man in the black hat lay face down, defeated in the dirt, while the challenger caught hold of the donkey's rope. He continued to smirk as he walked toward the gatekeepers and handed them his piece of metal with his initials.

One man placed it in the coals and soon it was red hot. It took two men to hold the donkey down while the challenger grabbed the iron with a tattered-looking oven mitt between his thumb and forefinger. He smashed it hard against the creature's flank. Victoria looked away as the braying creature tried to thrash wildly, but the men held fast. The putrid smell of burning hair stung her nose. She lifted her eyes and saw it plainly—the initials for the man who had just won. They then heated it again and burned the wood of the cart with the same insignia. It was recorded in the book, and he was free to leave. He took the rope and led the donkey and the cart through the gate and inside. The conquered man stood, dusting the dirt from his clothes, avoiding eye contact with anyone around him as he straightened his black hat. He entered the gate and was soon gone from sight.

The injustice of it all made Victoria want to scream, but she dared not even breathe too hard. Gor was standing too close to her, and he was unbearably temperamental. Gor yanked her into the circle with him and gave a grunt. Victoria turned to look at Gregor, who stood several feet back from the line, looking down at his boots. The gatekeeper stepped up to them and stood, his red badge right in her face.

"Sir, I am sorry to waste your time. I don't really have anything worth fighting over." Victoria displayed her purse and pulled out the lipstick inside. "I will just give them to you, no need to fight," she quickly explained while presenting it to him.

When he did not take it, she looked up at the gatekeeper in confusion. Gor started to chuckle in amusement, and a few gatekeepers joined in. Men were approaching from the wall, not just one or two, but all of them. Everyone was gathering close, stopping right at the red curve of the circle, chattering loudly in excitement.

CHAPTER 9

AN OUTRAGE

VICTORIA GASPED AS THE realization hit her, hard enough to send the breath she had just taken in surprise right back out again, and she sputtered. She stepped back out of the line, but a gatekeeper pushed her back in. Their red badges now seemed to jeer at her. To Victoria's disbelief, at least a dozen men spoke, sounding the word she now feared.

"Bellum!" the men eagerly echoed. The gatekeepers started to motion for the first two to enter the circle and begin battle. Victoria was frozen as she watched the first man being driven into the dirt. Then the winner proceeded to the next contender. She was surprised to even see one of the gatekeepers had taken off his hat and had joined in the lineup. It was the longest series of fights she had ever witnessed.

More poured out from inside the gate while many of those women with the large feline ears whispered together as they looked down from the top of the wall, their tails swinging back and forth in curiosity. The crowd had tripled in size, their eager faces yelling. There were other creatures Victoria could not identify, but she did not have time to study them.

After a while, all the battles blurred into a haze of sweat, dirt, and blood. Her head pounded from breathing in all the dust kicked up and her legs ached from standing for so long in stiff anticipation. She watched a man with black teeth toss his opponent over their heads, and he landed with a heavy crash against a tree trunk. The remaining men stepped back, fearfully glancing at him as he roared out against the crowd.

The man with black teeth stomped right up to her and gave her a grin. It was the most terrifying smile she had ever seen, full of sinister glee. His rotten breath wafted over her, thick and moist. She couldn't resist the urge to step away, but was once again, she was pushed back into the circle.

"Bellum," Gor repeated with a smirk.

He stepped up to the man with the black teeth, jutting his chin so close, his whiskers tickled Blackteeth's throat. The gatekeeper motioned for the fight to commence, and Blackteeth clambered forward, swinging mightily. They went back and forth, swinging and ramming each other with their fists. Victoria was anxiously watching, unsure which outcome would be more horrendous. Gor snapped at Blackteeth's arm, sinking his teeth into his flesh. Blackteeth let out a painful bellow, and the gatekeeper hollered. Both men stopped and stood facing the gatekeeper. Victoria was once again surprised at the obedience among this mess of society.

"No biting. Hand-to-hand combat only," the gatekeeper corrected. "Another cheap shot and you are disqualified and forfeit the bellum."

Gor nodded quickly. Blackteeth held his arm, groaning. Many men were booing and making obscene comments.

The men squared up again. Blackteeth was angry now and caught Gor swiftly by the neck as he tried to dodge another swing. Gor was lifted off the ground, feet kicking. Somehow Gor brought his arm up and slammed it into the elbow joint of Blackteeth, making him release. Gor dropped down, tripping him at the ankle, causing Blackteeth to stumble momentarily. Gor was wrapped around him faster than Victoria could process. Gor had the man's arm yanked back behind him and looked straight at Gregor. Victoria felt the tension between the two, each staring back at each other with such intensity Gregor did not even flinch when Gor finished twisting Blackteeth's arm, snapping the bones. Gor's sadistic smile twisting his lips upward, showing that uneven bottom row of teeth. Victoria could not stifle the scream released from her own throat. It intertwined with Blackteeth's shout of agony followed by groaning whimpers to make a terrible melody to which Gor relished in pure delight. He stood on top of him, his face up toward the sky, arms outstretched. What was he holding?

Victoria gasped as his signet flashed in the afternoon sun. It was a *G*, but it was sloped and lopsided, angled where it should be curved and jagged where it should have been squared. Victoria thought it was very fitting—a broken symbol for a broken man. Then the crowd did something Victoria completely unexpected. They cheered.

She stood feeling indignant and terribly vulnerable. An itch on her hand made her scratch, and there was the patch of fur sprouting. She covered it with her skirting. She tried to hush her body, reminding herself to stay human. The pain was worsening, becoming more urgent.

"Bellum," Gregor's rigid voice sounded behind her. It was hoarse and cracked a bit at the end, and he cleared his throat and repeated it, stronger. Gor's eyes widened in disbelief. Victoria's usual beginning of transformation pain suddenly stopped, frozen as she held her breath.

"You are too late. Bellum must be called before the final challenger battles the defendant," a gatekeeper said dismissively. "If you wanted to enact a bellum, you should have stated earlier."

Victoria's heart sank, the panic rising inside again ignited the transformation. Gor chuckled and tossed his ring into the coals. She tried to breathe and focused on staying human. She focused on being human. *Remain human.* She repeated this in her mind over and over.

"Technically if a party of two or more arrived with the object in which the declaration of bellum is enacted, one must challenge the outside rivalry before turning in toward the party to proceed the challenge," Gregor said confidently.

"Yes, that is correct, young man, but the one from the accompanying party who must challenge the outside rivalry needs to be predetermined with a flipping of a coin to give equal opportunity, for it is not fair if one from the accompanying party must fight twice in a row to defend the same object in which declaration of bellum is enacted. It gives the other in question an advantage, fighting an opponent already spent. Flipping of the coin gives an unbiased result, turning the bellum over to the gods," the gatekeeper recited another passage he had surely memorized from the rulebook. "I am sorry but—"

"Not if any of the accompanying members are of royal blood," Gregor interrupted. "Royal bloodlines have only to defend their claim to enact bellum on said object once, coin be damned," Gregor said. With this, Gregor lifted a ring with his signet engraved in it, and everyone's eyes widened as it glinted in the sun. Victoria realized it was a *G*, *G* for Gregor. It had five spikes above the top to form a crown.

"Oh, forgive me, Prince Gregor. I did not recognize you in those common clothes," the gatekeeper said with a look of serious concern. "Please do not tell King Brutus."

"You little piece of—" Gor began, kicking the rocks underfoot angrily. "Parading your royal blood. You had this planned, didn't you? Well, no matter. It will be even more satisfying when I am smashing your face under my boot. You are aware even Daddy cannot punish me when I kill you? Did you read that in your little rulebook when you were busy plotting this? The laws of bellum protect both contenders from any backlash of the outcome as long as both entered the circle voluntarily. And you are clearly volunteering."

Victoria was stunned. She did not know Gor was capable of speaking with such intelligence, but also of the turn of events. Gregor was a prince! That meant he could save her, right?

As Gregor lifted his foot to step over the line into the circle, he faltered, hovering for just a second, but it spiked fear in Victoria. Nope, his title obviously provided no insurance. Then he stomped down into the circle and slipped his satchel off his shoulder and wordlessly handed it to her. Victoria shakily took it and fumbled to draw it over her shoulder. Without further hesitation he walked right up to look Gor in the face.

"Gregor, no. Don't fight him," Victoria found herself calling out. She hadn't meant to sound so fragile, and somehow this made their situation even more bleak. She understood why he did not even look at her.

"Gregor, don't fight him!" Gor mocked Victoria's voice with a shrill pitch, sending another jolt down her neck and to her fingertips and toes, churning her stomach painfully.

"Once you are within the circle, bellum can and must be enacted," one of the gatekeepers recited dryly. The other gatekeeper motioned for the battle to begin. Gor was talking a lot, making aggressive threats in a voice like nails scraping along Professor Carter's chalkboard in the library back home. Oh, how she wished she was there now, sitting with Mabel listening to his boring lectures. How she had taken the simplistic ease of her life for granted! She had been safe and blissfully unaware of all the terrible things in this world.

Gregor stood almost a head shorter than Gor. Victoria thought back to the time when she had first seen Gregor on the staircase in Charlene's ballroom. He was taller than most of the grown men there and seemed so large. Now here, surrounded by these wild men, he seemed small, which made Victoria feel even smaller. She shrank back and bumped into a gatekeeper who firmly pushed her back in place.

"Oh, thank you!" she snapped sarcastically at him. He just gave her a shrug. She was now directly in front of the fight, which she most dreadfully did not want to witness.

Victoria's heart sank. Gor growled toward her. Gregor stepped in front of her, blocking Gor from her sight momentarily. She began to pray in her heart. She prayed harder than she had ever prayed before, even harder than when Mabel had fallen off the tree in the garden and would not wake up for what seemed ages. But Mabel did wake up, and she had been fine somehow. Perhaps if she prayed hard enough, Gregor would be too.

Gregor stood, arms raised, fists tightly clasped. Gor made a silly little hop and skip toward Gregor, still wearing a hideous smirk.

"You are finally attempting to become a man. Takes time," Gor said. "Don't worry, I will allow you to wave at her through my window," he told Gregor while he gestured rudely toward Victoria. She cringed.

The crowd laughed, and she hated them all with their teasing faces and horribly perverse society. Where was this place? How could such anarchy not tear itself apart? She was pulled from her thoughts as the gatekeeper motioned for the fight to begin.

Gor and Gregor squared each other up, the same way she had seen all the others do. It seemed to be an unspoken rule to give the opponent an intimidating stare with a furrowed brow or to shift the neck from side to side while taking slow, calculated steps. Victoria looked from Gor's barreled chest to Gregor's narrower one. Gor stood taller, and he was built like five tree trunks had formed a human, two trunks being the legs, two trunks making a pair of arms, and the fifth forming his neck. His head seemed small in comparison, his beady eyes and large crooked nose even cruder in contrast to Gregor's chiseled features. But, alas, good looks couldn't win this fight. Victoria had a sinking feeling she was about to witness Gregor being bludgeoned.

Gor moved first, sending a powerful wallop at Gregor, and Victoria was relieved to see him dodge it easily. Gregor was able to slide under or skip back from the next several combinations Gor sent his way. Victoria's head pounded, and she realized she was forgetting to breathe. She made herself take a big gulp of air, and the gatekeeper closest to her chuckled. Victoria would have snapped something irritably at him, but she was too consumed in anxiety. She was wringing her fingers so tight, they were throbbing.

Gregor continued to dance around Gor, only avoiding shots and not taking any. Gor was getting red in the face, and he was starting to huff now. Victoria finally understood. Gregor was trying to wear him out, slow him down. Just as Victoria felt a flutter of hope, Gor sent a punch and stuck out his foot in the direction he anticipated Gregor was headed. Gregor stumbled, and Gor was on him in an instant. His blows were hard and the sound of them landing on Gregor's face made Victoria feel nauseated.

"Get up!" Victoria found herself screaming, her voice cracking pitifully against the cheering mob. Gregor blocked one blow and let the other fist land to slide his arms up around Gor's waist in a tight bear hug. Gor swung again, and Gregor grabbed hold of his shoulder, pulling him down closer. He kicked his leg and swung his free arm, sending Gor into a side roll, but not enough for Gregor to gain any leverage. Gregor squirmed away and was back on his feet. They danced again, round and round, while Gor swung and Gregor dodged.

"You fight like a coward!" Gor taunted. "Hit me! Try to land a punch!"

Gregor dove at Gor, grabbing him about the middle again and shifting his weight to free one of his legs to sweep Gor's knee, sending them both down. Gregor twisted around Gor and brought his arm over his head but did not make it around his neck. His bicep ended over Gor's forehead awkwardly as Gor began to shift to stand. Gregor wrapped his legs about him, holding on for dear life as Gor stood. Gregor bear-hugged his head, one arm slid down and covered Gor's eyes. Gregor's other arm waved in the air for balance.

"Poor, Gor, never enough. And you will always be nothing," Gregor said through gritted teeth. "You will never be a king."

Gor exploded in a howling, blinded rage, stomping about and grabbing for Gregor. Gregor now clung with both arms over Gor's face tightly. Gor staggered back and forth, not able to see with Gregor's arm covering his eyes. He huffed as he struggled to catch his breath while Gregor's other arm was pressed up against his nose and mouth. Gregor tightened his bear hug and shouted out in pain. Victoria did not understand why. She continued to watch with burning eyes and a tight throat as the crowd continued its onslaught of taunting jeers.

Gor caught hold of Gregor's leg and yanked it fiercely, flinging Gregor far. He landed heavily in the dirt, and as Gor stomped down on him with his mighty foot, Gregor raised his bicep, waving it frantically. The gatekeeper made some sort of signal, and everyone came to a spooky dead silence.

The gatekeeper looked at Gregor's arm and then to Gor's teeth, stained with blood.

"No biting," the gatekeeper repeated, and he signaled to the other gatekeepers. The crowd released a deafening cry of cheers, and Victoria could hear some mingled boos from those opposing the call.

"He tricked me!" Gor roared into the wild crowd. A few nodded in agreement, and Gor seemed to take this as a signal to begin shouting at the gatekeepers. The gatekeepers surrounded Gor, shaking their heads and ignoring his complaints.

Gregor stood shakily. The cut above his eye looked gruesome and his nose was swollen and bleeding. Blood slithered over his cheek, dribbling down off his chin and onto his chest, staining his shirt. Victoria ignored this and grabbed him as tightly as she could muster, not caring when she felt his blood smear against her cheek and wetting her hair. He weakly hugged her back.

"Listen, I, um . . .," Gregor said quickly as she felt his arm moving down into his bag she was still holding over her shoulder. The gatekeepers were all around them now, keeping Gor away and moving closer while he ranted about unfairness and cheating. He was hollering loudly, and the crowd was jeering at him. The entire noise was so overwhelming she let Gregor's tight but shaking embrace fold around her, his arms pulling her close into his chest. She could hear his heart pounding away fast and strong. And for a moment, they were not in a crowd full of corrupt backwoods bandits and vagabonds.

"I am sorry," she heard Gregor's anxious voice whispering in her ear.

Then the sobering sound of fabric tearing pulled her back into the present moment as the gatekeeper tore the sleeve from her right shoulder, and the gust of chilly autumn air hit her bare skin. Suddenly red-hot fire seared her flesh, stabbing with such intensity she screamed hysterically without control. Although she knew Gregor's signet was barely more than two inches wide, it felt as though her entire right shoulder blade was ablaze. She shrieked, and Gregor held her fast in his arms. Gor hollered all the while, his profanity actually matching the ones she was screaming in her head for once.

Then it was all over. The gatekeeper pulled the metal away, wiping it off and handing it to Gregor. He slipped it back into his bag quickly, trying to hide it from her line of sight. She appreciated his effort, but she caught a glimpse of that wicked *G* as it winked at her in the sunset before disappearing into the leather.

"Welcome to Omnia. What is your name?" The bookkeeper sitting at the heavy, leather-bound book asked her in with such a calm voice, it was a stark contrast to the commotion behind her. She could barely whisper loud enough to hear herself. He asked her to speak up and Victoria felt she would choke as she strained to muster any voice from her tight throat.

"Victoria Walton." Gregor said. She was startled when Gregor had spoken her full name, unsure how he knew it. She wondered what else he knew about her.

She saw him record it with long wispy lines under Gregor's name. The black ink staining the yellowing parchment was seared into her memory. She curiously scanned the long list. It took up two pages, beginning with his house number, then all the items inside. Apparently, he owned several horses and, oddly enough, a fine porcelain set. There was Victoria's name, the next item under the previous line with the word "mutt." She was the newest addition to his listed possessions.

She would have stomped her foot indignantly and begun a long speech of how backward she deemed this entire situation, but she was overwhelmed with gratitude she was not marked as Gor's with his atrocious, crooked *G*.

Gregor could not stand any longer by himself. His bloody face was swelling, and he leaned against her for support. She staggered under his weight, and two gatekeepers approached, grabbing Gregor together and carrying him into the city, leaving the crowd and the gate behind.

Gor was still rampaging. She dared not look, but she could hear him.

She followed as they carried Gregor's limp body over the cobblestone. She wasn't sure if he was breathing. She could barely comprehend the sight of the stone and brick buildings advertising their merchandise inside. She spied the strange creatures wandering through the streets. She-beasts were familiar and normal compared to these others. She was not even sure how she would even describe them to Mabel when she finally saw her again.

Soon they had wandered through the store fronts and entered a large garden, which ended at a beautifully designed stone bridge, a fast, large river flowed underneath. Once on the other side, the shops were replaced by homes, each home getting larger and larger as they continued to walk. She tiredly forced herself to look up as she realized they were now going uphill. At the top was a massive palace that Victoria took several long glances at between looking below at her feet to avoid tipping over.

The palace had obviously been magnificent at one point in time with brilliant white stone, but those days were long gone. The entire left spiraled tower was crumbling, the stairs peeking out through the wide holes and fallen roof. The palace's thick oak doors were only half constructed. The other half lay in splinters, the pathway covered in debris.

The ivy and rose bushes had long ago taken over, covering most of the remaining walls in a thick wall of green, the roses bursting in colorful pops of yellow along the cracked windows and tarnished rivets. The gatekeepers stopped at the trunk of a tree and unceremoniously dropped his body there. To her further surprise, they just walked away, back toward the gate, she assumed. She watched in confusion as they disappeared into the mess of buildings and people.

Gregor was still unconscious. It was getting dark. The sun was setting and casting shadows all around her. Two people—well, creature things—walked past, their eyes watching her curiously until they spied her burned shoulder, and they quickly moved along. She sat down beside Gregor, hoping no one else was going to come by. She worried Gor would be making his way here. He was so incredibly angry.

It was twilight before Gregor groaned and propped one elbow up to look about.

"They just left you here!" Victoria exclaimed and pointed toward the direction the gatekeepers were last seen. Gregor gave a small smile.

"That was good of them," he said. Then he chuckled at her puzzled face.

"Well, this is my place," he said. She looked around and didn't see any houses. She looked at him again, worried his head was damaged.

"Up," Gregor said, pointing above. She followed his finger and saw the floorboards of a tree house. Of course, there was a large *G* carved into the tree trunk. He looked back at her and gave a weak smile. His body obviously in a great deal of agony, but his eyes shone with a mixture of relief and triumph. She returned the smile.

"You are very brave." Victoria said. Her compliment seemed to give him strength.

He slowly stood, and Victoria helped him toward the trunk he was reaching.

"C'mon," he said, grunting in pain as he moved his arm. He pulled on a doorknob she had not noticed before sticking out of the bark. Curiously she saw the door swing out and there was a narrow staircase curving up the inside of the tree. He gestured for her to go first, and she began ascending the stairwell, holding on to the sides for support. She counted fifty-six steps till she reached the door at the top. She guessed they were high in the tree.

Gregor was below her and encouraged her to open the door and go through. She turned the knob and entered. It was completely different from what she expected. It was constructed with large windows and sturdy beams. Although she could see she was standing high above the ground, she didn't feel any swaying or even hear the creaking she expected.

"You built this?" Victoria asked breathlessly.

"Yes, well, I was guided by an old friend, an elf. But I do not trust him anymore. If you meet any elf, run. Especially one named Rhamy Lumpkin," Gregor explained quickly, weakly waving his arm toward the ceiling. Victoria felt strange listening to him speak so fluently after such a long journey of him being completely quiet.

"Before he turned on me, he helped me build this, teaching me how to carve the stairs into the tree while keeping it alive and growing steadily. This tree is older than the palace, older than any of these houses and will outlive us all. There is fresh water if you pull on that rope. Drop the pail down into the well below," Gregor said. Victoria followed his instructions and fetched some water. He finished drinking and he set the pail down while looking at her with his weak smile, relief leaking out from behind the blood and bruises.

"Get on the bed." Gregor said, pointing toward it. Victoria's eyes went round, and she felt like screaming, but she was too weak to try to fight him off. Her entire body was already trembling from hunger and exhaustion. Ignoring how dry her throat suddenly felt, she obediently climbed onto the bed. As Gregor removed his shirt, she forced back those stinging tears attempting to break through. She gasped at his horribly bruised chest and stomach where Gor's blows had landed heavily. She squeezed her eyes tightly as she listened to him pull off his boots. Then she felt her stomach clench as she heard him remove his pants, his belt buckle clinked against the floor. She held her breath as she waited for his approach. After several long moments of silence, she slowly peeked with one eye. Gregor was nowhere in her line of sight. She scanned the room to find Gregor had chivalrously taken the couch along the far wall. She gave a sigh of relief. Soon he was asleep, she listened to his breathing become slow and rhythmic.

The glass window in the ceiling let in a generous amount of light, and she could look about. She crossed over to the couch, looking at his sleeping form in the moonlight. His house was a bit messy but, overall, much nicer than she would have expected from a beast-man. The furniture was hand carved from solid wood with streaks of turquoise worked into it seamlessly. He had a lot more books than she would have guessed, and they were stacked around and lying open. He had written notes in them and circled many of the paragraphs. Then she spied his wardrobe. Most of the clothes were common, but there were a few pairs of brilliant red and black uniforms hung in a neat row. Over the breast pocket on each one was the same symbol the gatekeepers had on their badges. It held the silhouette of a slight sliver of moon. Above the suits on a wooden shelf sat a red silk pillow bearing the weight of a large gold crown with five distinct spikes, two smaller on either side and the middle one tallest and holding a single large ruby. It was simple and perhaps a bit crude. Obviously, these beasts were not very skilled in the art of fine metalwork.

She wandered about a bit more before returning to the bed and curled up there. His steady breathing seemed to soothe her. She fell asleep again.

Finally, when the sun was brightly burning through the window, she awoke. She had another, heavier blanket draped over her, and she wondered where it had come from. Of course, she was alone. Gregor had left her with all the questions and a creature staring at her from across the room. It was ridiculously small. For a moment, she wondered if it was a squirrel because of its size, but, looking closely, she realized it was indeed a dog. It was gray with a white underbelly and face with unproportionally large eyes and fluffy hair sticking straight up and out to the side. When it scurried across the floor toward her, she burst out laughing at its teensy paws. But soon it was in her lap, and she was petting it and letting it lick her neck and arms.

Gregor entered, his eye was still swollen shut, his face bruised and broken. He limped in with two bowls of some sort of food. She did not have the heart to bombard him with questions. She was also afraid. Was the real Gregor charming and sweet as she had seen at the ball or the quiet, icy-faced stone man she had now grown accustomed to?

He did not speak, and the silence was tantalizing. She just continued to pet the strange dog creature while Gregor fiddled with whatever he was cooking on the stove in the small kitchen area. She timidly looked up at him from time to time, and once she caught him looking at her, but he quickly looked back down. When whatever he was cooking was finished, he set the bowls down at the table and walked toward her. She flinched. He froze. She looked up at him in fearful expectation, once again her heart thumping painfully in her chest.

"I won't hurt you." Gregor reassured her.

"Eat," he said and gestured toward the table. "And I can answer your questions."

"What is his name?" she asked, holding the dog's two front paws up. The dog's tail wagged as Gregor patted his head.

"Milo," Gregor said.

"Milo," Victoria repeated more to herself than out loud. She stopped petting his gray fur, and she could feel her heartbeat rising. She tried to stop herself, but the questions were flashing in her head repeatedly. "What was that? What is this place? That was the craziest thing I have ever seen!" she said. Suddenly all the emotions smashed through the little restraint she had left.

"It is the only way to enter the city," Gregor answered quickly.

"Why? Why can't your home be normal, where people pay for their goods with money?" Victoria was shouting now. The dog was off her lap and hiding between Gregor's boots.

"I know. I do not believe it has a place in the future, but I grew up here and I understand it. This is the ancient way of the beasts, where the strongest survive and prosper. If you want something, you fight for it, and if you win, it's yours forever. No one can steal it from you," Gregor explained.

"And this 'it' being me? I belong to you forever?" Victoria demanded.

"Yes," he said.

She stared at him.

"I mean, technically . . .," he stammered, shifting uncomfortably.

"Oh, just technically, under beast law, according to everyone in this city, on this entire mountain, I belong to you?" She could hear her own voice, so shrill she sounded just like Mother, but she was too upset to stop herself.

"Only under beast law. I mean, I don't really own you," Gregor sputtered and pulled his hand up to scratch the back of his neck while he looked down at her feet. Victoria had never seen him so flustered.

"The same way you own that leather bag and this tiny dog?" Victoria said accusingly. "How many people did you have to beat up for him?"

Victoria asked. Milo's tail began to wag as she pointed at him, and he licked the tip of her finger playfully. This would have sent Mabel into a series of giggles if she had been here, but Victoria swept the thought away. She focused on Gregor's cheek because he could not seem to meet her eyes, keeping his head turned or looking down. It was starting to irritate her.

"Just one," he replied, then upon seeing her face when he sheepishly looked up at her, he quickly added, "No, wait, do not be upset." He took a long, deep breath and plunged into the next sentence. It was a bit of a mumbling mess, and Victoria stood from the couch and stepped closer to hear him better.

"Look, even your Queen Charlene abides beast laws to keep peace, but she does not let anything or anyone from the mountains enter her city—well, except your father. He was her kind of messenger. She likes to keep her humans in a safe bubble, unaware, so they are better servants, playthings, whatever it is she does with all her humans," Gregor said, tossing his hands in the air.

"What are you talking about?" Victoria asked. "Playthings?"

"Charlene isn't human, she is a monster," Gregor said. "*The flames burn red in their presence, the rose petals charr if they are near, the sun scorches their flesh.*" He spoke words similar to the poem she had read carved into the stone floor of the palace.

"So many beasts are suggesting getting rid of all humans, starve out the monsters," Gregor said slowly, trying to find the words to explain it gently.

"What?" Victoria asked, still confused.

"This is too much information, too fast," Gregor said. "You need to start from the beginning." He crossed to a case and plucked a leather book from the topmost shelf.

"This is your father's journal," he said, offering it to her. "It explains everything. And there is a man I want you to meet, someone who can help you with your transformations. His name is Plimsoll. If you are like your father, you can transform into any animal you wish, not just a fox, with training. Very rare gift your father had. We can travel freely through the Black Needles to meet him without a chance of someone taking you away from me. No one would dare break beast law here."

"I don't think Gor is going to listen to some ancient rule," Victoria said as she took the book, holding it like a teddy bear. She looked behind her shoulder through the window, worried Gor would be there outside below as they spoke.

"The ancient laws are not only sacred, but they are also upheld by capital punishment. If anyone takes anything that bears the mark of another, they will be killed the moment they are discovered in the way the one whom he stole from deems fitting. I have only seen one in my lifetime attempt to steal, and he wound up horribly maimed and terribly ashamed before meeting a bitter end. Not even Gor is that foolish," Gregor explained. "The only way he can reciprocate is to officially reenact bellum, and he and I would both need to agree to enter the circle again."

.Victoria's stomach churned. There had been more than a lifetime's worth of violence already. Gregor guided her to sit down at the table and offered her a bowl of food, but she grudgingly shooed it away from her, too upset to even consider eating.

"I mean, this was all your fault in the first place. You kissed me!" she snapped back at him. Gregor stared at her, looking surprised and a little deflated by her angry tone.

"I was trying to protect you," Gregor said.

"With your lips?" She asked, making Gregor flush.

"It was a distraction," Gregor said defensively. "And it worked. I snatched it right off your neck without you noticing." It was now Victoria who blushed.

"Look, everyone wanted the ruby," Gregor continued. "You have no idea how many times I saved you—"

"Why? Why does everyone want it?" Victoria interrupted.

"I do not know," Gregor said. Victoria looked at him in surprise. "Honestly, I do not. No one does. Charlene was so keen on getting her hands on it, so of course, everyone else wanted it too."

"Woah, wait. You said you saved me countless times? You were spying on me?" Victoria asked. "If you spied on me then why did you not know I was the fox back there in the woods?"

"I knew," Gregor admitted. "But I could not let Gor know."

"You knew the whole time?" Victoria asked suspiciously.

"Well, it took me longer than I want to admit figuring it out. Sorry about, um, flipping you on your back to determine your gender," he said. She felt her cheeks blushing pink and she shrugged, turning to hide her face.

"You ran up to me for help and I stepped on your paw, like a clumsy fool." Gregor said apologetically. Victoria was not sure if she should correct him or let him continue believing she had trusted him.

"Richard told Gor you and your sister were not his blood. Gor believed it until he saw you transform at the waterfall."

"And when did you first see me transform?" Victoria asked. "Were you watching me while I was naked?" She crossed her arms over her chest and gave him a frown.

"No, I" Gregor stammered. "You were not modest; I mean subtle. I mean, you transformed right in the middle of your garden!" Gregor said, taking a pause to breathe. "Rhamy saw you, he wanted to take you immediately back to his people, start your training to be used as some sort of weapon. I chased him off, but not before he tried to set fire to me."

"The blue fire, that was you and this Rhamy fellow?" Victoria asked, remembering the charred tree.

"Yeah, but he came back and I lost my temper while listening to their plans. I attacked and then Mason got involved. He demanded we give him the ruby, assuming we were fighting over it. Rhamy and his lot ran off with the information that Mason was looking for some sort of ruby, leaving me to fight. But when Mason realized I did not have it, he ran off too, for it was nearly sunrise. I heard the screams of the poor man Mason caught on his way home."

"Oh, that was the man found dead in the road on the way to Charlene's," Victoria said, piecing everything together. Gregor nodded.

"But they said they thought he was torn up like a large wolf ripped him up, wouldn't that be a beast then?" Victoria asked.

"I have noticed whenever one of the monsters step out of bounds and kill a human, without Charlene's permission, they just tear up the body enough to make it look like a beast so Charlene will blame us." Gregor said.

Gregor limped toward a drawer in the kitchen. He made his way back to the table slowly with a wooden spoon and once again stood in front of her.

"Then as the sun rose, you popped out of the house with the ruby around your neck, and there was Rhamy again, ready to swipe not just the necklace, but take you as well. I stopped him. I was hoping you were leaving, perhaps finding a new home. I was sure you had heard the fight but no, you headed straight for Charlene's, completely unaware. Gor had come in search of me after he got word and insisted on his plan to get the necklace, which you can imagine was horribly violent," Gregor said grimly. "I knew if I didn't get it, you would never be safe."

"Why did you care?" she asked. "And why did you risk your life to fight for me at the Bellum gate?" Gregor looked at her, his eyes steady on hers for only a moment, he opened his mouth and then shut it again. Victoria impatiently waited for him to reply. Gregor didn't say anything. He avoided her gaze as he put the spoon into the bowl and tried to place it into her hands. Her heart thudded painfully as her mind raced.

"What if you had lost?" she sputtered out loud finally, bursting into uncontrollable tears. As she flung her arms up to cover her face, she accidentally tipped the bowl and sent the food flying everywhere. Victoria was aware of his rigid body movements but could not see him well through her tears. He stood hovering over her as she tried to stop herself, which proved impossible, and more large sobs erupted from her chest.

He knelt down and began cleaning up the mess, pulling the bits of what seemed like oatmeal and berries into the bowl again, but the color was a vivid green and the berries were orange with blue leaves, so she wasn't even sure. She squatted down to help, stifling herself. He grabbed her hands, looking at her for the first time that morning with those piercing emeralds. Now both of them were sticky. She could fill the warm mash between their fingers as he squeezed her hands firmly.

"I am sorry," Gregor offered. She was taken aback by the pain in his eyes. "I never wanted any of this for you."

She was glad he had not answered her question. She was trying her hardest to push Gor's lopsided *G* from her mind, but the image of it flashed again, sending horribly cold shivers down her neck, through her spine, and to her toes.

He guided her to the sink, and she washed up while he finished wiping up the mess with a damp cloth. Then he found a handkerchief for her. He handed it to her and then focused on the ground while she wiped her eyes and blew her nose. Then she was even more upset and embarrassed, so she began to cry some more. She looked down at the handkerchief in her hand. It was just a neatly cut square of cotton. Victoria knew she could stitch a lovely thin lace around the edges. She could do that for the entire drawer of them because Mother had tediously sat and taught her each stitch. Thoughts of Mother and Mabel stung painfully in her mind and then anger started deep in her belly and rose into her chest.

"Why do you keep doing that?" Victoria asked, looking down at the handkerchief. She ignored the rest of the thought, pushing away the image of the perfect shade of blue cotton thread sitting in her crafting basket at home.

"Doing what?" Gregor asked.

"Talking about me like you know me," Victoria said.

"I feel like I know you," Gregor said, and then he straightened up and cleared his throat. "I knew your father." He gave a shrug. "Read his journal. Everything will make sense," he said. Apparently, he was finished with the discussion because he took the items from the floor to the kitchen.

She did not feel like she was done but she could not think of another question. Her mind was still trying to gather every bit of information he had just scattered over her. She only nodded and shifted to find the book beside her to open it. While she did so, she bumped her back against the wall and another sting from the burn made her wince.

She could hear him moving around. She opened the journal, recognizing her father's scribbles instantly. She could not help but smile, wiping the rest of the tears off her face.

Immediately she saw the first few lines and it sent her back, back to the tunnels with Mason. Here it was again. The same unmistakable, odd poem.

smile raises concern
blood flames burn
tainted black petals turn
stomach churn
silver to yearn
sunlight slowly fills the urn

She continued to read. Her father had written Charlene's name across the edge and underlined it. Then, in smaller letters, he had written in "Mason" and other names she did not know. She turned the page to read more notes. She studied the book for a long while until she felt her body crave movement. She shifted from the couch to the floor on her belly so she could kick her legs.

She read about five kingdoms. The first was beasts with a symbol of
a silver of moon, crudely drawn, indicating the kingdom's crest and flag.
Her father had not been a skilled artist. There were a few other sketches.
It was like the story he had told her in his last hour.

Then there were monsters, and even in the simple sketch she recognized Charlene's long hair and thin body. There was a list of their strengths
and then their weaknesses with a symbol for the sun. The next category
she did not know. It was labeled "Elves" with a leaf symbol on the crest.
These were strange creatures who were tall and thin and seemed to have
strangely formed ears with little points on the tips where a curve should
have been. She read about how the elves were born with vividly bright
colored hair and she looked at the drawings with purple and blue hair.
There was a smaller depiction of a baby elf with green hair, Victoria traced
the edge of it with her fingertips, assuming her father had used those
colored pencils he always kept at his desk to color it.

With narrow noses and high cheekbones, even the men looked too
feminine in her opinion. Victoria chuckled to herself at the dress-like robe
her father had drawn on them. They had elemental talents of some sort,
she could gather, because he had listed fire, water, and a picture of them
with plants growing under their fingertips and squiggly marks that he
seemed to use to indicate powers or magic. Then the fourth was written
"Elken Folk," and their crest was, of course, a hoof. It was half man, half
elk with majestic points. He had sketched a woman with no antlers, and
her lower half was a soft beige doe. He had even drawn a little baby with
the lower half of a fawn with spots sprinkled all over her hide. Father had
become a better artist as the pages continued. The fifth was titled "Avians."
Their crest was a single feather.

They were stunning creatures looking like angels with wings spreading over both pages. Their attributes were listed around the feather edges.

"Where is the sixth kingdom, the humans?" she called out without
lifting her eyes from the pages. "Why didn't he map it?"

"Humans do not have a kingdom. There are Charlene's humans and the nomads. I think you call them gypsies and I have noticed your people are quite leery of them and do not believe their stories." Gregor said. Victoria could not disagree; she remembered many times her mother crossing the street to avoid them in the marketplace. "The nomads are the remaining humans who have escaped Charlene's grasp. They travel according to the seasons, hiding," Gregor said.

"What?" Victoria asked, encouraging him to go on.

"Well, humans are relatively new. The five ancient kingdoms have been here many centuries earlier than them. Humans, non-magical beings or forms born without any natural talents bestowed from any of the planets, are seen as lesser than. If the celestial bodies did not see humans fit enough to bestow any magic on them, why should the five kingdoms give them space of their own? They are thrown into the lot with cattle, poultry, and the fish—useful, fast breeders, and made for our use and benefit," Gregor said, reciting something he was obviously taught in his childhood. Victoria had no idea how to respond.

"It is so insulting," Victoria said.

"Well, it should not be. You are not human either," Gregor gave this friendly reminder with a slight smirk. Despite her dire situation, Victoria returned the smile.

"It still is not right. Humans should be the sixth kingdom," she said.

"Yeah, I agree, but do not go spouting about it here. Only a human would say such a thing, and they are not particularly esteemed in these parts," Gregor warned.

"Oh, I intended to do just that, waltz right down main street here and start yelling for humans to be treated fairly," Victoria teased back. Gregor laughed.

"Why is there such a heated battle between the beasts and the monsters?" Victoria asked after reading several more pages.

"My pa, King Brutus had to go to war against Charlene. She was taking more and more land for herself and pushed all the beasts out of the valley entirely. She is vicious and manipulative and has killed anyone who gets in her way. Never trust her or anyone in her company," Gregor said.

"She seemed so polite, so warm," Victoria said.

"Oh, I am sure she is to her humans. They are her living food storage. Without their fresh supply of blood, she would wither and die," Gregor said.

"But I never gave her my blood. She never asked anyone I knew for blood," Victoria said, feeling confused again.

"I am sure she gets plenty from those who pass and from the infirmaries. Why do you suppose they drain all the body fluids from those who pass before setting them in the graves?"

"To preserve them for the viewings?" Victoria asked.

"Where does all the blood go?" Gregor asked. "Your entire society is just the same as ours, the strong feeding off the weak. Charlene loves how the paper money distracts the humans from the real currency being dealt under their very noses. Blood. The life source," he said, and she gave a shiver.

"Well, how do you beasts and the other three kingdoms get your blood?" Victoria asked, suddenly very concerned. Gregor laughed again.

"That is what makes monsters so insidious. The four other kingdoms see them as unnatural, cursed. They are the only creatures who need blood. Human blood gives monsters strength but sipping from a beast or elf would give them power. That is why the four kingdoms are wary around the monsters. If they were able to get a constant supply of just one of the other kingdom's blood, the scale would be tipped and they could take over the entire land. Beasts like the taste of humans too, but not so much the blood, but the flesh, which has led to a hideous trading between beast and monster. Naphtali is the main outpost where humans are harvested."

"Harvested?" Victoria asked in horror. Gregor grimly nodded.

"The elves and Elken Folk are strictly vegan. Avians and us beasts can sustain fine on fish and rabbits and cattle. But don't trust a beast on a new moon," he said.

"New moon? I thought the folklore was a full moon—" she began and then shut her mouth as Gregor shook his head.

"It is a rumor spread by beasts. They have the most control over themselves during a full moon. The moon gives our human side more control. It was a rumor started to take advantage of the superstition to get what we wanted, like sacrifices of gold and jewels and maidens," Gregor said.

"Maidens?" Victoria snapped the question like a dart.

"It is when the moon hides its face that we lose control, and the beast takes over. It doesn't matter how many hours I have trained and trained on transformation. Every time the moon disappears from the sky, I, too, rampage," Gregor said, careful to sidestep her question.

"Will I do that too?" Victoria asked.

"No that is what makes you so special, you don't have to answer to the moon or the sun, you are free. The only thing holding yourself back is your own discipline," Gregor explained.

"As for your questions about the maidens, that is a dark history. Past, it is all in the past. Charlene has most the humans now. They don't live in small tribes anymore. They are down in the valley in their civilized cities. They don't believe in monsters or other creatures. It only took her three generations to weed out the ones who remembered what we call 'The Collection.' Charlene has done her part well, erasing the truth and replacing it with fairy tales. We are forgotten, a whisper in the dark, only a nightmare," Gregor said.

"Three generations?" Victoria asked.

"Apparently, every so often, Charlene pretends she dies of old age and her 'daughter' who has been sent to finishing school for the last decade or so comes of age to take her reign," Gregor explained.

"How old is she then?"

"I do not know exactly," Gregor said. "Her son Mason is almost a century old."

"How old does that make you?" she asked.

"I am a bit older than Mason. I was young, but I remember the day his birth was announced because my father was so upset. He broke almost everything in the room. Having her own heir—he was so sure Charlene's quest to conquer land would become insatiable, which it did," Gregor explained. Victoria felt very strange sitting there, talking with an ancient being.

"You are over one hundred years old?" Victoria gasped.

"Yes," he said with a shrug. "Um, let me calculate it in human years," he said, touching his fingers and consulting some sort of invisible chart in his mind. "Puts me about eighteen or nineteen years old," he said, and then Victoria could read his face as he looked at hers full of pure astonishment. "Look, your father was even older than mine. Human lives are so short and they age so quickly, but they are able to breed faster. A human female can produce a newborn every year if she wants to. That is intense," he said.

Victoria was sure there was an entire other conversation about the fertility cycles of each of the creatures in their respective kingdom, but she did not want to discuss it, and definitely not with Gregor.

"What have you been doing for the past hundred years?" she asked, her eyes wide.

"Well, truth be told, I am considered one of the few youths of this place." Gregor said. Victoria looked at him with such bewilderment he chuckled. "It took me seventy years to reach this height and another twenty to be able to hold my own against the other, older beasts. I have never been able to venture far outside without my pa or another adult accompanying me. I am mostly kept inside Omnia, so I train for battle and read when I am not training." He said, motioning toward all the books. "This trip was the first I was allowed by myself. And even then, my pa sent Gor to retrieve me when I had taken too long," Gregor said in dismay.

"So how fast will I age, being a shape-changer?" Victoria asked.

"I have no idea, like I said, I have never met another shape-changer beyond your father, and he wasn't a fraction—I mean, um, excuse me, he was a full shape-changer," Gregor said. "Plimsoll will have more answers. Do you wish to meet him?" he asked cheerfully.

"Yes, I would love to learn how to transform as quickly as you do!" she said.

"Oh, Plimsoll didn't train me. He is an elf."

"I thought you said not to trust any elves," Victoria said.

"Well, Plimsoll is different. He is wise, and he is not biased for the elves, you father even trusted him." Gregor said.

"Well, who trained you?" She asked.

"My pa trained me, and Gor helped too," Gregor said and then added when Victoria gave him a look of disbelief, "Gor used to be less grumpy. This war has made him crazy."

"What did they tell you? How do you transform so quickly and without pain?" Victoria asked anxiously. "How do you control it?"

"It takes years, but the more you transform, the faster your body does it, and eventually you can almost ignore the pain," he said. "I had to transform every day for years to be able to do it now at will to prepare for battle. My pa pushed me hard because he was afraid Charlene would attack before I was strong enough. But most do not because it feels like torture, so they just wait until the lack of moon or a strong emotional rage makes them transform and lets themselves become its slave. It is much easier. But if you don't want to be the victim of your transformation, you cannot hide from it. You have to face it," Gregor explained.

"I was hoping for a magical potion or herb," Victoria joked and gave an exaggerated huff and leaned back against the wall, but winced again in pain.

"All my other cuts and bruises are healing. Why isn't this one?" she asked as she looked over her shoulder at the oozing wound.

"All the signets have silver infused in them. A cut from silver won't heal fast and will leave a scar," Gregor said.

"Does silver hurt all of us? All the nonhuman creatures?" Victoria asked.

"Well, everyone except elves, we are still trying to find their weakness." He said and made a fist in discontent.

"We need provisions for the trip to meet Plimsoll," Gregor said, changing subjects. "We will have to go into the marketplace."

"Are you ready to fight more?" Victoria asked with concern, looking at his swollen eye and bruised face. He gave another hearty laugh. She liked his laugh. It was contagious, and she felt her spirit lifting.

"No, there will be no fighting today," he said.

They climbed down the stairs, and he opened the door. The sunshine felt warm and bright against her skin. Now she was able to take in the entire sight of the city in awe. In the fading light yesterday, the city seemed dark and sinister. Now in the daylight, it was almost charming. Every building was handcrafted with different levels of expertise. Most of the homes were simple log cabins with an occasional fancier home.

"Those are the houses the elves or dwarves have helped build. Beasts are more warriors than craftsmen," Gregor explained quickly, but Victoria liked the quaint, humble charm. He seemed pleasantly surprised by her saying so.

He still limped, and they slowly made their way into the main street checkered with cobblestone and saw carts lining in the middle of the town square.

"If there is no money, why are people here in the marketplace?" she asked, confused. Gregor just motioned for her to listen. One of the she-beasts had a cart full of apples, her brand on her feline ear clearly visible.

"My master wishes for apples, and he offers these fresh fish," another she-beast said as she approached the first. Then she turned and showed her mark on her large feline ear. The first looked over the fish and nodded, and they made a trade. She looked at the other carts and noticed everyone was trading, using their brand to begin the discussion. Victoria had a thousand questions, but she stifled them all down and just watched curiously. Gregor excused himself and disappeared into one of the large shops, and she stood content to just continue to watch this bizarre society.

"Let me see your insignia!" a feminine voice pierced through the rest of the chatter, and Victoria jumped. She looked beside her to see one of those she-beasts standing so close that her fur brushed against her arm. It was the closest she had ever been to one of these creatures, and she was comparably small, the she-beast being at least a foot taller. Another three joined the first, and they were talking to each other excitedly.

"Well, do not keep us waiting," another said, snapping her jaws shut impatiently. Her small kitten nose wrinkled, and her whiskers trembled a bit as Victoria stood frozen just looking up at them. They were tall and thin. Their faces were mostly human but covered in a soft peach fuzz, and their noses were pink and the triangular shape of a cat's. But they had human-like eyes, cheeks, lips, and chins. Their large, pointed ears sat on top of their heads just like a cat's, but they had hair falling all around them. A perfect blend of human and feline. She could not help but continue to examine them from head to toe. They had fingers with a pair of thumbs and regular human legs with five toes peeking out from their laced sandals. Every inch of their skin was covered in a soft peach fuzz, each one colored differently. Three of them were striped, and the first one who had spoken to her had spots.

They each had a tail, and Victoria resisted the urge to pull on it to see if it was, in fact, attached. She knew Mabel would be so angry when she found she missed out on seeing these strange and beautiful creatures.

"Have you never seen a belle before?" the one with spots spoke again, shaking her head at Victoria. Her whiskers whipped against Victoria's forehead playfully.

"Well, show us then. Show us your insignia," another one snapped.

Victoria felt their hands grazing over her bare shoulder. Their fur stopped at the palm and on the underside of each finger and thumb, so their fingertips were just like hers with the little ridges and everything. But their nails were long and pointed and sharp, so she let them continue to touch and poke her shoulder and look at the healing scar until they were satisfied.

"That is a nice-looking one. It is clean and crisp, should scar nicely," the spotted belle said again.

"Everyone it is talking about yesterday at the gate! I am so sad I missed it! But I heard all about it. If any beast had declared bellum for me against Gor, I would be so flattered! You are so lucky to be his, and he is a prince too!" One of the other belles had her hand on her hip and was talking so fast Victoria wasn't sure she caught everything she had been saying, but she gathered enough to know these ladies here must not leave the city too often.

"There is a huge world outside of here. You shouldn't be an option for bellum. We should be able to enact bellum ourselves!" Victoria said. At this, the belles began to laugh.

"Honey, bellum is for us too. Belles can enact bellum to other belles. We usually do not, though. We are much more civilized. We just flash our insignias and let our beast's name do all the heavy lifting. All that clawing and biting, no way. It would mess up my hair."

"No, that's not what I meant. I mean, we should not be objects for them to bellum over," Victoria said.

"Well, then who would decide which beast we belong to?" another one asked, confused.

"You! You could decide. You pick which you wanted to be with!" Victoria said in disbelief.

"These humans have such strange ideas." The spotted one was obviously the leader of the group. She laughed again, and the others followed.

"I don't know, that actually sounds nice," one belle said sheepishly. The others all turned toward her, eyes narrowed.

"Oh, you choose. Okay, well, Priscilla, go ahead. Choose. How would you know which one is the strongest if they didn't fight?"

"Well, it sounds like in the human world that doesn't matter," Priscilla said.

"Yes! Because we have money, men and women—I mean, beast and belles can make money and buy stuff that way, not fight for it."

"So you have this money and you use it to get things. Okay, I understand. What is money shaped like? Is it made from metal or from solid oak? Does it have a point on it for stabbing?"

"Yeah, I think we should let money decide our bellums. It sounds strong," another said, imitating swinging something heavy.

"No, no, money is made from paper," Victoria explained.

"What? How is paper going to beat someone up?"

"No, it means you trade the paper for what you want and there is no fighting at all."

"Well, you fight for the money though, right?"

"No, well, I guess sometimes some people do. Usually, you can earn money by trading services. Like what the slaves here do. People get paid money for it there, so everyone is free. Each thing or service is an agreed upon amount of the paper money."

"This sounds like bellum but with more steps, and now counting is involved?" the spotted one said.

"Yeah, this is just confusing. How do you know which one is the strongest?" Priscilla added, now sounding less convinced of the idea.

"You don't, I guess, I mean some wrestle for fun or compete in sports, but once again, it's usually just for fun. No one really cares who is the strongest."

"Well, if no one knows who is the strongest then how does your species cut out the weaklings?" the spotted one sneered, and now all four of them were closing in on her, stooping over her with their sharp teeth glinting in the sunlight as they spoke. Victoria was now feeling a bit uneasy with this whole conversation. She wondered when Gregor was returning.

"We have plenty of weak people living among us. They are often very nice and usually make great friends," Victoria replied, making sure to keep her tone light and soft. She needed to deescalate this situation.

"I don't understand. You befriend the weak? You do not enslave them?" the spotted one asked, but her tone insinuated she did not want an answer. It was more riddled with sarcasm.

"Everyone is free, and they earn money according to their talents and craft," Victoria said quickly, trying to scoot away from them in vain.

"I do not understand how humans have survived this far," another said.

Victoria nodded politely and let out a breath of relief as she saw Gregor approaching. All the belles chattered as he walked toward them.

"Hi, Beast Prince," Priscilla said with a giggle and a little wave and a deep curtsy. All of the others, except the spotted one, joined in and giggled. Victoria stood there in disbelief, watching them swoon over him, and he gave a short smile with a nod.

"Hello, Nagini," Gregor said, nodding to the spotted belle. She gave a short curtsy back.

"Just meeting your first demesne," Nagini said. Her tail flicked as she spoke. Gregor slowly stepped toward Victoria, taking her hand and pulling her back behind him protectively, which alarmed Victoria. She stood ready to run, her legs shaking slightly.

"It is a terrible shame you chose a human over a belle. Perhaps for the next one you will consider one of my daughters, your own kind," Nagini said with a sneer.

"Don't be so upset, Nagini. Humans have such short lives—" Priscilla started to say matter-of-factly, and Nagini sent her a scowl that silenced her immediately.

"I just don't understand why Gregor would go against Gor for this," Nagini said, flicking her wrist dismissively toward Victoria.

"I don't care about this human," Gregor said coldly, matching her condescending tone when he used the word *human*. "I just wanted to take something from Gor. I realized I was finally strong enough to stand up to him."

Nagini did not say anything, but her face was full of knowing glee. She chuckled, and Gregor gave a full smile as he grabbed Victoria by the base of the back of her neck and steered her forcefully away from them.

As soon as they were out of sight, Gregor dropped his hand, but it was too late. Victoria was spitting mad.

"You are the most—" she began a flurry of insults, but he covered her mouth quickly, pressing her into the nearest corner. She could feel the cold stone against her back and his pleading eyes burrowed into hers.

"Listen, it is not safe for anyone to know you are a shape-changer. Here that is a myth, like how humans think of unicorns. If anyone knew, they would . . . well, you would not be safe," Gregor warned.

"But I am your 'demesne,'" Victoria whispered back, embellishing this new word she learned with plenty of sarcasm. "I thought they couldn't touch me."

"We can't let any word get to Charlene. Also, we can't let my pa know. He would definitely—" Gregor stopped himself, his face soured at the mention of his pa. "No. Um. You look human and luckily you smell human," he said.

"Wait, what? What does that mean? What do humans smell like?" she asked curiously.

"You are not concentrating on the important point here. You have to pretend to be human for your safety," Gregor said.

"Okay, fine, I am human," she said, feeling silly announcing it. "I thought I was human, so it should not be too hard to just continue being me."

Gregor looked relieved and dropped his hand from her face.

They resumed walking, and Victoria gasped as a burly man with the lower body of an elk stepped alongside them with his four powerful hooves clopping on the cobblestone. His majestic rack of antlers almost smacked a few of the street signs.

"Hello, Brawn," Gregor said, and he listened while the creature spoke to him in another language she did not recognize in the slightest. Gregor tensed and his face darkened. Gregor replied with sounds all garbled and too fast for her to decipher anything. Then Brawn nodded at her and trotted away. Victoria stared after him, watching his graceful movements and unsure if she would ever be capable of describing any of this to Mabel. Thoughts of Mabel stung. She knew they would be in a tizzy looking for her. Mabel was probably unable to sleep, and at this point, she probably assumed Victoria was never coming back.

"After meeting Plimsoll, may I go home?" Victoria asked in a shaky voice. She had been terrified to ask, but she finally was able to get the words out. Gregor looked at her and put his hands in his pockets.

"I can escort you home right now if you like," Gregor said, but he kept his eyes on the ground ahead of him. Victoria now understood he did this when he was feeling uncomfortable.

"Really? Right now? We can go home right now?" she challenged. It sounded too good to be true.

"If that is what you want," Gregor said, casually kicking a rock to the side with his foot as he walked. His limp was still noticeable, but he seemed to be moving smoother. His nose stayed pointed down. Victoria turned the options over in her mind.

"I better meet this Plimsoll first. I want to master my talent," she said after a long moment.

Gregor seemed to perk up. His step was lighter, and his small smile returned, but he pushed it back into a neutral position, once again masking his emotion. The entire thing had played out in a millisecond, and it was the first time she realized perhaps Gregor liked having her around. Worse yet, he did not want to let her know. She felt a flicker of emotion. What was this she was feeling? She felt an odd rush, an excitement she could not place, at the thought. She shook her head, pretending to gather her hair, unwilling to acknowledge it.

"Then we go home?" she asked, at the risk of sounding redundant, but she needed to hear it again. She stopped walking and stood on tippy toes so she could meet his eyes.

"I promise," Gregor reassured her. Victoria felt a weight lift off her chest, and despite all the pain in her shoulder, she impulsively wrapped her arms about him in an appreciative hug. He gingerly wrapped one arm awkwardly around her, his hand landing on the small of her back. Victoria realized it was inappropriate, so she quickly pulled away. She looked at her shoes, and he looked at his for a moment. Then he grunted and gestured toward the road, and she nodded, and they were back to walking again.

"What did that Elken Folk say?" she asked.

"My pa wants to see me," he said with a sigh. "We better go or else he will come looking."

"Right now?" Victoria asked, feeling anxious. "I am a mess. I have not had a proper bath—"

"I know, calm down. We are going to the bathhouses now," Gregor said.

"Bathhouses?" Victoria asked in disgust. "Like, as in multiple people, um, bathing together?"

Gregor chuckled again, a deep, hearty one. "Do not worry. They divide it. You will be with the belles, that means—" Gregor began to explain.

"I know, beasts are the men and belles are the women. I am your demesne belle."

"No, you are not a belle. A belle is a she-beast. She cannot transform. She is stuck in a half-and-half form forever. It matters not if she was born of beast or bitten. Either way there has never been a female who can fully transform into a beast. That is what makes you so special—you could become a fully transformed she-beast if you wanted to."

Victoria wanted to ask more questions, but Gregor handed her a package she just now noticed he had been carrying since Nagini had cornered her. She was glad they were far from her. Gregor pointed toward the opening, and she went inside, and Gregor went in the opposite door. Inside it was hot and steamy, and it took several moments for her to find her way to the pools. They were hot springs naturally occurring from out of the ground, and this building had been built around it, blocking in the steam and offering privacy. There were several other belles there, and at first, they looked at her suspiciously, but Victoria quickly learned to show her shoulder. They nodded and moved on without comment.

She slipped off her filthy clothes, dropping them into the separate wooden tub others were putting their clothes into. After lathering them with soap and fiercely scrubbing them, she dunked them several times into the rinsing tub. Then she pulled them up and hung them on the clothesline provided.

As they dried, she ventured deeper into the steam to the pool where the water was hot and relaxing. When she got inside, she suddenly realized she was sore from the top of her head to the very tips of her toes, and the hot water seemed to soothe it all away.

There were multiple soaps in the bag Gregor had given her, and she relished every moment of finally getting clean.

At one point, she must have fallen asleep because she woke to the splash of a belle climbing into the pool. Victoria opened her eyes to see the bare back of a belle as she dipped her face into the water. She was striped beautifully, the pattern connecting down her spine from her ears to the tip of her tail, looking more like a tiger than a common house cat. But rather than the intense orange typical of tigers, her stripes were black and white, complimenting her tangled, curly black hair. When the belle turned her face toward her, it took every bit of restraint Mother had driven into Victoria over the years to keep herself from gasping out loud in horror as she looked into the black hole of an empty eye socket. The remaining eye rested on her curiously.

"You have stirred up quite the commotion." the one-eyed belle said, studying Victoria from head to toe, which seemed much more intrusive with the singular eye.

"Um, yeah, I did not mean to," Victoria said sheepishly, trying to look anywhere but at the hole.

"Gor was beside himself, he hasn't lost a bellum in nearly eighty years," she said with an amused smirk.

"I am Victoria," Victoria introduced herself, partial to anyone who would smile at Gor's misfortune.

"I am One-Eyed Giselle," One Eyed Giselle said. Victoria nodded, once again trying not to look at it, but since they were both undressed, there was not any other place to look politely, so she ended up staring back into the black abyss.

"Yeah, I know. It happened when I was human. Gruesome, isn't it?" One Eyed Giselle said, gesturing toward her face. Victoria shook her head but couldn't find any words to string together.

"I was around before Gregor was born and I have watched him grow all these years into a savage, selfish beast like his pa, but today I saw an entirely new Gregor," she said. "You have changed him, somehow." One Eyed Giselle stared at Victoria, once again her one eye piercing farther than any pair had done before. Victoria wanted to ask more questions but One-Eyed Giselle was obviously done speaking because she began to swim, diving under the water and receding into the thick, steamy fog.

Victoria stood and wrapped herself in the towel from the bag and was delighted to find a lovely blue dress was folded neatly inside and some slipper shoes with soft leather soles.

She brushed her hair slowly with the exquisite comb. It was engraved with flowers and vines and even had a little butterfly embellishment attached to the handle.

When she finally emerged from the bathhouse, Gregor was leaning against a tree, looking as clean as she felt. His hair was combed and swept to the side, no longer hiding those emerald greens beneath the wave of dark brunette strands. He was wearing a crisp white cotton shirt and some nicely tailored pants, and his shoes looked like the ones she wore but of course much larger.

"Listen, we are going to my pa," Gregor said. "Please know anything he says or does is not in any way to be taken personally."

They walked along the path paved with tiny pebbles of white, and on either side were thick bushes with thorns so sharp she caught her hand and winced. She stepped into the middle and kept her hands close to her side as she walked. The bushes held no leaves, just a tangle of thorns on the spiraling vines. She looked forward to a large ruin in the distance. It looked structurally unsound as it sat lopsided on the hill. She guessed the original design was a castle made from white stone, but too much was crumbled to be sure. Large holes stood gaping out the sides, and furniture and rugs could be seen sitting inside. The courtyard was littered with all sorts of old and stained furniture and other objects. It was a sad remnant of once former glory.

She would rather return to the snarling branches than approach it.

"We are going in there?" she asked him. He nodded, and she sat for a moment, catching her breath. She now noticed that the dusk was settling in fast. Gregor pulled a cracker from his pocket with a gleeful smile and set it in her palm. Victoria looked at him with her head to her side, puzzled.

The moment the buttery golden round winked in the open, flecks of lights flew over her and close to her hands and face. They zipped about, faster than she could blink. They all buzzed about in her palm, eating the entire thing in seconds, down to the last crumb. Instantly, all the lights disappeared. Small poofs of sparkling dust shimmered around her.

"Fairies," she breathed happily, trying to catch another glimpse of them. After a few moments of searching, she gave up. They were fast. She giggled, and Gregor joined in with his pleasant chuckles. He handed her another cracker. The dazzling lights returned.

One faerie clung to her sleeve. She brought it up close to her eye to get a better look. It was a small woman, no bigger than Victoria's pinkie. She fluttered her delicate butterfly wings as she rose into the air, a continual flicker of vivid purple with each flap. She had long, wavy golden hair and pale glittering skin. Her indigo eyes were large on her tiny face, but the strange proportion somehow added to her splendor. Small, plump lips and rosy cheeks made her look angelic. Victoria could not believe her eyes, and she just stared down in awe, savoring every detail so she could explain it fully to Mabel.

It was fascinating enough to sacrifice another cracker as the rest of the little flock once again surrounded her. The entire swarm covered her hand. A dozen sparkles danced up her arm in celebration, tickling Victoria softly. She laughed out loud, feeling sparks of weightless happiness. The dust covered her face, making her sneeze twice. They whispered to each other with high-pitched tones that sounded like rushes of wind passing by her ears in a melodic tune. They seemed to communicate through song, and Victoria welcomed the pleasant noise. Each faerie was so unmistakably different. Each had its own unique face and features. The women wore flowing silk gowns. The men only wore trousers, their shiny chests proudly displayed. They all shared the same golden dust, which seemed never ending. It floated all around her and settled on her hair and skin, giving her a shiny glow. She smiled as they danced for her in midair, the men twirling the women with great gusto.

"I guess you don't get as cold as us humans," she said, wondering if they even knew what she was saying. She felt oddly relieved to find something sweet, a glimmer of hope, in such a dark place. Interrupting this calm was a low howl in the distance. All the faeries turned pitch black. Their golden, sparkling skin turned a darker hue—even the whites of their eyes—letting them slip into the shadows. If Victoria had not witnessed it happen right in front of her face, she would have been oblivious to the dozens flying right by her. The last noise she heard was from a panicked flutter of one's wings near her ear, hiding behind her hair. As the growls got louder, they all hid themselves among her hair and behind her shoulder, their delicate wings whirring softly against her skin, tickling her pleasantly. More approaching snarls made Victoria sink into the bush and watch with shallow breath. Several large beasts clamored into the courtyard out of the forest as though the dying sunlight stirred them awake. She was horrified at the sight of more beasts. There were over a hundred in the crowd gathering.

They were a hideous mix of wolf and man, with long hind legs and a tail. The paws on which they stood left massive prints in the dirt. Large muscular arms dangled low. The coloration of fur was in such variety between light browns to speckled blacks. Some were spotted and others were striped. They held some human qualities in that they stood upright on two legs, although some hunched further than others. Several faces were furrier with long snouts while others held more of a humanly demeanor. Their sharp fangs glistened with fresh blood, chilling Victoria.

One beast tried to join, but the group parted, and he stood alone among them. Victoria gasped in horror as she recognized him; it was Gor.

Victoria knew which beast was King Brutus immediately, not because he was the only beast wearing a bright-red cloak, but because he was the largest one there. He stood with the golden crown on his head, bolder and larger than the one she had seen in Gregor's wardrobe, but it was the same design.

"How is he so massive?" Victoria asked.

"The older a beast is, the bigger he grows," Gregor whispered back to her. By the looks of it, Brutus was the senior of everyone.

He stood proudly, and the beasts paid special respect to him, never turning their backs on him or crossing his path. He was able to transform faster than even Gregor. A beast, and then suddenly a man replaced him. He was taller than average and bulkier, but he looked like a normal person, except for the scar. Victoria assumed it was a claw mark. It started on Brutus's forehead and slithered down the side of his head close to his ear and then sliced down his cheek, continued to his chin and snaked down his neck. She followed the scar down his chest and was horrified it did not end until it reached his navel. Then she quickly looked away, because he was undressed.

"Where did he get that scar?" Victoria asked Gregor.

"When my pa was young, he was attacked by a beast, and it would have devoured him, but he happened to be wearing a necklace with a ruby." Gregor paused as Victoria gasped. "He said he held it up toward the beast and it ran away. He was nearly dead but survived because he transformed, but when he returned to the place he was attacked, it was gone. He suspects it must be your necklace, the one Charlene wants, but he wants to examine it himself to see."

The beasts transformed into human. Most took several long minutes, grunting in pain. Only a few were able to change quickly. Victoria was relieved to see some belles approaching with baskets of clothes.

Although she did not hear what they were saying, she saw Gor fall to his knees, begging for mercy. The others stood silent. None moved while the king stood staring down Gor. Victoria was unsure what was said, but after the king said one word, Gor threw himself before Brutus flat on his belly, face planted into the earth. Brutus leaned down, listening to what Gor was saying intently.

"If you change your ears into a fox's, you can hear what they are saying," Gregor said, and he showed her his ear, which he had turned into the beast form. It looked lopsided with one large chestnut ear protruding from the top of his head, but she wanted to try. It took her a long time to concentrate.

Victoria suddenly felt very stupid. Gregor gave her an encouraging nod, and she continued to command herself to transform her ear. She missed a few more minutes as she struggled to make them change, but after it was complete, her large fox ears were able to tune into the conversation, but her nose was now fuzzy, too, somehow. Gregor chuckled, and she defensively elbowed him in his ribs.

But she stopped when she could hear not only the two men's deep voices, but also the faeries' wings beat. One faerie whispered to the other, and Victoria realized their voices were too high for her to understand them before.

"Fly! It's the Beast King!" they screamed in terror.

The others gasped in awe, fluttering away. They were gone, and although their departure did not lessen the light, she felt darker inside. A part of her wanted to call after them, ask them to stay with her, but a sharp tone from the hill brought her back into focus.

"He turned on me! Gregor is the traitor," Gor said defensively. Brutus listened to Gor's frantic mutters, patiently waiting for them to stop. "The girl—she is the daughter of Richard and can transform."

"You failed to bring me the ruby, your one assignment," Brutus said flatly.

"No!" Gor screamed, looking to the crowd for the mercy he could not find in his king. Everyone stepped back, revealing the cobblestone courtyard that was shaped in a lopsided circle, most of the stone on the edges worn away.

The king stepped toward a large chain and gave it a heavy yank and dropped it, stepping out of the circle as well. A low grumble echoed from inside the single tower adjacent to the rest of the castle ruins, and the group fell into a hushed silence. Gor stood up abruptly and took a preparatory stance as something slammed him into the ground. The crowd cheered and yelled explosively. It was as though a shadow was fighting him. Victoria could not see the culprit that tore into Gor's chest and bit into his leg, sending squirts of blood into the air, but some of the red drizzled down its face, and Victoria could determine it was some sort of animal. The nearest onlookers stepped back, wiping the red from their faces as Gor screamed in agony. He was shaken back and forth and flung high into the air. Whatever held him, it was larger than even Brutus, and its roar seemed to stop Victoria's heart. A bell rang, and Gor collapsed in relief.

Brutus stood from his chair, and the creature retreated to the tower, knocking one onlooker off their feet. She was unsure if it was intentional or if it was just unable to control its size.

Gor crawled out of the circle slowly, and some of the crowd jeered while others cheered.

"He has survived thirty seconds against Samson!" Brutus announced.

"Gor, because of your long-standing loyalty, I will give you one more chance to join the others in the search. Let any man who brings me the hollow ruby be rewarded greatly!" Brutus said with outstretched arms. The crowd cheered, but as a noise from the distance rumbled, they all scattered. Gregor pushed Victoria down, deeper into their hiding place and put his finger to his lips.

CHAPTER 10

AN EYESORE

A BLACK CARRIAGE WITH a white handkerchief dangling over the side and drawn by two black horses pulled up from the forest path. It was large and expensive because of the carved wood and the golden embellishments along the edges. The footman jumped down and quickly opened the door as Brutus stood looking surprised. The rest of the beasts were gone, except Gor, who was still on the ground.

Victoria gasped as she recognized Charlene's bright-blond hair flowing around her pale face, her red lips drawn in a frustrated frown. Gregor ducked down and gestured for her to follow so they could get a better look.

"She never comes here," Gregor whispered, turning to listen intently.

Brutus wandered over toward her, his teeth gritted, and hands clenched. She looked down at Gor and then back at Brutus with a wordless sneer.

"Why did you send Gor to interrupt my masquerade ball?" Charlene asked.

"Well, obviously I had no part in whatever you are speaking of, but once I found out about it, I immediately punished him," Brutus lied smoothly, gesturing over toward Gor.

"Your kingdom is thriving," she said sarcastically, stepping over Gor to reach Brutus in her bright-pink, shiny high heels.

"Keep your dogs on tighter leashes, or I will have to put them down," Charlene said.

"Sounds like this visit is more than just one ruined tea party," he said in a flat tone once they stood facing each other. Gor continued to crawl away, avoiding eye contact with Charlene. Only Brutus held his shoulders straight and looked directly into her large blue eyes without hesitation. Victoria could not believe they were fearful of Charlene. Her slender body seemed delicate, so vulnerable.

"One of your dogs attacked a human in the valley. You know more than anyone that humans are skittish. One dead body will send them all into a frenzy. Someone left the corpse on the road, the main road. Hundreds came across it before I had even heard about it."

"I will talk to my men."

"That is poaching. How am I supposed to produce a large supply if your men keep taking snaps here and there, sending widespread panic?" She paused until Brutus nodded.

"And another thing—I am missing a girl. She robbed me and ran," she said. "Since I have yet to find her inside the valley, perhaps she was foolish enough to take up the side of the mountain."

"Why should I bother to clean up your mess?" he asked. "What did she steal?"

"It is none of your concern," Charlene said. "No one steals from me."

"What is in it for me?" he asked.

"Just do it!" Charlene snapped, rubbing her temples with her fingertips. "She has red hair and should be easy to find."

"I will keep an eye out for this girl," he said with a nod.

"No, she needs to be found. Tonight!" she said, looking at him suspiciously. "Unless you already have seen her?"

"I would never lie to you," he said.

"You just did. I know for a fact that Gor and Gregor went toe to toe yesterday and Gregor won." She raised her eyebrows, and a sly smile slid across her face. "Gregor has become quite the warrior. Perhaps it is time he meets my Mason. I think they should finally have a playdate after all these years, don't you agree?"

Brutus only snorted, the frown on his face turning down into sheer disdain.

"Maybe later," he said coolly.

Charlene laughed, relishing Brutus's obvious discomfort. "So, back to my question, why are you lying to me about the girl?" She gave him a satisfied glare.

"I have only heard of it. I have not seen Gregor or the girl for myself yet," Brutus said. "What about the dwindling meat supply?" he asked. "Surely you were meaning to discuss it since you rode all the way out here."

"What is there to discuss?" she asked.

"You have only been sending us half the usual portion, and most of them are old and weak."

"We are having a bit of a shortage, but soon—"

"Your ladies have been saying that for over three deliveries now," Brutus interrupted.

"Give me time—" Charlene began to explain before Brutus cut her off again.

"I think you have grown soft, keeping all the humans for your little pets down in the valley, playing dress-up with them, and inviting them to your parties."

"Hush, Brutus. You will get a larger supply soon. Our farm is just undergoing new management since the nomads attacked."

"Whispers of you losing control have echoed out. Perhaps you need some more of my beasts to protect—"

"Last thing I need is more dogs," Charlene snapped back.

"Just offering some help," Brutus said.

"Quiet! Brutus, I am handling it. All right, I know beast law. I know Gregor has won the girl fair and square—no matter. All I want is the necklace. Tell him I will give him anything he wants for it. Perhaps he would be interested to know that I have the girl's sister." Charlene nodded, and the footman pulled a small frame from the carriage. Mabel stumbled and fell into the dirt at Brutus's feet. Victoria felt her throat tightening as though she had just tried to swallow a rock.

"Surely you can commission any silversmith in the valley to custom remake the piece you lost. What is so special about this necklace?" Brutus asked suspiciously

"This one is sentimental." Charlene said.

"Oh is it?" Brutus asked. Charlene ignored him and pushed Mabel further in front of her.

"Not very much meat on this one," Brutus said, nudging Mabel with the tip of his boot.

"I am trying to decide the best way to dispose of her mother as well."

Victoria grabbed at the soil beneath her hands in fury as she helplessly listened to them discussing her family's fate. Gregor held her shoulders firmly as though he could read her thoughts. She allowed herself to release a slow breath, listening intently to the rest of the conversation.

"Perhaps I will let you raid their estate, make it look like a nasty robbery—if you do so quietly. She is proving a bit more difficult to remove."

"A human is giving you trouble?" Brutus asked with a small smirk.

"I can't just pluck her out of her home. This one is very social. It is a delicate situation," Charlene explained.

"Anyway, I am taking the sister to Naphtali tonight. Tell Gregor I will be there until the Full Moon Maze Run, and if he isn't interested in a trade by then, I will sign her up as a participant."

"Yes, Your Majesty," Brutus offered sarcastically and gave a mocking bow. Charlene's eyes flashed with anger, and suddenly Brutus was staggering back. Victoria blinked a couple of times, trying to piece together what had just happened. She looked from Charlene back to Brutus, who now was on his knees with a clasped hand on his cheek. Four long, deep scratches bled diagonally. Gor ran off, despite his injuries, his whimpers echoed through the trees, leaving Brutus alone at Charlene's feet.

Brutus gave a low guttural groan but dared not move as he watched Charlene daintily lift the folds of her dress and step into the carriage with the footman's assistance. Then the footman returned to shove Mabel into her seat, and the door slammed shut. The noise sent a jolt down Victoria's spine and into her toes.

Charlene gave one last glance out the window, her porcelain face and bright-pink lips brilliant in the pale moonlight, before the horses pulled the carriage into the dark forest.

"Find the necklace, it has to be the one I have been looking for all these years," Brutus commanded as Gor crawled back into view.

"I told you I would keep Gregor far from her. She never saw him," Gor reassured Brutus.

"Yeah, you did good." Brutus patted his head. "This whole plan would be perfect if you had not lost the necklace!" he scolded, and Gor bowed his head.

"I will find it," Gor said, and he howled up at the small sliver of moon, which looked ridiculous as he was in his human form. Apparently, Brutus thought so too because he promptly delivered a punch in his gut.

"Knock that off," Brutus snapped. "Now come get something to eat. You will need your strength to face the Goblin Queen," he said. Gor remained hunched over in pain and waited for Brutus to disappear back inside before he followed slowly.

A loud bark made her look around, and all the beasts were springing in from the forest now that Charlene was gone. Then Victoria gulped and clambered quickly to her feet, following Gregor.

"Keep the men from feeding when they visit the valley," Brutus could be heard yelling at someone from inside.

"Your ears!" Gregor reminded her and waited for her to transform again to a normal-looking human. "Listen, whatever happens—I, um . . .," Gregor grumbled. He was tight and rigid, the stone-cut jaw set again in place. There was a long pause while he tried to find the words to describe or explain what was about to take place, making Victoria even more anxious. Unable to finish his sentence, he just sighed and said, "I won't let him hurt you." But his voice quivered. The look in his eyes was unmistakable because she had seen it when he had stepped inside that red circle. It was fear. And with that rousing speech, Gregor opened the door to the palace and guided her inside.

It took every bit of self-restraint to keep from screaming. Her heart was thumping faster in her chest than she thought possible. The only thing keeping her in place was Gregor's reassuring nods and the squeeze of his hand pulling her along.

Although the walls, the furniture, and the curtains were, in fact, beautifully crafted, they were in dire need of repair. It was like walking into an abandoned estate. Autumn leaves lay scattered over the exquisitely woven rug and pure marble floors. Porcelain vases held flowers, but the flowers were long dead, having withered and dried in place. Portraits on the wall were covered in a thick coat of dust and cobwebs. A large chunk of the wall had crumbled, and the moonlight shone in against the tapestries.

"This is where the Beast King lives?" she asked in a hushed whisper. Gregor shrugged and continued through the corridor. They passed by others, and Gregor gave a gracious nod to each one, everyone spying Victoria curiously, but no one spoke. As they entered what once must have been a spectacular ballroom, Victoria was greeted with a ghastly sight. A large table was centered in the room and a mishmash of chairs was scooted up to it. There were broken dining chairs, a desk chair, some stools from the kitchen, a settee sofa, and even just a massive stump that had been dragged in from outside. There sat many beasts, all in their human form, waiting for their food to be served.

"Gregor!" Brutus said when he spied him. He stood and stomped over to meet him.

Brutus grabbed hold of Victoria, turning her around and pulling her sleeve off her shoulder enough to reveal her blistering burn. The other beasts cheered, and one gave Gregor a cup filled with some sort of red liquid and a slap on his back.

"That's my boy! Finally got yourself a real bellum under your belt," Brutus said.

"But I lost the necklace—" Gregor's shameful confession was cut short by Brutus's fist. Gregor stumbled back, the drink in his cup sloshed around, spilling to the floor. Blood squirted from his nose.

Gregor apologized as he held his nose. Blood oozed over his fingers. Victoria gasped in sheer astonishment at the brutality. She looked from Gregor's face to Brutus's and tried to find some similarity. They had the same brow line, eye shape, and square jaw. Both had thick necks with the same square chest and round, broad shoulders, but Brutus was much swarthier in comparison.

"You come back with that necklace or don't come back at all!" he shouted. Gregor squared his shoulders, ignoring the blood trickling out his nose and dripping down onto his chest. He looked him directly in the eye.

"Just keep Uncle Gor out of the way and I will be able to get it done," Gregor said, casting a sidelong glance at Gor, who immediately began to yell. Brutus shot him a look, and Gor fell silent, leaning on the arch of a deteriorating column in frustration.

"Charlene visited before you got here. She is taking the sister to Naphtali, hoping that means something to you?" Brutus asked slowly, scrutinizing Gregor's reaction.

Gor smirked at Victoria. She pretended to not see him.

"Why would I care?" Gregor asked with obvious annoyance. Brutus looked over his son. He gave a relieved sigh. "You look awful," Brutus chuckled.

"It's been a rough one," Gregor responded. Then Brutus laid a heavy hand on Gregor's shoulder, shaking him slightly as he steered him around toward the table.

"Well, let's eat!" Brutus said and gestured toward the chair on the right side of the throne that was pushed to the head of the table. The throne was oversized and embellished with plenty of jewels and designs carved into the wood, so it looked silly sitting about two feet taller than the table. Brutus climbed up on it, his legs dangled down, and his boots ended up on the table. He tapped them in delight as the food began to arrive. He called loudly for someone to get him something to drink. After a while, Brutus left and came back inside, yanking a heavy chain behind him. It looked odd, Brutus walking a floating leash and collar, but she could hear Samson breathing, a raspy gurgling sound. She imagined his nose must be severely disfigured to sound such a way. Everyone moved, diving out of the path of the invisible beast.

"C'mon, Samson," Brutus said as he locked the chain into place against the far stone wall. As he stepped away, Samson followed, his claws and chains scraping on the marble floor quickly as he sprang for Brutus. Brutus tried to block, but Samson grabbed a hold of his forearm, lifting him up into the air. Brutus twisted and laid several heavy punches wildly.

It was a strange sight watching Brutus dangling in the air, punching at what seemed nothing.

Brutus finally broke free and dropped to the floor. He rolled back as Samson sprang again. Samson's chain came to an end, yanking him back. Everyone could hear the gasp of his breathing; the collar had choked him.

"Down boy!" Brutus said with a chuckle, getting to his feet. All the other beast men looked at him with fear on their faces. He wiped the blood off his arm with the rag one of the belles anxiously held out for him. Although he could not reach the table, his hot breath flowed over and hit her face, sending her hair into a whirlwind every time he exhaled. No one dared sit any closer, and that side of the table remained empty despite the lack of room on the other end. The men just crowded together.

"We need about two dozen men to go with me to face the Goblin Queen," Gregor said. The men looked at each other nervously.

"It can wait for tomorrow. Tonight, let us drink and be merry!" Brutus called happily. The men let loose some cheers.

"Pull that girl over here. We don't want her freezing," Brutus called out, giving a hearty laugh. They turned to Gregor expectantly. To Victoria's great indignation, Gregor grabbed her by the waist and sat her on his knee, which resulted in another wave of hooting and laughter. Brutus drank deeply and slammed his cup down as the men continued to cheer.

"Let the dinner be served!" Brutus hollered loudly. Musicians began to play, and belles filed in to dance and pour drinks. Their dresses had rows of beads sewn on every hem. The beads would tinkle and chime as they shook their hips. Despite being perched on Gregor's lap like a trophy, Victoria was momentarily mesmerized by their exotic beauty and graceful movements.

Then her senses returned when one of the men slapped one of the women on her bottom. Victoria gasped at the indecency. She wanted nothing more than to punch Gregor in his smug-looking face, but she reminded herself of his promise. So, she sat, waiting for the party to end.

But she refused to eat any of the food offered because she could only stand so much humiliation. She was not going to be fed like some pet. She squirmed, her stomach churning in disgust at the thought the meat could be from Naphtali.

The celebration all around her was intensifying. The music was fast and everyone was drinking and laughing loudly. Soon the king was stumbling to his feet and dancing on the table, pulling the belles to join him. They were all now dancing and singing along to the song, which was in a different language, so Victoria had no idea what they were saying. Soon they were kicking and dancing so hard that whatever was left of the food went flying everywhere.

"What is the reason for the celebration?" Victoria asked.

"This is just an average dinner." Gregor said, confused.

In the confusion, Victoria appreciated the chance to be overlooked. Gregor slid her in the chair beside him and cast her an apologetic glance, but the moment was interrupted by his father jerking him up by his collar and Gregor falling in rhythm with the steps. Everyone shouted as father and son were suddenly locked in a sort of dance-off, both kicking their feet and swinging their arms, eyeing each other intently.

She was surprised to see Gregor could in fact dance in rhythm, if it was to this savage music, in this odd jumping and thrashing manner. It was unlike anything Victoria had seen at the proper balls and at first, she was unimpressed. But as she continued to watch, she realized there was a certain level of skillful mastery needed to accomplish each step.

She found herself clapping along and then stopped herself at the thought of Mabel being transported right now through the dark forest as she sat here being entertained. She slumped back in her chair, wary of Samson's chain and the men staggering around. It was harder to see because most of the candles were burning low now and no one had given thought to change them out.

Samson continued his eager scratching toward the steak several feet from his reach. He was whining and panting even heavier. Victoria could no longer endure his suffering. She slid out of her chair and carefully scooted the steak toward Samson with her foot. She was unsure how far his reach was, so she continued to push it slowly until she saw the steak begin to move on its own, assuming he had snagged it by his claw. Although she could not see him, the steak soon disappeared bite by bite with loud smacking noises.

Samson sniffed; she could hear his paws shifting eagerly. She tossed another toward the end of the chain. The meat vanished in midair.

"You are hungry," Victoria said, tossing another piece. It, too, was engulfed in one bite. Feeling a bit entertained, she threw the next one as high into the air as she could. She could see the chain jump and hear Samson's short snort as he caught it. She giggled as she saw the meat hanging half-eaten in the air. It was a strange sight she guessed she would never get accustomed to.

She stood on the nearby chair and sent the last slab of meat as high as she could throw. Samson leapt up, the chain jerking tight. He gobbled it while still in motion, making her laugh out loud. Samson grunted and snorted playfully.

Victoria started back toward the safety of the end of the chain, but Samson gave a slight whimper in reply. She stopped and turned around, facing that collar floating in the air.

She could feel his breath hot on her face and reached her hand up. Resisting the urge to run back, she stood, slightly shaking. She felt his face pressing against her palm. It was large, and she could feel it was lopsided. Half of his forehead was sloped and furrowed. With both hands on his face, she could feel his uneven eyes. One was severely smaller than the other and propped higher, too close to the eyebrow. Although she felt sparse patches of hair, he was mostly covered with rough, bumpy skin, and she was surprised when she realized he had a human nose. It was large and knobby, and the bridge was flattened down, blocking proper airflow. His nostrils constantly flared with each breath and his mouth had to hang open to compensate. Understanding now why he was always panting; she felt a pang of sympathy toward this large, disfigured beast underneath her fingertips.

Then his slobbering, wet tongue came out of his mouth, wiping up her face and into her hair. She sputtered. Pulling down his head to avoid another flood of drool, her fingers ran across his large sharp teeth protruding from his mouth.

"Ow!" she whimpered, pulling her hand away to look at her cut finger. The blood ran down her arm. Samson licked at it instantly, and she hid her hand behind her back. "You have very sharp teeth," she said. Samson began to growl, and her heart quickened, fear flooding back into her.

"Okay, you fed it, now step back," Gregor's tight voice cut through the commotion of the party happening behind her. She could feel his hand on her shoulder. Victoria ignored his hushed whispers of concern and gave Samson another pat.

"He is fine," she said.

She lifted her other hand and held his face between her palms, giving him a good scratch behind his large floppy ears. She could hear the music coming to halt, and a silent hush had fallen over the crowd. She felt all their eyes burrowing into her back, and she gave him another pat for the satisfaction of turning around to see all their mouths hanging open in astonishment. She looked down at her hand and realized the cut Samson had given her was completely healed, perfectly new smooth skin had formed immediately after he had licked it.

"Get back, you mangy rat," Brutus stomped over and slapped the chain on the ground. Samson dashed back into the far corner. Then Brutus turned on his heel and looked at Victoria squarely in the eye. "Are you sure you don't want to trade for the other sister?" Brutus said, his eyes squinting as he looked at her. "This one seems odd."

"She will do," Gregor said dryly, pouring a pair of cups full of the red liquid and handing one to his father. He raised his, encouraging Brutus to drink.

"She refuses to even dance or drink with us," Brutus said, continuing to stare at her dubiously over the rim of his cup. Then, to her mortification, he pressed the cup up to her lips, demanding she drink from it.

She gritted her teeth and turned her head, intent on not letting him bully her any further. Gregor stood there looking unsure what to do, frozen in between Victoria and his father.

"Drink it!" Brutus said. Victoria continued to lean back, keeping her lips tightly closed together. The rim of the cup was cutting into her cheek painfully, and she finally slapped it out of Brutus's hand.

The cup clattered against the marble and rolled a bit before coming to a stop. The sound echoed through the silent room. It was at that point Victoria realized every soul in the room was staring breathlessly at her. Gregor looked pale, his eyes wide and lips dry.

Brutus lifted his arm and then caught himself.

"Oh, I apologize. You discipline your demesne as you see fit," he said and stood aside, leaving Gregor in the spotlight. All the beasts and their belles looked at him, waiting.

"I will deal with her later," Gregor said.

To Victoria's pure bewilderment, Brutus's hand lifted and he slapped her with the back of it, hard enough it sent her sprawling. She fell to the ground beside the cup. The red liquid puddled there, soaking into her skirting. She knew it would stain forever. Brutus found himself a new cup and clicked it against Gregor's, who stood looking appalled. He looked to her and then back to Brutus the war raging inside obvious.

"I said I would take care of it myself," Gregor said, his voice shaking in anger.

"The human would forget why she is being punished if you wait too long, they don't have much in the way of brain capacity," Brutus said, slapping Gregor on the back.

Brutus gave another one of his hearty laughs, which Victoria now loathed. The musicians struck up a louder, faster song, and this sent the crowd into another flurry of excitement. Brutus turned Gregor around and walked him back to the table where they joined back in with the merriment.

Victoria sat where she had fallen, appreciating the moment of being overlooked while she concentrated very hard on not letting herself cry. She turned to see Gor fumbling beside her. He gave one glance at Victoria and rubbed his eyes in his drunken stupor.

"You deserved that!" he grumbled. "You made me the laughingstock of the entire pack! They all think I am a fool, but I did not lose the necklace to the goblins. You did," he said, throwing his goblet at her, but his aim was lacking, and it clattered against the floor. Samson growled.

"Hiding in the shadows, those blasted elves standing guard!" Gor said, spitting in outrage. "I lost my best men fighting them back. We never got even a foothold! All for what? For nothing! Your pa messed everything up. He had Lily, I know he did," Gor rambled on, and Victoria looked for Gregor, but he was nowhere in sight. She wondered if he was still in the room.

"But I wish I could have seen their faces . . . Charlene's face . . . when they all realized you were gone, taken right under their noses!" Gor chuckled at the thought. Then his face soured again. "But now Gregor gets the glory! And I am once again nothing!"

Victoria had been watching his rant while slowly scooting toward Samson, hoping Gor would not notice how his chains were now overlapping.

"If I can't get reward for you . . .," Gor said, staggering forward in his drunken rage. She noticed the red blood vessels in his eyes seemed to be pulsing. "No one will!" Gor said, springing forward and catching her about the throat.

She sputtered, gasping for breath. Trying to squirm from his grip, Victoria noticed Samson's chain scraping slowly toward his turned back. Suddenly Victoria could see the outline of Samson's teeth digging into Gor's arm. Gor's grasp was lifted as he shrieked in pain. A growl escaped from Samson as his claws tore across Gor's face, catching his eye and pulling it from its socket. Blood poured out. The eye soared through the air, landing right in front of Victoria, with a light splash hitting her. Lifting a shaking hand, she wiped at her face. Quickly realizing its slime now sat on her cheek, she shrieked in horror.

Gor floundered about, trying to land a punch on Samson. He was tossed into the air and screamed until smashing into the ground. He groaned and turned onto his back, covering his face as Samson barked angrily, ready to lunge again. Victoria huddled in place.

"What is going on?" Brutus's grumpy voice thundered over her shoulder, and he grabbed ahold of the chain, slapping it hard against the floor again. The entire party was now a huge commotion and even Brutus's booming voice was lost among the noise. Samson shrank against the wall, whimpering.

"Your stupid mutt attacked me!" Gor screamed as he crawled away.

"You attacked first," Victoria mustered in her loudest voice, which still came out shaken and small.

"Shut up!" Gor warned her, his empty eye socket glaring at her harder than his remaining eye. Brutus gave a hearty laugh.

"Hey! Now you match Giselle!" Someone yelled. The other men joined in a round of laughter, and Gor got to his feet, shaking from anger. He started to stomp toward Victoria. She sat frozen in place as he grabbed his eyeball from near her foot. He gave her a furious glance as he popped it into his mouth. Victoria gagged. He spat it out, covered with his spit. While he fumbled, trying to shove his eyeball back into place frantically, the others roared hysterically. He finally rammed it back into the socket, and blood oozed out the sides. His face was in a dreadful state and some of the torn skin peeled down his cheek. This only incited more uproarious mockery.

"Stop laughing! She can shape-change! She was a fox in the woods!" Gor yelled. "You will get yours!" He pointed at Victoria and then to Samson. His eye rolled wildly around, cloudy and discolored. "Very funny!" he screamed into their faces. "I will have respect!"

"What do you mean she can shape-shift?" Brutus asked. "I thought Richard had no offspring."

"Pa, Gor was obviously trying to hurt my, very human, demesne, he should be brought to justice," Gregor said. His voice was bold and loud as his fists were clenched.

"Nah, Gor was just having a bit of fun," Brutus said with a chuckle. "I think he got his punishment." This comment incited more laughter and Gor glared angrily. "No, she can change into a fox! I saw it with my own eyes!" Gor insisted.

"If that was true, Gregor would know about it too," Brutus said.

"Pa, come on, he needs to be punished for trying to steal the life of my demesne. At least give him time in the stocks!" Gregor said.

"Gor, go sleep it off, buddy. Save your rage for the Goblin Queen," Brutus said.

"What?" Gregor asked.

"Yeah, let Gor fetch the necklace back from the goblins tomorrow. That is his punishment. You get a day off to lounge and get better acquainted with her," Brutus said. He made another rude gesture toward Victoria, and she wished she had not seen it. As Gor slumped out of the room, he turned to give Victoria one more threatening glance.

She caught a glimpse of Gor's eye. Miraculously, it had fallen into sync with the other, slowly resuming color. Although still murky and gray, she assumed it would heal in time.

"I have had enough tonight," Gregor said, taking another long chug from the cup. "Night, Pa."

"Does any of this have truth in it?" Brutus asked in a smaller whisper, pulling Gregor in closer.

"If she could do all that, I am sure Gor would have fought harder for her at the gate," Gregor said. Brutus laughed again.

"Are you sure you don't want to trade her? This one might be trouble-some," Brutus said, and both men guffawed at the remark. Gregor chuck-led and took another long chug from his drink. Victoria was sure any normal man would be nearly dead with the amount of alcohol Gregor and his father had consumed. They both were only staggering a bit.

"No, this one will do," he said casually, giving Victoria a little wink that sent Brutus into another fit of laughter. Brutus stood looking at Victoria for a long moment. She could see him calculating something in his mind.

"We won't be going to Naphtali," Gregor said, and Brutus laughed.

"I hope not. Charlene is planning on staying for the maze run," he said.

Gregor motioned toward Victoria to follow, giving her the dignity of walking herself without poking or prodding. She was relieved when they stepped out of the castle ruins and into the crisp night air. She took several deep breaths, letting the foul stench of odor and ale clear from her nostrils.

Gor's gleaming red eyes peered down at them from the tower window, and he ground his jaw angrily. Victoria consciously ignored him and did not even give a sidelong glance toward him as they set down the path on foot.

They walked in silence, apart from Gregor's ragged panting. He was managing to walk much better than she had anticipated after all the ale he had drunk. She stumbled on the dark forest path, and Gregor tried to help her regain her balance. She smacked his hand away with a furious huff. The moon was hidden in the thick canopy overhead, further blanketing everything in black. They walked on until the castle ruins were far behind. They were now in an orchard, walking along the barren trees. The fallen leaves crunched underfoot.

Distant howling flowed on the wind, and she quickened her pace and tripped over what must have been a large rock. She landed on her knees painfully. Gregor stopped and looked around cautiously before squatting down.

"I am so sorry," Gregor apologized as he traced her reddened cheek with his finger, the mark from Brutus's hand still visible. "I would never hurt you."

"You did hurt me, Gregor," she said angrily, smacking his hand away. "I have never been so humiliated in my life."

"I had to pretend like you are a worthless human," his voice faded as he stroked the strand of hair dangling down her cheek. When he tried to tuck it behind her ear, she pulled away sharply.

"Get away from me," she said defensively. "Humans aren't worthless," she said flatly. "I can barely control turning into a tiny fox. Why would men who can transform into oversized destruction machines care?" she asked.

"They can't know how special you are," he said. She pushed him away.

"You have had enough of this drink," Victoria said shortly, tugging at the flask he had in his hand.

"I have not drunk much. I pretended to drink to oblige my pa." He said. Victoria tossed the flask out into the snow.

"I am so sorry I could not get Mabel free from Charlene tonight," he said, leaning back against the nearest tree.

"We are going to get some sleep and we will try again tomorrow. It is the least you could do," she said coldly.

"I could not save your pa," he said sadly. "But we will save Mabel though. I stole the key to the maze off my pa. It opens a door to escape." He held up a tiny gold key. Victoria breathed a sigh of relief.

"You had a plan!" she said, happily. Gregor gave her a coy smile.

"This can help us now, but with training, you can be the most powerful being, more powerful than me, Brutus, Charlene—you could end this entire war!" Gregor said. His eyes shone in the dim moonlight.

"But Gor knows," Victoria said.

"It is our word against Gor's. He only saw you transform into a fox and that can be ruled out with the one he killed," he said. "We just have to convince everyone you are human until you are strong enough—".

"Cuddles," she interrupted impulsively.

"What?" Gregor asked.

"The fox Gor killed was named Cuddles," she said, her voice cracked with emotion.

"You can speak with them?" Gregor asked in awe.

"No, no, I had named her," Victoria said.

"Your pa could talk with all the animals, another useful talent of being a shape-changer. I am guessing that is why you were able to calm Samson and not lose a hand to him, you have the skill," Gregor said. Her heart thudded painfully at another mention of her father.

"I did not hear Samson speak," Victoria said.

"Yeah, but you communicated with him in some way, anyone else would have been ripped to shreds. I know, I have seen it."

"Well, if my father was so powerful, why didn't he just end the war himself?" Victoria asked.

"He was bitten by a mermaid before he could." Gregor said.

"A mermaid?" Victoria laughed out loud. "Now you are rambling like Gor."

"If mermaids are real, aren't they sweet and beautiful sirens who sing lovely songs? They would not bite." Victoria laughed as Gregor looked at her with sincere concern.

"Mermaids are vicious." Gregor said. "One bite from a mermaid will strip any being of their abilities. Only elves and your pa could really talk to them. I can't hope to ever pronounce most of their savage language," he said.

"That is what killed him. Sure, Gor broke many of his bones, stabbed him, and bit off his pinkies," Gregor stopped himself as he read Victoria's horrified expression. He cleared his throat.

"But without his abilities, he was as weak as a human and could not heal fast enough. Your pa was strong, and he never revealed where he stashed the mermaid he found."

Victoria's head spun.

"Why would Gor bite off his pinkies?" she asked, emotions rising as the memories were triggered, her father's bloody stubs dripping through the bandaged wraps. "What did you do—you just watched?"

Gregor huffed and slumped down deeper into the leaves, his back hunched, head lowered. The chilly wind was picking up now, and the moon was weak behind the clouding sky, so everything was turning into gloomy shadows, matching Victoria's mood. He looked so exhausted as he relived the memory, as though the weight of it might crush him.

"I was his guard," Gregor admitted. "My first real assignment. My pa has always treated me as a child. For years I tried to prove myself beyond the reputation of 'princeling.' So, I was anxious to take the job, show him I was ready to join the war," Gregor said and crinkled a leaf in his hand. Victoria sat beside him, the hard dirt crunched under her, but she could barely hear it. Everything had faded away, except the words Gregor was speaking. She clung to each one, listening intently.

"When your pa was brought in, I did not know who he was or why he was in our prison. I did my guard duties, bringing him water and food and not letting him escape, but it was no effort at all. He was already deteriorating. At the time, I did not know it was a mermaid bite. I did not see it. He kept his calf covered. Then we had hours to pass, just us. He began to explain the war, that beasts weren't supposed to win. It was bigger than the beasts and monsters. He wanted all five kingdoms to work together and add humans to the kingdoms." He paused and looked at her and gave a small chuckle.

"Just like you said, a sixth kingdom." He gave a sigh before continuing. "He changed my entire plan for my future. I was not destined to remain in the pack of beasts, always in my father's shadow. I could help build something bigger and better, freedom for everyone," He said with another sigh. This was heavier, and Victoria feared he was done speaking. She needed him to finish while his tongue was loose and without the usual restraint he painstakingly kept propped in place.

"Then Gor came in, and he tortured him for information, for any knowledge on Charlene that would turn the war. Gor discovered the bite, and he knew what it was. He knew your pa had found a mermaid. Charlene has been hunting them mercilessly for years. There are none left. Except those under the care of the elves and they refuse to share, those slimy, leaf-licking . . ." Gregor went into a frenzy of insults, and Victoria rolled her eyes. She sighed and waited until he was finished.

"No one has seen one in such a long time, except your pa. He must have somehow convinced the elves to give him one. But he did not tell anyone. He knew if Gor got his hands on the mermaid, he would not just use it on Charlene. It would be a powerful weapon turned against all the kingdoms. Beasts would reign supreme." He tossed the crumpled pieces of leaf into the air, watching the chilly breeze carry them away.

"I felt helpless while I watched Gor torture him. The only thing I could think to help was convincing him to let your pa go, suggesting he would take us to the mermaids. But he just went straight home to you, his girls. That is all he cared about. That is the only reason he survived and clawed his way back. To see your face." Gregor said. She felt her anger at him dissipating but quickly caught it again, the burning in her cheek still resonating.

"Gor was ready to tear your whole house apart, we saw Mason spying from the bushes. And then we spotted Rhamy. Like I already told you, I watched them watching you. You and your sister huddled together during his funeral as you laid his body to rest." Gregor closed his eyes and tipped his head back on the tree trunk. Victoria felt a cold wave wash over her, knowing it was not from the chilly wind. It was from inside, that icy stab spreading from deep in the center of her soul. She remembered the funeral. It was the gloomiest day of her life. Mother refused to cry, and Mabel could not seem to stop. She wrapped her arms around herself and looked at Gregor, waiting for him to go on. He did not for a while. They sat together, looking up at the dark sky and listening to the wind shake the trees and rustle the leaves irreverently.

"But soon I realized you did not know anything about a mermaid. You did not even know about the war. Your pa had done his job. You lived in a blissful bubble, free of worry or cares. Even after everything, I failed. I failed your father. I failed you. You are still here in this mess, and if they figure it out, the necklace won't matter anymore. Even beast law, even my insignia, can't protect you if Charlene finds out." Gregor looked miserable, and he continued to cradle his head in his hands. Victoria sat looking at him with shaking hands and a thumping heart.

CHAPTER 11

An Unexpected Flight

THEY SAT THERE FOR what seemed like an eternity until, apparently, they both fell asleep because the next thing she knew, it was bright early morning shining in on her face. She opened her eyes, and once again she felt the licking of Milo, his fluffy hair tickling her neck. Then she remembered they had finally made their way back to Gregor's tree house, climbing the steps wearily. She was tucked into the bed in his tree house. When she sat up and looked around, she realized Gregor must have slept on the couch because a blanket and his pillow were in a wrinkled pile.

Gregor came into the room. His face was all healed and his limp was nonexistent. He had two more bowls of vivid green mush with the orange berries with blue leaves.

"Please tell me what this is," she said groggily as she sat up and took a bowl between both her hands, pushing Milo from licking her face.

"It is a sort of grain like you have in the valley. I think you will like it. I made it into a mush, and these are otricoli berries. Their slight tangy sweetness compliments it well," he said cheerfully as though last night's confession did not loom over them. She was waiting for him to talk about it, but he seemed intent on keeping her focused on the food in her hands. So, despite her impulse to throw it on the floor again, she listened to the grumbling of her stomach and took a small bite. It tasted like oatmeal, and the orange berries were strangely delicious. He seemed content to sit with her and eat together, so she allowed the peaceful moment to linger.

Then he stood and slung that leather bag with the *G* that matched her scar over his shoulder. He stood looking at her for a long moment as though he was trying to commit the image of her to memory.

"My aunt, One-Eyed Giselle, told me you met yesterday. She has agreed to come bring you more fresh food tomorrow and keep an eye on you." He said with a bit of flourish. Victoria was not amused. "She helped raise me. She would laugh at that." Gregor stammered quickly. He cleared his throat.

"Anyway, I should be back with Mabel before too long." He said but his voice was a bit shaky. "But if I do not return, she said she will deliver my final wish, for my trusted friend Brawn to escort you to Plimsoll or home, whichever you choose." Gregor turned to leave, and Victoria slammed the bowl down hard enough to get his attention.

"I came up with a plan to save Mabel," Gregor said.

"Well, she is my sister. I have to help," Victoria said.

"I know you think you are helpful, but Naphtali is a dangerous place. Then add the fact Charlene is there and the maze run is scheduled to commence tomorrow night—" Gregor tried to explain quickly, stepping to the door. "You are no help until you have read the entire journal and these other books." He gestured toward the stack he had set on the table, which Victoria just now realized was sitting there.

"I won't be caught up reading while Mabel faces this maze thing."

"See, you do not even know what the Full Moon Maze Run is. There is so much to learn before you can expect to even have a chance of being more helpful than a liability," Gregor said.

"I am coming," she said flatly.

"No, you are not," he said.

Victoria stood and pointed to her cheek. "You owe me!" she said.

Gregor looked at her face, and although the mark was no longer there, he knew what she meant. His face softened, the shame clearly visible. He could not bring himself to look at her in the eye, and Victoria knew she had him. She stood and crossed to gather the cloak and boots Snal had given her. She gave Milo another pet and followed Gregor.

They started out walking as the sunlight weakly popped over the tree line, the frost covered leaves crunching a bit under their feet.

"Please, prepare me for the city of Naphtali." Victoria asked.

"It isn't a city. It is a harvest outpost, a collection site," Gregor said. "The nomadic humans who have been captured and those who Charlene pulls from her city get funneled there to be, um, harvested," Gregor said with a heavy grimace.

"Harvested?" She gulped, feeling her hands shaking and anger rising inside.

"Yes, a living supply of fresh blood. They extract blood from them as often as they can without killing them so they can continue to produce," Gregor said, his face souring.

"And when they can't produce any longer?" She struggled to find the strength to take another step and sat down on the nearest overturned log, covered in a thin layer of frost.

"Every full moon, they host the maze run," he said, and she put up her hand. She did not wish to hear anymore. Her imagination running wild at the thought of Mabel being put in a maze made her stomach clench.

"It is a horrible and shameful place," Gregor said.

"When you become king, you will change it?" she said encouragingly. Gregor gave a half-hearted chuckle and then sighed.

"Yes, I am called the Beast Prince but not because I am next in line. I am the son of the current Beast King. Any beast can overthrow the king and assume his throne at any time. If I want to be king, I have to enact bellum against him. But with a demesne that large, it is a death bellum," Gregor said. "Two enter, and only one is allowed to leave alive."

"Has anyone tried against your father?" she asked. Gregor nodded, beckoning for her to stand and continue to walk.

"A few," He said, obviously not wanting to relive the memories any further.

"What happens if your father dies outside the bellum, from old age or disease?" Victoria asked.

"That is unlikely for at least another century," Gregor said. "My pa is in his prime, but that would be a bellum tournament. Any beast could try for it, and it would not be a death bellum because there would not be a reigning king to defend." Victoria nodded, standing and falling in step beside him. They continued to walk.

"Why are we going to Naphtali without the necklace?" she asked. "As much as I hate Gor, we should be helping him track down the Goblin Queen, so we can trade the ruby for Mabel."

"That will not be necessary," Gregor said as he lifted a small black velvet bag from his pocket and tossed it to her. She loosened the ribbon of the drawstring, the small key winked at her in the gray winter light.

"But this isn't a sure thing, Mabel still has to get inside the maze," she said.

"I will get Mabel out secretly. When she doesn't come out, they will assume she got—"

"Eaten?" Victoria said, her voice rising. "There is a chance, a very high probability, that she will get eaten! We should go get the necklace. It is the only way to make sure Mabel is safe."

"We do not have time. The maze hunt is tomorrow night. We do not have time for any detours." He said.

"Well, at least let me hold the key," she said. Gregor slipped it back into his pocket and began to walk again. "That way you have to take me with you, you cannot leave me somewhere behind."

"No, we only have one shot at this, and I have been in the maze before. I know where the door is. It is small and hidden and won't open without this key," he said. "It will be the best way to save Mabel."

"Wait, why have you been in the maze?" Victoria froze as the implications lingered heavy in the air.

"Before I met your father, I was not a good man," Gregor said. He hung his head in shame, shoving his hands deep into his pockets. Gregor stood before her, vulnerable. He was scared of what she thought of him. Victoria looked at him, from the top of his messy hair to his loose cotton shirt, down past his large belt fastening his trousers, then to his boots. They were muddy and scuffed. All the lingering anger she felt toward him faded, feeling as though this was the first time she was truly seeing him.

Everything clicked into place, like the time Victoria had been constructing a puzzle in the parlor, but half the pieces had been scattered under the rug. She had just overturned it and found the unsolved portion of Gregor. She selected her next words very carefully.

"You are a good man," Victoria said. He did not meet her eyes, but Victoria had come to expect that of him. He was incredibly brave when faced with physical confrontation, but any sort of emotional encounter seemed to make him cower behind that stone-set jaw of his, becoming rigid and silent.

"But giving the necklace to Charlene is the best way to save Mabel," Victoria said, refusing to take another step.

Gregor looked at her with a frown. He cast a glance up to the heavens and then back down at her. "You are so stubborn. Do you really think she is going to just hand over Mabel after you give her the necklace? The key is our only shot, and since you do not know where the door is, you are going to get Mabel and yourself killed," Gregor said.

"Give me the key," Victoria demanded, her hand outstretched.

"You can carry it for now," Gregor explained and shook his head as he pulled the velvet bag from his pocket and dropped it into her hand. She opened it to make sure the key was inside, causing him to suck his teeth at her mistrust. She tucked it inside her skirt pocket with a satisfied smile. Victoria started walking again, and Gregor fumed behind her.

"You do not know the way to Naphtali, and I will not take you until you promise not to try to negotiate with Charlene. You must remain hidden and let me save Mabel," Gregor said.

"Well, then I will just ask for directions. I am sure someone is bound to come along and want to help me give Charlene the location of the exact thing she has been canvassing this entire cursed mountain for!" Victoria said forcefully. "I am sure she knows where the Goblin Queen lives?"

"You are going to get everyone killed," Gregor said.

Victoria kept walking. She could hear him sputtering behind her. She just continued to walk, determined to save Mabel herself. Then she could not hear Gregor's footsteps any longer. She looked back to see she was completely alone. The forest seemed much larger without him, and the shadows in between the brush seemed taller now.

"Very childish," she shouted back. She was sure he was hiding nearby. So she continued onward with her arms crossed and nose pointed high in the air for the proper dramatic effect, confidently.

After another few minutes, she slowed her pace.

"Gregor, I know I am stubborn," she said, letting the last two words be drizzled in sarcasm. "Just come out here and let's discuss a real plan together. We do not have time and Mabel is alone and—" Then something heavy landed on her shoulder, and she looked down to see a massive talon affixed to her, lifting her lopsidedly into the air. Another talon took hold of her other side, and she was flying up high past the treetops while she let loose several screams of hysteria. She spied Gregor being suspended in the sky by what looked like a giant owl. He was thrashing about wildly, but the bird kept flying despite his best efforts. There was a thin, shiny rope wrapped about Gregor's throat, and it seemed to be causing him pain. She wondered why he did not just transform—his weight alone would be impossible to carry. Then he could just drop to the tree canopy below. The creature turned, and Victoria screamed some more as she looked into the face of a human with the wings and markings of an owl. From his knees down, he had bird legs with powerful talons. She looked up above her and only could see the dark copper feathers of the bird creature holding her.

Perhaps she lost consciousness, but the next moment, she woke to the blasting chill of a mountain peak coming into focus. Realizing she was at the top of the Black Needles, she tried to gasp for air. It was hard to pull any in, and any she did stung like icy knives sliding down her chest.

Soon they landed on a carved-out balcony on top of a staggering tower that was adjoined to a grand palace as white as the snow blanketing it. There was no way to enter unless by flight. The sides were completely smooth, and there was not a single door or window for the first hundred feet of the building.

When they landed, she collapsed, her shaking legs unable to support her weight.

The owl man who had carried Gregor paid him no mind, but the eagle who had been carrying her looked annoyed with her, his piercing eyes searching her over. Then he turned to the owl, and they chatted in a strange language.

Then they just flew off, leaving them standing there at the edge of the stone balcony with nowhere to go.

Gregor was frantically scratching at his neck, trying to break the glinting cord. She quickly ran to him and tried to unlatch the heavy clasp.

"Oh, this is hot!" she exclaimed, letting it slip from her fingers. She gingerly grabbed it again, ignoring the burning sensation, and it took several long moments for her to finally release it and fling it away like a silvery serpent. Her fingers were singed as though she had been playing with a hot piece of coal. Gregor's neck now had a nasty burn encircling his entire throat. Luckily it was a thin, threadlike piece, so the burn was not very wide, but it was deep. Gregor was bleeding just above his Adam's apple, and the droplets trickled on his shirt.

Then she turned to the side and released her breakfast in its entirety down the side of the cliff. She had to hold her hair tightly because the wind was trying to throw it around. Gregor crawled to join her at the edge of the stone railing and retched. At least she was not the only one feeling the sensation. When they both were finished, they slumped down and sat clawing for their water bags from their satchels. Victoria was so grateful Gregor had packed such a large amount of water and that they had not lost them on the flight.

"What is this?" Victoria asked, touching the metal choker with the tip of her shoe, churning it in the dirt, and the wind took the upturned dust quickly away.

"A pure silver collar. It is near impossible to transform when wearing one," Gregor said, spitting a few more times over the edge and coughing.

Victoria staggered to her feet when she had the strength to stand and quickly gathered her skirting before it was taken by the wind. She grabbed at the collar with the edge of her skirt while holding the rest of her dress down with her other hand.

"Hey, it doesn't burn when I hold it in fabric," Victoria said.

"Yeah, it is only hot to direct skin contact. But if they try to place it after we have transformed, our hair will protect us. It is only useful to capture someone before they turn. Thankfully, they are very rare because they are made from pure silver, so I have only heard stories of them. I had never felt the burn of one until now. Toss it over the edge. I don't want this thing anywhere near me," Gregor said, and he turned around to retch again.

Victoria shoved the silver chain into the velvet bag that held the key, sending a sidelong glance toward Gregor to make sure he didn't see her stash it. Soon they were crouched together under the one alcove on the balcony. It was meant for decoration but did a decent job shielding the chilly blast of the wind from their faces.

"Why don't you rub your spit onto your neck and heal yourself?" Victoria asked.

"It won't help against a silver wound," Gregor said. Victoria was not sure what that meant but left it alone.

"What were those things?" Victoria asked.

"Avians," Gregor huffed. "They must have been spying on us. I was worried they would get involved. I should have not shown you the key. We could be halfway to Naphtali by now, but you had to stand and argue, distracting me!" Gregor snapped.

Victoria huffed at him and crossed her arms. "This is your fault. If you had just told me where to use the key, we could both work together to save Mabel," she said.

"Well, if you weren't so emotional and impulsive, I might have trusted you with it," he returned with an angry grunt, and they sat with their backs turned to each other for a long while.

Victoria took a deep breath and walked to the large door on the side of the tower. She rattled the massive knob in vain. She tried to sit away from him, but the chilly wind blast seemed to cut through her dress folds and her thick, green cloak felt nonexistent. She had to pull on it to reassure herself she was in fact wearing it.

Defeated, she slid back down beside Gregor, who did not acknowledge her in the slightest although their shoulders were touching. She pulled out her father's journal from her bag and began to read. After some time, the wind began to howl even louder, and she burrowed closer to Gregor's warmth but refused to break the silence until she read some disturbing passages.

"I am still mad at you, but it says here Avians are not one of the vegetarian kingdoms," she said, her voice cracking a bit.

"Nope, they are not one of the vegetarian kingdoms," he repeated flatly. Victoria shuddered.

"But they are most likely wanting the necklace," he assured her.

"Which we do not have," Victoria said glumly.

Gregor did not reply. After a while, the winter's chill was just too much. Gregor wrapped one arm about her, and she had abandoned trying to read altogether and buried her face into his chest because her nose was numb. She was too cold to worry about his bloodstained shirt rubbing against her hair. She pulled her legs up against his side, and eventually he brought his legs in from the edge of the alcove. They were like a wadded piece of taffy shoved underneath a tabletop, forgotten.

"Are they just going to let us freeze to death?" Victoria asked, struggling to pronounce the words through her chattering teeth.

"I will transform, and my fur will keep us both warm but before I do, I wanted to tell you," Gregor said and then paused, his voice tight from his clenched jaw.

"I have heard stories of the Avians . . ." He stopped himself and embraced her in a full bear hug, and she was not sure if it was to try to get them warmer or if he was trying to show affection.

"Whatever happens, I would never forgive myself if we died without you knowing—" he said and then the door flung open.

CHAPTER 12

A BIRD BRAIN

OUT STEPPED THE MOST spectacular creature Victoria had ever seen. She was tall with long black hair and had high cheekbones and lips seemingly chiseled by a master sculpture artist. Her large deep-set eyes sparkled like two golden coins under a heavy lash line. A massive pair of wings adorned her back, and at first, Victoria supposed it was some sort of costume, but as she turned, Victoria could see they were real. They seemed strangely too large for her small frame but then she reminded herself that birds have rather large wings, when she compared the rest of their bodies in proportion. Each movement the bird woman made was as though she was not making actual contact with the ground, although her brown-and-white wing tips swept the floor.

She wore a simple brown dress with a white bodice. There were absolutely no ribbons or lacing, not even a flourish of the stitches. It was the plainest dress she had ever seen in her life, yet the creature wore it with more confidence than Charlene had worn her exquisite ball gown.

"I am Elizabeth," she said, ignoring her hair sliding along her face in the wind. Her bizarre accent made it hard to understand, and Victoria had to sort the words out quickly in her mind before she nodded.

"I am Victoria, and this is—" Victoria began politely.

"I am not listening," Elizabeth interrupted. Her voice resonated into Victoria's ears, and she wished she would speak some more. She turned and, with a flick of her wrist, gestured her expectation for them to follow her inside.

It took a bit to convince her cold body to move, and she lopsidedly made her way to the warm entrance. Victoria could feel the heat rising out of the building, enticing her inside. Gregor followed, walking just as stiffly.

Despite the abysmal cry from her muscles, Victoria could not stop shifting her neck so she could continue to stare in astonishment at such an interesting creature. Elizabeth looked in every way human, walking on two human legs, which was odd because the other two Avians had bird legs and talons from the knees down. She had two human arms crossed tightly. From her shoulders jutted that lovely pair of long, powerful wings. They were decorated with the unmistakable spotted pattern of a female peacock, the black, brown, and white spots with just a splash of teal green near the base where the wings connected between her shoulder blades. Victoria reached out to quickly touch the feather closest to her, rubbing the silky strands between her fingertips.

"Why I never!" Elizabeth said, snatching her wing from Victoria's reach, looking at Victoria as though she tried to start her ablaze.

"I am sorry. They are so lovely," Victoria offered.

"Indeed, they are," Elizabeth said, straightening herself. As she turned to walk away, Victoria noticed she had a fan of tail feathers protruding from the base of her spine, right above where Victoria was sure her bottom began. The tail feathers were folded down, covering the back of her skirts down to the floor, and a few trailed out behind her like the train of a dress.

"And who are you?" Victoria asked the snowy white owl-looking Avian who just entered from one of the doors in the hallway. She recognized it as the one who had carried Gregor.

"Newel," he said and gave a gracious bow before falling in step with them.

"Watch out. They are feather-snatchers," Elizabeth said rudely, yet her voice was as though Victoria's ears were being wrapped in silk. It was soft and smooth.

"Oh, here you can just have one," Newel said cheerfully, and to Victoria's amazement, he yanked a feather from his wing and gave it to her. It was so incredibly soft and pure white as the snow.

"Oh, this is magnificent. Thank you!" she said, and he gave another bow with a wide smile.

"He is much nicer," Victoria whispered to Gregor, sending a wayward glance at Elizabeth. Gregor nodded in agreement with a small, amused smile. Just then another door opened, and the copper-colored bird who had carried Victoria stood with a gracious smile.

"What is your name?" Victoria asked, curious to see how he acted, trying to find a normal range of behavior for the Avians.

"I am Joshua," he said. Victoria looked at him and realized he was the one who had carried her. His coloring and the shape of his talons looked like an eagle's.

"It is a pleasure to meet you," Victoria said, giving him a curtsy. He saw she held a feather in her hand from Newel and asked if she wanted one of his as well, to Elizabeth's dismay. She nodded vigorously, and soon she was carrying two shiny feathers, one white as the snow and the other a lovely gold. It changed from gold to copper as she moved it in the candlelight.

Then following behind Joshua was a thin man without any wings.

"And are you, um . . . human?" she asked as she looked at his sun-kissed skin and bright-white, blond, curly locks. That is when she noticed his ears, slightly pointed upward where they should have been symmetrically rounded. The tip was subtle enough she had easily overlooked it before.

"I am, um, let me find the word humans use for us," he said, taking a moment to think. "Yes, I think you call us the word 'elf,' but—" he stopped short when he spied Gregor. Gregor stood looking at him, his nostrils flared. In an instant, Gregor sprang at the elf, swinging both fists in a furious rage. Gregor began to transform mid-fight, and soon he was a beast, blocking most of the hallway and shaking the poor man from side to side in his mouth. The man hollered out in a dismal cry of pain. Elizabeth stood back, leaning against the wall, looking almost bored while Joshua and Newel tried desperately to break the fight up. Suddenly there was a flash, and Gregor's entire chest was on fire. Gregor let out a howl of pain. He dropped to the ground and rolled until it was out, and the smell of burning hair stung her nose. Victoria realized the fire had come from the man. He was holding a strange blue glow in his palms.

By this time Newel had pulled the man to the side, flapping his wings hard to separate him from Gregor. Gregor was still snapping and growling. Victoria rushed over to Gregor because Joshua was now flapping his wings and screeching, keeping a worried eye on Gregor's fangs. The commotion had gathered the attention of other Avians, and they were rushing in with spears and arrows drawn. But Gregor was so intent on the man, he caught poor Joshua by the wing and whipped him out of the way in one powerful motion. Then an arrow grazed his neck, shearing a tuft of hair and making blood trickle. The Avian who had let loose the arrow was reaching for another quickly.

Fearing for Gregor's life, she darted to place herself between Gregor and his prey. She lifted her arm up as high as she could reach. She closed her eyes to help her ignore his snapping teeth. Her heart thumped painfully against her chest, but she was pretty sure Gregor would not hurt her.

Then she held her hand in place, shaking a bit but denying herself to give in to the impulse to pull away.

She placed a hand on Gregor's snout and then pulled it down. She continued to pull his foaming jaws toward her until his large ears were pressed against her chest, making him listen to the pounding of her heart. She stroked his hair softly, trying to calm him. Soon it was Gregor's human head between her hands. He was breathing hard, and his forehead was still hot to the touch. Everyone stood watching. Victoria looked around to meet their puzzled gaze. Soon whispering erupted between them, their eyes shifting from her to Gregor and back again.

Joshua walked toward them with a bit of a limp. He was banged up from Gregor's assault but somehow managed to retain a smile as he handed Gregor his torn clothes. Gregor dressed himself best he could while muttering under his breath, sending scowls over Joshua's wings to the man.

"Who is that?" Victoria asked as Gregor finished putting on his shirt.

"Rhamy. Rhamy Lumpkin," Gregor said with a sneer, brushing the burned hair off his chest.

"Beast Prince, always a pleasure," Rhamy Lumpkin said sarcastically while he clutched his nose, his other arm dangled beside him limply. It was obviously dislocated or broken. Either way he continued to groan and grimace in pain. The Avians whispered all around her as she stepped back from Gregor to pick up her bag.

"What are you doing here?" Gregor asked.

"I was invited here, same as you," Rhamy said. Gregor scoffed but allowed Joshua to continue to lead them down the hallway, Newel pushing the grunting and groaning Rhamy further ahead, placing a greater distance between them. But they ended up in the same circular room, seated at the largest table she had ever seen. One of the Avians served refreshments as another tended Rhamy's arm by wrapping it in a sling.

Victoria looked down at the table. It was covered in pieces and figures.

At first glance, Victoria thought it must be a complex and intricate game of some kind. It was similar to the board in her father's study, but upon further examination, she realized the pieces were made from precious metals, gold and silver, and studded with jewels. The pieces were placed on a network of carved grooves and embellishments to make a very detailed pattern. As she examined it further, she realized it was a map.

Victoria continued to stare, mindful of her elbows. She did not want to bump any of the tiny, handcrafted trees or buildings. There was one small sliver of it she recognized. It was the valley at the base of the mountains. Her hometown. It was such a small portion, her entire world she had spent her childhood roaming was represented by the carved wood in a space no larger than her hand. The rest of the map was foreign, and she gawked at it.

"Sis Meta," one of the Avians said as they placed a cup beside her with a gentle nod. Victoria heard the phrase, as they were walking here, with their fingers pointed at her. Then someone else repeated it again to another Avian, and then they both stood staring at her directly with wide eyes. They continued whispering.

"Why do they keep calling me that?" Victoria asked Joshua as another Avian gave her a curtsy and whispered it again.

"It means soother. You soothed the beast and now they think you are an enchantress," Rhamy said from across the table. Joshua confirmed this with an excited nod. He was about to open his mouth when Gregor's gruff voice cut in.

"Don't speak," Gregor shot the words at Rhamy like daggers. "You do not get to speak to her."

"Oh, does Gregor decide who you talk to now?" Rhamy asked curtly, turning to face Victoria squarely, cutting Gregor from his line of view. "I did not realize beast law included speech." He said "beast law" with mocking embellishment.

"I can talk to whomever I wish," Victoria responded quickly, squaring her shoulders. "I am especially curious to talk with you and ask how many times you tried to break into my home."

"Oh, I see he has wasted no time in spinning the story in his favor," Rhamy said. "Did he not mention it was he who attacked me? I almost lost my leg to the infection after he bit me. Now look at my arm!" he said, clutching his injury.

"The council is about to meet," Elizabeth announced.

"Who is the council?" Victoria asked.

"It is supposed to be one ambassador from each of the five kingdoms. But we have not had a meeting with anyone sent by the Beast King or Monstress in nearly a century." Elizabeth gestured for all of them to follow her. Seeing as she did not want to be pushed back out on that ledge again, she obediently followed.

"Monstress?" Victoria asked.

"The mistress of monsters, we just threw it together and made a little nickname; she hates it," Rhamy chuckled.

Newel and Joshua assumed positions between Rhamy Lumpkin and Gregor. The lineup ended up pushing Gregor the farthest behind, and he seemed anxious, which made Victoria wonder if she should be more so. She oddly did not feel very concerned. Joshua and Newel seemed perfectly civilized.

They crossed through a large cavern with children playing. A few older Avians watched the younger play. She noticed the children did not have wings. The boys had talons instead of feet, but the girls looked completely human. The boys dressed in brightly colored clothes and the girls were all in plain brown or white linen. Then there were several teenaged kids sitting around. The odd scene made Victoria stop and stare. They were balding on the top of their heads, and their skin was peeling and flaking. Each of them held a large hump on their back, forcing them to hunch a bit forward. But they did not hide their splotches on their faces.

"Are they sick?" Victoria asked Elizabeth and gestured to them.

"No, of course not," Elizabeth said with another look of annoyance.

"They look very sick," Victoria said in a whisper, glancing back at them.

"You do not know anything. They are Avians coming of age."

"Have you ever heard the tale of the ugly duckling?" Rhamy asked.

Victoria nodded, and then when she caught his eye, she realized he had made a joke and, despite herself, she could not resist a small giggle.

"Oh," Victoria said after a moment. "This lady I know, Charlene, from the valley below, has an Avian. Her name is Ann, and she works as a servant in her palace."

"What? Charlene has an Avian?" Elizabeth stopped walking and stared straight at Victoria, the first interest she had taken in Victoria all day. "This is a serious matter. Are you sure?"

"Yes. She looks just like they do. Wait, how do you know Charlene?" Victoria asked. Elizabeth was no longer listening to her; she was walking and writing something down.

"The Monstress, the Mistress of Monsters, she has your generation of humans call her Charlene currently," Rhamy said. Victoria was grateful for the information but still was wary of him, so she did not reply.

When Victoria looked, she saw one of the mothers come to the children. She had long white hair and beautiful white wings with skin delicate and soft. Victoria smiled to herself at the thought of Ann. She would be beautiful someday soon. Elizabeth rushed them forward down another hallway.

"Just continue on." Elizabeth pointed in the direction. "We will discuss that matter later."

Eventually the large hallway ended at two massive red doors with engraved designs all along the edges. The large golden handles sparkled in the torchlight, and two of the bird people pulled the doors open.

"Stay here, Beast Prince, only those who are trusted are welcome beyond this point," Elizabeth said while two Avians blocked his path, their spears outstretched but their eyes were filled with fear.

"He is fine," Victoria said. "I trust him with my life."

"If it was up to me, you would not be here either," Elizabeth said

Victoria entered the large room, feeling vulnerable without Gregor. An Avian sat on a throne at the very end of the room with other thrones arranged on either side. They walked past crowds of Avians. Victoria noticed all the eyes were on her, and they rustled their feathers in impatience as she slowly made her way down the aisle.

"That is my father, Eryngo, adviser to the queen," Rhamy said, pointing to the tall man with curly platinum blond hair, the same hair color as Rhamy's. Both had clean-shaven faces. Beside him sat one particularly beautiful elf with a large crown on her head. It was intricately designed in pure silver, which Victoria had taken a point to notice.

Her long brilliant ombre lavender hair fell in waves of ringlets with jewels woven through in a delicate pattern. She wore a flowing light blue gown with a long train. Victoria recognized the leaf symbol from the journal carved on the ring she displayed proudly on her finger.

The third elf Victoria was unsure what position he held because he sat quietly. He wore a similar crown as the queen, but it was bolder. His hair was a vivid blue and even his eyebrows and short beard were the same shade. Victoria could not help but gawk until a large creature caught her eye and she recognized him.

It was the same Gregor had spoken to in Omnia. Victoria tried to remember his name. He stood taller than any other in the room, and his arms and chest were bare. Under his belly button, a coat of light tan fur grew thick covering four powerful legs with hooves black as night. A large rack of antlers stood as though tree branches out of his head. He had thick, stubby curly ringlets of hair on his head and wore a goatee of the same dark russet hue.

She could barely blink as he started forward, walking as he shifted his weight from one front hoof to the other. To his left stood a she-elk. Her bosom was covered by a decorative bralette of jewels and woven leaves. Her long thick waves of brunette hair flowed to her belly, almost completely hiding her bare stomach and back. She had large brown eyes. She wore a necklace of flowers, and its design reminded Victoria of the first tender shoots and leaves of spring. Her arms and right cheek bore painted patterns onto her skin with a reddish dye. She had the same emblem on her neck under her right ear as the man. As Victoria looked closer, she identified it as a hoofprint. The same symbol was carved into the thick wooden crest hanging behind them.

She looked to the Avian throne, where a feather was centered in the middle of their crest emblem. Victoria noticed two thrones were left empty. One was carved with the familiar design of the moon and the other had the sun she had seen in the journal.

"No place for humans?" she asked in what she deemed a whisper, but the entire crowd fell silent, trying to stifle their snickers. Elizabeth was the only one to give a haughty laugh out loud.

"Humans? Humans do not hold the brain capacity to be a part of the council," she declared with conviction. The crowded hall grunted in agreement. Victoria took a long moment to ward off her intense flush of anger and swallowed the series of responses flooding her mind.

"This throne is for Brutus, King of the Beasts," Joshua explained quickly, pointing to the carved moon symbol.

"And this is the Monstress's throne, Charlene," he said, pointing to the sun emblem.

"Where are they?" Victoria asked.

"We are at war," he said curtly.

Joshua imploringly looked at Victoria to not ask another question. She held her tongue. She looked respectfully down at the marble below her feet as Elizabeth began the introductions.

"Empress Theron, Richard's daughter, Victoria, is here," Elizabeth said and bowed low. Victoria quickly followed with the same proper curtsy she had been taught since she was old enough to stand. This seemed to please the Empress because she smiled slightly.

Empress Theron was a tall, thin old woman with long white-and-gray hair parted in the middle and sweeping down to her waist. Her wings were white with gray tips. Her reddened, sagging neck made Victoria think she resembled a stork. She stood from her throne.

"Daughter of Richard, I welcome you here today," she said and spread her arms in unison with her long white wings in a receiving gesture.

"We have all gathered together. I am Theron, Empress of the Avians. Ursinia, queen the elves, her husband Jonquil, and her adviser, Eryngo." Rhamy's father and the queen's husband stood in unison and bowed deeper.

"Lord Brawn and Lady Danika of the Elken Folk with their newborn, Emilia," she continued as the Elken nodded toward her, a small Elken girl with golden hair shyly standing behind her mother's rear legs, white spots freckling her coat.

"I have heard that you have already met the Monstress and the Beast King. We celebrate your escape in both encounters," Empress Theron said.

"Thank you," Victoria said. She once again tried not to stare at every creature in the room impolitely, reminding herself to close her mouth.

CHAPTER 13

A BIASED COUNCIL

"WE LIVE IN UNCERTAIN times. War and destruction plague this land. Your father encouraged us to raise our expectation of your mother's kind by showing us humans have more courage and intellect than we thought conceivable. We realize you possess the shape-changing capacity as he had and want to make you into a powerful ally. I know you are considered the Beast Prince's demesne under their beast law, but we hope to reach an understanding with him. Rhamy Lumpkin has vouched for the Beast Prince today. He says he can be trusted, and I sure hope that is correct. The Black Needles must have peace again." Empress Theron now rested her hands on Victoria's shoulders, a slight smile crossing her face.

"We have gathered here in this sacred place full of only those trusted to also hear the location of the Princess of the Sea," Empress Theron announced. "So please, speak now." Everyone in the room watched eagerly as she approached a table and motioned for Victoria to do the same. A large parchment map with labels and every lake and river in the

Black Needles were crossed out with a red ink. Victoria noted the map had her small village circled with "Richard" written in black ink over the area. She followed the roads to Charlene's estate and noticed it was completely drawn in red with Charlene's name in large letters. Then she gazed over the map, and her eyes rested on King Brutus's palace ruins.

"Is this us here now?" Victoria pointed and asked. Empress Theron nodded. They currently stood on the peak of the tallest mountain of the Black Needles.

Her mind was trying to memorize the map, so when Theron spoke again, she reluctantly pulled her eyes away.

She looked at Victoria and again at the map expectantly. Victoria looked to Rhamy, and he exchanged a look of confusion. Others gathered closer, watching. She raised her hand to move a strand of red hair from her eyes, and everyone gasped at her movement. She dropped her hand back to her side, and Elizabeth huffed angrily.

"Where is she?" Elizabeth asked. "Where did your father take her?"

"Um . . . I am not sure you know this, but my father is no longer with us," Victoria said nervously and added the last part, unsure how much they knew.

"We know that!" Elizabeth said impatiently. "He died from her bite, but where did he hide Lily?"

"I never saw a mermaid," she said nervously. They sighed and looked to each other in distress.

"Did Richard leave any clues at all?" Ursinia asked. Victoria mulled the question over in her head. She looked about nervously and tried to stay her fidgeting hands. All their eyes turned to look at her, anxiously waiting.

"I don't know," she admitted. The entire room gasped and whispering broke out.

"Why couldn't Richard have had a son?" one deep voice asked, echoing in Victoria's head loudly. The entire room exploded into a series of fights at this comment. Their voices echoed off the marble walls and hit Victoria's ears, making her shrink away from the crowd. She covered her head and Empress Theron squeezed her shoulders.

"Princess Lily, uh . . .," Empress Theron said, clearing her throat worriedly. "She is the answer to our salvation. She is the last mermaid, our only chance."

"Why is one fish so important?" Victoria asked. "Just ask the elves for another one from their hidden stash."

"I am afraid Charlene has raided 'our secret stash' as you call it. There are no remaining mermaids," Ursinia said in dismay. "Charlene's hunger for power grows and she is conquering more and more of the other kingdom's land. She must be stopped."

Empress Theron turned to walk out of the council room with Victoria. Once they were in the hallway, Gregor stood up from the ground, his hands had been tied behind his back. He looked furious.

"Let Gregor loose!" Victoria said. At this point, Elizabeth had followed them out and was standing with her arms folded with a sour expression.

"Only precautionary, don't want a beast running freely through my palace," Empress Theron said.

"I did not want to be here. I was choked and carried here without my permission," Gregor said, lifting his chin to display his neck burns. Theron gave a sidelong glance at Elizabeth, who looked annoyed.

"You took a collar?" Theron asked.

"We didn't have time to cordially invite them," Elizabeth shrugged. Empress Theron, although looking very distraught, did not push it any further. Instead, she summoned for someone to bring in a sort of medical kit, and Gregor let them apply ointments while they continued the discussion.

"I might not know where this mermaid is, but I have the need of your help," Victoria said. "Charlene has my mother and sister."

"Charlene has your family?" Theron asked.

"Yes," Victoria was relieved she was listening.

"Well, *had* your family," Elizabeth sneered.

"Yes, I am afraid Elizabeth is correct. I am sorry, my dear," Theron said.

"I am sure they both are still alive," Victoria said. "You are not going to help me?"

"Richard must have had some sort of plan?" Empress Theron asked, pushing her face right into Victoria's. Their noses almost touched. Victoria shook her head, pulling away.

"Did he at least teach you how to morph?" Elizabeth asked curiously.

"No," she said, and once again her answer was greeted with sighs of concern.

"I will not help you look for the mermaid until we rescue my sister and my mother," Victoria said, trying to stand up tall and look confident.

"No. You already told us you have no idea where the mermaid is, and both your mother and sister are already dead. You just have not accepted it," Elizabeth said.

"I have someone who will help you master your transformation; his name is Plimsoll." Empress Theron explained. "Perhaps this is all we can do for now." She gestured, as a man walked into view, and Victoria gasped.

"Hello, Victoria," a familiar voice made Victoria feel like she was whirling around the room in tight circles.

"What are you doing here, Professor Carter?" Victoria asked the one they were referring to as Plimsoll suspiciously. Gregor looked at her for answers.

"This is my teacher. He has been teaching me and Mabel history, math, and harp," Victoria explained. "My mother hired him right after father's death, worried we needed a formal education without father around to teach us himself." She remembered all the long lectures he had given them, the monotonous voice of his reading from the large books.

He now wore the same robes as the elves, and his head was completely shaved smooth.

Gregor looked even more stunned than she did.

"How did you enter the house without me seeing you?" Gregor asked. "I was there, standing guard . . ." Gregor's voice dropped off as he tried to understand.

"You are very young, Gregor. You get distracted easily. It was hardly an effort to slip in and out daily without you seeing me. I knew if you saw me, you would instantly know she and Mabel possessed the same talent as Richard, and I had yet to trust you with such a secret. But you have proved yourself trustworthy and noble, Rhamy tells me. Everything would be perfect had you not lost the necklace to the goblins," Plimsoll said.

"You were watching us the entire time?" Victoria swung around to look Rhamy Lumpkin in the eye. Gregor looked ready to pop off his seat, but Plimsoll glided closer to him and rested one hand on his shoulder knowingly.

"I assigned him to follow you. I needed to get Victoria somewhere safe we could train without the fear of being found," Plimsoll said. Victoria was still reeling.

"Mr. Carter—I mean, Plimsoll, why did you not just tell me everything and start training me there at the house instead of reading all those boring history books?" she asked, flinging her hands into the air.

"You were not ready. I wanted to give you knowledge and teach you important lessons of the past while preserving your childhood for as long as we could, to give you better judgment and a strong moral compass. You and Mabel are the only ones of your kind, and we must tread very carefully," Plimsoll said in a calm voice that did nothing to help settle her.

"You could have warned me before we left for the ball," Victoria said. "Hey, so you are going to Charlene's place? She might want to kill your entire family!" Victoria ranted.

"I did not expect a piece of jewelry to strike her interest. I also did not expect Gor and Gregor to enter the palace. I assumed it would be just a ball, another childhood milestone," Plimsoll said. "All of it is in the past. Let us eat and then we can get some sleep. Tomorrow we can go to the training courts, and we can begin your transformation practices," Plimsoll said.

"Do you know what the necklace does?" Victoria asked.

"No, the mere fact Charlene is so keen on it makes us all wary," Plimsoll said.

Everyone nodded in agreement, and soon they were moving down to the dining hall. They chained Gregor to the heavy wooden chair and Victoria anxiously sat beside him.

"Is this really necessary?" Victoria asked with a huff as she shook his chains. Elizabeth just nodded.

Victoria couldn't identify most of the food, but she was too hungry to turn away. The first thing she tried was a bright-red lumpy jam with black flecks, which she took for strawberry seeds. She spat it out immediately while Rhamy laughed.

"Is that food?" she asked, the intense heat still stinging her tongue.

"Yes," Rhamy said, scooping a spoonful onto a slice of toast and eating it. "Fire beetle is an acquired taste." Victoria's stomach lurched.

"Okay, what about this? Is this really beef or is it unicorn meat?" she asked sarcastically as she stabbed at a seared steak.

"That is beef," he laughed heartily.

Victoria breathed a sigh of relief, cutting herself a bite. The juicy flavor danced in her mouth, awaking her senses she had almost forgotten in the past few days of hunger.

"This is delicious!" she said, taking another bite.

"These are the famous steaks of the renowned Avian chef. His marinade is a secret, but my father and I have concluded the special ingredient is goblin blood," Rhamy said with a smile. Victoria stopped chewing immediately. Rhamy laughed quickly before she could lift her napkin to spit, the joke now apparent.

"Really?" Victoria asked, feeling ashamed of her gullibility.

"I hate goblins," she said between bites. She wanted to ignore Rhamy, she was still so upset he had spied on her and Gregor's obvious loathing of him made her leery, but Rhamy had said he trusted Gregor to the council. And Rhamy's hearty laugh was contagious.

"One is not so bad, but, as you know, they usually hunt in a horde," Rhamy said, lathering another piece of toast with a thick layer of fire beetle jam.

"Gross!" Victoria said, and Rhamy exaggerated taking a big bite, moaning as he tore the bread with his teeth. Then he laughed and she giggled, despite the irritated glance Gregor cast.

She imagined trying to explain it to Mabel, knowing she would probably laugh so hard her eyes would water. Then the image of Mabel sitting in whatever prison Charlene had put her in at Naphtali landed hard.

Victoria looked at Gregor, who had only taken a few bites while he eyed Rhamy angrily. Brawn stood beside him, and they spoke again in the same language she had heard them speaking before. Gregor seemed less tense speaking with him, and she realized they must be longtime friends. Elizabeth ate quickly and seemed annoyed to be sitting at the same table as them. Plimsoll took a chair across the table from Victoria.

"All this time, you never bothered to tell me you were an elf!" Victoria said with a huge sigh.

"All in due time. If it was up to me, you would not have been plunged into this world for a few more years after I had a chance to explain things properly from the beginning" Plimsoll said.

"Okay, you teach me how to transform into anything, and I can go save Mabel and my mother," Victoria said excitedly.

"Training of this magnitude should take at least a decade or so to master, and perhaps we will be ready for battle before the next generation of humans start producing their offspring, increasing her supply of blood and giving her another tier of supply to handle another region of monsters to join her army," Plimsoll said.

"She has been turning her humans at an alarming rate. Although they are weaker than a monster born of monster parents, they still are formidable," Ursinia added.

"When they get old enough, it does not matter how they became a monster. Remember, Charlene herself was bitten long enough ago that it does not matter," Plimsoll said.

"Wait, so if you plan on me training here, what about Mabel and my mother?" Victoria asked. "You yourself keep saying Mabel is a shape-changer, but you do not seem too keen on saving her."

"Well, if she really is at Naphtali like you said, there is no chance of rescuing her. She will be dead in a fortnight. We do not have to worry about Charlene using her as a weapon against us," Empress Theron said as politely as she could, but Victoria was now raging. She stood.

"You all are willing to let her die as long as I am here to be your puppet?" she said, feeling uneasy, and her temples pounded as she looked at each person there in the room, many not wanting to meet her eyes, except Gregor.

"I do not think Victoria is interested in staying that long here," Gregor said, standing best he could with the weight of the chains. "But we can stay for some training sessions."

Victoria nodded her head quickly, then stopped. "No, we do not have time. You said yourself the maze run is tomorrow night," Victoria whispered to him.

"I can go and try to get Mabel. You stay here and train," Gregor whispered back.

"Wait, you said try," Victoria said, her voice rising. "Like you have already decided with everyone else here that she is already gone."

Gregor shook his head. "Victoria, you have nothing to offer, no weapons, or even basic defense skill. There is no way for you to help Mabel right now. If you train, you can become formidable. You help Mabel the best by staying here," Gregor explained softly.

"Well, my training does nothing for Mabel if she is dead," Victoria said, no longer whispering.

"Thank you for the history lessons," she snapped at Plimsoll before gathering her bag.

Everyone looked at them with concern, and two of the Avian guards were now drawing out their swords. Victoria felt that was a little dramatic. Strangely, Plimsoll looked calm. He spoke to Gregor and Brawn in the same language they were using during the dinner. Gregor nodded with a heavy sigh. Victoria watched as Gregor slipped off his insignia ring, bearing the *G* Victoria was starting to despise, and placed it in Plimsoll's outstretched hand.

"She is my demesne, and I leave her in the hands of Plimsoll until I return," Gregor said forcefully. He dared not look at Victoria, but she sent him a terrible scowl anyway, huffing angrily.

"I am not to be passed around like some pawn piece!" Victoria shouted.

"No, I am sorry you are staying. By official Avian decree and by the beast law, Gregor has the authority to enact bellum proxy in his stead to Plimsoll," Empress Theron said. "We can't risk you falling into Charlene or Brutus's hands, especially if Gor convinces them of what you are."

Victoria was reeling at the thought of them all spying on her and now trying to control her. She shook her head and began to back out the door.

"I am afraid you are staying here, fraction," Elizabeth said with a hideous smirk drawing over her beautiful face.

"Elizabeth, please do not use that sort of slander in my court," Empress Theron said with a strict click of her tongue. Elizabeth fell silent, bowing her head. Victoria was not even sure why she should be offended and just continued to try to leave.

Two Avian guards pushed her with the spears back into the room, and Victoria looked at Gregor for help.

"Gregor, you can't let them do this!" she pleaded.

Gregor looked at her timidly. "I'm sorry, Victoria. It's the best I can do," he said. "I will get Mabel and bring her back here," he promised, but Victoria no longer trusted him. She cast another scowl at him, making sure he saw it this time.

"She has his mark, but she controls him," Ursinia observed out loud, looking from Gregor to Victoria in confusion. Plimsoll sat where he was, watching everything with that continued strange look of calmness, as though he were watching a simple play and was merely curious.

"Plimsoll, please. You know my mother and sister. Are you not even going to discuss an attempt at a rescue?" Victoria asked.

"My dear, there are larger things here at play," Plimsoll said.

She was pushed down three more hallways before they placed her in a small room with a bed and a hot bath drawn up. They shut the door behind her tightly, and the moment their footsteps receded, she stomped around, rattling the doorknob. Tired, she looked out the large glass window to see the entire mountain below her. The view was incredible.

Despite the beautiful landscape before her, she still huffed and puffed until she finally sat down on the bed. There was a fresh new dress with thick wool stockings and heavy cloak they had laid out for her. She looked down at her own ripped and ragged dress. The claw marks from Joshua's talons had all but tattered her sleeves.

Then she looked to the bathtub, the hot steam rising from the water. It would be nice to finally wash off all the dust and grime from the flight here. She hoped they never did that to her again. But Gregor had basically given them permission to do whatever they wanted while he was gone—who knew how many flying trips they would subject her to. Her stomach lurched at the mere thought.

She undressed and stood before the giant mirror, inspecting her shoulder. The bubbling skin had all but healed, no more flaking or blistering. Only the clearly imprinted fancy *G* with the crown embellishments remained raised against her soft, peach skin.

She felt another rush of indignation. She clawed at it again and again until the *G* was gone, covered in a mess of torn skin and scabbing blood. Then she stepped into the tub, reminding herself it was mere necessity, but soon she was submerged and soaking with her eyes closed, feeling slightly relaxed.

There was a knock on the door.

"Who is there?" she asked, poking her head out of the bubbles.

"It's me, Gregor," Gregor said.

"Do not come in!" she yelled as she scampered out of the bathtub and quickly found the robe they had laid out for her. Only when she was decent did she call out for him to enter, making sure her arms were crossed tightly and she was standing as tall as she could.

"Victoria," he said softly. He tried to step farther inside the room from the doorway, but she put up her hand and he stood still, filling the doorframe. His hands were bound behind his back. Guards were with him, but they kept themselves in the hallway respectfully, giving some privacy.

"I am going to get Mabel and bring her back here. I need the key," he said. Victoria pulled it from the pouch, careful to keep the silver collar hidden. She held the key out.

"Take it," Victoria said smugly. Gregor just looked at her while he shifted his shoulders to emphasize his restraints. Victoria huffed while she unbuttoned his chest pocket, deliberately slow as she dropped the black velvet pouch inside. She patted the pocket three times. He just stared at her all the while, looking utterly dumbfounded by her audacity.

"Please concentrate on the training tomorrow," he said anxiously.

"Take me with you. She is my sister. I need to be with her," Victoria said, crossing her arms again.

"I can't do that," Gregor said sadly. "My hands are literally tied. They are escorting me out of the castle. They don't trust me. Newel is flying me down to the bottom, and from there I can travel quicker at nighttime as a beast. There is a blizzard coming, and if I do not leave now, I will be caught in it. You would only slow me down." He sat looking at her, begging for a kind word or some sort of expression of forgiveness. This further infuriated her, but she knew her feelings needed to be pushed aside for Mabel. She took a deep breath and started again.

"Please, Gregor, you could easily break through those restraints, you are so big and strong," Victoria said with the softest voice she could muster, walking her fingers along his chest.

"Stick to being angry, you are terrible at flirting," Gregor said, unaffected by her attempt at charming him.

"You can't just leave me here. Take me with you. After all, I am your demesne," she said the last word with taunting exaggeration. At this, Gregor flared his nostrils and furrowed his brows. He stepped closer and bent to pull his face close to hers.

"You are right. You are mine, and I am commanding you to stay here," Gregor said, his voice low and menacing.

Victoria flinched. Gregor's face softened immediately as he read fear on her.

"I am not yours! I will never be yours!" she said and slipped the robe down to display her shoulder, all torn and the G no longer visible. His eyes widened at the bloody wound but he did not say anything.

"Get out!" Victoria screamed and pointed to the door.

Gregor nodded, and as he left, Victoria could not resist the anger rising inside her. It was red-hot and started in the pit of her belly and rushed through her chest and throat until she was spitting the words out, her tongue sizzling as it pronounced them with so much disdain it burned.

"I hate you," she heard herself say.

Immediately she regretted it as she watched his face fill with complete misery after the look of initial shock faded, as though she had pierced his chest with a dagger. He shut the door with his head bowed low in defeat.

CHAPTER 14

A TRICKY ESCAPE

SHE SAT THERE FOR a long moment, thinking of her own justification and awfulness. She did not hate Gregor. Even when she was boiling mad at him, like she was right now, she worried about him. Why was that so? She should hate him, but she did not. In fact, she perhaps felt the opposite. Then she pushed that absurd notion away.

She played the encounter over in her mind and suddenly realized the door did not make that distinct clicking sound of a lock when he left. She ran to it. As the handle turned, she smiled. Peeking out the hallway, she was relieved to see only one guard, Joshua. She gave him a small wave, and he waved back with a large smile.

She bounded back into the room and shut the door tightly. She quickly dressed. She pulled on those thick wool socks. She stroked the cover of her father's journal. She stood and gave one last glance at it sitting on the bed before she slid out of the room.

"They gave you guard duty?" she asked casually, leaning against the wall. He stood tall and straight with a spear in his hands. He nodded.

"All night you have to stay here and watch my door?" she asked, trying to use her most childlike voice. He nodded again.

"I adore this feather you gave me. It is so soft," she said, stroking the feather against her face. "Thank you for giving it to me."

Joshua gave another wide smile as he nodded quickly.

"Well, I was so angry at dinnertime I did not actually get anything to eat," she said. "I may have lost my temper a bit."

"A bit," Joshua said with a laugh.

"Yeah." Victoria laughed back. "Do you think I could go down to the kitchen and get a snack?" she asked.

"Look, I am sure you really are just hungry, but I cannot allow you—" Joshua started.

"Oh, look I am not even wearing shoes!" Victoria pointed to her socks. "Where am I going to go? I don't have wings," she said. Then she loosened her sleeve and revealed her wounds where his talons had scratched her when he had carried her in the air.

"I mean, it's the least you can do after giving me this," Victoria said, grimacing dramatically and moving her fingers along the scabbing ridges of the scratches. Joshua's sincere concern spread across his face, and Victoria continued to pout until he nodded. He carried his spear in his hand and marched cautiously, eyeing Victoria for any sort of escape ploy.

She began to chat pleasantly, asking plenty of questions about him and encouraged him to continue speaking. By the time they reached the kitchen, he had left his spear against the doorway as they entered. She continued to listen to him, asking more and more questions to fuel his ego as she fixed two large sandwiches, interrupting him occasionally if he preferred cheese and which sauces he wanted.

By the time they were seated, and he had his second cup of whatever dark purple liquid was stored in the glass bottles, he was no longer even wearing his armored plate about his chest. It sat on the table, and he leaned back relaxed as he spoke, his wings drooped lazily on either side of the chair.

"And even after all those hours of dancing, Elizabeth didn't choose you?" Victoria asked in the most empathic voice she could muster.

"No, I assumed the triple back flip would have impressed her! But she still has not chosen!" Joshua said in discouragement, resting his chin on his hand.

"That means you still have a chance, perhaps you should show me your dance!" Victoria said. He perked up at the notion and stood excitedly and soon was whirling about the room. Victoria, despite her eagerness to find a moment she could slink away, got momentarily distracted by his spectacular display.

"You are a fantastic dancer!" Victoria said and clapped her hands to the rhythm he was making with his stomping feet and singing. Victoria thought of how much Mabel would enjoy this performance and that stone caught up in her throat again, making her stand. Joshua paused and looked at her.

"I want to learn that dance move when I get back from the ladies' room," Victoria said in an embarrassed whisper. He nodded understandingly and pointed the direction to the nearest facility.

The moment she was inside, Victoria ripped off all her clothes and shoved them deep into the basket, hiding them under the towels and other things. She transformed into her fox form, wondering for a moment if this escape plan was worth all the pain. Then she remembered how terrified Mabel looked with Charlene's cold laugh echoing in her brain.

She felt a new depth of courage fill inside her, and she burrowed deep into the basket on top of her clothes. It was a full ten minutes before Joshua came knocking, and when he did not receive a response, he slowly opened the door.

"Um, miss?" he said in confusion. Victoria felt bad she was tricking such a polite man, but once again Mabel flashed before her eyes and she bent down lower in the basket.

"Oh no, I am going to be in such trouble," she heard him mutter under his breath and then the heavy footfalls of him running down the hall. Victoria sprang from the basket and sprinted along the bottom of the wall, careful to stay low and in the shadows.

She saw stairs and headed for them. She gave a huff and pushed her paws to keep running. It was much harder to go down steps with her small legs.

"There must be over a thousand!" she panted to herself out loud in discouragement, but all that reached her ears was a small yip.

A small door popped open along the wall.

"Get in here!" Rhamy Lumpkin was suddenly picking her up. He was in some sort of tunnel and pulled her inside just as they heard the Avian guards yelling and entering the stairwell. Victoria was kicking him and snapping at him. He covered her snout with his hand, clenching her jaws together.

"You won't get out. The bottom is locked, bolted tight, and even if you got that open, it is a sheer hundred-foot drop below. It was built for those with wings," Rhamy Lumpkin said.

Victoria shot another glance up at the guards flying down the spiraling stairs.

"Go, go!" Rhamy said, and he lifted her up and pushed her into the tunnel. Rhamy almost didn't fit back inside. His shoulders hit the walls, and he had to adjust them at an angle to slide along. Rhamy pulled the rope he had fastened on the knob and pulled the door shut. They could hear the Avians flying past them. Their swords scraped the stone as they descended, echoing loudly inside. She could hear Elizabeth's voice echoing down the stairwell.

"She lied, Joshua! She could be anything!" Elizabeth sounded so angry, and she could just imagine Joshua's sad face. Victoria felt a pang of guilt but continued onward. "Grab that moth, it could be her!" Elizabeth's command made Victoria want to burst in laughter.

Crawling on his belly, Rhamy was making slow progress while Victoria pranced along, using her large fox eyes to see almost everything easily. She was keenly aware they were at a bit of a downward slope. Soon she popped out of the other side, and she waited for him. Once he was standing, he towered over her, and she looked at him. Behind him, the mountain face was cut away and replaced with large windows so the sun could easily fall into the room, but the sun had long set, and the moon was nearly full, sending another chill through Victoria.

I am coming, Mabel, she whispered to the moon in her mind.

"If you would allow me?" Rhamy Lumpkin asked, and she nodded as he picked her up, hiding her in his jacket.

The middle of the room held rows of about two dozen softly padded cribs holding different colored eggs. Some were soft blue, some were green, and others were spotted. Each looked to weigh about five to eight pounds. They were the largest eggs Victoria had ever seen.

"The hatchery. This is where Avian babies are born," Rhamy whispered to her. She looked out the little gap in his jacket carefully but there was only one lady rocking an egg in the corner, and she barely looked up.

The hallway from the hatchery was silent and dark. Victoria guessed everyone else was fast asleep in this part of the castle. He led her into a laundry area and was pulling out dresses and holding them up, trying to eyeball her size.

"Here, how about you transform. You will need your legs for the next part of the journey," Rhamy said, handing her a brown dress. Victoria looked at him.

"Well, what did you expect, to remain in fox form the whole time? That was not a very good plan," Rhamy said laughing. Victoria went behind the hanging sheets and transformed, once again stifling the painful screams that wanted to escape her lips. She curiously looked to her shoulder and noticed the self-inflicted claw marks were healing. The *G* would once again be clear against her smooth skin. Irritated, she shoved her arm into the dress and pulled the sleeve over it. Rhamy then found her a thick white fur cloak. Luckily there were some boots. They were a bit big on her, but when she pulled on a pair of thick wool socks, they didn't seem too loose.

Rhamy lit a candle, and its light led the way up a spiral staircase. As he guided her forward, she stopped.

"We can't go up. We need to go down," Victoria said.

"Trust me," Rhamy said. Victoria hesitated, Gregor's warning repeating in her mind.

"We will let the lady choose," Rhamy said as though addressing a large crowd. "Should we go the way I know is an exit, or should we wander around here in the dark looking for 'down'?" Rhamy asked with more sarcasm than she appreciated.

Victoria felt leery, but soon they were going up the stairs. When they reached the last step, the hallway widened, so Victoria could join his side. She looked down and gasped. It was not a candle burning brightly, but a ball of fire that sat in his palm.

"How are you doing that?" she asked, poking the flame. "Ouch!" she exclaimed, yanking her hand away and sucking on her fingertip. Rhamy laughed loudly.

"Why would you touch it?" he asked, looking at Victoria with a baffled expression.

"Well, you are holding it!" Victoria whined. Rhamy closed his hand, and the fire extinguished with a small puff of smoke. Darkness surrounded them like a heavy blanket as he drew her hand into his, squeezing tightly. The pain subsided. Slowly, her eyes adjusted. The high ceiling had a row of small windows, and the moonlight weakly cast its light through them.

Victoria was reminded they were inside the mountain in this castle carved from the inside out. All those years of staring at the highest peak of the Black Needles with a shudder, and now she was standing inside, fear dissolved.

"I am fire. It is my totem," he explained, his brilliant blue eyes sparkling as he pulled his face close to hers. "Just like your totem is a fox," he said.

She wondered why everyone here seemed to lack personal boundaries.

"You have not done anything but run us all over the castle. Get us out, and then I will tell you thank you," Victoria said.

"I want a gift wrapped in a bow," Rhamy said as he led them into a smaller room that smelled like rotten fruit and expired meat. He opened a hinged door, and it dropped open with rusty creak.

"Get in!" Rhamy said. Victoria looked down it, but it was pitch black.

"Where does this tunnel go?" Victoria asked. As she spoke, she heard the clatter of boots and spears.

"Get in," Rhamy said.

Victoria began to pull herself up and suddenly Rhamy's hands were pushing on her bottom, stuffing her inside. As she turned to chastise him, she slipped off the sloped edge. She let out a scream as she hit a slick hard surface underneath her, and she continued to slide. It was sticky in some spots and smelled awful like rotten food, but she did not have to breathe it much longer because the slide was picking up speed. She laid her head back, tucking in her arms, afraid she would hit something. The chute spit her out into a pile of mush, all stinky and gooey. It was rotten food. In the moonlight, she could tell it was an assortment of rancid vegetables and the fat or spoiled pieces of meat. She quickly tried to stomp out of the pile, knowing Rhamy was behind her, but she sank in the muck up to her thighs and she wanted to vomit. Rhamy shot out and missed her by a few inches but sprayed her with the juices. She was now covered in it, and she began to laugh. Rhamy sat up and looked around, and she continued to laugh as she spied a limp celery stick hanging off his shoulder. He joined in, and they laughed together for a long moment. He lifted his hand to pull the lettuce leaf that was clinging to her neck, and this stirred another round of laughter until they both heard a noise behind them.

Victoria turned to face the largest boar she had ever seen. It snorted, ruffling the hair on her head. They both scrambled to their feet and headed for the fence. Victoria sprang up, hoping to climb, but it was made of heavy timber and her fingers could not grasp well enough. She slid down and ducked as the pig smashed its head against the fence, missing her by less than an inch. The creature was about to smash her again but squealed wildly and began to stomp and snort furiously as Rhamy clung to its thick white-haired back.

He was riding the boar! It was in a rage and was kicking and running about, and the commotion had awoken the others in the pen too. It gave a mighty thrash of its neck, and Rhamy fell off its back and onto its snout, holding on by its tusks. The creature ran full speed toward the fence, fully intent on smashing Rhamy into it, but he dropped to the side just as the creature made impact, splitting the wood with a loud series of creaks and cracks.

Victoria climbed through the space as the dazed boar staggered a bit. Rhamy was right behind her, and together they ran. In no time, the other pigs were beating against the broken fence, and as they disappeared into the forest, Victoria saw the first boar's head poking out, escaping its pen.

When they were finally far enough away, they sat on the frosted ground, catching their breath, and laughing.

"You are crazy," Victoria said. Rhamy just continued to laugh. "Thank you for getting me out of there!" she said.

"You sound like you are saying goodbye," he said with a gesture toward his wardrobe, which Victoria had yet to notice—heavy snow boots and a thick winter coat. He was ready for travel. "I can't let you venture all through the Black Needles alone," he said with another heartwarming smile.

Victoria was so relieved she felt like crying, but she took a breath and regained herself.

"All right, Naphtali is this way," He said as he stood.

"But I don't have a key to the door, and I don't have any strong powers yet," Victoria said.

"We will figure it out," He said. Victoria liked the refreshing change of pace and fell into step behind him.

"Why doesn't the king of the elves command your kingdom? Is he sick? He did not look sick, but is he unable to rule for some reason?" Victoria asked. Rhamy laughed.

"The husband of the Queen?" he asked. Victoria nodded.

"I guess technically he is a king, huh?" Rhamy said, more out loud to himself while he pondered the idea. "I forget some other species are predominantly patriarchal."

Victoria looked at him expectantly, waiting for him to elaborate.

"The elves are the most successful kingdom and will continue to be as long as we maintain our honored matriarchy. Females are far more superior in compromise, and their egos don't blind their decision making. We watch the beasts clash their pride, destroy themselves with petty rivalries and that ridiculous bellum tradition," Rhamy said, gesturing toward Victoria's shoulder. Although it was hidden under her cloak, she found herself trying to cover it with her hand self-consciously. She wondered if he had been there and seen it play out.

"Don't worry, soon that will mean nothing," Rhamy offered kindly. "We are astounded they have survived this long. A couple centuries ago, their species was almost extinct, a roaming lone beast bit Brutus. With the newfound power, he appointed himself King and sought petty revenge on the villagers who had bullied him in his youth. But it was not enough, he wanted more, aggressively biting all the humans he could get his teeth into, all fractions. Sure, he has produced a few purebloods, like Gregor, more powerful, more dangerous. But their numbers are already dwindling again because of their savage, dog eat dog lifestyle. It is a doomed species."

"You must read a lot of history books." Victoria said.

"Nah, I am not much for sitting still for too long." Rhamy said. Victoria gave him a puzzled look. "Oh, these are my memories. I was there." He explained. Victoria looked at his smooth youthful face, astonished.

"You have to stop judging time by the humans' teensy scale." Rhamy said with a chuckle. They continued to walk while Victoria tactfully formed her next question.

"So, it was your Queen who told you to spy on me and my family?" Victoria asked, hoping he would answer truthfully. He nodded.

"And you saw Gor kidnap me and have been silently following me since?" Again, he answered her question with a simple nod, unbothered by her angry scowl. He just kept walking.

"She is the wisest among us. Often, she commands us to glean information before acting. Listen, it was not just me. After we heard word, that Richard was dead, we stood guard to protect you."

"Funny, that is what Gregor said about you, that he had to keep you at bay." Victoria said. This comment made Rhamy laugh loudly.

"Gregor could not possibly fend off all those who wanted to torture you for information on the whereabouts of the mermaid. We let him think he was in control of guarding your balcony, he was useful at stopping those few who fought their way past our battalion in the forest. It was us who kept you safe. You are welcome." Rhamy said proudly. Victoria rolled her eyes, unsure if she believed this story. At this Rhamy stopped short and stood huffing.

"I lost my best friend to a monster!" Rhamy's voice faltered, cracking with emotion. Victoria hung her head, ashamed she had been so callous.

"We were there to protect and observe until we saw you transform. Then we knew Richard had lied. He was so convincing that you and your sister were not his blood!" Rhamy said, making a fist. "After that I wanted to tell you everything, force Plimsoll to begin your training. If Gregor had not stopped me, you and Mabel would be safely hidden among my people right now. But no, he is young and dumb. He would not listen to reason and continued to guard you like some lovesick pup,"

The pain obvious on his face, he turned away and hid it by stomping through the snow. Victoria continued behind him, ashamed. She dared not tear at such a tender wound any further, so she pushed all her questions out of her mind. Neither spoke. Only the crunch of snow underfoot echoed into the forest.

She wondered how many had died on her behalf while she attended to her daily routine unaware. Well, not completely unaware; she had been so sure it was just in her mind, the haunting faces outside her window and the noises interrupting the night. The constant feeling of being watched. She cringed at the thought of someone standing under her window in the shadows. She shivered again and let long silence ease the tension before she finally spoke.

"I am sorry. I did not know," she offered her apology. She understood the long, silent walk that followed.

"Was it you who gave Snal the warm clothes and boots to give me?" she asked. Rhamy nodded glumly. "Thank you," she said.

Sooner than Victoria expected, Rhamy resumed his usual smile, generously shedding joy back into the journey by opening a small jar he was carrying in his sack with an exaggerated gesture. She laughed; it was more fire beetle jam.

Victoria noticed he was careful to steer clear of any serious discussion by throwing snowballs and climbing trees excitedly as they moved down the mountain face. He started telling her a series of jokes that she did not understand. After he would laugh at them himself, he would explain them. Most of them were elvish references. She enjoyed hearing more about his kind but enjoyed his laughter more.

Rhamy stopped at the rivers edge, the thick layer of ice made the slow running current underneath barely visible. Rhamy chose a pooled area and stood there staring down.

"Do you see that?" He asked anxiously. He bent down and wiped the snow away with his hands, revealing the ice underneath clearly.

"What?" Victoria asked nervously.

Suddenly it gave a tremendous crack. Before Victoria could reach out to grab him, he slid in between the two large chunks, disappearing below the surface. The last moment of fear on his face replayed over and over in her mind.

"Rhamy!" Victoria yelled out in fear. She plunged her arms down, hoping to grab him out. But the water was not cold, it was hot. It was so hot Victoria pulled away in surprise, the steam now visibly rising.

Rhamy popped up, spraying her with water and laughing. Victoria found herself laughing too.

"You may wish to remain stinky, but as your traveling companion, I am begging you to at least rinse the rotten food from your hair." He said.

"You will freeze when you have to trudge in your wet things!" Victoria scolded him.

"Fire elf," he replied.

Victoria reluctantly began to unbutton her cloak.

"But do not look at me." She said shyly, Rhamy dramatically turned away, making sure to shield his eyes with an exaggerated gasp. Although he made a big spectacle of teasing her, Victoria appreciated that he kept his head turned until she was completely submerged in the water.

The steam rose and wavered in the chilly night air. Victoria scrubbed her hair and then as she flipped it to one side, she spied the stars overhead. She paused to look up at the dazzling array in awe.

She saw thick clouds were rolling in and the stars were slowly being swallowed by them. Soon they would be completely blocked from sight.

Rhamy slumped down deeper into the water, making bubbles like a child would in the bath. Victoria laughed at the sight.

She was smiling as an arrow slid past her head, only an inch from her skull. There was a golden flash in the sky.

"Run!" Rhamy said, popping out of the water and sending a fireball toward the direction the arrow had come from. The fire burst and Victoria could see the distinct outline of Elizabeth, flapping away from the flames. This gave Victoria time to pull on her dress. Rhamy sent another fireball. She sprinted with her shoes and cloak in hand, through the snow as more arrows rained down on them. Her feet stung from the cold ground. Victoria glanced up when she heard Elizabeth, flying close above the treetops, screeching loudly.

Before Victoria could register that the arrow was zooming straight for her heart, it turned to ash, burning so brightly she had to shield her eyes. She looked to Rhamy, who winked at her.

"Thanks!" she said breathlessly, and Elizabeth screeched in frustration, reaching for another arrow. They ran as fast as they could, sprinting through the trees and stumbling down a hill.

"Elizabeth! You are making a mistake!" Rhamy yelled up at her. Her only reply was another arrow grazing his cheek as he narrowly ducked away from it.

Elizabeth swooped down, weaving between the trees, and painfully smacked her wings. She had to fly back up over the tops to stay with them.

"We are safe as long as we keep in the trees," Rhamy said and Victoria took the moment to pull on her boots. Elizabeth dropped down between the trees and folded her wings, running toward them.

"Sometimes I am wrong." Rhamy said with a shrug. Victoria jumped over the hill and let herself slide down in the soft powder. Then she cried out as she hit into a thick slab of ice painfully at the bottom. She looked around in panic at the clear landscape of an ice-covered lake. Rhamy dropped beside her and hollered for her to run. They took off over the ice, toward the other edge of the lake, aiming for the thick tree line. Elizabeth was already back into flight, pulling another arrow tight across her bow.

"Keep running!" Rhamy screamed and pulled to a stop, igniting a fireball in his hand. Victoria continued to run until she heard a distinct snap. Rhamy had formed a bow of his own completely from fire and was shooting vivid blue arrows with the fireballs on the tip to rain down on Elizabeth. Her golden shield blocked most of them, but one caught the bodice of her brown tunic, and she swatted at it fiercely. The fallen fire was crackling on the ice and billows of steam were whirling around. It was a dazzling display and Victoria paused to look at it. Rhamy shot another arrow, and it pierced her wing, sending Elizabeth down in a spiral. There was a cloud of her feathers floating in the air. Victoria continued to run.

She looked back to see Elizabeth setting a trumpet to her lips, letting out a call for rescue before falling to the ground unconscious.

Another shower of arrows erupted over their heads, and Victoria felt a sting as one whizzed past her, slicing her side painfully. She fell as Rhamy disappeared into the trees.

The other Avian was now over her, covering her with a thick net. She fought to get free, but it was tangled all about her. She screamed, and he yanked her to her feet. She turned to see it was Joshua.

He looked angrily at her. Victoria knew she probably deserved it, but his glower stung a bit. She struggled hard despite knowing escape was unlikely with Joshua's obvious determination. He carried her above the trees with the rope in his talons and dropped her near Elizabeth. He anxiously knelt beside her and inspected her wing.

"Your foolish actions now have put her life at risk," he said with annoyance as he tied Victoria tightly to the nearest tree still in the net.

"What are you doing?" Victoria asked.

"I can't carry both of you, and her life is more important," he said. "I will send someone to retrieve you—that is, if we can get back before the blizzard hits."

He tenderly picked up Elizabeth, and Victoria was moved by the sincerity in his eyes and the desperation to get her safely home. She could not be angry. He flew away, the wind from his wings whipping soundly into her eyes.

"What blizzard?" Victoria screamed at him, but he was already gone.

CHAPTER 15

A TEMPEST

THE NET WAS THICK and tightly woven together, and she knew even her fox form could not slide through the tiny holes, nor could she bite through the thick net. She was sure it was infused with some sort of metal. She screamed out in frustration then felt the ping of pain from her side. She looked down to see the long gash the arrow had given her. Blood was oozing out. She wrapped her arm about it awkwardly as she started to shiver. The wind began to pick up and the first few snowflakes began to swirl about her face. She huddled into her cloak tightly and leaned into the tree, hoping Joshua would return.

Soon the wind was blowing the flurries all around her, and if she had not been tied to the tree, she was sure she would be lost in a whirl-wind of white. Keeping her eyes tightly shut to avoid the constant thrash of ice and wind making them tear painfully, she drifted in and out of consciousness.

She wasn't sure how long she had sat there, but when her ropes released, her numb limbs sounded out painfully as she tried to move. Feeling herself being lifted and carried by someone in a thick fur cloak, relief wafted over her.

"Rhamy?" she asked. "Joshua?" She waited for a response, but the howl of the wind stifled any answer. He was stomping his way through the storm. Her eyes were still tightly shut; the icy blast had pounded them relentlessly. It was too painful to try to move, her body registering different varieties of numb and painful stabbing sensations all over.

Then, after some time, the howling of the wind was muffled, and her face no longer stung from its thrashing. She was laid down on something soft, and she tried to sit up but was unable to find her balance. As a fluffy blanket surrounded her, she snuggled into it. She was unable to fight off the need for sleep. She felt herself drifting away.

Something warm was against her cheek as she woke. She opened her eyes slowly, running her fingers through the fuzzy blanket. It was too dark to see her hand in front of her face, but she could hear the steady stream of wind whistling through the narrow entrance. Outside, the blizzard raged on viciously, smashing itself against the cave. Snow flurries spun inside, sprinkling the doorway in a shower of glittering white as small slivers of the moonlight filtered their way through the storm. Victoria thought it looked like a giant saltshaker. She smiled to herself, knowing Mabel would giggle at that thought.

She was in a sort of narrow tunnel by the echoing noise, perhaps a cave because she could hear a distant drip of water from the depths. She turned to follow the noise and looked down further inside, it opened into a large cavern with a strange greenish blue glowing pool of water.

As the blanket stirred beneath her fingertips, she froze. It was breathing. She stumbled back, trying to make out the creature, but it was too dark. It was big and hairy, and she was grateful it was fast asleep. It gave a rumbling snore, and Victoria crept away. Covering her mouth to stifle her shaking breaths, she tiptoed around it. She looked to the storm outside and then again at the thing she was sharing a cave with. It gave a heavy grumble. Victoria stood trembling in fear. As she took another step backward, she displaced a pebble. Its clatter rang in her ears loudly. She could hear the thing begin to wake. Victoria gasped and dashed out into the night, grasping her cloak tight about her.

"Rhamy! Joshua!" she screamed out desperately. "Rhamy!" she again called in vain. She was sure they were nearby. She just needed to find them. Perhaps the animal inside there had eaten them. She screamed again, panic wringing her throat and settling in a gnarled knot in her gut.

The wind dove under her cloak, and the folds ruffled about. She forced them down quickly, holding them fast against her legs. A broken piece of branch spun in the wind and slammed into her painfully. She stumbled and fell into the snow, the white haze all around.

Disoriented by the chilly air whipping into her face, stinging her eyes, she was unsure which way to go. Her hands burned in the frigid snow. She tried to feel around in the darkness, reaching for anything.

She stumbled to her feet, using the nearest object to help her stand. It swayed under her weight, and she realized she was holding on to some sort of horn. A snort escaped the creature's mouth, and it rammed her, striking her down into the snow. She was unable to make out more than its large white figure, but she then recognized its squeals. It was one of those boars. As it charged again, she rolled away, its tusks missing her throat but goring deep into her shoulder. Warm blood splattered over her face. She shrieked and tried to fight it off, but it snapped her side in its jaws. It shook her furiously, its hot, stinky breath washing over her.

She screamed in agony as it dropped her. As she heard it snort, charging to trample her deeper into the snow, she cried out in desperation. A roar echoed through the storm, and the swine gave a series of high-pitched squeals. She crawled away from the noise. As the last screech faded, Victoria held her breath, only the winter storm whistling in her ears.

"Victoria," a voice spoke, piercing through the icy blast. She recognized it instantly, it was Gregor. A mixture of relief and reluctance flooded over her as she called out. She reached out toward him, clinging to his neck as he bent down. His arms gathered her against his chest, and he struggled against the wind. He grunted as he trudged through the snow. Victoria closed her eyes. They felt too cold and frozen to stay open.

It seemed to be a long trek, his heart throbbing loudly in her ear. When Gregor reached a narrow entrance, he sat her down. She blinked several times, and when she opened her eyes, she found herself again in the safety of the cave. She felt a rush of embarrassment wash over her at her own stupidity. Gregor stood at the entrance, snow swirling around his bare body. The wind whistled by and created an eerie melody that blended with Gregor's heavy breathing.

He stood looking at her with a furrowed brow. His tight frown made Victoria shift uncomfortably. His large frame now took up most of the only exit as he faced her, standing as best he could with the low ceiling.

"Are you trying to kill yourself? Get me killed?" he asked in a voice a lot louder and harsher than it needed to be in the small space as he pulled on his pants. He stooped down and yanked a candle from his bag. He lit it by scraping the blade of his knife along an odd stone. The flickering light made their shadows dance against the cave wall.

He crossed his arms over his chest, obviously waiting for her response. His unbuckled belt hung down.

"I woke up in a strange, dark place next to a terrifying monster!" she snapped back defensively.

"I am many things, but I am not a monster," he stated flatly, his voice dangerously low. Victoria had offended him. Once again, she lamented at her own foolishness, forgetting those words meant something completely different here. He stood staring at her, huffing. There was a long moment while Victoria tried to sort through her thoughts to find the right defense or excuse, but she came up short.

"I am sorry," she offered sincerely. "I should have listened to you."

Disarmed by this response, Gregor lowered his arms. He stood now looking a bit ashamed of his overreaction.

Then he realized his belt was still unfastened. As he fumbled to slide the tail of the strap over the bar of the buckle, Victoria noticed the deep puncture wounds on his forearm.

"You got a—" She was not sure how to describe it, so she just pointed. He looked down and huffed in annoyance.

"This is what I was trying to avoid," he muttered to himself and began to lick it. Victoria gasped in disgust as he continued until all the blood was gone.

"How did you find me?" Victoria asked.

"I saw the Avians circling in the sky," he explained. "I was furious; I just knew it must have been you. You just can't seem to listen to me, ever."

She watched his skin mend right before her eyes, the bright-red flesh threading back together. Soon only smooth peach skin remained, all traces of injury gone. Where the fresh new skin had grown, an uneven lighter patch splotched his tanned arm.

He looked at her while she sat awkwardly holding her injury. She followed his gaze. Her blood oozed down the front of the cloak. Pain began to register.

"This was my favorite cloak," she sputtered. Gregor gave a slight smile at her joke despite his concerned expression. It was the first smile she had seen on his face in what felt like forever.

She sighed and gingerly pulled away the fabric to see white bone sticking out of her shoulder, glinting in the candlelight.

She screamed frantically, falling on her back as she stared at it in shock. His face flashed in alarm. He lunged forward, forcing her down.

"No," was all she could make out between hyperventilating moans.

"Calm down, it's not your bone. It's the boar's tusk," he said forcefully. Before Victoria could scoot away, he held her still and ripped it from her flesh. She gasped in agony, kicking her feet, as blood began to pour. The tusk dropped on the floor with a clatter, and Victoria felt she might vomit from the seething pain.

"If I do not heal you, you will most likely bleed to death. Your healing properties are not evolved enough yet," he said, kneeling over her and pressing on the wound forcefully with his palms. She shook her head as the pain flooded through her.

"Don't touch it," she shrieked, delirious from the excruciating pangs bolting through her body. "You are making it hurt worse." She tried to scoot away.

"You are going to die," he said in a harsher tone, yanking her back to position himself over her. Gregor caught her flailing arms in his hands, holding them down. His face rubbed against her cheek as he lowered his head. As his tongue touched, it seemed to shoot hot sparks out along her skin. She tried to squirm under him. She winced as the sting was sharp enough to bring her to tears. She groaned, but it did not last long. Soon her wound was numbed entirely. Gregor held the white ivory up for her to see. She took it in her hand, accidentally grazing his fingertips as she did so. Their eyes met. His emeralds sparkled brightly. She examined the tooth fragment in her hand. As she stared at the smooth bone, the wind whistled relentlessly against the cave opening, and she could hear the boars squealing in the distance. She looked back up to Gregor, his eyes still on her.

"Will those things attack in here?" she asked.

"No," Gregor said flatly. "I marked the territory outside."

She was uncertain how to respond, surely, he did not mean urination.

She breathed in relief as the pain faded away. He let her go, sitting back on his heels. She eyed him as she slowly propped up on her elbows. He gave her a small, gloating smirk as she watched her shoulder mend.

"Better?" he asked. She felt flushed. He pointed toward the gash from the arrow, on her side below her ribs, with an inquiring gesture. She gave a single, reluctant nod slowly.

He lowered his head and when he touched her with his tongue again, she flinched in surprise. It was hot, and it sent a quiver through her. As he worked his way over the lesion, he slid a hand under to turn her slightly to reach the remaining parts. He stopped to pull a foreign fragment from her flesh, and Victoria grimaced. He drew his face close again, licking the wound until her pain stopped. He pulled away, wiping the blood from his lips with the back of his hand.

He placed a hand on her leg. She jumped. He continued to pull the cloak away, revealing the wound on her thigh.

As he moved down her body, Victoria stopped his forehead with her hand. His eyes met hers again, sending a thousand butterflies in her stomach into a fluttering mess. He impatiently ducked under her hand.

As his muscular neck and shoulders bent over her, she debated to say something, anything, but nothing came to her rescue. She wondered if he felt the tension, too.

She guessed the blood was a prized taste to his animal side, and perhaps it was not such an inconvenience as she assumed. She remembered her slight fascination with the smell of blood while she was in fox form, although she doubted she would ever let herself indulge upon it. Her suspicion was correct as he not only licked the wound but cleaned the blood-stained skin all around. The familiar sting radiated and soon numbed as it healed seamlessly.

He looked up at her, waiting for her to further invite him toward the final injury. Bloodstained lips were less intimidating than the fangs she had seen before. To prove she was unafraid, she lifted a hand and brushed her thumb against his chin, wiping a drop of blood away. There was a small flicker in his eyes. Victoria secretly liked the way it made her squirm.

Victoria leaned back, exposing the scratch on her neck. He placed a hand on either side of her body, trapping her between his arms for balance. As he bent over her, his chest hit against hers. He was so close Victoria worried he felt the rush of tingles working up her body too. His ear brushed against her cheek. His tongue seemed hotter now, dragging along her delicate skin. His scruff tickled her, and she could not hold back a soft giggle, putting a hand on his chest.

Gregor paused at this, slightly pulling away. Victoria apologized softly. She turned her head, further inviting him to continue. The sting felt oddly comforting, knowing the numbing sensation would follow soon after. She could actually hear her skin mending because it was so close to her ear. She let out a breath of relief as relaxation flooded over her.

No longer distracted by the pain, she was now aware his body was slightly quivering over hers. He looked up into her face, their eyes meeting again.

"I did not mean what I said back at the Avian castle," she said. He continued to listen, his intoxicating breath hitting her chin and neck. He raised an eyebrow, waiting. He continued to listen, his mouth drawing a small smile.

"I do not hate you. I . . ." she began again and then lost the words, becoming too shy to say anymore as he moved closer. His lips trembled near hers, so close Victoria knew she had only lift her chin slightly to connect. He let out another stilled breath, a soft eager pant.

She felt another frenzy of shivers, as though her whole being was shifting under the tension. Her face felt hot and yet her body was yearning to lean into his warmth. She knew if she did not stop him, he would be on her within a few seconds and yet she could not bring herself to pull away. She found herself savoring the moment.

She recognized the look in his eyes—hunger. She was not naive. She had seen this look plenty of times on the men she passed on the street, the way their eyes lingered a moment longer than proper, and she would pretend to not notice. But this was the first time she liked it. The tingly sensation she felt as she placed her hand on his chest excited her in a way she had never known before.

When his lips brushed against hers lightly, she let herself give into them. They were soft and surprisingly gentle. It was truly her first kiss because she had never counted that ridiculous, sloppy mess he had laid on her at the ball.

This held more magic than she had ever anticipated, and she found herself pushing into him, demanding more. He intertwined his fingers into her hair, gently tilting her head while he maneuvered over her in determination. Letting his body drop down on top of her, Gregor let out a soft grunt. Gregor's lips were faster now, pressing firmly with each slight shift of his chin. Pinned under his weight with his lips covering hers, she felt delightfully conquered. Then another groan of pleasure escaped his throat, which made Victoria tremble enjoyably.

She realized she had been holding her breath and released, opening her mouth a bit and Gregor took this as an invitation to tug a on her lower lip passionately. His hand now was sliding over her, and this took Victoria by surprise. She jumped and pulled back. She felt a rush of bashfulness.

"Thank you for healing me," she said in a soft whisper, barely loud enough to reach her own ears. Her words proved startling to him. She could read his disappointment clearly.

"Victoria," Gregor breathed, his steely gaze seemed to release more of those butterflies.

"I do not know how things work in Omnia, but for me, this is very inappropriate behavior. This sort of thing is reserved strictly for a couple after they have taken the vow to be each other's until death," Victoria quickly explained. Gregor continued to look at her, but his emotion was hard to read. "We have not made such a vow," she continued.

"I take this death vow right now," he said eagerly, and he dropped his face closer, his lips brushing against her neck, tickling her a bit.

"No, it doesn't work like that," Victoria said, stifling the small giggle wanting to bubble out. "There is a large ceremony, all our family and friends attend. I wear a white dress . . ."

Despite how wonderful it felt to have all his attention, she knew she needed to resist. She dropped her hand from his chest and tried to scoot away from his tantalizing musk. A chill washed over her as his warm body pulled away. He gave a small cough to clear his throat, trying to hide his uneasiness by shifting about, finding his shirt. She realized he was struggling to determine where to sit in proximity to her. Finally, he settled against the wall, resting an arm on his knee and leaning his head back.

Victoria looked down at herself, trying to shake off the tension. Her dress was so torn, most of her midsection was exposed. The remaining bloodstained cloak was torn and ragged. Fiddling with it to cover herself proved impossible, so she gave up. Turning her attention toward taming her frazzled hair, she felt even more at a loss at the end of the struggle. She glanced up and realized Gregor's eyes were still on her. She felt her face blushing, and she looked away, hoping he did not notice. There was a long silence between them, the spitting storm continued to echo.

"Gregor?" she finally asked. Her voice seemed loud, shattering the stillness. After a small grunt in reply, he sat up, opening his eyes to look at her expectantly. His steady gaze made her nervous again, and she wished she could control the wild thoughts popping up in her head.

"Thank you for saving my life," she finally said. He nodded and leaned his head back against the wall but kept his eyes open to stare at the candle's flame. Feeling a sudden rush of self-consciousness, she tried to conceal it by looking away. Soon she fumbled with the fraying hem of her cloak.

"I am glad you are okay," he said with such sincerity, she met his eyes. Then he began shifting about and Victoria could tell he was now uneasy under her stare. She liked the satisfaction of making him squirm for a change.

As the candle dwindled, the increasing darkness covered her like a thick, damp blanket. She sat impatiently. The blizzard continued to blow insistently while thoughts of Mabel edged into her mind again, and this time she could not push them away. She hoped Mabel was not afraid and alone. Poor Mother, always so cautious and protective, losing both her daughters was probably sending her into a downward spiraling tizzy. She wondered what Mother had said to everyone asking about their disappearances. Thinking of everyone, faces flashed a crossed her mind, until one face came into clear view. It was Henry's concerned face she imagined, looking for her among the crowd and not finding her. She wondered if he would be as bold as to ask Mother. Mother would no doubt be most unpleasant toward him. Victoria felt another wave of urgency wash over her. She needed to find Mabel and get home soon.

She looked toward Gregor; his face turned into the faint light. His breathing indicated he had fallen asleep. She rubbed her arms again, hoping for more warmth.

The winter hogs once again rummaged about the woods nearby with their loud squeals echoing in her ears. Each loud rustle would stir her into a stance to best defend herself. When the tune of the blizzard resumed uninterrupted, she settled back down just to be frightened again by another noise momentarily.

"Calm down. I will not let anything harm you," Gregor said with a bit of mumble, barely conscious from sleep. Victoria rested against the wall, finally ignoring the noises from outside. Sleep found her and tried to lure her into a restful state, but the chill of the night rattled her awake. The blizzard seemed to become a wild animal, thrashing itself about, and snow now shot into the shelter furiously. Victoria shivered violently, she pulled her knees to her chest and wrapped her arms about herself. It was useless, her teeth rattled painfully as her jaw chattered. Her entire body was trembling. She looked toward Gregor. He looked peacefully unaware of her predicament. Once again, she noticed the dropping temperature. Her breath wisped about her lips as if puffs of smoke.

She timidly crawled toward him in the dark, touching his arm gently. His eyes opened and looked at her. His emotion was lost in the shadows.

Unable to decipher his mood, she whispered, "I am cold, sorry, I don't mean to be—" she apologized, afraid he was annoyed, or worse, think she changed her mind about the other thing. He did not say anything, only gave a slight grunt as he lifted his arm and pulled her close.

He shifted himself partly underneath her and wrapped his arms about her. She rested her head into the space between his chest and neck, pressing her body along his. His skin seemed hot against hers, and immediate warmth enveloped her.

Perhaps this is what they spoke of, the comfort of sharing a companion to cling to during the storm of life. The sacred bond of a married couple was not just the act of marrying in the church, it must be this complicated mess of emotions too. She wondered if beasts believed in some form of marriage. She doubted Gregor, the Beast Prince, would get on one knee and propose. She ventured as far to imagine trying to introduce him to her mother, bringing him to her church. His bulky form shoved into the church pew made her laugh in her mind. No this could never be her future.

And yet, she let herself enjoy the heat between them. Only until the sun came up, just to survive, she reminded herself.

She could hear his heart pounding fast in her ear. He lay perfectly still and rigid, so she knew he was wide awake too. She dared not speak, in the fear of ruining the moment.

No longer shivering, she was finally able to find sleep.

CHAPTER 16

AN INFESTATION

AS THE MORNING RAYS shone into the opening, Victoria awoke. She could see the blizzard still raged on, but the sun was poking through, trying to ebb its force. Gregor slept on, uninterrupted by her small movements. She was nestled between his arm and side, her face buried into his chest. She did not immediately pull away, she let herself enjoy his heat for a few more moments.

Then she sat up, straightened her cloak, and once again tried to smooth her hair and weave it into a decent-looking braid. She gathered fresh snow into both their waterskins and ate the snowball she had formed in her hands. She waited. He woke slowly, taking his time to sit up.

"Are you hungry?" he asked. She nodded to him. He stood and walked toward the cave opening, pulling in the large boar from the cold.

"You brought it back here?" Victoria asked as Gregor reentered the cave, dragging it behind him.

Victoria scooted closer, looking at the boar's head in fascination. It had thick white hair, and the beady, lifeless eyes stared wide open in a cloudy haze. With four gray-and-black-striped hooves, she decided it was a strange-looking creature. She picked up the bloodstained tusk Gregor had pulled from her shoulder last night and held it over the remaining stub, piecing the two halves together in fascination. Then she gulped at the torn jugular.

"How did you become . . .," she paused, unsure if she should continue. "A beast?"

His eyebrows furrowed as he finished slicing a large chunk of flesh. Victoria could tell he did not want to discuss it further, and she shut her mouth.

She managed to find a somewhat comfortable position against the rocks and settled in, feeling more like an animal than a human in the current surroundings. He piled a few stray pieces of wood together and pulled some hair from the creature as tinder. Soon the crude campfire was ablaze. As the light flared all around, it cast their shadows upon the walls.

"I was born as a beast," Gregor finally spoke. "My ma was human, so I am like you, a fraction, but I was raised in the pack, so I am more beast than human," he said in a huff.

"Fraction?" Victoria repeated, remembering Elizabeth used it as an insult.

"That is what they call any offspring that is half magical being and half human," he said. "It is not kind," he cautioned.

"Where is your mother now?" Victoria asked.

"My pa tells me she died soon after I was born," Gregor said.

"Oh, I am so sorry," Victoria said. Gregor accepted her sympathy with a slight nod. "Are you going to be punished for helping me?" She was almost afraid to ask. He looked at her and then back at the ground.

"Yeah," he said with a shrug after a strained pause.

"Why don't you leave?" she asked. Gregor blinked at her, the idea almost startling him.

"There is no other place for a beast, except his pack, but the Avians will soon know I broke my proxy bellum, and there is a punishment," Gregor said. "When I gave my ring to Plimsoll, the terms were for you to be in his care until I returned. The proper procedure dictates he returns my ring before I can claim you again."

"What is the punishment for claiming me again without Plimsoll's knowledge or the ring?" Victoria asked, worried.

"A dozen days in the stocks," Gregor said.

"What? I am sorry. I did not know this," Victoria said in desperation. "I will go for you. It was my fault. When we get back from saving Mabel, I will go in your place."

He gave a hearty laugh; it was not his usual tight and rigid voice. He was finally at ease. "It doesn't work that way," he said.

"We are going to get Mabel before the moon maze starts," he said. His look of determination drove the hope she seemed to have lost somehow back into her heart, and she could not resist wrapping her arms around him in a tight hug.

He returned the hug, lifting her into the air as he stood. She only could see his soft lips. It was impossible to resist the urge to place hers upon them. As they pressed together, the last bit of shyness withered away, leaving space for a new sensation to sprout, weaving through her as though lush green ivy and blossoming into large blooms with a dazzling burst.

He shifted so he held her in one arm while he slid the other arm down her back, and it startled her.

It was then she felt the overpowering shyness return and pulled away. His lips followed hers and tried again for another kiss, but she turned her head, feeling too bashful.

He set her back down, but he looked at her with such intense, smoldering eyes she was unsure if her feet made contact with the cave floor.

Victoria felt pleasantly muzzy. Her heart felt too large for her chest as it thudded loudly, she worried he might hear it and give herself away.

They exchanged glances while she began to gather her things and he busied himself with cutting more meat for breakfast. She was surprised on how delicious it was and ate her fill. Gregor showed her how to slice more meat as he cooked it. He then wrapped it for the trip, sliding it into his satchel.

After breakfast, he stood and wandered down to the edge of the pool below and washed his knife and hands. Victoria joined his side to get a closer look at the odd greenish water. Upon further inspection she realized the water itself was not green, but the strange mushrooms growing on underneath the surface were an array of greens and blues, they glowed softly. As Victoria looked down into them, something glinted. A drip from the ceiling hit the still water and while the ripples moved over the mushrooms, Victoria blinked several times and leaned closer. She could not believe her eyes.

"Gregor!" Victoria whispered. "Whose cave is this?" She asked cautiously in a whisper, whipping around suspiciously.

"Why, what do you see?" Gregor asked.

"Do you not see that?" She asked while pointing to the water.

"What do you see?" Gregor repeated.

"Mabel's mask!" She said. "Don't you see it? Did Charlene bring Mabel here?" She felt stupid pointing to it when it lay just a few inches from her fingertips, its pink ribbon tangled about the mushroom stems. She began to reach for it but Gregor grabbed her hand before she pierced the surface.

"What are you doing?" She asked. "Mabel must be around here."

"Don't grab things from the water." He said.

"But you just touched the water, you just cleaned your knife." She said, confused.

"Yes, but I am not reaching for anything." Gregor said.

"I do not understand." Victoria replied.

"Those are fool's gold shrooms." Gregor said, nodding toward the eerie glowing greenish blue mushrooms under the water. There are a few spores about these mountains. You see what you want just beneath the surface of the water, but it is a trap. The farther you reach, the deeper down it seems to go, always just barely out of reach. Many have drowned eagerly trying to grab at whatever they are seeing. Then the mushrooms feed off the remains."

"So, you do not see her mask?" Victoria asked.

"No," Gregor replied.

"Well, what do you see in the glowing green water?" She asked quickly. Gregor looked into the water and gave it a momentary glance before pulling his face away and sheathing his knife.

"Well, what do you see?" Victoria asked again.

"Doesn't matter." He said.

"Well, her mask isn't important to me, my mother just bought it for the masquerade. Why isn't it an illusion of Mabel down there?"

"These are little, they aren't strong enough to make you believe there is an entire person. Not yet. If you see any like these but bigger than your fist, then do not even go near the water." Gregor cautioned.

"What if I had come down here before you? I could have drowned." Victoria said with a gasp.

"I was watching." Gregor said calmly. "I find it strange it wasn't that ruby necklace you so desperately clung to."

"Were you testing me?" Victoria asked. Gregor gave a smirk.

"Mabel is way more important to me than some jewelry piece." Victoria explained. "Anyway, we should destroy these, I mean, we shouldn't just leave them around to grow bigger and kill someone." Victoria said.

"Be my guest, go on in and start tearing them out." Gregor said and offered his knife to her, with another smirk. Victoria eyed him coolly and took the knife, when she looked back toward the water suddenly it was a commotion of movement. They flashed orange and yellow. Under their glowing caps were two little beady eyes and a tiny mouth. They thrashed their stubby arms about wildly. The mushrooms were uprooting themselves and running on their squat little legs back further down the cave. Gregor chuckled again at Victoria's shocked expression. She handed the knife back to him.

They continued to watch the retreat. The littlest one tumbled underwater and was now on its cap, its fat legs kicking frantically. Victoria could hear it crying.

Victoria, ignoring Gregor's warnings, stomped into the water with a splash and grabbed it. It was barely bigger than her pinky.

"It's alright, little fella." Victoria said. The little mushroom rubbed its eyes and looked up at her, the orange flashing subsided. Then Victoria heard a soft, squeaky voice, very faintly. She held it up to her ear, closer.

"Do you hear him?" Victoria asked Gregor. "He is asking for food." When Gregor did not respond, Victoria looked up to see him looking dumbfounded.

"It is just squeaking," Gregor said.

"No, he is clearly asking for food," Victoria challenged. She walked back to their makeshift campsite and tore a little snippet of raw meat from the pig's head. She held it up for the mushroom and he took it graciously.

"He likes it!" Victoria said and laughed. Gregor was still looking at her wordlessly.

"You have better hearing than I do, how can you not hear him?" Victoria asked as they both looked down at her palm, the mushroom now laying on its back, the pinch of meat had stuffed it so full it had fallen fast asleep. A contended green now outlining his tiny form.

"Is he speaking full sentences?" Gregor asked.

"No, its mostly just one word." Victoria explained.

"Plimsoll told me you might be able to do something I wouldn't understand! You can communicate with animals," Gregor said excitedly.

"Well, I am keeping this little guy!" Victoria said. Gregor did not say anything, he just shook his head in disapproval.

She gave one last look down to the pool of water and sneered at the pink mask gleaming at her, sitting perfectly perched on the top of a mushroom cap.

Soon they were wandering through the snow.

A muffled cry in the distance startled them. They stood and looked toward the approaching man. He was limping and slashing a flaming sword in a panicked haze. Two boars snorted at him, encircling him against a tree. He continued to slash madly; each strike weaker than the last. One boar grabbed his arm and pulled him to the ground, fiercely biting into his flesh. The flaming sword melted the snow beneath it.

"Rhamy!" Victoria screamed and turned to Gregor.

"Please, he is my friend," she asked. Gregor looked back at Rhamy and then back at Victoria before deciding. Finally giving into her pleading face, he rushed toward the scene, transforming as he ran. Victoria followed behind, gathering his clothes for him. He barked loudly at the boars. They stood their ground, striking the snow with their hooves and lowering their heads aggressively. He pounced, slashing the nearest across the face. It whimpered and scurried into the forest with a loud series of oinks. The other charged, and Gregor dodged as it squealed. Rhamy set the hair on its back ablaze and then stumbled and fell weakly into the snow from the effort.

Victoria ran forward, pulling him onto his back. Brushing the snow from his face, Victoria gasped.

"Rhamy?" she asked.

"Victoria!" he said in a soft whisper, his energy almost completely spent. "I finally found you."

"What is he doing here?" Gregor asked, and they both looked at Rhamy, who now slumped back into the snow, his flame sword extinguished.

"He helped me get out of the Avian castle, but we got separated when Elizabeth and her flock attacked us," she explained.

"You trusted this elf?" Gregor said, infuriated.

"Well, you left me and um . . . I . . .get dressed!" Victoria stumbled over her words as she held out his pants for him. As he pulled on his trousers, she turned her attention to Rhamy.

"Please, get up Rhamy." She pulled under his arm and helped him to his feet. Leaning against her, they slowly made it under the thick trees offering protection from the chilly wind. She helped him onto a dry log under a thick pine. His arm was bleeding, badly torn up. She looked to Gregor while he pulled his jacket on.

"Could you—" she began to ask, but Gregor immediately stopped her with a violent head shake.

"Not a chance," Gregor said flatly. Victoria continued to check for other wounds. Thankfully there were only bruises and cuts. She tore a bit of her skirt's hem and used the strip of fabric to bandage his arm best she could.

"I think he is going to be all right," Victoria said. She could tell Gregor was annoyed.

"I still got some fire in me!" Rhamy said with a bit of a snicker, but he fell into a weak stupor and slumped against the log.

"He is your knight in blazing armor," Gregor said. Victoria did not appreciate the mocking tone and pretended not to hear it.

"I do not know how you survived the storm out here," she said.

"Fire elf!" Rhamy said wearily, taking several more sips of water. "I am relieved to find you in good health," he said. His usual polite demeanor restored; Victoria welcomed his familiar voice. "How did you survive?"

Victoria blushed; a tingle worked its way along her spine as she relived the moment.

"Cave," Gregor said to Rhamy, gesturing in the direction where it lay behind them. Victoria was a bit set off guard at his casual tone. Now she worried perhaps their kiss had not been as special to him as it had been to her. Then she silently scolded herself; she would not be one of those women who fretted needlessly over a man and tried to decode his emotions by his unrelated actions. She had seen it a million times with her mother's friends during the gossip sessions they discreetly held during their tea parties in the parlor.

They let him rest until he was able to sit up without shaking.

Finally, when Rhamy stood, he looked at Gregor as if acknowledging him for the first time. He did not say a word to him but watched him closely. Gregor returned the stare with a hint of disgust forming on his raised lip and flared nostrils.

"Are we ready to rescue Mabel?" Victoria asked.

"It is impossible now without a better plan. Between the boars and the storm, we have been driven off course. We should not be walking through this part of the mountain," Rhamy said. "Come with me. My people have horses; if we go there, we can regroup and be more prepared."

"She is not going anywhere with you!" Gregor said, standing up defensively.

"Oh, and I should leave her here with you? You have no supplies, and you are on foot!" Rhamy said.

"This was your plan; you help her out of the Avian's shackles to replace them with your own!" Gregor said and then he turned to Victoria. "You cannot go with him."

"Stop!" Victoria said. "I am going to get Mabel, and I welcome both of you to accompany me. But if you two wish to argue instead, I will continue forward on my own. We do not have time to stand around arguing!" She angrily trudged froward.

Rhamy followed close as Gregor trailed behind. Victoria remained an anxious lead, thoughts of Mabel helped fight off the cold seeping into her toes. She once again lost track of the time as they walked, she wished she had her father's pocket watch. It sat uselessly on his desk, in his office at home.

"We need to warm our feet before we go further. We do not want our toes to rot," Gregor said as he sat in the snow and pulled his boots off. Victoria followed obediently and rubbed her feet in her hands. Victoria huffed in pain as a series of needles poked at the tips of her toes, which were alarmingly red and somewhat swollen.

"Let me help with that," Rhamy offered pleasantly. He took her feet in his hands, and a warm yellow flame below his hand covered her toes.

"How is this flame not burning me?" she asked.

"I can adjust temperatures according to need," he said, his voice a bit louder than necessary, and she realized he was gloating for the benefit of seeing Gregor glower. Soon her feet felt warm and cozy, and Rhamy turned his attention to her boots, drying them completely before handing them back to her.

"Can you warm my friend?" Victoria asked, pulling the little mush-room from her pocket. He looked bluer than before now. Rhamy held his thumb and forefinger on either side and soon the little mushroom was his normal greenish hue.

"A fool's gold mushroom." Rhamy said. "I have never seen one up close before."

"Yeah, I heard it crying for help so I grabbed it." Victoria explained.

"Interesting. Has it told you its name?" Rhamy asked. Victoria was taken back by this question.

"Has he told you?" Victoria asked.

"I am not a shape changer; you are the one who would be able to ask." Rhamy said.

"Well, I did not think to ask." Victoria admitted. She turned toward it and asked.

"He calls himself Rumi." Victoria said.

"You speak to them in their tongue too. Fascinating," Rhamy said.

"What do you mean? I just asked it like how I talk to you, plainly," Victoria said.

"Nope, you were squeaking," Rhamy said. "There is great power in you. One day you are going to trust me enough to let me help you." He said, giving Victoria a knowing look.

Victoria slipped Rumi back into her pocket.

"Thank you, Rhamy," she said pleasantly as she drew her boots back on. She looked toward Gregor. He was obviously irritated, evident by his short, stiff movements. Rhamy stopped and pointed in the distance. "We need to make it to that ridge before nightfall." It was a hill that sloped high, and trees grew on the top thick and close together.

"Well, we need to make it to Mabel tonight before the maze run begins, so we are going as fast as we can," Victoria said.

"Yes, indeed I know our goal, but we must make it to the top of that ridge before the sunlight shadows this valley." Rhamy did not offer any further explanation but trudged faster down the hillside. Rhamy's anticipation made Victoria nervous.

"Do you know why?" She looked at Gregor, and he shrugged.

"I have never come through this way to get to Naphtali." He said.

"To the top of that ridge," Victoria repeated, looking up at the steep hillside. She estimated that it would take longer than they had sunlight.

They plodded onward and were halfway up the side of the ridge as the sun started to touch the distant horizon.

"Please hasten your steps," Rhamy encouraged them. Seeing the fear in Rhamy's eyes, Gregor pulled Victoria over his shoulder and sprinted up the hill. She tried to sort through everything being upside down and caught a glimpse of something moving in the valley behind them.

Gregor stopped for a moment, peering behind him.

"Don't stop to sniff—run!" Rhamy shouted in exasperation toward Gregor, and his stern tone made Gregor's feet fly up the slope.

She looked down as a shriek sounded in the valley below. Small black figures were emerging from the trees and gathering. They were naked little creatures. Their greasy black skin shone in the rising moonlight. They varied in size, but most averaged about two and a half feet tall. She recognized those thin, knobby arms and legs. They seemed to carry most of their weight in their overly plump bellies. As they turned their heads upward to echo high-pitched screams into the darkening sky, she saw their ugly faces.

"Goblins!" she breathed. After their last encounter, Victoria was sure they were demon spawn from the depths below. The bright white of the snow cast even more of a shadow on the dark creatures.

Their cries sounded devilish and hastened Gregor's feet to the top of the ridge and into the safety of the tree line. He sat her down gently. She looked down to see Rhamy still several yards away and said a silent prayer he would make it undetected. Thankfully, the creatures seemed terribly excited and were busy dancing about as they gathered wood into a large pile near the shore of the frozen lake.

Rhamy finally landed in the snow beside Victoria. Immediately he warmed Rumi as she presented him eagerly. Then Rhamy removed her boots and began to rub her cold feet.

"Oh, thank you," she said. They were more swollen and brighter red. Their state made Victoria cringe. She grimaced as they began to thaw.

"What are they doing?" Victoria asked in a shudder, looking down at the creatures below as they continued their chants and stabbed at each other with their crude spears.

"Gathering to eat," Rhamy said.

"And I would hate to be poked to death by a hundred of their little forks," Gregor said this with a look of disgust and began to remove his own boots to warm his feet. More goblins came from the forest a few at a time, and soon they pulled instruments out and began to play on their eerie pipes, flutes, and drums. They lit the large woodpile, and the flames rose in a peculiar green hue. Some jumped onto overturned stumps and danced a little jig while others swung from the low tree branches, cackling to each other.

As Rhamy rubbed her feet, soon they returned to a normal temperature, and she was able to wiggle her toes once more.

"Thank you!" she said. Rhamy gave a large smile and took up her boots, once again drying them. The chilly wind whistled through the trees on the ridge, and their unprotected backs got the brunt of the cold. Rhamy started to light a fire.

"A fire would expose us," Gregor said, pushing Rhamy's hands down harshly into the snow with a sizzle. Victoria nodded in complete understanding while resenting the fact. A loud explosion of cheers and chants from below woke them from their weary state; the goblins were bouncing about excitedly. Many took up the drums in a fast rhythmic beat as more goblins came from the woods.

"Woah, that is a huge goblin!" Victoria said, pointing at the creature stepping from the forest, surrounded by the little goblins.

"The Goblin Queen," Rhamy said. "Strange, she usually only leaves the drey to feast on some poor fool caught in their clutches," Rhamy said this as a dozen goblins emerged, carrying a long pole with a figure tied to it in the most barbaric way.

The figure had pale peach skin, and Victoria realized it was a man as his head dragged along the ground. He was tied by his hands and feet, swaying from side to side as the mob of creatures carried him toward the green fire. Busily they set about preparing a crude roasting spit.

The man screamed in terror as a few of the goblins prodded him with their sharp three-pronged spears and gawked at him with hideous faces. Victoria gasped as she caught sight of the man's face.

"That is Henry!" She could not help but run toward the slope, but Gregor caught her, pulling her back into the shadows.

"Victoria, we can't help him," he said.

"I have to!" Victoria said in desperation. Gregor looked back toward the scene and furrowed his brows. "You can stay here, I am going," Victoria said, and she leaned over to grab the dagger she knew he kept in his boot.

"Fine, only if you promise to stay here," he said in aggravation. Victoria nodded quickly, and she offered back the dagger. But he was already pulling off his shirt. Rhamy drew his fire sword.

She was about to argue she could help, but another look at the goblins below persuaded her to sit. Gregor began down the hillside, shifting in the shadows. Rhamy followed. Victoria watched as the goblins noticed the beast descending on them. They dropped Henry. He fell to the ground painfully and he rolled, trying to break from his bonds. The goblins ran around and sometimes stepped right on him. The goblins grabbed up their forked spears and shrieked in a high-pitched manner, preparing for a fight. Rhamy lit his sword with a blue flame just as he slashed the first row of them. They shrieked in surprise.

Rhamy beheaded a few on his first swing. Others jumped on his back, and he had to fling them off. Some landed in the fire. Their burning black flesh made the smoke rise in murky coils. The putrid smell hit Victoria's nose, and she gagged.

Gregor roared, and many fell over each other in momentary fear, but the goblins seemed to gather strength from each other and soon surrounded him with their bloodred eyes full of delighted glee. He thrashed his claws, severing many in half and breaking the forks into unusable pieces.

Victoria brought her attention back to the fallen Henry, now lying in the snow still bound to the pole, forgotten by the distracted goblins. He was wiggling uncomfortably, trying to break free. Victoria looked at the dagger in her hand and pushed herself down the slope.

Victoria continued to Henry undetected and started to cut at the binds on his feet.

"Victoria?" Henry whispered in hysterical surprise.

"Shh," Victoria whispered back, not wanting to attract any attention, but it was too late. Three goblins broke from the mob trying to stab Rhamy and bounced over eagerly to surround Victoria. She whipped the dagger in front of her and jabbed it at the nearest goblin. Their faces were covered in bumps and notches. Most had scars and poorly drawn, blotchy tattoos, making their bodies look even filthier than they already were. Their large red eyes shifted on her as their lips curled in wicked smiles. Then she realized she recognized one. The little tuft of hair on his head and the markings—he was the same who had beckoned her into the thicket only days before, but it felt like a lifetime ago. Then she second-guessed herself. The probability this was the exact one, out of the hundreds here on this frozen lake, seemed highly unlikely. But then he let loose in a hideous cackle and pointed at her excitedly to its buddies. He flicked its tongue at her and was the first to leap toward her, jumping higher than what seemed possible for such a disproportional creature.

Aiming for the squishy middle, her dagger struck as he was in midair. His blood was almost as bright red as his eyes, and lots of it spattered over Victoria's arm. A sickening smell rose from the entrails of the goblin as it fell back into the snow, still alive and screeching in agony. She had no time to quiet it because a second goblin shot its fork toward her. She barely missed its jagged points, and she crouched to cut at the black arm that threw it. She sliced the arm off with one swift motion, and she was stunned, momentarily staring at the black limb twitching in the snow. The goblin looked at its remaining nub and began to shriek angrily, throwing itself against her leg and biting at her calves as though a rabid dog.

While trying to kick it away, more blood doused her skirt. It clasped down deep into her flesh with its yellow pointed teeth, and she drove her dagger into its head. She did not have enough vigor to slice deeply, and she heard the tip hit the bone. The creature continued to chew at her leg. She pulled the dagger's tip out of its flesh and drew it high above her, clasping two hands on the hilt. Dropping all her weight behind the blow, she sunk the dagger deep, piercing into its skull. The goblin fell over with its teeth still chattering.

She stepped on the creature to hold him fast to retrieve her dagger, but as she bent forward, another jumped on her back, pulling her hair in a wild frenzy. She swung about, but the goblin clung tighter as though a mere child playing a game. Victoria threw herself down into the snow and heard him gasp as the wind was knocked from its chest. She swung blindly above her head, trying to hit him away, finding its eye with her thumb. She drove her nail inside. The goblin shrieked. She flinched as warm drops of blood slithered through her hair.

She stood, wiping the dripping blood from her forehead and looked at the goblin. Gagging and finally retching to the side, she vomited over another attacking goblin she had not noticed approaching. He still attacked, disregarding the slime that now covered his body. When Victoria kicked, its thin arm whipped out and pulled on her skirt, wiping her own vomit back onto her clothes. She dashed back over to the fallen goblin, yanking the dagger from its skull after a series of hard tugs. When she finally wiggled it loose, she stabbed the goblin climbing up her leg. He fell into the snow.

Ignoring his cries, she returned to freeing Henry, wanting to wake from this nightmare. When his bonds were cut loose, Henry grabbed the nearest weapon, and whipped a goblin in the head, stabbing it through its open mouth still screeching in anger. Henry then pressed his back up against Victoria's, both held their weapons ready. Victoria could feel Henry trembling. Then there was an excited cry as something huge was barreling into the battle.

"Get to the ridge!" Victoria pointed, and Henry nodded. They both took off toward it. The queen stomped at them, letting loose a blood-curdling bellow. She was taller than all of them, which was a stark contrast to the tiny goblins running around her feet. She was a large, lumpy blob with a couple of double chins and beads of sweat dribbling down her forehead. Worse yet, she wore little clothing and Victoria could see her underarms were incredibly hairy. Her big, sausage-like fingers were armed with threatening claws, and she used them as weapons, slashing madly. She kept snapping her pointed teeth viciously. Victoria screamed and ducked several of her swipes, trying to maneuver around her.

A large burst of vivid blue fire sizzled into her backside, and she swung about in a rampage, knocking a goblin over and stepping on another unfortunate one in her path.

"Run!" shouted Rhamy, and he flung another barrier of fire. Victoria and Henry continued toward the slope and began the climb up to the top. The path upward made them both quake, and they leaned on each other pathetically. Slowly they scurried, and, midway to the top, they both fell exhausted into the snow.

"I think this is far enough," Victoria said, and Henry collapsed beside her.

Rhamy made several barriers with flames while Gregor slashed and bit his way through the throng. They fought the remaining goblins surrounding them while the rest cackled angrily from the other side of the flames. Rhamy kept the barriers as long as he could as Gregor fought his way through. Rhamy started up the slope, reaching for Victoria, but she pointed to Henry. He helped Henry to his feet, wrapping his arm over his shoulder. They pressed onward.

Together they finished the rest of the steep slope into the tree line. Victoria looked eagerly for Gregor. Gregor was far below, goblins pulling on him from every side.

"Gregor!" Victoria yelled. She started back down the hillside, the dagger feeling even smaller now, but she had to try. Rhamy drew another flaming arrow and began to shoot them into the goblins, but for each he shot, another two seemed to replace it.

Gregor broke free from the pile riding him and staggered up the hillside. The queen was now running full speed toward Gregor. She slammed into him, tackling him down into the snow. All the goblins circled, their screeches piercing the night in victory. Victoria screamed.

Rhamy pulled back another flame arrow and while he let it loose, suddenly a shower of arrows rained down behind his, piercing many of the goblin's flesh. Victoria spied three archers on horseback, letting loose another series with such accuracy, Gregor clawed out of the horde without hesitation. The goblins used their own bodies to shield their queen from harm. While the archers continued their assault, Gregor was able to break free and make his way up the side of the hill.

Victoria did not recognize any of the scruffy faces, but they knew Gregor, beckoning him forward by name. Each rider offered a hand, one pulling up Rhamy and the other two gesturing toward Henry and Victoria.

"Gregor, can you keep up with our horses?" one man asked with a chuckle, and the others joined in a hearty laugh. At first, Victoria thought they were being mean, but as soon as they galloped forward, Gregor stayed easily in the lead. Soon the goblins were far behind, their eerie screeches fading in the drum of the horse beats. Victoria held one arm about the rider as to not fall off. She looked to see Henry clinging to his rider, following the beast Gregor with wide eyes.

They rode through the snow for longer than Victoria had expected. As they finally reined to a stop, she looked about at the endless expanse of forest. Her legs stung. The rider hopped down, light and nimble, turning toward her to offer a hand.

"Ow!" she groaned as she slowly swung her leg around. "Thank you," she said, forcing a smile through her grimace. Half-limping, she made her way to Henry, who was also having a hard time walking properly because his legs were shaking so terribly. He probably had not eaten in days.

He grinned at Victoria as he raced to her. Victoria grabbed him in a tight embrace, tears welling in her eyes. Then Henry kissed her, first he kissed her cheek and then her other cheek and suddenly he was on her lips. She pulled back quickly, but not fast enough. Gregor's fist flew through the air, sending Henry reeling back into the snow.

"A savage!" Henry yelled, trying to pry his sword up toward Gregor in defense. "You shall not gorge on our flesh this day!" He shakily lifted himself until he stood leaning on Victoria's shoulder, brandishing his sword weakly.

"No, Henry. Gregor is not going to hurt you," Victoria said, sending a warning glance at Gregor. She tried to pull the sword away. Henry resisted.

"Get out of here!" Henry yelled, still waving the weapon best he could. Gregor frowned, anger on his face.

"He is a friend," Victoria quickly explained.

"Who is this?" Gregor asked.

"Henry works with the horses in the stables back home—" Victoria started to explain, but when she turned to look at Gregor, she realized his clothes were still crumpled in his hands. Shamelessly, Gregor stood impatiently waiting for further explanation.

"What are you doing here?" Victoria asked Henry, bewildered.

"I saw it—I saw the creature take you away from Charlene's palace," Henry said.

"My father did not believe me. He did not see it. No one else saw it. I started to wonder if I had imagined the entire thing, but you did not return. Your mom was screaming for someone to find you, so I took off on Nutmeg at the first light, following as best I could. I was thrown off Nutmeg and got lost, and then those creatures got a hold of me."

"You came for me?" she asked, grabbing him in another hug. "Henry, you are so brave!" Victoria could hear Gregor give a huff, but she did not look.

"How did you escape?" Henry said, looking over her with wide eyes. Victoria supposed she was a sight to behold in her tattered clothes, wild hair, and wind-burned cheeks.

"I did not escape. Well, I definitely tried but failed, twice," Victoria said with emotions welling up inside her. "You know, I will tell you all about it later," Victoria said. "Let's get you fed."

A few women approached, offering soup and warm blankets. Victoria wondered where they had come from, looking around again at nothing but more forest. As Gregor approached, they cheered. The women swarmed to offer him blankets and soup. He thanked them with a smile, both hands holding a steaming bowl awkwardly. One of the riders slapped him on the back, spilling some of the soup into the snow with a sizzle.

"This is Daryl, leader of the last remaining free humans," Gregor introduced the man as he unwrapped his scarf from his face. "This is Victoria," Gregor said. Daryl stepped toward Victoria, and she offered her hand. As he gave it a kiss, she noticed his crooked nose. "And this is her stable boy," he said, gesturing toward Henry. Victoria did not like the condescending tone Gregor used. Henry did not seem to notice as he gave a tired half wave

"Hello, stable boy," Daryl said.

"And a fire elf," Gregor said in disdain, and the others gasped, looking at Rhamy fearfully.

"Why would you trust one of their kind here?" another rider grumbled.

"I have no idea," Gregor said, eyeing Victoria. The women shuffled from Rhamy. One even yanked back the blanket she was in the middle of presenting him. The men eyed him closely, lifting their fists toward him.

"He is my friend," Victoria said, stepping toward him and holding his arm to display that he was indeed harmless. The humans whispered to one another, now glaring at her suspiciously.

"Is he your lover?" one asked accusingly in a harsh tone. Gregor and Henry both gave loud objections at the allegation.

"No, he helped me escape from the Avians. He is going to help me get into Naphtali," Victoria said.

They all broke into whispers. Gregor shook his head. Victoria realized she should probably have asked Gregor what their story was before she shouted it to a crowd of strangers.

"You have been there, to Naphtali?" Daryl asked anxiously.

"Was there a man named Eric there?" a woman asked quickly before she had a chance to answer.

"No, I haven't been there yet," she answered, but no one seemed to hear anything except the word "Naphtali."

"My son, Jacob—did you meet a young man named Jacob?" another asked, pulling on her arm.

"My sister, brunette, stands about this high. She has brown eyes and answers to the name Martha?" another man asked.

Soon the questions flooded over her as the people stepped closer to her, pleading for answers. Gregor stepped in front of her, blocking the hands waving in her face. Many more were asking about loved ones, and she could no longer hear individual voices. It was now an unintelligible hum.

"Please, everyone." Rhamy stood on a stump and used a commanding voice. "We do not have time—" But they all booed him, and snowballs flew at his head. He clambered down from the stump and disappeared. Victoria was trying to call after him, but the crowd continued their onslaught of asking about their loved ones. She kept shaking her head until Daryl stepped into view and cleared his throat.

"Calm down." Daryl commanded and the crowd fell into silence. "What do you need, Gregor?"

"Keep the stable boy safe, will you? And I am going to need a horse," Gregor said with a sigh, casting a sidelong glance at Victoria. She smiled back at him, glad they did not need to have another argument about her going.

"And what about the fire elf?" Daryl asked. Gregor shrugged.

"I would like to help rescue Mabel," Henry said.

"And you could use my fire," Rhamy volunteered.

"No, neither of you are coming," Gregor said.

"We might need them," Victoria said.

Gregor shook his head. "Too many people will just get in the way. All of us running around will get us caught."

"I am sick of waiting. We must act!" someone from the crowd yelled, and the others joined in a cheer.

"No, Gregor will go now. He has told me Charlene is there right now. It is near impossible to save anyone while the queen is there. We must wait and come up with a plan after Gregor has updated information on Naphtali," Daryl said. The crowd dispersed slowly.

"Please, just keep an eye out for my boy," Daryl said, his voice dropping low in urgency. "Daniel."

Gregor gave him a reassuring nod. They clasped each other on the back of the neck, pulled their foreheads close, and they gave a low grunt. Someone brought over a horse.

"Nutmeg!" Henry shouted in delight. "Where did you find him?"

"He was wandering around. We guessed he was yours," the man holding the rope said. He held Nutmeg's rope fast as Victoria grabbed a hold of his saddle and pulled herself up, swinging her leg over successfully after two tries because the horse kept neighing and stomping.

Her face flushed with embarrassment as she tried to pull Nutmeg in control with the reins, but he would not allow her to direct him. He reared up, and Victoria screamed, clinging to his neck in fear.

"Calm down," Henry's voice pierced through the commotion. He grabbed hold of the reins and pulled the horse back down, allowing

Victoria to quickly slide off before the horse tried to nip at her with his oversized teeth.

"Oh, yes, horses do not seem particularly fond of me these days," Victoria said.

"I remember," Henry said with a laugh. It was so good to see a familiar face, and Victoria could not resist hugging Henry again, once again amazed he faced the mountains alone to find her.

"Horses have never been keen on changers. They were leery of your father too," Rhamy said with an inquisitive examination of the horse's face, pulling on its lips and prodding near its eye curiously.

"We will never make it on time," Gregor said, looking up at the horizon. The first edge of the moon was sliding into view.

"I will take the horse," Henry volunteered, saddling up and steering the horse about expertly.

Before Victoria could begin to climb up, Rhamy cut in.

"I promised you I would help you get Mabel and I do not break my promises," Rhamy said. He climbed on the horse with Henry.

"Then why are you taking my horse?" Victoria asked, puzzled.

"Well, I know Gregor is not going to let me ride his back." Rhamy said with a hearty laugh.

Gregor did not look too enthused about the situation, but another glance at the sky made him just shake his head. He undressed, stuffing his clothes and satchel into the saddlebag, while Victoria once again looked away. She worried someone would notice her blushing cheeks.

As Gregor changed, Victoria realized it was all normal to her now, but Henry had yet to see a transformation, he was too busy fighting the goblins before to see it. As Gregor turned, Henry screamed.

"Oh, sorry, sorry. Gregor is a beast, but he is not the one who took me. It is all very complicated," Victoria hurriedly explained as Gregor stomped near them. She completely understood his wide eyes and horrified expression. Gregor bent down, and Victoria swung her leg up over his back and held about his thick, hairy neck. He leaned forward and ran on all fours, picking up speed. Henry obediently guided the horse to follow, his mouth still hanging open.

CHAPTER 17

A NASTY TWIST

AS THEY APPROACHED, VICTORIA saw the walls of Naphtali made a perfect quatrefoil with rounded edges meeting in four distinct corners. Each had watchtowers stationed above. It looked like an inescapable prison. She shuddered, knowing Mabel was down there somewhere among those rows of buildings. Then she spied the maze, with tall and thick walls. As Victoria looked at it, she realized she recognized the design. It was a large scale of the small green hedge maze below the balcony on Charlene's estate, the maze she had stood staring at with Mason. Shivers were sent down her spine as she thought of how close she had stood to him, unknowing he was a monster.

As they approached the edge of the tree line, Gregor stopped and bent low so Victoria could climb off him easily. Henry pulled the reins of the horse until its hooves stood beside him. Gregor quickly transformed and dressed while Rhamy laughed at Henry's reaction.

Victoria walked around the horse, once again taking care to avoid his mouth.

"Where is the door?" Victoria asked anxiously.

"Go along the wall until you see the small keyhole. You will have to open the door to the maze, it only opens from the outside," Gregor explained to Henry and dropped the key into his hand. Henry looked to Victoria, and she nodded.

"We have to save Mabel" she encouraged. Henry gave a sigh and then hugged Victoria tightly.

"Please come with me," Henry said. "It is safer outside here."

"She is safer with me," Gregor said. Henry once again looked at Victoria, concerned.

"I have to help get Mabel out," Victoria said.

"How are you going to help?" Henry asked frankly.

"I do not have time to explain," Victoria snapped.

Henry looked reluctant but finally started forward.

"I'll go with Henry, in case you need a smoke signal to find us at the door," Rhamy offered. Victoria passed Rumi to him. He placed him in his front pocket. Gregor nodded and Victoria gave them a small, anxious wave.

Victoria and Gregor headed toward the main gate. Two men stood there, and Victoria watched them greet Gregor with smiles and jolly jokes. He stopped to chat for a bit before they let him pass without question. Naphtali was a place of hard stone and brick, from the buildings down to the cobblestone below their feet.

Victoria shivered at the sight of the rows and rows of small houses. All the humans were walking in lines being directed by three ladies, two Victoria recognized. They were Gretchen and Hannah. Victoria gasped as she looked into her familiar burnt sienna eyes. The third lady had large blue eyes with a sprinkle of freckles across the bridge of her nose, her blond hair set in a perfect wave of curls. All were wearing flowy blouses and trousers tucked into their thigh-high laced boots. It was a strange out-fit, and though it was a masculine compilation, they wore it with graceful femininity. She was yanked from her observation by their taunts.

"Oh, Hannah, do you see the Beast Prince is here?" Gretchen said in a snooty tone.

"Oh yes, looks like he is here for the maze run, not to see us," Hannah said in a dramatic declaration.

"You never come here anymore. When did you become too good for us?" the blonde said, pretending to pout.

"Well, you know, he has his own demesne now. He doesn't need to pay us any mind," Hannah said.

"Victoria, your mother would be upset if she saw how far you have let yourself go." Gretchen said mockingly, tugging on her torn dress hem.

"Hello, Gretchen, Hannah, Jezebel," Gregor acknowledged them while trying to push his way through the line of humans and head to the maze. Hannah stepped in front of him, placing a hand on his chest flirtatiously.

"What are you doing after the maze run?" she asked with a little gig-gle. Gretchen was ruffling his hair.

"Maybe later, ladies," Gregor said, shifting away from them.

"You are about to miss it," Gretchen said, and then she turned her eyes on Victoria. "And there is a special guest tonight." Victoria did not like the way she laughed after saying that.

"Or Victoria can stay here with us. We are about to harvest the next lot. We can just toss her into the line," Hannah offered.

"No, it's okay. She can come with me," Gregor said casually.

"You will get her back, silly. It is just one jar," Gretchen said, holding up a pint jar with red liquid inside. As Victoria realized it was blood, she felt her stomach lurch, she looked to the line of humans, and they all looked as scared as she felt, shaking in the winter air with their faces pale.

She carefully spied each face, looking for Mabel, until she felt Gregor's hand gently grasp hers, pulling her along.

They crossed through the other rows of houses and to another gate, where he was met by more guards who recognized him, and they discussed the latest news of Omnia for several minutes before they followed the crowd to the seating overlooking the maze.

"We will have to wait until she is released into the maze before we can open the door and pull her through," Gregor whispered.

"You are a beast. Can't you just talk to them like you have been doing with the rest of the guards?" Victoria asked.

"You do not understand. I have purposely transformed over and over in training to be lucid when I am a beast. It is not easy, and I would not have suffered it if my pa had not pushed me since I was very young. Most don't know what they are doing when they are transformed. There will be no talking, only screaming," Gregor said. "We must remain hidden."

"Where is the door?" Victoria asked.

"It is up there. There are a lot of twists and turns on the inside, but here on the outside, it is just down there," Gregor said, pointing down the long wall. Victoria did not see it yet. They were still too far away.

"No, this thing is massive. How will she just magically know where to go?" Victoria asked.

"I will transform and go in and guide her," Gregor said. "Please, just promise me you are not going to go in, no matter what," Gregor said. Victoria nodded quickly, but Gregor looked at her, unconvinced. She continued to anxiously nod, knowing full well she was about to transform as soon as he was over the wall.

"Do not follow me," Gregor said, giving a stern look. His hand was on Victoria's shoulder. Victoria gasped in anger and tried to shake his hand off, but it was heavy and clutched her harder, squeezing her collarbone painfully. She looked down and spied the hand. It was too burly to be Gregor's.

"I won't let her go anywhere," Brutus said. His gruff voice made Victoria cower under his grasp.

"What are you doing here?" Gregor asked.

"I came to stop you," Brutus said, his voice spiking with anger. "I found my key was missing. I could not let you come alone while Charlene was here. It's too dangerous, son. She is a monster. Not just any monster—she is *the* monster. The worst one."

Gregor looked like the illustration Victoria had seen in a storybook she had read to Mabel so often she had it memorized. It was of a child caught with his tiny fingers inside the pie sitting to cool on the windowsill. It would have been comical if it was any other parent, but Brutus did not seem the forgiving type.

"It's back to strictly Omnia duties for you," Brutus said. Gregor gave a groan.

"For the next decade," Brutus said, and Gregor shut his mouth and dropped his head in defeat. "Gather your demesne. Let's go. Go this way. Her patrol is on watch on the other side," Brutus said and pushed Gregor toward the gate. Victoria stood unyielding.

"I am not leaving my sister here," she said, her voice cracking as she tried to retain a whisper.

Brutus looked at Gregor expectantly. Victoria clenched her fists and prepared for the worst.

Gregor squared his shoulders and looked Brutus in the eye.

"We are going to get her sister," Gregor said. Victoria felt a wave of gratitude toward Gregor. Brutus did not have a chance to reply as a laugh pierced the crowded stadium around them. Charlene and Mason came into view. Gretchen was whispering, as usual, with Hannah behind them. Their hushed tones seemed more sinister now.

"Hello. It seems you are lost. The good seats are over here," Charlene said with a smile.

Brutus looked irate, his wild eyes seemed to burn into Gregor's before he slowly turned his head and popped on a crooked smile. He good-naturedly bowed to Charlene.

"I was just telling Gregor he did not have the time to stay and watch. He has a prior obligation to attend to," Brutus said, nudging Gregor to head for the forest.

"Nonsense, nothing can be more important than family-bonding time." She said with a smirk.

Brutus obediently followed, Gregor behind him and then Victoria. She shook in the horrible mixture of fear and frustration. It took all her strength to start to shift her feet and follow behind, dropping her hand from the wall. She knew Mabel would be on the other side, fighting for her life at any moment.

As they approached the stairway that led up to the podium overlooking the maze, Victoria hoped Henry had found the door.

Music with heavy drumbeats now pounded on the platform opposite them. It was filled with more beautiful women, playing instruments and dancing around.

Victoria realized they were all monsters, all those rows and rows of ladies cheering. She recognized some from the ball and even some she remembered seeing at her house for tea. Sure, there were a few men, and Victoria guessed they were monsters, too, but they were few and far between.

A few beast guards stood watching, but it was the large hairy forms below that caught her eye. They were unruly, barking and scratching furiously inside their small cages. Victoria instantly understood what Gregor had mentioned before. Whenever she saw Gregor and even Gor in beast form, they both had complete control over their beast instincts, being able to stand and keep their individual personalities intact. These below had no such control. They panted aggressively on all fours, their eyes rolling around wildly. They slammed against their gates again and again despite the sharp metal points welded to the heavy iron, catching blood and fur.

Then she forgot all about the plan when she looked ahead. She gasped. There was Mabel sitting on a comfortable-looking chair and eating. Mabel had been cleaned up and dressed in a fancy gown, her hair braided and curled into a complex updo. With vibrant pink lipstick and matching nail polish, she looked like a smaller version of Charlene.

"Victoria?" Mabel gasped, jumping out from her chair. Charlene clicked her tongue, and Mabel immediately sat back down and shut her mouth. Mason took a seat on the other side of Charlene. Charlene gestured, and they all took seats, Victoria rushing to the one nearest Mabel.

"How have you been?" Victoria quickly whispered. Mabel looked at her but then looked down at her lap, not daring to speak. Charlene was watching closely. Her smug smile irritated Victoria.

"Come, come, sit here right by your father," Charlene beckoned Gregor. Gregor glumly stepped forward and sat down. Gretchen and Hannah remained standing, which was more unsettling.

"I thought you said you were not coming. You have not accompanied me in many moons," Charlene said to Brutus.

"Somehow, I found myself here," Brutus said, sending a sidelong glance to Gregor.

"Did you bring my necklace?" Charlene asked Gregor.

"No, I was hoping to trade something more valuable," Gregor said. At this, Brutus huffed in agitation.

"There will be no trading," Brutus said.

"Well, let's listen to what our boy has to say," Charlene said, her hot pink lips twisting into a cruel smile.

"Charlene," Brutus said in a low guttural burst, a warning.

"I am open for negotiations," she said.

"I want the girl," Gregor said, gesturing to Mabel.

"Oh, you want the complete set?" Charlene laughed. "Both of Richard's daughters?"

"Yes," Gregor said.

"Now why would you want two? Isn't one handful enough?" she asked. "Are you sure you don't want to just trade? This one is more obedient," Charlene said, once again gesturing to Mabel. "I heard of your little debacle at the Avian monastery. And again just now, she has consistently defied your commands," Charlene said. "Unless she is worth more than a slave?"

"I offer a year's worth of my servitude in return for Mabel," Gregor said, bringing himself to one knee and bowing his head. Charlene laughed out loud at Brutus's horrified face.

"No, no human is worth that!" Brutus said.

"Interesting," Charlene said, considering the notion.

"That is off the table. Gregor is not allowed to leave the pack. What do you want for the girl?" Brutus said, obviously trying to finish the conversation as quickly as possible.

"Hush, Brutus, let Gregor speak for himself. He does not need Daddy anymore," Charlene said.

"Let me ask you this, Gregor. What do you want for your Richard's daughter? You can have anything. I have everything," Charlene said. "Want your own castle? I have several scattered along the coast, you take your pick. No one will bother you there. I have chests of gold and precious stones. I have plenty of ladies much more beautiful than her."

"What do you want for the girl?" Gregor asked, repeating the question. His face was once again as though chiseled from stone, his body rigid.

"Gregor, do you ever wonder where your mother is?" Charlene asked. Victoria tilted her head, wondering where Charlene was headed with this.

"No," Gregor said.

"Why not?" Charlene asked.

"Because she is buried near my house in Omnia," Gregor said. "I look at her memorial stone every day."

"Oh, I see," Charlene said, exchanging a glance as Mason smirked alongside her, the only one understanding the comical aspect of the conversation.

"Is that what he told you?" Charlene said. "Do you have any pictures of her, any portraits, not even a carved bust?"

"Charlene," Brutus said again, but this time Charlene flicked her eyes at him, and he fell silent.

"Do you want to know the truth?" she asked. Gregor looked at her and then to Brutus.

"Tell me," Gregor said.

"Perhaps I could tell you and you give me Victoria in exchange," Charlene said.

"No, I don't trust you. You are a liar," Gregor said. Brutus nodded in agreement.

"I am the liar?" Charlene said, turning to Mason and they exchanged another glance. Then she looked to Brutus, watching him stand there glaring at her.

"Let's cease this poorly executed charade. We all know neither of these girls are human," Charlene said, her tone no longer sweet and soft. "I know you have come here in hopes of snagging both of these shape-changers to someday use against me, take my empire for yourself," she said accusingly, her voice now shrill.

"Mabel is human," Victoria spoke up loudly. "She has no ability. She is of no use to you."

"Oh, and when did you discover your abilities?" Charlene said. "Yes, think about it. I am guessing Mabel will bloom sooner than we anticipate!"

"Is that true, Victoria? Will I be a fox like you someday?" Mabel asked excitedly. Victoria shook her head, but Charlene heard.

"A fox? That is an interesting totem," Charlene said.

"Gregor, do you really think she stays because she wants to be with you? What sort of future do you have if she is forced to be your property? Just give her to me now. I can replace her sevenfold with those who will worship you," Charlene said, gesturing toward Hannah and Gretchen, who both smiled.

Victoria felt Charlene was just taking shots in the dark, hoping to stir up something she could use to negotiate. Gregor's face was still like stone. He had not given any indication he was even listening.

"I know the first love always seems the truest, but that is a terribly painful lie only fooling the young and naive," Charlene said, once again sending Brutus the cruelest of smirks. Brutus did not give her the satisfaction of letting his face register any emotion.

"Just make a trade, son. Let's go home," Brutus said, casting a defeated look to his shoes.

"Yes, it seems your father is growing wiser. Perhaps there is hope for him yet," Charlene said. Brutus sheepishly looked up at her and then returned his face to the ground. Victoria was astounded Charlene could reduce such a large and muscular man into a pitiful-looking schoolboy. His hands were in his pockets, his head was low. Charlene grabbed hold of Mabel by the neck and pulled her from her seat, tossing her beside Gregor. Mabel staggered on the edge of the lifted platform. Victoria screamed.

Gregor barely caught her by the arm and pulled her back onto even footing. They both stood facing Charlene.

"All right, you can have Mabel if you answer a riddle," Charlene said, her tone again light and cheery. Her face seemed to reset back to its pleasant and perhaps even friendly smile. Everyone turned to her in anticipation.

"Gregor, Gregor, born of beast and fame. His desires and appetites he could not tame." Charlene paused for effect. "But what was his mother's name?" Charlene was standing very close to Gregor at this point. Her hand pulled on the one strand of hair that had come loose and dangled down his forehead. She replaced it back with the others and smoothed them together by running her nails over his scalp. Gregor flinched under her touch.

Victoria was distracted by the distinct sound of a horn being blown as the unfortunate humans were forced inside. Most began desperately fleeing into the depths of the maze, while others tried to climb the gate. Their cries tormented Victoria.

Gregor looked to Brutus, who stood looking pale, his mouth agape.

"I don't know. The stone is unmarked. We always have just called her Ma," Gregor said finally after a long pause.

"I am sorry you do not know. Truly I am," Charlene said, sweetly caressing Gregor's jawline with a stroke from her slender fingertips, the hot pink nail polish sparkling in the moonlight. She dropped her hand and turned to Brutus. "Tell him the answer and let him claim his prize," she said. Brutus looked at her suspiciously, but Victoria could see a glint of hope in his eye.

"Charlene," Brutus said after a long moment. Her name seemed to cut his mouth as he spoke it. He pressed his lips together fiercely afterward, pain distorting his face. Gregor stood looking as though he might never regain function of his arms or legs. He truly looked carved from stone now. His eyes were filled with disbelief as a most dreadful groan escaped his lips, and Victoria shrank from the sound of it. He looked at Brutus, and Brutus confirmed it with a single nod.

"Come home with me. I will teach you all the things your father never could," Charlene said. She opened her arms wide and gave another smile. This one was softer and perhaps the only sincere one Victoria had ever seen because the tiny folds around Charlene's eyes actually creased.

"Bring Victoria, and the sisters can live with us, one big happy family," Charlene said. Brutus looked like someone had knocked the wind from him. He stood trembling, struggling to fill his lungs.

"I volunteer myself," Victoria said. "I will go with you. Just let Mabel leave with Gregor." She stood as tall as she could and tried not to flinch as Charlene turned and focused her eyes on her.

"That is fine with me," Charlene said with a chuckle, and then Victoria felt the chilly blast of wind against her shoulder as Charlene had sliced through her dress sleeve and cloak in one graceful flick, revealing the *G* on her shoulder. She stood there holding her dress bodice up, clinging to the fabric and cowering under everyone's gaze. She hated how vulnerable she felt, and she could once again feel her face flush red with fear and embarrassment.

"But that is not your decision to make, dear," Charlene said with a small giggle of delight. "Gregor?" Charlene said, mockingly gesturing toward Victoria.

Victoria looked at him intently, mouthing the word *yes* and nodding her head, begging him to make the trade.

"No," Gregor said.

"Gregor!" Victoria hollered in frustration. Gregor avoided her eyes.

"Oh, she is mouthy. I would never once let any demesne speak to me in such a tone," Charlene said. "These are one of the things I could teach you, how to demand respect."

"Through the years, you have killed too many of my friends." Gregor said, as he spoke Victoria could see this stirred up awful memories.

Presently Charlene's smile faded. She flicked her wrist, and suddenly Mabel was falling. Charlene had pushed her off the platform in such a swift movement it was not until she heard the thud of Mabel hitting the stone floor below did Victoria process what had happened.

"Mabel!" Victoria said in a gasp, and she ran to the edge to see Mabel trying to sit up while she clutched her twisted leg. Victoria replayed the sound in her head, the heavy thud had a distinct crack, and she knew the noise all too well after all the carnage she had witnessed lately. Her leg was broken. Surely Mabel was in agony.

"Mabel!" Victoria screamed over the blasting bugle blowing into the chilly winter wind. The drumbeat now pounded faster as the beasts were released.

Victoria instantly began to transform, knowing her fox form could at least survive the jump and slide along the edges with greater ease. Gregor, of course, beat her to it. He sprang from the platform and transformed in midair, shedding his clothes in the process. He landed near Mabel and bits of pants and shirt and jacket landed around them in strips.

"He is a talented young man," Charlene said. "Brutus, I am pleasantly surprised. I just wish you would have let me see him before now, or at least given him my letters," Charlene said in a voice dripping with sentiment. Victoria was unsure if Charlene was being sincere or only pretending. Either way, Brutus was shifting closer to her, his head still down. As they shared the moment, Victoria took her chance to start slipping away.

"You know I couldn't. You tried to drink him dry twice when he was just a baby," Brutus said. "You couldn't control yourself."

"I learned," Charlene said, gesturing toward Mason. Victoria finally understood the look Brutus was giving Mason. It was the look of pure loathing. Mason and Gregor were only half-brothers. The jealousy burning in Brutus's eye was probably just as hot as the first day it sparked into existence, proving a lingering obsession. Victoria shook herself loose from the conversation as the final pain from her change hit.

Gregor was scaling the wall as best he could with Mabel over his shoulder. The walls were tall and had been smoothed with precision; even Gregor could not find holding. He was having a hard time jumping high enough to clear the top. He was on his seventh try as the first beast rounded the corner, and Gregor had no choice but to set Mabel down and face the oncoming brute.

Victoria felt herself sinking down, down until she was beneath the folds of her dress.

"A fox? That is all you have mastered?" Charlene said. "Pathetic really. All that power wasted on one so undisciplined, unmotivated."

"Grab her, Mason. After Mabel dies, I am sure Gregor will reconsider my proposition, especially if we keep his property safe for him," Charlene said.

Victoria slipped under Mason's hand, over his arm, and across his shoulder. As she jumped toward one of the beasts below her, Charlene's nail tugged along the tip of her tail.

Victoria looked behind her to see Charlene's fingers close in a fist and her eyes flash in irritation. Victoria had been quicker, literally by a hair. She landed on one of the beast's shoulders and sprang away before he could catch her in his teeth. She ran under his legs and dashed around the corner, careful to keep the wall to her right side, following the path to Mabel.

"Oooh, she is quick in her second form," Victoria heard Charlene say, intrigued. "Oh well, we tried to save her." She settled back into her seat. Gretchen handed her a tall glass of red liquid, and Victoria told herself it was wine.

The cobblestone floor below was icy cold and frozen hard. Even her padded fox paws felt the chill. She had to sprint away from another beast as it turned to snap.

She turned the corner and saw Mabel leaning against the wall as Gregor struggled to hold off a big black beast, slashing at him furiously. Victoria leapt, sinking her teeth deep into his ear, tearing it clean away. The beast howled in pain, and Victoria ran further up his back, latching deep onto his neck and spinning, tearing a large piece while dropping to the ground. The beast fell, scratching in agony. Gregor's beast form looked at her and gave an impressed grunt. Victoria spat out the cluster of hair and blood.

"Victoria!" Mabel said through a clenched jaw. "It hurts so much."

Victoria looked down to see Mabel's ankle was already beginning to swell. Mabel stood up lopsidedly. Gregor picked Mabel up, Victoria safe in her arms, and once again tried to jump, missing the top by an inch. Another beast barreled into their path. Gregor sprinted right for him, and Mabel screamed in alarm.

Gregor hopped up past the beast's snarling face and used the back of his neck as a steppingstone. He tossed Mabel up onto the top of the maze, and Mabel landed painfully on her bottom as the beast caught Gregor by the foot, yanking him back down into the maze.

Mabel crawled weakly through her tears, dragging herself along the half-foot slab of capstone with unsteady hands. Victoria was trying to help her best she could, but she was too small to really do much. Another beast was barking below now, jumping and snapping at them. She heard the scoffs from the platform. Charlene's was the loudest. Their deranged laughter made Victoria's stomach squirm. This was all a joke to them, some cruel game. Victoria could see bright blue flames burning the buildings beside the maze. Victoria felt her heart leap as Charlene was running to attend to the fire, leaving the platform.

Mabel continued on with Victoria's encouraging yips. As loud shrieks echoed from inside the maze, Victoria was reminded there were other poor souls suffering an unspeakable fate.

.

Mabel continued, Victoria guiding her to the doorway. She could not see him, but she hoped Henry was there. The beasts were below, snapping and snarling along.

Finally, they came to the curving wall that connected to the outermost one, which was much taller. Victoria knew the doorway could not be too far ahead, but now she worried how to get down to it. There were three beasts following behind them. The others were occupied with easier prey. Their screams vibrated through her ears and down her spine.

Victoria wished she could transform into something powerful enough to save everyone.

"How are we going to get down from here?" Mabel asked breathlessly. Victoria was looking around. She could see Henry waving below, he had found the door. She could not see the door until Henry opened it. It swung outward, outside of the maze. She realized the door was made from stone and was perfectly flush with the wall so she would have never noticed it. It was a small passage, and she realized Gregor would have to transform to get through, leaving him vulnerable.

"Victoria, you should escape. You are so little; you can jump and land in Henry's arms safely. Go, save yourself!" Mabel begged. Victoria ignored her, trying to determine a plan. Henry kept looking up at them. The drop was just too high. Mabel would break another bone or two and probably crush one of Henry's. They would have to wait for Gregor. The beasts were snarling and jumping up toward them, trying to grab hold of Mabel's dangling foot. Mabel picked Victoria up and held her close like a teddy bear.

Gregor came around the corner, three more beasts snapping at his heels.

Mabel pushed herself off the ledge. She cried out in pain as her leg flopped. Gregor crouched down and then jumped up, catching her. Even meeting halfway, it was a big drop, and they landed with a heavy thud. Mabel turned away from his fangs, still afraid. The nearest beast snatched Mabel from his arms. Gregor lunged, sinking his teeth deep into his leg. The beast whimpered and dropped Mabel. She ducked down and shimmied through the doorway as another beast's paw sliced the door. Another beast pushed the first aside and tried to get through, forcing his head in, snapping at Mabel's awkwardly dragging foot. Victoria nipped at his nose, and he tucked back just enough for Mabel to clear the passage safely. Although the beast could not fit more than his head and neck, he kept reaching his paws through, slicing the snow in a fury.

Victoria peered over the swiping hairy arm to see two beasts tackle Gregor. He let out a cry of pain before his face was covered in a mosh pit of hair and teeth.

Victoria slipped back through the door, missing the beast's claws and sending her teeth deep into the side of his exposed neck. As he reeled back, she sprang up and over his face.

"No, Victoria!" Henry yelled, and Mabel gasped.

Victoria jumped on top of the pile, sinking her tiny razor-like teeth again and again until one was distracted enough to chase her, leading him away from Gregor. She bolted down one row and then another before she double-backed toward Gregor, leaving the beast behind in a confused daze. She leapt up to the raised claw about to swipe Gregor, piercing his flesh so deep her skull shook as her fang hit bone.

The beast howled and shook her hard, and then Victoria was sailing through the wind, smashing against the heavy stone. She slumped down, dazed. She heard Gregor and the beast fighting, but she could not focus on what was happening. She knew she needed to get out of the doorway. She tried to concentrate on moving toward it. She looked at her hand and wanted to laugh. It was her human hand but tiny. She pulled it up to her face, and it looked ridiculous next to her other three paws. She could feel her face changing, transforming back into human. Her tail was shrinking, and the pain was making her head even fuzzier. She crawled slowly, putting one hand and then a paw in front of another, pushing herself forward toward the doorway.

The pain was causing her to shake, but no matter how much she tried, she could not retain her fox form. She felt her legs and back sound with the fire-like pain shooting down to her toes. The winter air stung her delicate bare skin, and she continued to crawl. A beast ran toward her, his jaws wide as he came at her. She closed her eyes, bracing for the impact of his sharp teeth. Suddenly Gregor was there, and he blocked the beast, slashing at it with his claws, sending it back.

Gregor took the moment to shove her through the door and Henry slammed it shut. The hinges creaked loudly. She could hear a heavy thud and a yelp from the other side.

"Gregor!" she screamed.

Henry pulled Victoria to her feet and wrapped her in his jacket. She stood shaking with Mabel.

"We have to get out of here!" Henry said, and he brought Nutmeg around and pushed Mabel up into the saddle.

"Hurry!" Henry said.

"Yeah, get on, Victoria!" Mabel shouted.

"I've got to go back. I have to help him!" Victoria said.

"There is no time," Henry said. "They are coming!"

"You go. I am going to transform again. I can get back through the door and help him," Victoria said, raising her arms. The jacket hung open, and the cold winter air hit her body while she concentrated hard on being a fox again. Her head felt fuzzy, but the pain would not start, and the transformation would not begin. She stomped her foot angrily.

"Come on!" she screamed.

"Keep your clothes on!" she heard Rhamy say. She turned and caught him staring at her with no regard for privacy.

"Get the door," he said dramatically. Victoria rushed to open the door. Mabel gasped. Both his hands were bright blue and sizzling. Rhamy gave her a wink as he stole one more look before crawling through. Victoria flushed with embarrassment, quickly fumbling to button up the jacket's front as she watched anxiously.

There were howls of pain and the distinct smell of sizzling fur. Suddenly Gregor's human hand shot through the door, and Henry and Victoria grabbed a hold, pulling him out. Then Rhamy Lumpkin crawled through the door. A beast paw was reaching out of it, sliding around, while its owner released a series of barks and growls.

"They are coming! Run!" Henry said. Hannah and Gretchen leaving their comfortable spectator seats now, looking angry.

Rhamy Lumpkin let loose several neon blue fire arrows, catching Gretchen in the thigh and Hannah in the collarbone, slowing them down. He jumped on top of the horse with Henry and Mabel, and they started to ride away. Gregor pulled himself to his feet, ignoring his many bites and wounds. He grabbed Victoria by the hand, and together they ran. They reached the tree line, and as they ducked below the hanging branches, Victoria felt icy cold fingers wrap about her throat, yanking her away from Gregor.

She was lying on her back, Mason above her and his fingers still choking her. Gregor slammed into him, taking Mason down into the frozen, snow-covered ground. Victoria watched their heated wrestling match, unsure how to help. Soon they were both covered in muddy snow and muck.

When they broke free, they scurried to their feet and stood facing each other. Stepping in a circle around, they stared at each other, churning up more snow into mud. The muck squelched softly as it wiggled over Gregor's bare toes.

"Oh, how I have despised watching her fawn over you, the son she never got to raise," Mason said. "Well, I do not see what the fuss is all about," Mason said, looking him up and down and then giving a scoff. Gregor continued to furrow his brow.

"I always was annoyed with you but never understood why," Gregor spat back.

Mason laughed heartily, looking up at the sky before suddenly slamming into Gregor, sending him down onto the ground painfully.

Victoria watched as Mason moved faster, his speed and agility quickly overtaking Gregor. But as Mason pinned him down, Gregor began to transform, and soon the fight was evenly matched, monster versus beast.

"I thought we could get along now, brother," Mason said as Gregor slammed him against the nearest tree trunk and then he lifted a hand to his ear, indicating he was waiting for a reply.

"Oh yeah, dogs can't speak," he said. Gregor bit down onto his shoulder and shook him hard. Mason yelled in pain.

"Drop him!" Charlene's voice cut through the commotion. Gregor ignored her command, continuing to shake Mason, shredding his flesh into bloody chunks. Mason was shrieking in agony.

"Brutus, do something!" Charlene cried out as she came into view. Victoria gasped at Charlene's face. It was burned, melted, one of her eyes were black and charred Victoria doubted she could see from it. Her skin had bubbled from the heat and slide down off her cheekbones in a saggy mess. Her nose was only a black stub. Her hair was singed clean off with only one small patch remaining at the top of her head, it stuck up wildly. Charlene's arm was burned to a crisp, dangling uselessly to her side, the fingers were gone, burned off entirely.

Brutus stood looking at her with fear on his face. Victoria was not sure why Brutus was afraid, obviously Charlene was in no shape to fight. He stood with his arms crossed and let Gregor continue for another long moment before he gave one short bark. It was a strange noise to hear coming from his human mouth.

Gregor instantly dropped him, standing at attention toward Brutus. Charlene looked intrigued.

"I've got to remember that command," Charlene said, her teeth gritted in pain.

"It won't work for you," Brutus said. "Only works for the king."

It was as though an invisible white flag had been waved as Brutus stepped slowly toward Charlene and bent down, allowing her to drink from his neck. She only took a few gulps before pulling back, her face already began to mend. Brutus grabbed Victoria without any comment and slung her over his shoulder. He clicked his tongue and beast Gregor followed behind. Charlene stood there watching them go as Mason lay on the frozen ground at the toes of her white fur-lined, high-heeled boots, writhing in anguish. Gretchen and Hannah came to her side, holding their injuries.

"Well, don't just stand there. Fetch some blood for us before we expire," Charlene said.

"Should I gather the sisters? We can overtake the younger shape-changer," Gretchen said breathlessly, clutching her wounds.

"No, not while the fire elf is with her," Charlene said, she was staring at Brutus and Gregor walking away.

The last sight Victoria had was the upside-down view of Charlene's odd look of amusement.

CHAPTER 18

A FOOL

THEY WALKED FOR A while in silence. Victoria, despite being hauled like a rag doll over Brutus's shoulder, snuggled into him because Henry's jacket only went mid-thigh and, turned upside down, it slid up further.

After a while, Brutus took off his own large jacket and threw it over her bare legs and held it in place with his arm slung over her thighs. His other arm swung bare in the winter's chill. She very much appreciated this kind, unspoken gesture. His skin was like his son's, hot to the touch. She wondered if it was a beast trait or just special to their family. Soon the only part of her that was cold was her bare feet.

"Son, remain a beast so you do not catch your death headed back to Omnia. Another blizzard is coming," Brutus said. Beast Gregor nodded.

"And your demesne forgot her clothes too," he said, flicking the hem of his jacket against Victoria's leg. "You both need to take account of your transformation locations, so you are not left naked when the fight ends.

Think," Brutus said with another flick. This one he gave to Gregor on the tip of his nose.

It was a heavier flick then he had given Victoria, and although it obviously stung, Gregor did not flinch.

"Gor is still out there trying to get the necklace from the Goblin Queen. I have not had one report back," Brutus said, and then paused with a meaningful grunt before he continued. "And the Avians have declared war on us, thanks to you and your breaking proxy bellum with Plimsoll."

Gregor bent his beast head. They continued to walk alongside each other, Victoria still swinging against his back for perhaps another mile or two. She was too terrified of him to ask to be set down to walk on her own. It was a clear night, the full moon stirring all the noises of the wildlife into full activity. She kept herself calm by repeatedly singing the lullaby her father had always sung to her in her head. She tried again in vain to figure out what the words used to be, so she just sang the gibberish she always had.

"You are a reckless fool," Brutus said harshly, coming to a stop to turn to him and give him a hard stare. "But I have to admit you got it done. You ended up with both the shape-changers. Your plan was lacking. You should have let me into it. I could have helped, you know, but I respect you trying to do it on your own. First your own bellum and now this," Brutus gave Gregor a slap on the back with his free arm. "This one needs to learn the discipline of staying in form," Brutus said. Victoria was growing irritated. Brutus never seemed to address her, speaking of her as though she wasn't slung over his shoulder.

"And in time we can make more," Brutus said in a greedy chuckle, and Gregor's large beast head snapped to look at him, which made Brutus give a hearty laugh.

"Don't worry, pal. You, I meant you." He gave Gregor's hairy head a rough tussle.

Brutus took another deep sigh and looked up at the sky. Victoria craned her head to catch his face in the brilliant moonlight, hope gleaming in his eye.

"Things are changing. This could be the end of Charlene's reign of terror," he said. "Listen, I know there was a lot said down there with her. Once we set up a camp, we can discuss it in full. I am sure you have plenty of questions," he said, his gruff voice hitting a gentle tone. "I can smell your nitwit comrades up ahead." He turned and dumped Victoria into Gregor's hairy arms.

"Here, she can stare at your ugly mug for a while," Brutus said. "If her bare feet touch this frozen snow, she will lose all her pretty toes," he warned.

Gregor pulled her close to his chest, holding her in both his arms. She was not sure if she was just relieved to be right side up again or away from Brutus, but she felt grateful to be near Gregor, though she would never admit it out loud. She buried her face deep into his hairy chest, inviting his warmth. She looked up once to peer at his snout, teeth, and large pointed ears bathed in the light of the moon. Although his eyes were small and beady, they were still the same shade of emerald green. His beast form was indeed hard to look at. If she had not known it was Gregor, she would be writhing in torment being carried away by such a hideous creature.

But then she remembered the wild, furious beasts she had seen back at the maze. Their hair was wired and frazzled, their demeanor much more menacing, many of their teeth broken or rotten.

She shifted to look over his wounds. His fur was matted with so much blood, but she was unsure how much was his. By his ragged breathing, she could tell he was in much more pain than he was willing to admit.

She was so grateful he had rescued Mabel. Her heart was light in her chest, and it was all thanks to him. She was not sure how to tell him of her appreciation. Simple words did not seem enough. Perhaps she would bake him a cake. Yes, a chocolate cake with plenty of frosting.

They continued to walk in silence as a few of Brutus's men could be seen ahead, setting up a makeshift campsite. Then she spied Mabel, Henry, and Rhamy Lumpkin among them.

"Give me my key, boy," Brutus said to Henry. Henry dutifully handed over the key and backed away timidly.

"It might be useless now," Henry said respectfully.

"Yeah, you might be right," Brutus said.

"I hope there are clothes in that saddlebag," Brutus said. Mabel began to search through it, and Gregor came up behind her, grabbing the bag with his teeth. Mabel quickly backed away from him, and he disappeared into the distant trees to transform in private. Victoria rushed forward to finally embrace Mabel.

"Victoria!" Mabel said. "You have no idea what I have seen these last couple of days! Oh gosh, you are a mess!"

"Your foot!" Victoria said in surprise. Mabel was sitting down, and her foot stretched out, but it did not look as swollen as it should have been.

"Oh yeah, it feels much better. The pain subsided, but I still can't walk on it," Mabel said.

"I heard the bone break," Victoria said. "You should be in complete misery. I guess it is true. You really are going to become a shape-changer too."

"Yes!" Mabel said with a huge laugh. "I was hoping I would!" Mabel happily twirled her hands several times in the air, and Rhamy clapped his hands.

"Well, also one of those guys licked my ankle and it feels much better now." Mabel said, pointing to one of the beasts. Victoria gave him a grateful nod. Human Gregor came back clothed, and he handed her a pair of wool socks.

"I am sorry I could not find any shoes for you," He said. "I will carry you to the campfire." He offered. She let him.

She put the socks in the pocket of Brutus's jacket she wore. She wanted them dry while she slept so she needed to avoid getting the soles wet from damp mud around the fire.

"Let's get going, boy. The army needs its commander. You have proved resourceful. You will join me at the front after your time in the stocks is over," Brutus said. Gregor nodded his head dutifully.

"Rhamy, you saved my life back there. We are now even," Gregor said, taking Rhamy's hand in a firm shake. Rhamy smiled overzealously and gave a good-natured chuckle. "Henry, get these two home to get their ma and gather their things," Gregor said. Victoria looked at Gregor in surprise.

"What?" Brutus's voice sliced through the moment.

"Charlene will be coming for your ma. You need to get her out of there. You have the entire day. Charlene can't move until sundown, but hurry," Gregor said, keeping his back to Brutus.

"Son, she is your demesne. Her mother is none of your concern. Just tell her to come. She has to follow. You will need her to give you water while you are in the stocks," Brutus said, aggravated.

"You are free to go," Gregor said, looking at Victoria and ignoring his father defiantly. "My mark should keep you safe on the road," Gregor said.

"No, that is not an option," Brutus huffed. "We need both of them."

"No, Pa," Gregor said. "She is mine, and I say she goes free. She and her sister," Gregor said.

Brutus stood facing Gregor, his eyebrows furrowed. "What was all this for then?" Brutus asked, squinting hard at him with gritted teeth. Gregor puffed out his chest, squaring his shoulders. They stood staring at each other, jaws jutted, teeth clenched, knuckles cracking as they formed tight fists.

The tension caught everyone unprepared. No one dared breathe when Gregor began to open his mouth. It was at that moment Gor and his men came spilling into view, shouting angrily.

"There he is!" Gor yelled. Brutus turned, listening intently. Gor walked right up to Gregor. Brutus stepped aside and let Gor punch him squarely in the jaw. Brutus let out a confused chuckle.

"Whatever it is, I am sure he deserves it," Brutus said.

"He is a traitor! We found the Goblin Queen. I lost four men to her. *Four!*" Gor repeated himself, shouting so hard spit foamed at the edge of his mouth. "And I lost three fingers!" It was then Victoria noticed half of his right hand was missing. The pinky, ring finger, and middle finger were gone, leaving gross rounded stubs in their place. Although it had healed, the fingers had not grown back.

Suddenly Victoria realized she had just assumed the beasts were nearly immortal. Now she realized although they could heal quickly by licking their wounds, if a piece was torn from them, it could not regenerate unless connected again before the healing process, like with Gor's eyeball. There were no fingers to reconnect. They had gone down the gullet of some goblin. Victoria did not hide her smile at the beautiful the irony.

"Don't look so smug!" Gor said, turning to backhand Victoria. Gregor clicked his tongue, and Gor let his hand pass near her face, only displacing a few strands of hair. Gor looked back to Brutus.

"See how he protects her? She has cast some spell upon him. She is called the Sis Meta by everyone now. I have heard the rumors," Gor said. "And he, no doubt, has her necklace too, holding it for her until she commands him otherwise!"

At this, Brutus looked at Gregor. "Is this true, boy?" he said, his face distorted in a mixture of confusion and anger.

"No, I do not have it!" Gregor said.

Brutus looked at him, bringing his face close to his so their noses touched. "Check his bag!" Brutus said.

Gor tore the bag from the other soldier's hand eagerly, dumping everything into the frozen snow. It was a mess of food, his journal, his writing pencils, candles, and his water skin. Then Victoria spied the nymph harp, the very one she had dropped near the goblin's nest entrance. It was the same harp, she was sure. The vivid green and the delicate strings made Victoria curious as to what else was in his bag. Gor gasped angrily and scraped along the bottom and shook it again. Brutus stood, looking annoyed at Gor. Gor looked up to Brutus and then back again at the scattered contents.

"It is here, I just know it!" Gor said.

Gregor laughed. "Gor, you seem to be hitting the ale harder every time I see you." Gregor laughed again. Victoria listened to the sound of it suspiciously. Gregor never laughed in such a forced manner. It was full of nervousness. Now Victoria stepped closer, watching Gor's frantic flipping and tossing of the satchel. There was something bulging inside in the flap of the bag, sliding around lightly as Gor twisted it and rummaged angrily. She had almost missed it. The movement was so slight, but Victoria knew the exact weight from all the hours it had hung about her neck.

"Son, I am sorry I once again distrusted you," Brutus said. "You have proven yourself time and time again. Perhaps you are smart. Perhaps it would be a better incentive to bring the girls' mother with us." Brutus put up his hand to silence Gor, who looked like he was about to burst from hysterical anger. "Gor, once again you failed to complete the simplest of tasks and lost four men, and, worse yet, you tried to blame it on Gregor. You are relieved from your command."

"No! No! He has it! He has the necklace! He is under her spell! She is a witch!" Gor was screaming now, shaking uncontrollably.

"Get him out of here. You three, escort Gor back to Omnia and make sure he stays there." Brutus said, motioning toward his soldiers. "The rest of you are reassigned here with me,"

They grabbed Gor by the arms and hauled him away kicking and screaming. He was so infuriated he began to transform, and Victoria quickly pulled the black velvet pouch from among the messy pile of Gregor's satchel and displayed it for the soldiers to see. They nodded in appreciation and forced him down. One soldier had to keep his face in the snow as he tried to bite her, still with human teeth. Victoria ignored the stinging on her fingertips as she clasped it around his neck. Gor released a new set of screams as the silver collar clung to his neck, the itching burn making it impossible for him to transform.

Gor shrieked, and he tried to kick at her but they pulled him away. Brutus stood laughing at the entire thing while Gregor looked at Victoria in disbelief. Brutus stroked his scruffy chin while he considered her over again, as though seeing her for the first time.

"I have underestimated her for the last time," Brutus said to Gregor. "In the morning, go get the ma and whatever else she wants."

Gregor nodded, sending a small triumphant smile to Victoria under his bowed head. She gave him a nervous smile back, afraid Brutus would change his mind, but he did not. Rather he called for a fire and some supper. Victoria picked up the nymph harp and gave it a strum. Mabel soon had it in her hands and was playing the two simple songs Professor Carter had managed to teach her back in the library.

CHAPTER 19

A HERO

SOON THEY WERE SITTING beside a roaring bonfire. The soldiers began to pull out food from their packs. Victoria found herself instinctively taking over the process after watching the men's dirty hands about to touch the food. Mabel hobbled over and sat down to help, falling in line with her, counting the number of mouths. They set to work, making about two dozen sandwiches. Victoria's dismay, only ale was provided as drinks. She was grateful to scoop some pure white snow into one of the metal cups and set it near the fire. Soon she and Mabel had hot water, which warmed their bodies delightfully while the rest of the men heavily consumed the dark amber liquid. Rhamy Lumpkin downed two cups without hesitation, and the soldiers cheered. He passed another to Henry, who curiously took a sip and then coughed several times, sending the rest of the men into fits of laughter. Henry forced another swig and resisted the urge to sputter. Rhamy patted him on the back while the rest cheered. Brutus pulled a flask from his bag and gave it a heavy chug, passing it to

Gregor. Victoria was alarmed by all the drinking and pulled Mabel close to her near the fire.

But as the cups emptied, filling the bellies, the men began to grow louder, laughing and stomping around, dancing in the moonlight. Mabel continued to play the harp until Rhamy took it and strummed it expertly. He began to sing a silly little shanty with an accompanying jig. Soon the rest of the men were learning the words and joining in. Mabel clapped happily, and even Victoria could not keep a serious face.

Rhamy Lumpkin grabbed Victoria, twirling her and leading her in a series of complicated dance steps. Soon Victoria was laughing, and Mabel was begging for a turn, but she could barely walk, so Rhamy scooped her up and flung her about. Henry took this moment to cut in, and his human hands were warm, not hot like Rhamy's, so it made holding them more comfortable. There was not any sticky sweat rubbing between them. They twirled about for a while, trying to fall in rhythm with Rhamy's dancing. Victoria was watching Gregor out of the corner of her eye the entire while. He sat with his father, looking positively miserable. They had been muttering to each other with their heads bent low in a serious conversation. She imagined they were discussing all Charlene had revealed. Gregor's face looked solemn, only lifting his eyes to take another shot from the flask.

She continued to dance. After a while, they were bursting with laughter. Rhamy was distracted teaching an eager Mabel how to slide her swollen foot safely in tune. Everyone else was busy refilling their cups from the barrel. Victoria took this time to slip away, following the hoofprints of Nutmeg and the other horses. They had wandered into a glen. Their search of grass proved fruitless among the snow and ice glistening in the stillness. She gingerly crept to Nutmeg, trying to keep him calm as she found Gregor's satchel. He had shoved it deep into the saddlebag during the commotion of dinner, but she had noticed.

As she slid her hand over the large clasp, her fingers ran over the embellished *G* to admire the fine craftsmanship. Suddenly she felt his hand on hers, his arm reaching over her shoulder, trying to pull the bag in one swift motion. She yanked it back and accidentally elbowed his ribs in the process because he was standing right behind her. She could smell the ale on him. This time she knew he had drunk too much because he was straining to remain upright.

She turned to face him, holding the bag defensively and casting what she hoped was an intimidating glance. She followed the lining and found a small gap where the thread had been cut. It was tiny, and she doubted anyone else who had not spent hours working with thread would have even noticed it. She tore it larger until her hand fit inside the bag's lining. As she brought the ruby necklace out, she stood dangling it in front of his face. She held her lips tight and pulled her shoulders back as she had seen all the beasts do whenever they were in the middle of a confrontation. She had to slightly tilt her neck up so she could look him directly in the eyes. Her bare feet stung in the snow, but she ignored them. She waited for an explanation.

Gregor looked as though the air had been knocked out of him. He stammered a bit. Victoria waited. She could feel the burning anger steeping deep in her belly and rising up her throat. The noise of the crackling fire and the merry laughter seemed distant now. All Victoria could hear was Gregor's short breaths as he stood looking down at her.

"You have had this since the goblin brambles?" she asked finally, her voice shaking as she tried to control the rage and maintain a whisper.

"I, um, yes. Let me explain," Gregor muttered. His speech was a bit slurred. He was trying to keep his voice low and grab the necklace; both were a failing attempt. Victoria whipped her hand back from him. He dropped his arm.

"We could have traded this for Mabel! She almost died! You almost died!" Victoria tried to control her voice, but it was shrill and continued to crack. Gregor placed his hands on her shoulders, whether to make a point or just to keep himself steady, she was not sure. He was looking her in the eye this time. The ale had washed away his reserve.

"Listen, we cannot let Charlene get what she wants. It must possess some unknown power. We cannot let anyone get it," Gregor said, casting a suspicious glance around. "I was going to take it to Plimsoll, but I fear the bridge has been burned," Gregor said, casting a pointed look at Victoria. She huffed back at him.

"I can't even trust you. What else have you been lying about?" she asked, throwing her hands up in frustration. She did not wait for his response. She was already pushing herself up on the nearby stump. Her feet felt painfully numb, and she could no longer ignore them. She shook off the snow and rubbed them and then pulled on the wool socks she had kept in her pocket.

She now held her knees to her chest. He slumped against it, sliding down and settling in the snow, one arm slung over the top to keep himself from falling back. The horses were nickering and had wandered away from them.

"At first I was envious of you," Gregor said. His voice was low and shaking. "You with your perfect life," he said it with such disdain that Victoria shifted uncomfortably. As he spoke, his eyes looked weepy from the alcohol. For the first time, Gregor spoke freely. All his inhibitions had been washed away with the strong drink, and he was pouring his soul at her feet. Victoria was unsure if she should say anything and nothing was coming to mind, so she just sat frozen under his steely gaze.

"As I, I—Well, you have met my pa, and my ma apparently is not dead, but worse, much worse," he continued. Victoria was worried he might begin to cry in defeat. Then he took a heavy breath, as though pulling himself from the depths of his despair, and he lifted his head. "But the longer I watched you, the more I knew you deserved it. You are kind and gentle." He looked at her with such intensity, she almost flinched. "Treating everyone with more respect than I had ever seen in my entire existence. And they did not need to fight and scrap and step on each other for it. You gave it freely to all, and somehow you had plenty to give," he said. "Soon your delightful smile and cheery laugh was all I lived for. I eagerly waited for you to read out loud to Mabel every night. Listening to your sweet voice sustained me."

Gregor had his eyes closed now. He was muttering, more to himself than her. She was not even sure if he was aware anymore that he was speaking.

"You listened to me read?" Victoria felt a flush of embarrassment with a pinch of anger at the invasion of privacy.

"I was on a recon assignment. I was doing my duty," Gregor said defensively, and then he shook his head. "No, it had turned into more than that," he said, shaking his head before resting it on his elbow propped up on the stump. Victoria thought he was done—perhaps he had fallen asleep—but then he started speaking again.

"Several times I almost came out from my hiding place to introduce myself hoping you would show me even a shred of affection you showed for everyone else in your life," he confessed. "But I would see Rhamy, or Mason, or another one of them. They all were always there, watching, waiting. If I made a move, they would attack, thinking I was going for the unknown weapon. It was a dangerous situation. Soon I became your protector. Each time they were about to make a move, I was there to stop them. Your balcony with the large glass windows was the weak point of your home, and it was the place they continuously tried to enter, Rhamy during the day and Mason at the night, to search your things. So that is where I posted guard. I stood in the shadows of your balcony, defending you against all of them. There were many. The only one who had gotten past was Rhamy. He and I used to be friends. He used it against me to slip an elvish sleeping potion in my water skin to get past me, but when I awoke, he had not found anything he thought was worth stealing. He could not figure out what Charlene wanted. He took advantage of my trust.I continued to post guard. One night I caught Mason entering your room while you were sleeping. I yanked him out, and we fought until we both were near dead, but I had done my job. You were safe. Sorry about tearing your blanket." Gregor nodded; his chest puffed a bit in pride. "But you were safe," he repeated in a mutter, more to himself than anyone else.

"That was you?" Victoria asked. She was overwhelmed and had no idea what to do with all this information, and despite her anger at him, she somehow found herself holding his head against her chest, rocking him slightly from side to side as she had done so many times for Mabel, but this time felt different.

She wasn't just comforting him. She liked his face close to hers. His breath made her tingle oddly, although she would not admit it out loud ever to anyone.

Victoria looked down at Gregor, covered in all the bruises and bites from the onslaught of beasts he had kept at bay. There was blood splattered on his ear. She looked at his jawline, the moonlight hitting his cheek.

"Victoria?" Mabel's timid voice shattered the moment. Victoria whipped away from him, her socks sinking into snow. Her toes felt the squish of the melt. She shivered as she looked toward the campfire. It was burning low now, and Mabel was hobbling about on her weak foot, arms wrapped about herself, calling for her.

"Victoria!" she called again. Victoria started toward her and gave one last look back at Gregor, who remained frozen where he was, gazing longingly at her. She hurried to Mabel, secretly savoring the sweet words Gregor had spoken as she helped Mabel get nestled into the blankets the soldiers had given them. Victoria's heart was still beating fiercely in her chest. She longed to wiggle free from Mabel's clinging cuddles and find her way back to Gregor. But she stopped herself, knowing it was completely inappropriate. She felt an odd mixture of shame and exhilaration.

She fell asleep with her head blissfully calm. Her body felt warm and tingly despite the wet socks.

She awoke to the footfalls of Gregor. He had found his way back to the campfire, and he laid down his blankets near her, not in touching distance, but close enough she could see his small, sly smile before he laid his head down.

In the weak morning light, they gathered themselves together. Brutus and his soldiers agreed to wait in the forest as they collected Mother and their belongings. Victoria was relieved. She was sure Mother would already be overwhelmed enough without hosting a small army.

"Can we please go home now?" Mabel begged as she and Victoria climbed up on Nutmeg. She was not sure how to explain everything to Mabel, so she just gave her a warm smile.

Henry started to walk the horse down the slope, headed back for the valley. Victoria felt a burst of energy as she realized she could see her home below. Nutmeg seemed less tense now and walked in a slow, easy gait. Henry slowed until he was side by side with Gregor. Victoria looked behind her to see them exchanging glances and muttering to each other. She eavesdropped with her fox ear, turning to hide it under her hair.

"I know she seems to trust you, but I know what you are," Henry said in a low hush. Although Victoria did not look back, she knew Henry was angry by the agitation in his voice. He struggled to keep the whisper.

"You are cursed, a vagabond, a scourge. You will only bring sorrow and suffering to her," Henry said as she heard a rustle of fabric. Looking back, she saw the odd stance between the men. Henry was grasping Gregor's collar and tried to pull his face close, but he stood smaller and shorter, so the threat seemed more comical than plausible. Gregor did not say a word and merely stared at Henry until he timidly let go, unsettled by Gregor's silence. Victoria was touched by the concern Henry had shown for her. She also was impressed by his bravery; she supposed a lesser human would not dare threaten Gregor. Then she thought of Gregor, who had shown a tremendous amount of reserve, allowing Henry to say such things without knocking him unconscious. She wished they would stop bickering and concentrate on the task at hand.

Soon they were through the main road without notice. It was so early in the morning that no one had passed, except a few sleepy farmers. Victoria led them through surrounding fields to her house.

Although her stomach was empty, she felt a rush of energy from being so close to seeing home again. She jumped off Nutmeg and sprinted toward the familiar gate, ignoring the snow wetting her socks, and opened it with much gusto.

There was no one in sight. Victoria led the way into the yard. After searching she opened the door to the house. It was a mess of overturned furniture and broken glass. Emily sat up from the chair she was lazily lounging in.

"Oh, you two came home?" Emily asked.

"Emily!" Victoria exclaimed. "What happened?"

"Your mother told everyone to leave. She won't get out of her bed." Emily said. She looked exhausted. "Then the men came, they stole everything worth taking." Emily said, looking around the destroyed house.

"Oh, Emily!" Victoria said sadly.

"I hid while they robbed the house. But I do not have anywhere else to go. So here we are." She gave a huff. "Oh, I see you brought friends." Victoria looked to Mabel, who shared in the concern. They ran upstairs. The halls were dark and dusty, making Victoria sneeze. Mabel rushed toward Mother's room. Victoria quickly followed. Mother lay asleep in the bed, and Mabel stroked her nose. Mother stirred, smacking her hand away.

"Stop, Mabel," Mother mumbled. Then her eyes sprang open. "Mabel! Victoria!" she said, jumping up to gather them in her arms. She knocked the candle off the nightstand and onto the floor. Mabel screamed and that brought the men running to the doorway. Mother ignored it and continued to squeeze them much tighter than necessary, and tears streamed down her face.

"I thought you were dead!" she cried into Victoria's hair. After several long moments, Victoria coughed, spying the fire blazing on the rug. Rhamy came into the room to scoop up the fire. By the time Mother had gotten a hold of herself, she turned toward the commotion. She screamed as she saw Rhamy. Then she screamed again as Gregor's large frame filled the doorway.

"Mother, Mother, it is okay. This is Rhamy Lumpkin," Mabel said.

"How do you do, madam?" he asked, pulling her hand to his lips and giving it a kiss. Victoria then motioned toward Gregor.

"That is Gregor. He brought me back—well, after he helped kidnap me," Victoria said, suddenly realizing it sounded very confusing. "Henry came to rescue me. He is putting Nutmeg back into the stables."

"What?" Mother shrieked.

"Everything is going to be fine," Victoria said, stroking Mother's arm to calm her. "But we need to see Father's things." Mother barely mustered a nod.

"Give us a minute," Victoria said, shooing both of the men from the room. She ignored their looks of confusion as she shut the door, leaving them to stand in the hallway to stare at one another awkwardly.

CHAPTER 20

A LULLABY

WITH MOTHER PROPERLY DRESSED, they made it down to the dining room. Soon they were eating all the food Emily had gathered onto the table. Mother watched Rhamy and Gregor with wide eyes, looking back to Victoria every few moments with a puzzled face. Henry had now joined the others at the table.

Victoria dropped Rumi into the nearest cup and gave him a little warm water and placed a sugar cube into his outstretched arms. Mother watched Rumi munching on the sugar grains with wide eyes. Victoria thought she saw one twitch a bit. Mabel giggled as Rumi leaned against the edge of the cup, as though relaxing in the bath.

"Who are these men? Are they suitors?" she asked. "And why is Henry eating at our table?"

"Henry deserves much more than just a meal, Mother. He was the only human who saw me taken and did something about it," Victoria said.

Mother looked at Henry with astonishment. Henry humbly shrank from Victoria's recognition.

"Rhamy is a fire elf," Mabel squealed in delight. Victoria hushed her, not wanting to be interrupted. "Gregor is a beast," Mabel continued, unaware Gregor's head twitched a bit as she revealed his secret.

"A beast?" Mother asked.

"Yeah, but he doesn't eat human beings," Mabel explained while Mother's startled expression widened.

"What about you, dear? Are you unharmed?" Mother asked.

"Victoria was almost eaten by goblins," Mabel burst out before Victoria could stop her.

"Oh, I see." Mother's teaspoon quivered in her hand as she tried to remain calm and collected as they stood talking causally about impossible and impractical things.

"But everything is okay. We are here safe and sound," Victoria quickly added. Patting Mother's back hurriedly, Victoria hoped to coax the color back into her face. "But we do have to leave before sunset."

"Because Charlene and her bloodsucking minions will kill us if we are still here," Mabel said. Victoria sighed at Mabel's horrible delivery of the news. Then again, they did not have time to sugarcoat it.

"Why is your father's cufflinks in that teacup along with that thing?" Mother asked.

"Oh Mother, you see Father's cufflinks?" Victoria asked, her voice trembled a bit with emotion.

"This mushroom, his name is Rumi, makes you see what you want in the water he is in. Since you want Father back, you see his cufflinks." Victoria explained.

"I don't see cufflinks at all. I see hair. I see your fox hair in the cup." Mabel said.

"That's probably because you want to be able to change too." Victoria said after a moment of turning it over in her mind. Mabel nodded quickly.

"I better go tell my family I am still alive," Henry said, patting his face with a napkin. "Thank you for the breakfast."

"We are leaving today, and the horses will need new owners," Victoria said, handing him the proper paperwork. Henry looked baffled.

"No, I couldn't," Henry said.

"Yes. They do not much like me anymore and where we are going, we won't need them," Victoria said.

"Where are you going?" Henry asked.

"It's best if you do not know in case Charlene finds you and asks," Victoria said. "Thank you for coming for us. You are truly brave." Victoria could not help her eyes tearing a little at the thought of leaving everything and everyone behind.

Victoria walked him out, but he did not leave. Instead, he guided her to the garden. Somehow, they ended up at the bench, right below that bent tree.

"Don't cry. I will see you again, right?" Henry said. "You are only leaving for a little while?" He looked at her curiously.

Victoria quickly nodded. "Oh yeah, it is only until the war settles down," she lied, steadying herself and giving him a big smile, forcing back the tears.

"Oh good, because I did not see cufflinks or hair in that cup. I saw a ring," He said and gave her a knowing look. Victoria was caught off guard and tried to stop herself from gasping out loud as he knelt down before her.

"Look, Victoria," Henry said. His voice was quivering now, and Victoria was alarmed. "I went into the mountains looking for you not because it was the brave thing to do. It was because I could not see myself in a world without you." Henry said pulling her hand into his. "Victoria, I love you, and I want to be your husband," Henry said.

Victoria gasped and began to open her mouth, but Henry quickly went on before she could say anything.

"I know right now your whole life is turned upside down and somehow that beast-man owns you, but I am talking about after all this is over, when this war ends and when they all go back to the mountains. When you can return to me, please know I am here waiting for you," he said. His eyes shone with emotion. "Because I have always loved you."

Victoria stood frozen; his words echoed in her head. Henry stood, and he gingerly pressed his lips against her cheek.

"Oh! Um, they are in Father's study, making quite a mess. Come quickly!" Mabel said.

Victoria was unsure how long Mabel had been there, but when she looked up, Henry was already greeting her casually as though he had not just dropped a thousand-pound burden on Victoria's chest. Thankfully Mabel was there, smiling enough for the both of them.

"Mabel, you have a terrible habit of interrupting," Victoria said, secretly grateful Mabel was here to cut her loose from the unexpected suspension that held her fast. Victoria pushed Mabel ahead of her, knowing she was about to say something stupid, and she did not want Henry to be in earshot.

"He wants to be your husband!" Mabel said in a singsong whisper right on queue. Victoria hushed her.

"But he looks at you the same way Gregor does. Does that mean Gregor wants to be your husband too?" Mabel asked.

Victoria sputtered at the question. She left Mabel to comfort Mother, needing a break from her inconvenient questions. Victoria and Henry rushed to the study. She was careful to keep her hands close to her side in fear he might reach for them again.

As she stepped into the dusty room, she took a moment to pause, remembering Father sitting at the desk. But now it was overturned, papers were flung everywhere and the lamp shade was torn. Gregor and Rhamy were turning things over and pushing stuff around. It seemed so irreverent that it was all Victoria could do to not let loose a shrill shriek.

"Careful!" Victoria said, grabbing the vase from Gregor's large hands. She was sure he would drop it. "Easy!" she said, pulling the stacks of paper from Rhamy, worried he would start it on fire. "Please be gentle," Victoria said.

"Look, it was already like this before we entered," Rhamy quickly explained.

But they now moved about the room cautiously. She looked from the bookcase to the drawers. Victoria noticed Rhamy leaning on the walls, studying inside the frames of each picture. Gregor moved the furniture about slowly, looking under the large pieces. Henry sat at the desk and neatly stacked each loose page after he looked it over.

"How can I find something he spent years looking for unsuccessfully?" She paused at this. Frustration swelled inside.

"Because he did find it," Rhamy reassured her.

"How am I supposed to fulfill a task that is not even mine?" Victoria huffed, flinging her hands in the air.

Rhamy kept looking and Henry kept stacking while Gregor slumped into the nearest chair. He looked as tired as she felt. Everyone needed rest.

"All he left me was a necklace and a pebble!" She fumed a bit and pulled on the golden chain absentmindedly, quickly dropping it and hiding it under her collar again, wondering if anyone had noticed. Thankfully they all had been looking away. She slumped back down in his old leather chair, covering her face with her hands. She felt like she wanted to cry and yet kick something hard.

"A pebble?" Rhamy asked with a raised brow. She guessed he was trying to lighten the mood with his tone.

"Show me this pebble," Rhamy demanded. Victoria stood up from the chair and propped a hand on her hip, annoyed at his pathetic attempt to distract her. "Show me this pebble," Rhamy Lumpkin said, his eyes ablaze with hope.

Victoria did not want to climb all the stairs to simply show him a rock. But his inquisitive brow coaxed her out of the chair, and she wearily dragged her feet along the floorboards. She glumly directed them through the house and up the stairs. She was flabbergasted at the amount of dust that had accumulated on the steps. Leaves scattered the wooden floor and the moldings. Victoria groaned in sheer exhaustion as she closed the large window at the top of the stairs. By the look of the floor, it seemed the window had been open for a while.

They continued down the hallway, and she ignored the crunch of leaves under her shoes. Soon she turned the knob, listening to the hinge creak in its familiar way. Suddenly all these little details were a comfort. She liked the way the third board from the door squeaked under her foot.

She had never invited a man in her room, with the exception of her father, and now three stood inside. It felt strange and invasive having them look at her collection of things. The thieves had taken her jewelry but left the rest untouched. Had her room always been this small? All of her shelves full of her favorite things seemed unimportant now, as though she was seeing everything in her room for the first time as an outsider. Her face flushed in embarrassment as Rhamy squatted at her large dollhouse, making one of the dolls dance about on the veranda playfully.

"I don't play with those anymore," she found herself saying. She closed her mouth and tried to not speak, further incriminating herself. She held her tongue as Gregor looked at her rows and rows of journals. He began to pull one from the shelf, and she slammed it back into place quickly.

She was glad she had practiced making her bed every morning under Emily's strict guidelines. The day she had left for the masquerade ball, she had made her bed out of habit and had neatly tucked in the edges and perfectly fluffed the pillows. It looked a bit dusty, but still beautiful. If she was alone, she would have plopped into it, ignoring all the dirt and filth she was covered in. She would have napped for the rest of the day. She pushed those thoughts aside.

She turned their attention to the dresser where she kept the pebble. She picked it up and tossed it to Rhamy. He rolled it about his fingers and then he licked it once. Victoria wrinkled her nose in disgust.

"Yeah, before he died, he handed me this pebble. He had completely lost his mind." Victoria sat up as the images of the night played out again in her head—his trembling white fingers placing the pebble in hers, his assuring tone. She was glad Rhamy Lumpkin spoke to interrupt the part in her memory where his chest stopped heaving.

"Where did he get this?" Rhamy asked.

"Oh, it is just a pebble from outside. There are a thousand in the riverbed," Victoria said. She was too tired to continue playing this game. She wondered if it would be rude to ask them all to leave.

"And where does this riverbed lead?" Rhamy Lumpkin asked, interrupting her momentary stupor. She turned to give him a weak shrug, but his eyes flickered in excitement.

"To the lake on the edge of our property," Victoria said. Gregor was staring at them now, looking from Rhamy's hand to Victoria.

"The lake!" Victoria said. Suddenly her feet did not seem so heavy, and her head cleared. She paced to the balcony, flinging the doors open wide to ignore the mountain peaks. She did not look at the heinous face of the hillside. She dropped her gaze below it to the lake. She had been so fearful of the Black Needle Mountains that she had rarely looked out, even to the lake on the edge of their property.

"He gave me the answer. He gave it to me long ago!" Victoria felt overwhelmed. She raced through her room to grab the pebble from Rhamy, and then she sprinted down the hallway and took the stairs two at a time.

"What is going on?" Mabel asked as they rushed past the dining hall.

Rhamy quickly explained it to her.

"You mean to tell me you have been looking for a mermaid all this time and none of you thought about the large body of water right next to the house?" Mabel asked.

"How have you become so outspoken in the small time we have spent apart?" Victoria asked.

Everyone followed her outside and down the pathway. Over the bridge, she was careful to walk on the other side, away from the broken railing, and approached the river, following it down to the large lake.

Gregor stood on her right, and Henry stepped to her left. Victoria felt strange standing between them. She shook it from her mind and concentrated on the sparkling water in the weak light of the morning. She called out loudly.

"Princess Lily!" she shouted out expectantly. It was at this point that Rhamy and Mabel stood beside them, with Mother and Emily following curiously, completing their little group.

Mabel joined in, her high-pitched voice cracking as she screamed at the top of her lungs. Rhamy joined in. It was not until Henry started to shout that Gregor was calling, too, making a point to yell louder than Henry. Henry and Gregor looked at each other and screamed in unison, each trying to outdo the other. Victoria covered both her ears, stepping back from them.

Mother watched with her thin lips agape at their desperate screams at the water, but Victoria ignored her judgmental expression. She looked at Mabel, and Mabel looked back at her and gave a shrug. Soon Henry and Gregor's clash settled, and only the gentle, rhythmic slapping of the small waves against the rocky shore could be heard.

"Mermaid Princess Lily, I summon you to come forward!" Victoria said again, trying to place more authority in her voice. After the second shout brought no response from the still lake, Victoria finally let the exhaustion of the journey take its toll. She dropped to her knees, screaming out for any reaction from the green blue.

She frantically tossed the pebble in her hand as far as she could. When the small plunk gave no satisfaction, she scooped handfuls and threw them into the pond without any sense of direction. The water and mud sprinkled her face and hair, staining her dress. She burst into uncontrollable sobs, turning her face from everyone. Someone bent beside her, and Victoria was relieved when she felt Mabel's small hand on her back, giving her those reassuring pats, Mabel always gave.

She was painfully aware everyone was cautiously gathering around her with concern. Her face was red from embarrassment, and she collected herself forcefully, sniffing a few times.

Finally, silence resumed, spreading the anxiety and tension. Victoria let a few more of her tears roll down her face and wiped them away. Victoria saw Mabel look toward Rhamy for answers, but he just shook his head. By now the sun was higher in the sky, its weak winter light casting a false sense of hope. It was mocking her alongside those cursed mountain peaks.

Victoria felt despair, and even Mabel's warm hand on her shoulder could not soothe the chill edging up her spine.

Mother stepped out in front of them all. She had been standing so quietly Victoria had forgotten she was there. She continued to the edge, her shoe sinking into the hardened mud, and she waded forward in the water until she was up to her knees. Victoria and Mabel both stood to try to collect her, but Rhamy put up his hand.

Mother began to sing. She was singing Father's lullaby, but she, too, did not know the words, so she sang the incoherent nonsense Victoria and Mabel had always sung. Victoria was surprised she remembered it at all. Mother had not spent much time with them in the last couple of years.

"What is she doing?" Gregor asked. Victoria sighed in embarrassment.

"Mother?" Victoria asked slowly, stepping closer to the edge. The cold water hit her toes, and the chill made her shiver. "Let's get you inside," Victoria said, motioning toward Mother, trying to persuade her to shore; surely, she had lost her mind.

Mabel was crying now, hugging herself in dismay. Mother ignored them and continued to sing. It sounded bleak against the lapping of the cold water, hopeless and pitiful.

CHAPTER 21

A SHIMMER EXPLAINED

THEN TO EVERYONE'S SHEER astonishment, Rhamy joined in. He joined the second verse with Mother on cue, and he sang the same gibberish Victoria had always known. His steady and clear voice struck the chord boldly.

Victoria dared not breathe. She listened intently as together they entered the chorus of the lullaby and then began the third verse.

Rhamy's native elvish tongue pronounced the words clearly, and Victoria realized it was in a different language. She closed her eyes, welcoming the sound. Its familiar melody calmed her heart and slowed her tears. Her fingers unfurled from their fists.

Bubbles broke the pond's surface. A vibrant mess of lilac hair was first seen, and soon her face came into view. Her eyes were bright blue with silver flecks that sparkled softly in the sunlight. Her chest was covered by the thick tangles of her hair rolling down in loose wavy curls. She was wearing a tiara adorned with seashells, pearls, and other jewels, and Victoria was sure this was the princess.

As she swam into the shallow water, her fin came into view. Sometimes her tail looked blue, purple, or green depending on how the light hit the glistening scales. It was a magnificent sight, and Victoria just breathed in relief. Soon Lily was sitting near her on the shore of pebbles, her fin ever shifting back and forth impatiently in the slight waves.

"Princess Lily?" Victoria asked.

Lily flicked her tail once again, splashing with impatience.

"I need your help with Charlene," Victoria said, and Princess Lily once again remained silent but now seemed even more annoyed.

"I do not think she speaks our language," Gregor suggested.

"Well, what language does a mermaid speak?" Victoria asked.

"Oh, I think I can help with that," Rhamy said as he stepped forward, looking a bit too snug. He smoothly spoke the words of an ancient language, and Princess Lily smiled. Her pearly white teeth were oddly bright for a creature of the deep.

Lily spoke with ease, her voice as smooth as her skin from her hips up, and her eyes flicked in fascination toward the small crowd gathered and back again to Rhamy. Rhamy chuckled a bit and nodded. Henry realized he was the source of the conversation and shifted his shoulders uncomfortably. Rhamy stood to look up at him.

"Princess Lily likes you. She will only help with Charlene if you will be there," Rhamy said with a bit of a grin toward Henry.

"What?" Henry asked with a nervous smile.

"Come with the horses, leave with a fish," Rhamy Lumpkin teased. When they all looked at him, appalled by his joke, he just shrugged. "She does not understand a lick of our language," he said in an upbeat tone, winking reassuringly.

"Well, great," Gregor said.

"Shh, she can understand your tone," Rhamy said, turning back toward Lily to offer a polite wave and nod, and turning back to cast a warning glance at Gregor.

"Look, I do not know why, but she has chosen you, a human, as her guide. Just try not to mess this up," Rhamy hissed and then turned back again, pushing Henry forward. Victoria tried to give him a reassuring smile as he stepped closer to the water.

"Sure, that is fine. "What does Charlene need help with?" Henry asked. Rhamy raised a single eyebrow at Henry's ignorance before turning back to Lily to conclude their discussion. She disappeared back into the water, and Rhamy turned toward the curious faces with his usual smirk.

"She is going to do it. She will come with us," Rhamy said.

"How are we going to get a mermaid close enough to Charlene?" Victoria asked.

As Victoria spoke, Lily appeared again and swam as close toward the shore as possible. When she was unable to use her tail anymore, she crawled on her belly, using her arms to pull herself from the water's edge. Rhamy offered his hand to her, and she spoke quickly with a heated tone. Rhamy nodded and looked toward Henry. Henry jumped to offer his hand, which she graciously accepted.

"Let's try to get out of here before we are spotted," Victoria said but noticed Lily was holding something green and lumpy toward her. Victoria gingerly picked it up from the mermaid's outstretched hands with thumb and her forefinger.

"What is it?" Victoria asked. Lily smiled. Victoria stared at it and gingerly used her handkerchief to wipe some of the grime away. A buckle emerged, and Victoria gasped.

"Is this my shoe?" Victoria laughed heartily and looked at Henry. "It is my shoe from when I fell into the river!"

Henry took a moment to recall the memory and joined in the laughter. He carried Princess Lily to the house. She wrapped her arms about

Henry's shoulders and pressed her chest into his in a hug Victoria thought was a bit tight. The mermaid was sniffing Henry's neck, and Victoria felt agitated at the indecency of it. Lily's eyes flicked in Victoria's direction, giving Victoria a coy smile before she tucked her head into his chest, shielding her face from the morning chill. Everyone followed, watching the mermaid in bewilderment.

They sat her down on the settee in the conservatory. Rhamy thought she would feel more comfortable surrounded by the plants and the humid air.

"Perhaps now we should get some rest?" Rhamy Lumpkin said. Henry was already nodding off on the chair next to Lily.

Mabel was helping Mother out of her wet clothes while Victoria showed Gregor and Rhamy to the guest room. She apologized that there was only one bed. Although it was large enough for both men, she could tell neither wanted to share. She did not stick around to watch the argument commence. Victoria walked down the hallway and passed Emily.

"Thank you for staying to help my mother." Victoria said to Emily. Emily just gave a nod.

"I am sorry I have been so difficult for you all these years." Emily said. "I was tough to ensure you would be raised properly. I was so sure you would marry well and take me with you, a life of luxury, caring for your children the way I cared for you. Now look at us. I guess we will all die in this hovel together." Emily said with a sigh. Victoria was not sure what to say, but Emily looked so sad Victoria was compelled to just squeeze her in a tight hug. Emily nodded and patted Victoria's back before making her way back to her room.

Victoria turned on her heel and marched up to her own room, finding her pillow to be the softest creation she had ever had the pleasure of touching to her cheek.

She woke with a start and instantly felt dread as she heard nothing, the pure silence sending shivers through her. She jumped from the bed and gathered her hair and tied it back as she cast a look to the sun outside her window. She had overslept, and they did not have much time.

Victoria came down the stairs, ignoring the roar of complaint every muscle in her body gave.

Mother was in the kitchen, and Victoria followed the sound of the clinking of pots and pans.

"We must feed our guests," Mother said. She was in her robe. There was no thought for her appearance as her hair was down along her waist, unbrushed.

"Mother, how did you know to call the mermaid?" Victoria asked, grabbing hold of the pan Mother was trying to place on the stove.

"Your father," Mother said. She took back the pan and placed it on the stovetop. Victoria stood with her mouth open as Mother began to slice vegetables. "*When surrounded by icy water, sing to find the princess within.* I always thought it was a metaphor."

"Why have you never told us?" Victoria asked.

"Victoria, you know your father spoke like that all the time. I didn't think anything of it. Your father and I agreed before you girls were born that you would be given a proper raising. We were supposed to do it together. I never imagined I would have to do it alone. I was unprepared," Mother said. The way she spoke the last few words, Victoria realized it was her form of an apology.

"The moment you disappeared from the ball; Charlene was in such a rage. Charlene ripped Mabel from my hands. I do not understand why she thought taking her would somehow get the necklace back. As far as I could tell, you and Mabel were gone forever. I was escorted back here to wait in this house filled with only memories. I was here, alone," Mother said. "I imagined you coming back so many times. I am still unsure if it is really you. I feel we have had this conversation before," Mother said. Victoria realized she was losing her again.

"No, Mother, I am here, truly here," Victoria said, grabbing her in a hug and then pulling away to grasp her hand tightly. Emily came into the room with another basket of food from the larder.

"We need you here, Mother. We need to feed everyone, so they have their strength."

"I am good at cooking," Mother said, giving a proud nod. Emily shook her head as she sat the basket down on the counter. Victoria sent her a grateful smile as Emily took a hold of the pan.

"Yes, concentrate on cooking. We will discuss the rest later," Victoria said as she pushed herself out of the kitchen.

Victoria decided they could have the entire conversation later when the battle was over. She shoved her emotions down and had successfully refocused herself by the time she got to the guest room. She opened the door and stepped inside to find neither Rhamy nor Gregor had won the bed. They had both climbed in on either side stubbornly and lay with their backs to each other. Most of the space was in between them as each clung to his edge of the bed.

"It's time to get up," Victoria said gently. They both groggily opened their eyes and then upon seeing each other, they both scurried off the bed to stand as far from each other as the small room would allow.

Gregor immediately rushed to her side, standing over her, his head bent so he could look directly down into her face. She was startled by his intensity.

"Rhamy told me Henry has made the death vow offer to you," Gregor said. She had to take a moment to mull over his wording.

"Oh, yes, he did propose," Victoria corrected.

"Did you accept?" Gregor asked as he stood hovering over her, his whole body was rigid, his breath shallow.

"No, I have not accepted," Victoria said. Gregor nodded, his shoulders releasing all the tension he was carrying, and he shifted back relaxed.

"Well, now you have two death vows, by my count, laid at your feet. How many more do you need before you decide?" he asked.

"Two?" she asked, confused.

"You have yet to accept or reject mine," he reminded.

"When did you propose?" she asked. He looked so taken back, as though she had slapped him across the face. Rhamy snickered. Gregor shot him a warning glance. Rhamy went silent.

"In the cave, during the blizzard. I gave you death vow," he said.

"I did not realize that was a proposal, I thought you just wanted to get me undressed," Victoria said. Gregor now got on both his knees and looked up, hands reaching for hers.

"Rhamy said human men kneel and beg for the death vow." Gregor said. "Am I doing it correctly?" Victoria gingerly placed her hands in his as Rhamy continued to watch with an amused expression.

"Stop calling it a death vow. It is called marriage," Victoria corrected, a bit overwhelmed by his urgency, but his unmistakable feelings made her cheeks flush.

"Yes. I want to give you marriage," he said eagerly, the new word coming off his tongue slowly as he tried to pronounce it. "You do not know me long enough to make such commitment." Victoria said.

"What do you mean? I have been watching you for many moons. I know everything about you." Gregor said defensively.

"Well, I just met you last week!" Victoria exclaimed.

"I saved you from that goblin when you tried to hold it like a baby, then again when you ran foolishly into their drey. I conquered Gor at Bellum Gate. I saved you from the boars and the blizzard, even after you broke Proxy Bellum." Gregor listed each with a slight nod of his head. Victoria bit her lower lip as he took a breath to steady himself.

"And I stood against my pa on your behalf." Gregor said with such emotion, Victoria finally understood the significance of his sacrifice. "What else must I do to prove myself?" Gregor asked.

"Well, it is customary to present a ring," Rhamy said, making a blue circle with his flaming finger. Gregor looked to Rhamy and then back to Victoria for confirmation. With the tension broken, Victoria pulled her hands out of his and dashed for the door. Gregor followed her with his eyes as she bustled away, her heart thudding so fast in her chest she thought she would topple over.

"Now is not the time to discuss these things. I can't just decide my entire life in this instant," she called back over her shoulder as she fled down the hallway her voice was higher than she would have liked. She pulled to a stop at the end of the hall and took a deep breath.

"You never told me about the ring!" Victoria could hear Gregor reprimanding Rhamy, followed by a low guttural grunt. Victoria assumed Gregor had punched Rhamy in the stomach.

Soon the entire bunch was sitting at the table. Gregor anxiously sat beside Victoria and kept casting suspicious glances toward Henry. Rhamy sat far from either of them. Emily was serving hot plates and Mother looked pleased with herself for creating a nice spread at such short notice. Lily sat with her fin brushing the floor rhythmically under the table. She asked Rhamy to explain each thing before she put it in her mouth curiously. She spat out the bread, and Rhamy translated she was saying it felt too dry, like trying to eat air.

"What is our plan?" Victoria asked. "Charlene can be here any moment!"

"No, no she isn't leaving her estate this evening," Mother said with a scoff.

"She made it very clear she was not going to stop until she gets what she wants," Victoria said.

"She has a party tonight at her palace. She could never cancel. It is a large event, and hundreds are coming," Mother said, pulling an invitation from her apron pocket.

Victoria anxiously read it. "That gives us time to prepare." Victoria breathed a sigh of relief.

"No, we have to strike there while she is playing host," Gregor said.

"We should play it safe, and, as much as I hate to say it, we perhaps should try to contact the nomads, Plimsoll, the Avians, maybe even ask your father for help," Victoria suggested. Gregor shook his head.

"That will take too much time. The nomads are our best allies, but they only have a small number of able-bodied men. My pa is not interested in a full out war with Charlene, he will not help. The Avians will just try to lock you up again and put off any form of confrontation until you have been fully trained. It could be a decade," Gregor said.

"Countless humans would be harvested in that time," Victoria said in a gasp.

"The only way to strike is tonight. Surprise is our only weapon," Gregor said.

Victoria had to agree.

"I think Rhamy is right. We should wait until we have a better plan," Henry said.

"Why are you still here?" Gregor asked him curtly.

"You can go tonight, but do not ask Victoria to put her life at risk," Henry said to Gregor. Gregor sent him an annoyed look, Victoria worried Gregor might pop over the table and slam Henry's face into his pudding. Henry could feel it too and avoided speaking further.

"We need to get Lily close enough to Charlene to bite her. We just need one nibble," Rhamy said. "Even if just one tooth punctures her flesh, the venom is potent. It should be enough."

"We will have to distract Charlene, somehow." Victoria said as she looked down into the teacup, Rumi looked up at her. He splashed in the water playfully, the little roots tapering off his short legs floated around in the water.

"What do you see?" Rhamy asked, looking from Rumi to Victoria.

"Nothing. I only see Rumi." Victoria said. Rumi gave her a wink.

"What is he saying?" Rhamy asked.

"I have a plan!" Victoria said confidently.

"Gregor do you think you could get Daryl to help us?" Victoria asked.

"If they know we had a mermaid, yes, definitely," Gregor said. Victoria nodded as Gregor stood and left. She watched him through the window, in his beast form, tearing through the fields and into the forest.

Victoria brought down one of her dresses for Lily.

"Luckily for us, Charlene's parties often have bright, colorful wigs, so your purple hair will be fine if we pin it up just so. We can hide your tail under the skirting. You are going to save so many lives," she said as she laced her corset and added the petticoats. Lily stared at the dress in fascination. Lily obviously thought it was the loveliest dress she had ever laid eyes upon because she kept touching the stitches and caressing the silky fabric. Lily winked at herself in the mirror.

Victoria was in the middle of dressing when she peered out her window and saw Daryl and his men arrive so she could not come down and greet them properly. They were armed and ready for battle. Gregor came into the view and spoke with Daryl, Victoria watched from behind the curtained window.

Emily led the men into the house. Emily had a good eye; she would be able to pick the right sized suit for each man.

Mother was pinning Victoria's hair while Mabel was sulking in the corner.

"Can't I come too?" Mabel whined again.

"No, you and Mother need to head into the larder to stay safe," she said.

"Then you come with us. Don't go fight," Mabel said.

"We have to finish this tonight. It is the only way to save Daniel and all those other children." Victoria sighed and tried to ignore Mabel's pouting face while she applied her lipstick. "They were terribly afraid and cold." Mabel admitted. "Just please be careful. Charlene is cruel."

Mother looked worriedly at Victoria. Victoria straightened her shoulders.

"Do not worry, I will return soon." Victoria said loudly, trying to convince herself more than anyone else. "I love you," Victoria said as she gave Mother and Mabel a hug goodbye. Both were wearing anxious faces.

As Victoria came down the stairs, she caught sight of Gregor, Rhamy, and Henry. Each stood, now clean-shaven and properly dressed as gentlemen.

Henry insisted on driving the carriage after he carefully placed Lily on the seat. Victoria helped tuck her tail under her skirts. Gregor climbed inside behind her and shut the door. When Rhamy opened it, Gregor loudly cleared his throat. Rhamy opted to sit up by Henry.

"Which gemstone do you prefer?" Gregor turned to her anxiously.

"For what?" Victoria asked in confusion. His random question had broken her train of thought, she was tediously trying to imagine herself transforming into something more useful than a little fox. She blankly stared at him.

"For your ring!" Gregor said.

"I am too terrified we won't even make it through tonight so I can't plan wedding details right now." She admitted. Her thoughts returned to the plan for tonight, she began to go through the steps again. She tried to untie the knot settled in her stomach.

"Do not fear, you hold more power than all of us combined, even Charlene. You must trust me," he took ahold of her hands and made sure Victoria was looking at him before he continued.

"As I trust you."Gregor said, pulling her hand up to his chest and placing his hand over hers. At this, Victoria could not resist leaning forward and grabbing a hold of his face tenderly. Gregor's eyes widened in delighted surprise as she kissed him. Gregor lifted his hand to hold the side of her face, his thumb near her ear and his fingers intertwining into her hair while he leaned toward her. Victoria reciprocated by further pressing into him, keeping their lips together. At this, Gregor grabbed her about the waist and pulled her onto his lap. The folds of her dress billowed out toward Lily and she smacked them down harshly. She sucked her teeth in irritation.

"Oh, sorry Lily," Victoria said, pulling herself away from Gregor. Victoria blushed as she sat back down on her own seat. Gregor scratched his neck and gave an agitated huff.

As the sun set, they made their way with the crowds toward the gates of Charlene's palace. The excited jabber and sweet-burning candles added to the happy demeanor. None of it pulled Victoria from the anxiety brewing in her gut. Victoria hoped their plan was good enough.

CHAPTER 22

A TERRIBLE PLAN

SHE GATHERED HER COMPOSURE and stepped inside the doors. She remembered the first time she had stood in that exact same spot—it was hard to imagine it had been a little more than a week ago. She had been so excited and filled with awe at the lavish palace, but now she only saw blood money spent by vanity.

Hundreds of people were arriving and wandering inside. Soon the ballroom was completely stuffed. She could not tell one person from another, and their masks further complicated the matter. Trumpets sounded, and all eyes turned toward the balcony.

"Presenting your honorable host, Queen Charlene," the official's loud voice announced.

Victoria stopped short, interrupting her own banter with a fellow guest. Charlene held her head high and gave short flicks of the wrist, greeting all the people looking back at her in awe. Her mask was different than the last one she had seen. This one was pitch black with a pair of menacing eyes, jagged and leering, further infuriating Victoria.

She eventually gave up trying to force herself through the crowd and just let herself stand in a line that had formed. It slowly moved forward. Eventually she was able to see Charlene sitting on the throne she undoubtedly designed herself. It was engraved with images and decorations on every inch of the marble. Gems and precious stones glinted from the high back. Victoria felt a pang of sympathy for the poor artist who had to endure the drilling commands and countless hours of hard labor to produce such a chair.

As she reached the aisle, walking toward the throne, people moved aside, whispering to each other in hushed tones. Soon the entire ballroom fell quiet as they backed away, leaving Victoria alone in the center of the stairs.

"You?" Charlene's eyes flashed. Her smile remained as she delicately tilted her head in greeting. Victoria gave a slight curtsy.

"Victoria! You have returned!" Charlene presented her to the crowd, lifting her arm in a dramatic gesture. The crowd clapped obediently, eyeing Victoria curiously. Charlene motioned her forward, and she stepped up onto the first three steps and gave another short bow. Charlene raised her eyebrows and smiled gleefully as if welcoming an old friend.

"Victoria, where did you disappear to?" Charlene's voice slithered into Victoria's ears like an unpleasant stream of cold water.

"Just needed time to decide whether I wanted to sell you the necklace or not," Victoria said while the guests watched with curiosity.

"Let us walk." Charlene said and she stood. They glided through the crowd, Charlene guiding the way out of prying eyes. When they were alone in the hallway, Charlene finally spoke.

"Oh, that is interesting Gregor and his father allowed you back here. I assume they are not far behind," she whispered.

"Just Gregor." Victoria. said, gesturing toward Gregor as he stepped out from one of the rooms and into sight. He walked down the hallway and soon stood beside her. Charlene looked him over thoughtfully.

"I would adore having the necklace, it is a marvelous piece for my collection." She said after a moment. "I am surprised your father would let you venture here without him."

"He does not know I am here, but if selling you the necklace will provide some peace between us, then it should be done." Gregor said.

"Indeed, it would be my pleasure!" she said. "Hannah, please go fetch the payment," she said. Hannah nodded and headed out of the room.

Charlene threw her hands into the air and then about Gregor's shoulders in a quick embrace as if blessing him. He gave a polite smile.

Hannah returned, but instead of a chest of coins, she held Mabel and Mother by their forearms. Victoria gawked at the scene, unbelieving.

"Please do stay and enjoy the party after this!" Charlene said, putting her hand out expectantly.

"I did not bring it here. It is outside in the carriage, in the front yard." Victoria said. Charlene looked about the hallway suspiciously. Gretchen and Hannah exchanged some whispers.

"Bring them." Charlene said. Victoria tried to give them a reassuring look.

They made their way out of the ballroom and down the hallway. As the doormen opened the front doors, Charlene grabbed Mabel and held her fast.

"Do not try anything funny." Charlene said. Victoria could feel the smooth marble steps under her feet and her heart pounding fast in her chest. She walked in front of everyone else, curving around the fountain and heading for the carriage.

"I'll go no further, bring me the necklace." Charlene said, pulling Mabel closer. It was so quiet all they could hear was the water flowing from the fountain. Hannah stood there, watching every movement Gregor made and him eyeing her back coolly. Mabel looked terrified.

Victoria opened the door to the carriage and had to step up with one leg to reach inside. She could feel everyone's eyes on her as her skirts rustled against the edge while she leaned in. She stepped down and shut the door, turning on her heel to walk back to the little group. The waning moon still held some light and it made the thin layer of snow and frost sparkle softly.

Victoria straightened her back and held her head up high, taking in several deep breaths to regain her composure. Then she tumbled forward, her foot had slipped on the ice and she went down into the snow. Everyone gasped and she looked up quickly to meet their surprised face.

"I am alright." She said as she grabbed a hold of the stone of the fountain's edge and a light splash met the quiet of the evening.

"Oh no!" She shrieked. "I accidently dropped it!" "You clumsy fool!" Charlene said, pushing Mabel aside and rushing forward.

Victoria reached into the water with one hand, waving it around. Her sleeve instantly soaking in the icy cold water while she avoided the ice riddled edge.

"I can't find it!" She called out in embarrassment. Hannah clicked her tongue. Charlene huffed.

Charlene was now at her side. She looked down into the depths of the fountain and ignored Victoria's repeated apologies.

"Are you blind? It's right there!" Charlene said as she cast a final irritated glance at Victoria. She plunged her arm into the fountain, reaching for the necklace. Victoria pulled her arm out of the water and stood up. She watched as Charlene narrowed her eyes and plunged deeper, reaching farther in determination. On cue, Lily lunged toward Charlene, snapping like a piranha. Her teeth reached Charlene's neck, the points of the ivory brushing the porcelain skin before stopping short. Her high-pitched shrill pierced Victoria's ears. Charlene smashed a fist into Lily's chest, sending her reeling backward with a huge wave crashing over the edge. Lily dove under the water and suddenly Charlene screamed. She was pulled down into the fountain, her skirts flipping up above her head and one of her shoes flew into the bushes as she kicked her legs forcefully. There was a series of splashing and churning water, Lily's tail came up out of the water and doused Victoria.

Then Charlene stood, yanking Lily out of the water above her head. Lily was chomping hard but Charlene had her about the throat, rendering her teeth useless. Lily struggled, both her hands trying to pry loose from Charlene's iron grip. Her tail splashed again and again against the water's surface, spraying everyone with the icy drops. It all happened so fast. Victoria had to take a moment to replay it back in her mind to sort it properly. Charlene whirled around to face Gregor.

"This was your plan?" Charlene asked in irritation over the noise of Lily's flailing tail. With a mighty heave, she tossed Lily out of the fountain and into the air. Victoria gasped as she watched Lily sail overhead, her scales shimmering in the moonlight. She landed on top of the carriage with a sickening plop and was still. Her tail hung down and her fin covered the carriage window like a curtain. Mabel screamed and tugged loose from Hannah's grip. Hannah let her go, laughing at the sight. Mabel was climbing up the side of the carriage to get to Lily.

Charlene bent down again to retrieve the necklace. Then again. She huffed loudly in annoyance, pushing her wet skirts out of her way. Gregor took the moment to tackle Charlene, but she was too fast. She slammed Gregor's head against the swan statue, and it exploded, a shower of marble and water sprayed all around.

"Hannah, get the necklace." Charlene said, holding the dazed Gregor. Hannah climbed into the water, her skirts immediately soaking and sagging heavily. As she began to scoop, she turned to look back at Charlene.

"I do not see the necklace anywhere." Hannah said in confusion.

"It's right there." Charlene yelled, gesturing with her head because both her hands were holding Gregor by his collar.

"I don't see anything but your crown. Why did you toss your crown in here?" Hannah asked.

"I did no such thing!" Charlene said. "It is on my head!" Charlene motioned toward the sparkling tiara on her head. She sucked her teeth and looked down at Gregor. Then after a very long pause, she laughed. It was a shrill noise that echoed against the cobblestone.

"So, you found yourself some fool's gold shrooms. I only know one place where they grow, so where did you find one?" Charlene asked as she stomped out of the fountain and yanked Gregor with her. Many of the guests were now filing out of the palace doors, curious of all the commotion. Victoria could see Daryl and his men mingled in with them, cleverly dressed neatly in her father's suits. She hoped no one looked too closely, some of the pant legs were a bit short on some of the men.

Her question would have to wait because at that moment Daryl and all of his men now flooded into the yard, waving their swords.

It was the first sign of fear Victoria had ever seen on Charlene's face, but the satisfaction lasted only momentarily as she quickly concealed her expression behind a series of commands to her horde. They came running from inside the palace, springing out from behind the door, flanking either side of Charlene. There were a few men, but most were women with flawless porcelain-like skin and bright lips, similar to Charlene's.

"It's over," Gregor said. "Surrender now and we will let you live."

"You think a few of these gypsies can defeat me? Perhaps I should fetch your father, we will see what he has to say about all this." She lifted a small silver whistle from her pocket and blew. He dropped to his knees, covering his ears and screaming.

Victoria could not hear anything, but Princess Lily wiggled on the top of the carriage, weakly lifting her arms to cover her ears. Mabel had crawled up to the top and was trying to help her.

Suddenly the whistle turned white-hot, melting under Charlene's fingertips. Rhamy stood twitching his fingers toward her. She dropped it, quickly scraping the burning metal from her flesh in disbelief. She grimaced at her burned hand. Gregor stood.

Only a few of her ladies attacked. The rest stood at Charlene's side, watching with somewhat bored expression. The nomad humans fought back with silver-tipped swords and spears. The ground seemed to quake under the fight The gypsy nomads were no match and Victoria panicked as she witnessed the bloodshed.

The party attendees were now peeking out the windows and some had decided to leave the ballroom and make a run for their carriages. They were all screaming in a panic

"It's over. Everyone will know what you are!" Victoria shouted. "Just leave now."

Charlene looked to the frenzied crowd of humans watching and back to Victoria. "You are right. I can never lie my way out of this!" Charlene said with an emotional crack in her voice. "Ladies, clean it up!" she said.

Her minions looked to her with excited grins, and when she gave a nod, they tore from their proper ladylike mannerisms and disappeared back into the palace. As they began to descend on the humans, Victoria could see them through the windows and hear their screams of pain. The monsters were sinking their teeth into their necks and feasting.

As the monsters fed on the humans they caught, they became faster and more aggressive. They ripped the limbs from the bodies of the few holding swords they had pulled from the decorations on the walls. Victoria watched the scene in horror. A few lucky gypsies overwhelmed a monster in the front yard long enough to dig a silver tipped sword into her chest. She let out an agonizing squeal as her chest began to smoke and smolder, the red-hot fire burning through her flesh and dress. She turned into a fiery ball sending the rest of the monsters into a frenzy.

Rhamy set many monsters ablaze. They had to tuck and roll several times for the flames to douse.

Gregor tried to wiggle out from her grasp. Charlene kicked Gregor in the face. Victoria rushed toward her. She easily caught Victoria's frantic swing in her hand, yanking her close to give a smirk. Her proud face gave way to a slight tremble as Rhamy plunged a flaming sword through her chest and into the large oak door, pinning her in place.

Charlene yanked the flaming sword from her own chest, releasing herself. She dropped the sword and shook her steaming hand, the skin charred. The sickening smell of burning flesh wafted to Victoria, making her sick.

Mabel frantically held Lily's face in her lap, trying to wake her.

Charlene clicked her tongue. She grasped Victoria's neck. Gregor charged, shoving himself between Charlene and Victoria. He landed two heavy punches to her face and one into her gut, sending her reeling back against the door. Her head rolled and Charlene gave a small smile, licking the blood from her cracked lip.

Suddenly Gregor's face was pinned underneath her heel. She moved so fast Victoria had to blink a few times to believe it. He huffed angrily as her heel dug into his cheek.

Hannah and Rhamy stopped fighting. Soon everyone was watching.

"Your plan failed!" Charlene yelled, looking down at the fallen friends. "Give me that necklace, Victoria," she said sternly. "Or I will crush his skull."

Gregor grunted in disapproval, but Victoria looked at the fallen body of Lily, who Mabel was still shaking in her arms.

"You would not kill your own son!" Victoria called her bluff.

"Yes, sure, I gave birth to him, but he is a stranger. Brutus saw to that personally. I brought him into this world, and it only makes sense I take him out of it." She pressed harder and with a sickening pop, her heel pierced through his cheek. Blood dribbled down the side of his face as he groaned in anguish.

"*Stop!*" Victoria screamed. She ran up to Charlene and obediently gave her the necklace. Victoria dropped beside Gregor and tried to pull Charlene's heel out of Gregor's face. Victoria's frantic movements were like a flutter of a butterfly's wing against the immovable force.

Charlene smiled as she twisted the clasp, opening the hollow ruby. Bending down, she plucked a hair from Victoria's shoulder.

She held up the small hair with a gleam in her eye. She placed hair into the hollow ruby and fastened the clasp back. She held it up and took a deep breath.

"Transform," she commanded, moving her foot so Gregor could roll away from her. Victoria's eyes widened in fear as the words hit her ears. Then there was nothing. Victoria laughed.

"That is what it was supposed to do? Control me?" Victoria scoffed. "Looks like your necklace is broke—" Victoria stopped short as the familiar cracking and rustling sounded behind her. She turned to see Gregor changing with intense fear on his face. Charlene looked just as surprised as Victoria.

"I can't control it!" Gregor said in horror.

Blood dripped from the hole in the cheek as he grunted. Hair popped over his face and covered the wound.

"Gregor?" Victoria asked.

"I was hoping to see what your powers could do without the limits of your weak mind, but I guess this works for now," Charlene told Victoria. "Smash your face into the wall," she commanded to Gregor. He stood straight, eyes shifting frantically, but his body could not disobey. All he could do was grunt as he rammed his head forward. As he pulled away, a gaping hole in the shape of his head remained in the wall. He stood toward her again, waiting for her next command with his arms down at his sides, his back straight as a soldier in uniform. Only his eyes were free to look around, the fear evident.

CHAPTER 23

A FINAL KISS

VICTORIA EYED CHARLENE, PANIC rising in her chest.

"I love this ruby!" Charlene said, and she swung the necklace back and forth teasingly. A white-blue fire arrow sliced through her hand, and she dropped the ruby necklace. Gregor was released. He fell to the floor unconscious.

"Gregor!" Victoria screamed. She dove to grab the necklace, but Charlene was too quick. She already had it back in her hand, and Gregor was in motion toward Rhamy.

Gregor threw Rhamy against the nearest pillar. Victoria watched in horror as he pounded Rhamy with his fists. Rhamy hollered for him to stop, but everyone knew it was useless. He defensively set Gregor's whole body ablaze. Victoria screamed at the sight. Gregor's fists began to catch fire, working up his arms, but he continued to punch Rhamy, ignoring the burns.

"Victoria, I really should be thanking you for bringing me the necklace and the last mermaid. The only thing you did not do was wrap them in a bow." Charlene laughed as she made Gregor pull Rhamy's arms tightly behind him, holding him in a terribly awkward angle. Charlene made a slight tugging motion, and Gregor broke both of Rhamy's arms. His screams echoed through the courtyard.

Daryl had broken from the crowd and started up the steps with five other men, all jeering at Charlene.

Charlene motioned Gregor to her side. Gregor immediately dropped Rhamy and sprinted toward her.

"Oh, first, put that fire out," she said. Gregor dropped and rolled until his hairy arms were no longer ablaze. The fur was gone, and the skin of his hands and forearms was all blistered and blackened.

"The Beast Prince protecting me!" she said with a smile as she turned Gregor to attack Daryl, who had no idea what was happening.

"Gregor, it is me. We planned this together," Daryl tried to talk to him. As he realized it was useless, Gregor sent him sprawling back, smacking two of his other men down.

"Rhamy!" Victoria rushed to the fire elf.

"Get out!" Rhamy cried hoarsely. "Don't worry about me."

Victoria shook her head, pulling his arm over her shoulder. "C'mon, Mabel. We've got to go," she said, straining under the weight of Rhamy. Mabel gave Lily one more shake, and Lily's eyes fluttered open.

"Leave me. You just have to save yourself," Rhamy insisted as he stumbled back against the wall, too weak from pain to walk. His arms dangled uselessly at his side. "I can't make fire. I can't," he said in panic. "I always have it come from my hands!" His face looked almost unrecognizable, and his nose was most certainly broken in at least two places.

"We are not leaving you behind," Victoria said sternly as Mabel gathered his other arm under her shoulder. Together they trudged down the steps while he moaned in pain.

As they looked for an escape route, it was a terrible sight. Monsters fought viciously against the remaining humans as the innocent were caught in between, getting slammed and trampled.

"We've got to get out of here," Victoria said. A crazed guard ran toward her, swinging his arms as a monster followed, whipping him across the chest with her sharp red nails. He fell face-first, and she sunk her teeth into his flesh. Victoria gagged as the blood splattered onto her face. Some landed on her lip, and the taste made her sputter. She quickly covered Mabel's eyes.

"Don't look," she said.

The monster heard her and lifted her head, wiping her mouth daintily.

"You could join us. Both of you are young and pretty," she said. Losing interest in the fallen prey, she stood to block their path. "It takes only one bite," she said, showing her pearly white teeth all flat and perfectly in a row.

"You have no fangs. How do you draw blood without fangs?" Victoria asked.

"Fangs?" she giggled, brushing her blond curls out of her face. "That would look hideous. The human jaw can bite through their own thumb, but they are too weak-minded to do it," she said, holding her thumb up for them to see. "But Charlene gave me strength to conquer myself," she said and bit off her thumb, holding the bloody digit between her teeth, blood trickling down her bright-pink lips, smearing her lipstick.

Mabel screamed. Calmly, she pulled her thumb from her mouth and held it up. She smiled widely and set the thumb back on the stub. They watched in amazement as the thumb reattached itself and seamlessly healed within a few moments.

"Don't you want to live forever?" she asked.

"Get away from us!" Victoria screamed.

She looked angry, and as she sprang at Victoria, Mason punched her squarely in the jaw. Her nostrils sprayed snot and blood. Mason nodded at Victoria. She was so surprised she did not even respond.

"Leave her alone, Jezebel," Mason said. She looked at Mason in disbelief.

"This has gone on long enough," Mason said. Jezebel ran off, looking at Mason with a mixture of fear and anger. Henry joined their side.

"Where in the world were you?" Victoria shrieked.

"Been a bit busy!" he said, gesturing toward the war in front of them. She looked down to see him holding one of the swords she recognized from the wall. The decorative tassels had metal bands engraved with Charlene's emblem. Victoria now realized it was the same symbol she had seen in the Avian castle in the mountain.

"Get him out of here!" she said to Henry, who nodded, pulling Rhamy onto his shoulder.

A howl erupted and Victoria turned her head toward the large palace gates as they burst open. A sea of beasts poured into the courtyard. They stood barking and snapping, waiting as Brutus stepped forward, his bloodred cloak billowing in the winter chill.

"Gregor, finish him," Victoria heard Charlene say coldly.

"What?" Brutus asked, looking from Charlene to Gregor and back again in confusion.

"Yes, I have my son back. You will not take him again," Charlene said.

Gregor stepped forward, and Brutus hesitated. As Gregor landed the first blow, Brutus only blocked, trying to spare anymore injury to Gregor, as his arms were bleeding from the burns now. Gregor slammed against him, offering no mercy. Brutus was forced to fight back. They came down the stairs, clawing and biting at each other.

Victoria heard a series of screams explode as a familiar growl echoed from outside the door. She looked to see Samson's outline breaking in through the wall, smashing many under his paws.

"Samson!" she screamed, and she could see him moving broken pieces of furniture and unconscious bodies in his path toward her. She held out her hand and found his face underneath her fingertips. She looked toward him, hoping she was meeting his eyes, but he was still invisible and it was impossible to tell. He whimpered underneath her fingers.

"Get them out of here," Victoria said to Henry, gesturing toward Mabel and Rhamy. Mabel looked confused as Victoria petted an invisible mass. She commanded him toward Charlene. He slipped up the stairs, and Victoria held her breath. Charlene watched the chaos ensue below with a confident smirk on her face.

Charlene was caught by surprise as Samson shoved his teeth deep into her shoulder. She screamed and wiggled out from his jaws, jumping over the side of the railing and landing off-balance on the ground below, looking around wildly for the transparent threat.

"Gregor!" Charlene shouted. Gregor dropped Brutus and started toward her. She turned as Samson landed on her. She flung her arms up, trying to protect herself against the invisible force. His claws dug into her arm, snapping the bone. She screamed, squirming away toward the door. She spied Mabel and lunged at her, catching her fast.

"Victoria! Call off your pet!" she screamed. Victoria shrieked to Samson, who stopped short.

It seemed the chaos in the courtyard faded. Victoria could only see Charlene with Mabel in her clutches.

"No, do not hurt her," Victoria pleaded, her voice shaking uncontrollably.

"I have had enough of your surprises," Charlene said, looking at her torn and broken arm hanging limply against her body. She glanced at Gregor, who stood now beside her, Brutus's limp body lying behind him. The other beasts stopped fighting. The noise faded to just the heavy breathing of Samson as all eyes were on Charlene.

"Looks like I win again!" she gloated. Victoria looked around the yard, the other monsters smiling in triumph as the beasts slowly transformed back into humans in defeat. Her eyes settled on Victoria.

"Gregor, kill Victoria!" Charlene said gleefully.

"Let her go, Charlene. You already won," Mason pointed out.

"Shut up, Mason. There is an example to be set for those who defy me," she said, crossing her arms expectantly. As the beast approached Victoria, fangs showing, Charlene still looked dissatisfied.

"Turn. I want you to kill her with your bare hands," she commanded. Her face was ugly for the first time, rotted by vengeance. Mason was still trying to talk her out of it.

Gregor's eyes filled with sorrow as his body unwillingly obeyed. Victoria tried to flee back, but she tripped over her skirts and fell. He knelt down, catching her throat in his hands. As his fingers gripped her throat, Charlene called out.

"Wait, wait. What sort of mother would I be if I did not let you give her a kiss goodbye?" She smiled, ignoring Mason's voice. Charlene's eyes were wild now, her lips turned up in a deep, hideous grin. Victoria felt his hand slide from her throat down her sides and wrap about her back.

"You have gone mad!" Mason cried out to Charlene somewhere in the background. As Gregor's eyes met hers, the fear was replaced by an intense passionate desire. His soft lips touched hers, and for a moment, everything else faded away. They were alone, pleasantly floating in a sea of nothing with only each other to cling to.

Charlene's cackle yanked them back to the awful reality. "Now strangle her!" she screeched, kicking high and sending her foot into Mason's mouth. "Shut up!" she said to him as he fell flat on his back.

As Gregor's hands found her neck again, Victoria gasped out desperately. She could feel his grip tightening.

"Gregor," was all she could muster from her collapsing throat. Gregor's hands paused, shaking under the spell.

"Kill her!" Charlene cried impatiently. Suddenly a bright blast of red filled the courtyard followed by a loud clash, like a thunderstorm, shaking the palace. Gregor's hands loosened, and he fell to the ground.

"What?" Charlene said in confusion, sitting on the floor with her legs sprawled. Her hair had been blown back, and her face was covered in red dust. The chain about her neck was now empty.

Victoria gasped for breath, coughing several times before she could figure it out. The ruby had exploded into a million pieces, showering down fine red dust. Victoria held out her hand to catch the falling particles, puzzled.

Gregor was unconscious beside her.

"Why won't you die!" Charlene screamed as she staggered to her feet.

"Once you are gone, we are going to free all those in Naphtali!" Mabel shouted. Victoria whipped her head toward her, fear striking as she opened her mouth to tell her to run. But Charlene sprung forward, grasping the unsuspecting Mabel.

"Victoria, look whom I found!" Charlene said, driving her teeth deep into Mabel's neck. Mabel shrieked in pain, trying to squirm her way from Charlene's iron grasp. Charlene sucked her blood with dramatic display as Victoria watched in horror, screaming uncontrollably. Charlene released Mabel's limp body, which slumped to the floor, her skirts collapsed all around her like a withered flower.

Victoria looked directly into Charlene's eyes in fierce reply. Her emotions overwhelmed her mind, and her body trembled with hatred and the only word settled on her mind was *revenge*. All the images of the night terrors collided with the creatures she had actually seen in the past few days. The fear that seemed to always linger inside her turned to red-hot anger. It was feeding strength she did not know she possessed. It was a sweet sensation as her stomach lurched in the familiar way.

She welcomed the pain as her limbs snapped, the new shape taking form. She bowed over and felt her spine breaking, ripping the dress from her body. The ground beneath shifted as she rose higher and higher. She looked down at Charlene staring in disbelief with mouth agape. Victoria welcomed the sound of everyone's gasps.

Once helpless to Charlene, now she stood over fifteen feet tall with a long, slender snout and large sharp fangs. She was covered in brilliant red scales, shining in the moonlight. She stood on her hind legs and laughed as she moved not one pair of arms, but two. Four sets of claws came toward Charlene, faster than Charlene could blink. With one swift movement, she was shredded from her neck to her thigh, the force knocking the entire throne stage askew. Charlene flew to the ground. Her own blood dripped from the railing above, splattering on her cheek. She struggled to get to her feet, the white flash of ribs showing through her open wound as blood poured all around her.

Victoria felt the rage sizzle in her throat, and she spat uncontrollably, spewing a huge billow of white-hot fire, the intensity causing even her a momentary pause. She summoned it to her command, catching Charlene in the middle of the burst. Shrieks of panic ignited from Charlene's burning body, and she wiggled about in agony until the fire was out. Kneeling on all fours, racked with pain, Charlene whimpered.

Charlene looked up to meet Victoria's gaze with an expression Victoria had never seen on her face, terror.

Victoria pulled Charlene into the air. Both pair of hands grabbed hold of Charlene—two grabbed her about the shoulders and the other two about her thighs. Victoria began to twist, waiting for the snap of Charlene's spine.

"Victoria!" Mabel called out weakly. Victoria froze. She had been so sure Mabel was dead. She looked down, realizing Mabel was moving. Victoria's heart swelled.

"We already won," Mabel struggled to say as she held out a shaking hand, revealing the mermaid bite, swollen from venom. She looked at the small movements Lily was making, a smile on her face, and then looked back to Mabel. She looked to Charlene, who was already looking pale and sickly, but not from the cuts or burns.

Charlene's screams dwindled, as though she was choking on her own words. She spewed foam from her mouth. Her face wrinkled into thousands of tiny folds.

Victoria dropped Charlene. She hit the marble floor with a dull thud and a slight crinkle. Everyone turned to Charlene as the venom stripped away her power, her curse. Her shrieks became shrill and weak. She tried to climb along the ground, pushing herself away from Victoria.

Mason stepped close to her, and she clung to his foot weakly. Her cheeks sagged and her face wrinkled past recognition. Age took its true form as her skin flaked away.

He squatted down to look in her frantic eyes. "Dust to dust, Mother," Mason said flatly, rubbing his busted jaw.

Long waves of blond hair turned from gray to a pale white and then fell off in a crumpled heap. The small, ragged form struggled under the weight of the dress; frail bones could not even lift the folds of the expensive fine silk. A soft gurgle escaped before complete silence.

Mason lifted the silk, displaying a delicate paper-thin skeleton underneath. Empty eye sockets gazed into the abyss blankly, the only remains of the great and terrible Charlene. He let the silk slip from between his fingertips and drape back over the pile of bones.

As Victoria approached Mabel, she realized the terrified faces of her companions. She tried to speak, but only a hideous growl ensued. Her friends jumped back. She stepped away and put all four of her hands up, trying to lessen their fear. She caught a glimpse of herself in the reflection of the tall windowpanes. She was a fearfully strange and magnificent dragon. She stared at herself and tried to steady her heart. She could feel her energy fading. It was exhausting to stay this large. She let herself give in to the impulse to fall on the floor, her muscles shaking weakly.

It was dreadfully painful to change back into a human without the anger and adrenaline pumping through her veins. She tore a curtain from the window as she collapsed to use it as a makeshift robe.

Victoria's attention turned to Mabel. She was looking sweaty and a bit pale.

"We've got a little problem," Henry pointed to the flames now consuming the building.

"Did I set that on fire?" Victoria asked.

"Yes," Rhamy answered, giving Victoria a look of amusement.

"You are a fire elf!" Victoria said.

"Yeah, even if I had working hands, I don't have enough energy to put out dragon fire," he said frankly. "Just looking at it hurts my eyes. I am not going to touch it."

"We've got to get out of here," Henry said and coughed from the smoke, picking Lily up in his arms. Mother carried Mabel. Rhamy followed slowly behind with his arms dangling.

"Samson!" Victoria called out. She heard the beast slurping and followed the noise until she saw the blood Lily had left behind disappearing.

"No! No, Samson! Don't lick the mermaid blood!" Victoria cried out, but she knew it was already too late. The beast's loud plopping over the wreckage prepared Victoria for his wet snout to rub against her hand.

"Samson, help me drag Gregor out of here!" she yelled. She pulled, but Gregor was unconscious and Victoria could not move his body more than a few inches. Samson was playfully licking her. She could see all the things being displaced by his tail.

There was a loud cracking as the entire column came down. Victoria felt its weight on top of her hips. She could not move. She coughed. The flames were hot, and the smoke was making her eyes and lungs sting.

"Samson! Can you get this thing off me? Why did you drink so much of Lily's blood?" Victoria lamented. Samson only gave a short bark. She could feel him pushing against the column, and it was moving slowly.

"Yes! Keep going, boy!" she screamed. The agony of the weight coming off her was so intense she wondered if she would pass out. In the direct rays of the rising sun, Samson became visible. He was the largest beast she had ever seen, making Brutus seem small. There were only a few thick patches of thin hair along his bubbly and splotchy skin folds where pockets of fur had begun to sprout. Although slumped over like a beast with a bald tail and long claws rather than hands and feet, his face was more human. His large, crooked nose sat lopsided on his face, and one eye was considerably smaller than the other, just a beady slit among the folds of wrinkled skin. Victoria ignored her impulse to look away. He leaned to look at her, his tongue hanging out of his misshapen mouth. Several fangs were missing, and the rest were discolored and broken.

"Yes, keep going, boy. Push this thing off me!" she said. She tried to think of transforming again, but her body was so weak and frail. It was hard to even stay conscious. Then Brutus was in her line of sight. He was pulling Gregor onto his shoulder.

"I'll come back for you!" Brutus said, seeing the large column across her. Victoria nodded, which sent her throat into another series of coughs. As he disappeared from view, Victoria tried to talk to Samson.

"You have to get out of here, boy. This whole building is coming down," Victoria said, lifting a hand to pat his paw. He just continued to lick her, ignoring the column completely.

He snarled as a large piece of wall came crashing down, and suddenly he was pushing the column off her and pulling her in the opposite direction from the large doors she had seen everyone else escape through. He grabbed her in his mouth, just forcefully enough to continue to pull her along without breaking her skin. She tried to help by pushing her feet, but the smoke was too much. Her lungs were burning. She saw the entire entrance collapse upon itself and realized Samson had found another way through the servants' gate. They lay on the frozen snow as the entire palace was now in flames. It looked oddly serene as the gentle snow began to fall over the valley, the little specks glinting in the light of the flames.

"You saved my life, boy," she said. "Thank you." But she had to stop talking to concentrate on breathing. Then a huge blast shook the ground. Fire and debris showered over her, and she felt Samson's slimy body on top of her and then darkness.

CHAPTER 24

A NEW DAY

WHEN VICTORIA CAME TO, she could see nothing. She coughed and coughed, trying to clear her lungs, and she shimmied and fought whatever was over her. She could feel the mixture of Samson's slimy skin and furry patches against her, but he was breathing shallowly. As she continued to fight, she finally poked up through the ash and the bits of furniture, wood, and stone over her. She gasped several long moments before she pulled herself out. Then she squinted in the brilliant sunlight. She stood alone in a sea of destruction. The entire palace was gone. Only ash and debris remained, the fire still smoking in the center of the wreckage.

"Mabel!" Victoria called out, coughing as she tried to strain her lungs to call louder. She had to lean on her knees and spew the smoke from her lungs. She felt very thirsty, and her head felt fuzzy.

She pulled the debris and furniture bits off Samson. There he lay in the sunshine, no shadows to hide his ugly, deformed face. More than she expected of his body was covered in skin than fur and the patches he had seemed smaller than she had felt when she had run her hands over him. He looked smaller than she had imagined. He slowly came to with Victoria's gentle shaking.

"What happened?" he asked.

Victoria gasped in surprise. "You can talk?"

"Aye, I can!" he said. As he looked at his hands and legs, he smiled. "Mermaid blood looks great on me!"

Victoria listened to his voice. It was thick with an accent she had not often heard but knew it was from a distant land.

"Thank you for saving me. You pulled me from the fire and shielded me from the blast," Victoria said and gave him a hug. He hugged her back. His lopsided face was mending. His eyes were almost the same size now and were proportional to his face.

"Where are you from?" Victoria asked.

"I remember the pain. Lots of pain, internal from being stuck in the change, and external from being hit a lot," Samson said, his face darkened. "They kept me in the dark and forgot to feed me often because they were so afraid of me. But you—you weren't afraid."

"Honestly, I was afraid," Victoria admitted.

"But you were kind rather than cruel," Samson said. "Then my newest memories are a bit befuddled. Were you a dragon, or was I having a wee mare of the night?"

"I was a dragon, but I could not hold it long. I was not strong enough. Then I almost died in the fire I had started myself," Victoria lamented.

"But you did it!" Samson said encouragingly. "You are a brave lass."

"I did this," Victoria repeated. "I did all of this." She looked around. There was no one in sight, only ashes and the fresh layer of powdered snow on top of it.

"Let's get home. I am not sure who survived," Victoria said while she tried to relive last night, collecting the memories into a proper order. She screamed out in frustration. There was no response. It was eerily quiet.

"Perhaps don't do that," Samson said. Victoria felt as though she was being watched, and she wrapped the curtains around her tighter.

"Let's get out of here," she said. Perhaps it was just her imagination or the ash in her eyes, but she thought she saw movement among shadowed parts of the trees. They had no other option than to head back to Victoria's house on foot.

"I wonder how much farther of a head start they have on us." Victoria tried to calculate the time of day with the position of the sun. "I wonder if the carriage survived," she thought out loud. She and Samson walked for a while in silence.

"How long were you stuck in between transformations?" Victoria asked. She knew he probably did not want to discuss it, but she was too curious to resist.

"Well, what year is it?" he asked. Victoria told him, and he stopped walking and slumped to the ground.

"Thirty-three years," Samson said in dismay. He now looked about himself with a look of sheer bewilderment.

"Brutus offered me to be a beast. It was supposed to be one bite to freedom. I was in prison off the coast, a little island where they put those away for life. Brutus showed up lookin' fer new soldiers, and it sounded better than rotting away in my cell," he explained.

"Oh, were you framed?" Victoria asked.

"No, I was not," Samson said frankly. "I was a bad man. Perhaps I deserved all those years of torment."

"No, you did not. No one deserves that," Victoria said. "You do not look thirty-three years old, unless you were sentenced to life in prison as a newborn."

"I don't look well over my fifties?" Samson asked. Victoria shook her head, looking at his smooth complexion, sprinkled with little freckles, the red flecks matching his orangey red tangled and curly hair. He had the straight stature of a young man.

"The change. It must have trapped my aging as well," he said. He was watching the building they were passing by with curiosity. The streets were bare, and rubble lay in their place.

"Here, put these on." Victoria had found some trousers, a pair of boots, and a jacket in the chaotic mess. He nodded to her graciously and quickly dressed. The sun was out, but it was still a chilly winter day. Most of the surrounding buildings were covered in debris and many windows were shattered, but for the most part, the structures still stood. Everyone was gone. The silence was frightening.

"Where is everyone?" Victoria wondered out loud. There was a pit in her stomach that stayed until she finally spied the gates to her own house. She entered the house timidly. There was no sign of life inside. Samson grabbed the candlestick on the hallway table, holding it up as they heard a rustling from under the couch.

"Oh, Victoria!" Mother yelled as she popped out from under the furniture.

"Mother!" Victoria was so relieved she grabbed her tightly in her arms, and they stood kissing and hugging each other for a long moment.

"We thought you had died in the fire that you had started," Mother added. Then she looked past her to Samson.

"Who is this?" she asked, pointing at him rudely.

"This is Samson. He drank mermaid blood and it cured him," Victoria said absentmindedly, looking around. "Where is Mabel?" she asked.

CHAPTER 25

A CRAZY CAT LADY

MOTHER GAVE A BIT of a squeak. Victoria turned in the direction Mother was facing to see a brilliantly white cat perched on the settee.

"Oh, Mabel!" Victoria said. "I see you are already mastering your first form. Oh, I do love your totem. So fancy!" she said, teasing Mabel's large, fluffy white tail. At this, Mother was sent into a series of sobbing fits. Victoria turned look at Mother and back at Mabel.

"How long has she been like this?" Victoria asked.

"I thought you were dead. You were gone and Mabel transformed. That fire-starting boy, he said it was permanent. Lily apologized in her special tongue before she left," Mother said.

"Wait, what?" Victoria asked. She sat down as she thought. The white Persian cat with large blue sapphire eyes gracefully curled onto her lap, looking up at her.

"I know you, Mabel. I know you think this is all fun and games being a cat now. Look at you—you are adorable, but permanent," Victoria said in despair. "And where was Lily going?" she asked.

"The fire boy went with her. They said they had to return her to her home." Mother said.

"She is the last one," Victoria said.

"No, Lily said she wasn't. Well, if the fire boy translated correctly. She said when your father had found her, she had volunteered to go with him to help, but it was her sister who bit him. She did not want him to take her, although he promised he would bring her back."

"Where?" Victoria asked.

"They did not say. He was excited to escort her home, but she refused to go without Henry," Mother said.

"Yeah, I bet he was," Victoria thought out loud. "Now all the elves will know. They will have unlimited resources to tip the scale in their favor." Victoria was unsure if they would rule with any more mercy than Charlene had. She had already seen their iron fist before and their bias against humankind. She sat petting Mabel for a long moment. Mabel was purring.

"Why were you hiding?" Victoria asked.

"We thought you were the robbers returning to take more stuff," Mother said.

Victoria looked around and realized the house was in even worse shambles now. Most of the pictures were off the walls and the shelves were bare. The furniture was sparse, and the rug was gone.

"What robbers?" Victoria asked.

"They were humans. They mentioned they lived in the forest, gypsies," Mother said. "Said they needed our things for their camp, something about hundreds of refugees coming. I could not resist all their convincing sharp blades."

"Naphtali," Victoria said. "Of course. With Charlene gone, it must have fallen." She sat smiling, letting the warmth of happiness settle over her. "Well, what is that?" she asked, pointing to a pile of flowers and a candle burning on a small table under Father's portrait. It seemed to be the only untouched part of the house.

"We thought you were dead," Mother said as Victoria stared at her own memorial.

"These daisies are from Henry. These red roses are from the fire boy. And these lilies are from the big one," Mother said. "Seems you had quite the list of suitors." Mother laughed, almost mocking her former self. Those days of embroidering handkerchiefs seemed a lifetime ago.

"They all think I am dead?" she asked.

"Well, honey, it's been several days!" Mother said. "I thought I lost both of you. Mabel just stirred from her catnap yesterday."

"Several days?" Victoria asked in surprise. Mother nodded. "Transformations of that size must take a great deal of energy, so much so I am unconscious for days!" Victoria wondered out loud.

"I cried and they cried. It was horrible watching the big one—"

"Gregor?" Victoria asked, and Mother nodded.

"He dug about in the wreckage for the first day until night, and his father pulled him away before what was left of Charlene's horde descended to try to find her remains."

"What do you mean 'try'?" Victoria asked.

"Well, Gregor's father . . . he found them. He scooped all her bones and ash into a bag and carried it off on his shoulder. It was morbid. I say let the dead lie," Mother said.

"Oh, Gregor!" Victoria sighed. She wondered if he was in Omnia right now, sitting in the stocks and thinking she was dead. Who was going to bring him water? Her heart thudded. She needed to find her bag and gather supplies, but her body felt so drained.

"Who wants some tea?" Mother asked. Samson eagerly replied. Victoria was happy to see Rumi sitting in a teacup, munching on another sugar cube. "The fire boy had broken arms, so I had to fish that thing out of the fountain with my bare hands." Mother said in disgust as she followed Victoria's gaze toward Rumi. Victoria wearily held out her finger to Rumi and he hugged it with his chubby arms, making her smile. Victoria leaned her head back against the settee in exhaustion.

"Victoria," Samson said anxiously.

"Yes?" she asked.

"We must prepare," he said.

"Yes, we must concentrate on preparations because I believe this is just the beginning," Victoria said.

"No, now. We must prepare now." He stood pointing out the window.

She crossed to the desk, pulling out her father's spyglass from the drawer. She was relieved it was still there. As the clouds pulled away from the peaks, she made out the very balcony the Avians had carved from the mountain, where she had stood. Squinting through the glass, she saw little speckles pouring from the cliff's face, growing larger as they approached—a huge flock of winged Avians taking to the sky. They were all headed in her direction.

"We are about to have company," Victoria said, lowering the glass with a steady hand, "and they are not particularly pleasant."

CPSIA information can be obtained
at www.ICGtesting.com
Printed in the USA
BVHW030334060722
641300BV00012B/1496